ANNA

SAMMY H.K. SMITH

SOLARIS

For everyone who has ever had to hide their true self
in order to survive.

PART ONE

PART ONE

PART ONE

CHAPTER ONE

IT WAS NATURAL now to wake, listen, check, and listen again, before moving on in silence through the wastelands. When it was light enough to see my breath in the air, I moved from the shadows of the ditch towards the larger, more isolated southern woods. It had been nine hundred and twenty days – or was it twenty-one? – since I made the decision to leave town and wander alone.

Leaning against the trunk of an oak tree, I searched my backpack for something, anything, to eat. Three unlabelled cans, a bag of rice, and two portions of Cheerios. My can opener had broken two nights earlier and there was no clean water for miles. Dry, chewy out-of-date cereal it was. *Yummy.*

I ate straight from the bag as I continued to move between the trees, carefully avoiding the main track. Resting for periods longer than absolutely necessary was an extravagance that led to trouble in the Unlands; I preferred to not be seen or heard.

So did he.

I didn't see him until it was too late. He grabbed my jacket and pulled me onto my back, pinning me in one fluid movement. I dropped my breakfast and pack, balling my hands into fists. The cereal lodged in my throat. Spluttering and coughing, my blows faltered as I struggled to breathe. A pitiful wail escaped my mouth; he clapped his hand over it.

Thrashing and bucking, I tried to get up, but he had me pinned on the shoulder with the weight of one knee, crushing me into the ground. The stench of mud and sweat stung my nostrils, but there was something else: a clean fresh smell I hadn't encountered since before the wars started. Like mint, but not.

The heels of my boots dug into the ground as I pushed as hard as I could to dislodge him while clawing into his jacketed forearm with my nails, squeezing and pinching his flesh. I couldn't reach his face. I slapped and grasped at the air, desperate to pull his hair, hit him, *get him off me!*

He stared at me. His eyes were dark brown, almost black. I dug my nails in harder and tasted more dirt, screaming under his hand as he straddled me. He pushed his weight onto my hips.

Anger welled and furious tears fell, wetting the hand still clamped over my mouth. My arms were free now, and I grabbed at that hand, slapping and scratching in blind fury. I fumbled for my pocket, but he was too quick. With a sharp movement he pinned my right arm to my side with his knee. Something pressed into my wrist sending a shock of pain up my arm and across my back. My slaps became punches, hammering every inch of him I could reach.

A flash of silver and two loud clicks. Cold metal encircled my left wrist as I continued to strike out.

No, no, *no!*

I spat and bit at his fingers, my lips curling back so far I thought they might split. He pulled the cuff around my left wrist sharply, smacking my shoulder into the ground repeatedly. Sweat rolled into my eyes, sharp and stinging. My vision doubled and I shook my head.

NO!

My right arm was useless, my left in agony, though I continued to fight. I was unsure just how long I struggled, but he didn't move, didn't make a sound. When all my strength finally ebbed away, I stilled and moaned, my chest and the back of my throat burning.

He reached down to my trouser pocket and pulled out my penknife, pressing the blade to my throat. My legs went cold as I lay paralysed with fear. The curls of his dark hair fell around his cheeks and he smiled. *Smiled!* Anger fired up again as he started to move his fingers over me, probing my mouth, pushing deep into my throat and making me gag.

Just get it over with!

He checked my face, my teeth, my hair, my skin. He had captured me, and by the rudimentary laws of the Unlands, I belonged to him. He hauled me to my feet and the metal of my shackles dug into my skin. I inhaled sharply.

To my surprise, he loosened the restraint. Rubbing the skin around my wrist, he smiled and nodded gently, treating me like a skittish colt.

I scowled and pulled as hard as I could. He slapped me

hard, the crack of skin on skin echoing like a rifle shot. The heat rushed to my cheek, the sting coupling with the warmth of blood on my lip. A sob escaped. Just one. I was proud of that.

"No more," he said, his voice incongruously soft.

I didn't reply. I remembered a warning from my childhood: *never speak to strangers*. Good advice. Relevant. Worthless.

"What's your name?"

I remained silent as he stared down and reached towards my tangled and filthy hair, brushing loose stands of hair away and running his fingers along my face. I flinched, conscious of his strength, of the metal that bound us, of my lost freedom. He rubbed my reddened cheek almost tenderly. His hand was soft and warm. I jerked my head away.

"Name?" He was firmer this time, grabbing my chin and forcing me to look up at him.

"Anna." My voice cracked with the lie. It had been so long since I had spoken aloud.

"Anna," he repeated, releasing his grip on my face. He bent to retrieve my bag. For a wild moment I considered attacking him. I could pick up the rock by my feet and crush his skull. It would be so easy; I'd done such things before, if only to a dying animal. I could do it again. The thrill of the thought left as quickly as it arrived. It wouldn't be easy. This was a human, however he might behave like an animal. He straightened with a knowing smile, darting his gaze from my face to my backpack to the rock.

From my bag, he pulled out my clothes, throwing them to the ground as though they were nothing. With our wrists joined, my arm was jerked and pulled about like a marionette's wooden limb.

All I need now is the painted grin.

He took out my small bundle of photographs and dropped the backpack. Rage rose in my chest, huge waves, swelling and towering. I balled my fists, ragged nails cutting into my palms, watching in horror as he flicked through the pictures, discarding them carelessly; they fell like maple seeds, spinning in the air.

He turned one over and a flash of my husband and me outside our home burnt into me. I looked so happy, so carefree. He turned over another. A big lump of cuddly white fur. Oh! I missed Oscar, his purrs and warmth at night. I tried to quell the rage. Pointless. It was pointless.

Finally, after gazing for what seemed like minutes, he turned the final one over and held it up for me to see. Our hands entwined, our rings clear in the daylight. I willed myself not to cry. Tears were weakness.

He stared at me and pulled his arm up to examine my left hand. It was bare. Jewellery had been valuable to the ignorant and desperate in the early days, and precious metals meant meals. I'd resisted for as long as I could, but he was dead, and I needed to live.

"Where is he?" The soft voice cut into me. "Soldier?" I shook my head. "Conscript?"

I nodded. Yes, my husband had been cannon fodder for a war, another number for the government to chalk up. Sent to the front lines and sacrificed to buy time for them to escape. All for nothing. The government had fallen, and afterwards, everything else had fallen apart.

"Dead?"

I nodded again as he secreted those last three photographs away in his inside jacket pocket. He turned his back on my scattered possessions and started to walk away. I resisted. He couldn't expect me to leave everything I'd carried around for the last two years. He moved to hit me again, but paused then reluctantly lowered it.

"I said no more," he warned, but I viewed it as a challenge and raised my chin.

Go on, beat me! A part of me wanted him to. I didn't know why; maybe I wanted to feel something, anything other than the rage that eroded me. I hated him, *loathed* him, this man who had captured and bound me. But with a heavy swallow I put aside my revulsion; I needed to discover all his weaknesses – he'd already shown me mercy. But for a man in the Unlands, he seemed in perfect health. No injuries, no disabilities.

He jerked me closer. I stumbled, the cuff pinching at the soft skin of my wrist. I gasped in pain and recoiled as the warmth of his hands on my sides drew me closer. His body dwarfed mine.

"Anna."

He called me Anna. I was Anna now. I must remember. They say you can tell someone's personality from a name. Anna was gracious. Anna was compliant. I had to be Anna.

"My photos. Please." I forced myself not to scowl, not to cry or shy away. My clear voice sounded alien, loud, wrong. Another person speaking. Anna.

"You speak when you want something." The amusement

in his voice was clear, though the cold eyes stared without emotion. He thought this was funny? I jerked away from his touch, scolding myself immediately. He didn't stop me this time, nor did he beat me. Instead he ran his hand along my bruised cheek, tracing his handiwork, his first brand.

There were stories in the Unlands of men who marked their women, initials or symbols and suchlike, the way farmers used to identify livestock.

"Please, my photos." I appealed to what I hoped was the softer side of my captor; six years couldn't have destroyed all shreds of his humanity. He said nothing, but continued to stroke my face. Without waiting for his response, I picked them up. I expected him to shout, to haul me up, to lose control the way I perversely wanted him to.

Go on, beat me.

He didn't, and instead allowed me to collect each and every picture. When I straightened, he held out his hand expectantly. I handed them over.

Good little doggy. I knew my master. I kept my head down and stared at the ground.

The ground was the same wherever I looked. Dry and cracked like crazy paving, the same everywhere but for the rise and fall of the earth like a paralysed sea. Overused, drained, poisoned. He smiled, removing a canteen and drinking deeply. I licked my lips.

"Where are you from?" His smile irritated me. Made my skin crawl. "For every question you answer, I will let you drink. Where are you from?"

There was a long pause as I stared at his boots, and

finally I heard him zip up his backpack. I had won, and it was my turn to look triumphant. I wasn't that weak. He started walking again, his strides longer and his pace faster.

We walked for hours. I was tired, hungry, thirsty, and I desperately needed to piss. Not that I would ever admit it to him. He didn't speak, but every so often he would stop and crouch, forcing me to follow suit. Grabbing handfuls of dirt, he rubbed it between his fingers and stared into the distance. There were three rabbits during the day. Typical. When I was alone I had no such luck. Watching them escape across the nothingness made me smile wryly. I said nothing. Someone had to have a lucky day.

I stole glances at him when I could. He was older than me, possibly thirty-five or forty? I was never good at guessing ages. As the day wore on, I knew where we were going and each step now filled me with dread. He was a wanderer, one who lived in the towns but scavenged the Unlands for supplies and cattle, like me. A fresh fear surged and caught in my throat. Did he intend to sell me? *Rent* me?

My legs buckled, my head spun, and I stumbled to the ground. My shoulder was almost wrenched from the socket as my arm whipped back. He stopped and pulled me up, wrapping his arm around my stomach, putting pressure on my bladder.

"I need a piss," I mumbled through gritted teeth. I could feel him against me. The skin at the nape of my neck crawled.

"Where are you from?"

Comply! You are Anna. Anna needs to piss too.

"Nowhere."

"Nowhere," he echoed, gripping me tighter.

"Home has gone. Bombed. Fucking destroyed." A slither of anger crept out through my mouth and across my skin and I sneered. "I'm going to piss, so let me go or I'll piss on us both."

He released the pressure slightly and led us to a nearby scrubland area. Tall ragweed plants were dotted like scabs on the ground. Staring over the wastelands, he waited.

Here? I had stupidly expected him to release me, give me some privacy. I struggled with the button and zip. I was left-handed; with only my right hand free I was useless. My bladder was ready to explode.

"Can you help?" my alien voice blurted out. "I can't undo my jeans."

I shut my eyes and remained as still as I could as he undid my trousers. His left-hand fingers lightly grazing my stomach, warm and deliberate, brushing against my skin. As he pulled down the zip, his fingertips lingered far longer than necessary. I did nothing. I was Anna. Anna is gracious.

"Thank you." I spat the words, and quickly swallowed. "Thank you," I repeated, quieter, demure. *I can't mess this up, or I'm dead.*

How I hated those words, and my pathetic quiet voice.

Afterwards, he removed his canteen and drank, watching me again, his eyes boring into mine. I looked away first. I tried not to lick my lips again. And failed. Again.

"What did you do before the war?"

The question caught me off-guard, but I would answer honestly. It would be *easier to maintain the truth than a lie*.

"Call centre, customer service." A waste of a life. If I had known the world was going to end, I would have done so much more.

He moved closer and raised the canteen to my lips. I allowed him control and sipped at the water. Nodding gently, a smile formed on his lips and he touched my bruised cheek once more.

"Anna from Nowhere who worked in a call centre."

As we continued, the dark shapes and crumbling stone of the town grew larger and soon dominated my line of sight.

I was his, to do with as he pleased.

No. *Anna* was his.

CHAPTER TWO

We ENTERED THE remains of the large nearby town, and humiliation and anger washed over me, seeing other people walking around acting as though a woman chained to a man was somehow normal.

I knew towns like this. I'd often walked along the streets admiring the window displays and wishing I had more money and less stress. Even during the civil unease and rationing, I waved my cash around, while members of staff smiled thinly at me with barely concealed contempt. I was a government employee, so my job and security was protected. The government would always need telecommunications. I was stupid and arrogant.

Now, in what was once the main street, I forced myself to look up at the building; it was the old library, the heart of this small town. My own heart sank when we entered: they had burnt all the books. I hoped there were other libraries, other records still intact somewhere.

Without pausing he led me to the only room on the top floor.

*   *   *

THAT FIRST NIGHT was hard. His room was scrubbed clean and carried that strange odour – the one I couldn't identify, the one that accompanied him like a familiar. It assaulted my sense of smell and rolled around my mouth, reminding me of the moment I had been bound. There was a double bed against the wall with sheets and blankets folded and piled at the end of the mattress, and chairs scattered about the room. There was only one window, high above the bed, and just the one door which he locked using a key hanging from a chain around his neck. I was scanning what was clearly to be my cell, searching for a way to escape, when he pushed me to the wall and lent against me, burying his head in my hair. I was glad he couldn't see my face. I hid my fear well, I think.

THAT NIGHT I realised my captor wasn't stupid and scratched simplicity off my list of potential weaknesses. He handcuffed my right hand and connected it to a long chain secured to the wall then, releasing the cuff that bound us, he prowled. Ten feet, he'd given me ten feet of freedom.

"This is home now, Anna."

All night he remained silent, sitting on a small chair in the corner, watching me. I didn't move from the wall, letting the hard brick support me, for without it I am sure I would have collapsed. I woke the next morning sitting with my head between my knees. Immediately I stood and checked my wrist. Still bound.

He was already awake, of course, and with me eyeing him warily as he approached, he took his hand from behind his back to present me, like a lover on St. Valentine's Day, with a gift. A hairbrush. *Anna, I am Anna, I should be gracious.* I wasn't. Instead I stared at it in disgust – what did I need a hairbrush for? I regret what I did next; it was ridiculous and cost me dearly. Taking the brush, I threw it with as much force as I could across the room and it bounced against the wall with a satisfying crack. I then screamed at the top of my voice, letting out the rage, the anguish, the pain and humiliation, in ear-piercing cries.

With one hand around my throat he squeezed until I felt all my weight leave my body and white floating spots crossed my vision. I wanted to die. I wished he would lose control and continue to squeeze until every breath left my body. He would then have done what I never had the courage to do.

Instead, as I slid to the floor, he let go and knelt in front of me. I coughed and spluttered for air. When I finally controlled my breathing he grabbed my hair and pulled my head back, exposing my throat. His eyes almost black and his mouth a thin line. He held his knife. I smiled. He didn't expect that and, as the blade touched my skin, I sighed and he stilled. I willed him to continue, I dared him, my gaze burning into his dead eyes, but instead of releasing me from hell, he simply, savagely and efficiently cut my hair. All of it. Chopping away at thick, matted and filthy strands until it curled just below my chin. My husband had always loved my long hair and I hadn't cut it since the wars had started, but now it was all gone. I didn't have time to mourn my loss, for he then hauled me over his lap and pulled up my top. I kicked and thrashed and wriggled like an eel, sliding onto my back and hitting out at him, finally doing what I should have done when he caught me – but he was too strong. One punch, that's all it took. One blow to my abdomen and I was winded, immobile. He flipped me onto my stomach and took the knife to the skin of my lower back. I didn't want to be branded, but he had other plans. He sliced, I cried, I begged and sobbed for him to stop. I made all sorts of promises that I'm now ashamed of, but he didn't stop. He didn't say a word as he carved deep into my flesh.

IN THE DAYS that followed he took me out of the town, wandering with him through the Unlands. No animal escaped his traps and the first day he caught a stoat and a squirrel, then each day after that we returned with at least two rabbits. He would sit for hours watching the same rabbit, waiting for it to approach. I wondered if he had watched me the same way and tracked me like a rabbit. We walked miles. My feet ached and blisters covered them, but I didn't complain because it was nothing compared to the pain, and shame, of my back.

He traded most of the food in the town. I never looked into the faces of his acquaintances. I did listen though, and his soft firm voice commanded respect. One man tried to touch me and my captor beat him. That was painful for both of us. As he kicked and savaged the would-be suitor he pulled and contorted me around on the cuff. He was silent as he delivered his blows. The man cried and promised not to touch me, crying out like a child, *"I'm sorry, I'm sorry."* Even though I knew the unwritten laws, it didn't stop me from pitying him. My captor kicked him to the ground and I jumped at the desperate pull on my jeans. The man had curled himself around me, gripping my legs together. I stumbled and fell on top of him; he stank, but this was a smell I recognised only too well. He was filthy and the slightest touch of him was like a film of oil on my skin. My back was bleeding now, the tacky warmth sticking my top to my skin.

My captor dragged me to my feet; he never lost his footing, and continued to kick the man. He was angrier than ever and grunted in satisfaction each time his kicks connected and the man wailed. I begged him to stop, I didn't want to see anyone die, I'd seen enough death.

He stopped, but I don't know if it was because of my words or if he had proven his point. Instead he watched in silence as the man crawled away sobbing. There were onlookers who didn't move, no one came to the aid of the injured man, no one came for me, but it was the former I felt for. A sharp gust of wind flayed at my skin and I grunted in pain. As he looked at me I winced, expecting a violent outburst of anger, but none came. Turning me around he lifted my top and exposed the bloodied and bruised skin of my brand. Hot, angry, throbbing. Every cell of my body ached and I wanted nothing but sleep.

With those cruel and yet now gentle hands he guided me back through the town, even carrying me a short distance like a child cradled in his arms. My arms hurt as I pulled them close to me. He wanted me to wrap them around him as a display of affection, but I wouldn't give him that satisfaction.

As we passed the remains of the secondary school I asked to be put down and to walk. There were thin and beaten prisoners clearing the rubble away. Men with guns and Kevlar vests surrounded the perimeter, barking orders and directing their work. When one prisoner dropped to his knees and collapsed, he was dragged away and replaced with a woman who sobbed. My captor stopped and watched me, watching them.

The woman: her hair had been cut off, all of it, not just below her ears but crudely shaved to the scalp. She wore the same yellow tracksuit bottoms and a white tee shirt as the others, and within moments of being thrown to the floor she started to work, scooping up armfuls of rubble and throwing them into the wheelbarrow at her side. Taking my hand in his, he guided me away. I looked back and connected with her. Her large brown eyes full of defiance, scorn and disgust.

HE TOOK ME back to his room where he continued the daily ritual of applying cream to my back. I didn't cry or sob again; no tears fell. He'd had his pound of soul and I wouldn't give him any more. I sat listlessly as he massaged the brand. I hadn't seen it. I didn't want to see it. It was sign that I was property, an emblem which stripped the last of my liberties.

At the same time every day he asked me a question about my life. If I refused to answer, he refused to feed me and refused me water. With the pain in my back, the constant hunting and my general apathy, I'd given in after two days. I told him the name of my husband, the name of our cat, my favourite colour. He laid me across his lap every day like a child and rubbed my back, touching my tattoo and tracing the lines of the butterfly. I couldn't stop shaking, no matter how hard I tried. His touch made me feel sick, I hated him more than ever when he asked the question:

"Do you miss him?"

What a question. The sharp flare of pain in my back as he touched me was nothing compared to the tight agony in my chest. *Did I miss him?*

"Yes."

I'd answered my question. He didn't ask anymore and after applying a fresh bandage he opened a tin and fed me the canned fruit with his fingers. *Good little doggy!* I'd performed my master's command and now I received my treat.

"Are you awake?"

I looked up from between my knees; I still refused to sleep on the bed, even though the tightness and scabbing on my back made it painful to sit against the wall. As I glowered, he smiled and reached down. I didn't know what to do but, remembering who I was, I accepted his hand and he pulled me to my feet. A sharp pull on my back made me grimace. He turned me around and pulled up my top. I didn't resist.

"How does it feel?"

Why, suddenly, did he care? I didn't have the strength to play games. I was tired, hungry, in pain and I wanted this fucking game to end.

"It hurts." My reply. *Truth is easier than a lie.* I am Anna.

He ran a hand through my hair and stepped closer. I froze. Grabbing my chin he lowered his face to mine. *That smell, again that smell.* I tried to twist away and involuntarily balled my hands into fists, but he tightened his grip and I stilled.

"Anna," he murmured. I closed my eyes. Better that I didn't see him, that way I could imagine I was somewhere else, with someone else. That I was someone else. His hot breath was on my face and the shaking started again. He noticed that too and stroked my arms in a seemingly calming gesture. It made it worse. As his lips touched my cheek and his stubble grazed my skin, I retched. Another win for him. He stopped and let go of my arms – I hadn't expected that, and opened my eyes in fear and interest. I couldn't sense any anger in him.

He left the room with a dull click of the lock. I was alone. *Alone.* I stood there aimlessly, finally taking a proper inventory of my surroundings. There was one chest of drawers, no boxes nor cupboards, only three chairs, a bucket, the small table and the bed. I sat on the bed and stared at the ceiling. Was this my life now? A prisoner with no chance of freedom and a master with no name?

Looking up, white and grey sky spread across the glass of the window. I stretched the chain and stood on tip-toes, pulling myself up. The tops of the ruined buildings cut into the sky, scarring the clean lines with their jagged edges. Piling up the bedding I stood higher and watched the streets below; people, they seemed full of people, milling and weaving through the narrow walkways. Women like me, grouped together and ushered by armed men, heads bowed and hands clasped together: no chains though, *lucky bitches*. The men laughed and joked, and there were boys playing football against the wall of the church. Two more women passed, alone, un-chaperoned and giggling with linked arms. One held up their hand and the glint of a diamond winked up at me. They were young, younger than me and seemed so… happy… and free. I stared and watched the world pass by until the emptiness was too much. Lying on the bed I closed my eyes. The mattress was soft and caressed my back. It was blissful.

I was lost in the first real sleep I'd had in months. In the wilderness deep sleep was an unwanted indulgence.

It was the weight on the bed that woke me and I scrambled up, sitting with my back to the wall and my knees tucked under my chin. My brand throbbed. I wouldn't lie down near him.

He carried a designer bag in pristine condition. I remember seeing it in a magazine once. I coveted it then. Now, not so much.

"For you." He handed me the bag and I nodded. The words stuck in my throat, but I said them anyway.

"Thank you."

He watched as I held it at arm's length. Did he want me to open it? Part of me was curious while the defiant side of me wanted to throw it back at him. But that hadn't turned out well for me in the past.

It was full of toiletries and clothes. I blinked in case they disappeared and I was in fact still asleep. They didn't, and I was awake. I don't know which was worse. I pulled out the first top, a blue tee-shirt, immaculate like his own clothes. As I went through the bag he sat next to me, just staring, watching me. He had brought shampoo and toothpaste, a small tub of face cream and make-up. Make-up? I looked at him with the lipstick and mascara in my hand. Smiling, he left again, locking the door.

I hadn't used shampoo in over a year. I unscrewed the bottle and sniffed: coconut, sweet and inviting. I remembered drinking coconut water with Stephen once, on our honeymoon.

He returned with a bucket of warm water. Beckoning me he sat on a chair and waited. I hesitated; did he mean to wash me? I walked robotically to him and knelt down, my chain snaking along the floor, and he knelt beside me as though we were both about to pray. Removing his jacket and rolling up his sleeves, he bent me over the bucket and, scooping up water in his cupped hands, he gently rinsed my hair. The angle at which he forced me pulled at my back, but the sensation of warm water trickling across my skin and down my face soothed the aches and I closed my eyes in pleasure.

I sensed him leave my side and then return. There was

the smell of coconut again. His fingers massaged my scalp and my skin crawled. I still pictured striking out at him, clawing his face, digging my fingers into his eyes, but I didn't. I needed strength for that.

"Do you like the clothes?"

I had to answer, I couldn't nod, and there was only one answer I could give; truth shouldn't come into my consideration, only pragmatism. Leaning over a bucket of water with my captor washing my hair, there was only one answer.

"Yes." I paused and remembered. "Thank you."

"You're welcome." He rinsed my hair and wrung the water from it. "How long were you alone?"

The question of the day; he had changed the rules. I was trapped. I couldn't ignore it and he knew that. Clever, I'd forgotten the first rule of combat; *never underestimate your enemy.*

"Two years."

"Were you lonely?"

Cheat! That was two questions. I remained quiet as he used a towel to rub my head. He expected an answer, and I had to give him one, but the truth was that I didn't know if I was lonely. I missed certain people, certain things, but lonely?

He waited.

"I don't know."

"Why do you not talk to me?"

"You hurt me," I replied, quicker than I meant to. Did he expect us to be friends? The man without a name, without compassion and, to judge from his eyes, without a soul? I crawled out of his grasp. The towel slipped to the floor and my coconut scented hair fell around my face.

"I protect you." He still knelt and I stared at him in confusion, unsure if he truly believed the lie that came from his lips.

"You hurt me!" I spat. *Gracious, gracious,* the words bounced around my mind but I angrily pushed them to one side. *Damn Anna, damn being gracious!* The rage was back: it had been quelled by my brand but now it returned and I stood up in fury and lunged towards him. I would scratch his eyes to stop him staring at me if I must.

He expected that, I think, for he grabbed both my wrists. I howled like an alley-cat, but he didn't try to silence me, not this time. *Beat me!* I wanted him to do it; the anger needed sating once more. But he didn't and that made me angrier.

His grip tightened as he tripped me. I landed heavily on my back and cried out in pain. He straddled me and I continued to growl and fight back – maybe I should have done this at the start, maybe I should never have given up. He pinned my arms above my head, knocking over the bucket of water.

"Enough." He took my wrists in one of his hands and placed the other over my mouth. I tried to bite but he pressed down firmly. "I protect you, you need taking care of."

I stilled again, frozen by incredulity and my eyes widened. He removed his hand and I spat at him. His patience snapped and he backhanded my face. *That's more like it!*

"That's more like it," I repeated aloud, kicking and

bucking. "Beat me, you coward." He raised a hand again and hit my face once more. Harder this time. I tasted blood and my teeth rattled. Then, suddenly everything drained from me again. The pain, the anger, my resistance, it seeped away like the water slipping between the floorboards and I stopped fighting. I waited for the next blow, but instead he leant over and kissed my cheek again and stood up.

"Get changed."

I did. I was weak. I was tired. *I was Anna.*

He took me hunting again. We didn't speak. My lip and eye had swollen but he paid me no attention and when we returned that night he didn't feed me or give me water. From experience I could last at least two days. I would win this round. He left me again that night, and when he returned I sat on the floor with my head between my knees and pretended to sleep while he stared at me.

Then, from outside, I heard a new voice call up to him.

"We need you, Daniel."

Daniel. His name was *Daniel.*

CHAPTER THREE

THE FOLLOWING DAY Daniel allowed me a few sips of water, and two days after that he fed me.

By the end of the second day I didn't care if I'd won or not, my lip was so swollen it seemed as though it would burst, and I could barely open my left eye. Every day he came to the room and watched me, sometimes for hours at a time, without moving and without speaking. I stayed on the floor and refused to look at him, I didn't want him to see the state of my face or the desperation in my eyes.

When alone, I took the underwire from my bra and tried to pick the lock of my cuff. I spent hours delicately moving the metal around, trying to find any mechanism that might budge or bend but there was nothing. On realising the futility of my attempts I forced the cuff down my wrist and across the base of my thumb, twisting, pulling and pushing it as hard and far as I could. The skin protested, wrinkling and then splitting as the metal anchored itself within my hand. I didn't care, I needed it off, had to remove it: but it wouldn't budge. No sooner had one side slipped down than the other slid back up, trapped. The weeping sore grew larger the more I moved, a scab I had to pick, each burn and twist making me gasp, but I had to remove it. All the while I considered why my captor, why Daniel, would have a chain on a wall like this: and then with cruel clarity I understood. He was a hunter, a scavenger, and I had been right, he'd been hunting for a captive for some time. I had been the stupid, lazy and weak girl he caught. I never used to be weak.

WHEN THE WARS and troubles started I was blasé and foolish. They played no in my life and I wasn't interested in politics. I wasn't the only one to feel that way, but I regret it now. If I, if we, if all of us had paid more attention then maybe, maybe I would still be working in a call centre, married with a cat and a huge mortgaged house in a small nondescript town. Maybe everything would still be all right.

The news built up and up and up: riots in the cities, the looting, the power cutting as the cyber attacks came – some perhaps from a bedroom in my road – the crazy spiralling violence as more violence was used to suppress violence, weapons flourishing like weeds; terrorism, inner city crime, vigilantes. That was when I, and all the other well-informed suburbanites, started to panic. The gangs on the street took more power and grew; fed with the fear of the masses the control they demanded started to rival the authorities. The police were useless and the military preoccupied. In our sleepy town, an air of restlessness threaded through everything and everyone.

And it wasn't just us. The rest of the world was in turmoil; suppression leading to oppression leading to rebellion, but the rebellion of the splintered. The countries fell one by one, and when we finally realised, it was too late. I don't even know who attacked first, but I remember watching the aftermath in China, and then their retaliation on India and Russia. It spread from there, like dominoes toppling. Our government reintroduced conscription for both sexes to fight the war abroad while anarchy simmered at home.

Stephen received his papers first and that's when it all became real. My life and soul ebbed away. I begged him to run away with me, hide somewhere the soldiers wouldn't find us. He'd finally agreed, but the day we planned to leave soldiers arrived and took him. We had been betrayed, and the only person who knew of our plans was my brother. *Blood is thicker than water* – that was the saying wasn't it? I never saw him again. I refused to speak to him or my parents, because they agreed with my brother's actions. Traitor, they call me: and I call them that too.

I never received confirmation of Stephen's death. He had been attached to the Maritime Regiment and when the war hit our borders all military bases were attacked first, followed by the power stations and water plants. I know he was in at the base that first day, but I never heard from him again. Two years after that I traded my ring for food, the pale skin the only reminder of our vows.

There was no point in working. With no communication networks, no power and no water, who needed me? I spent the next months trying to find some normality between the constant falling bombs. Some people thought it was the Middle East who attacked us, others thought it was the Russians, but no one was sure and we weren't exactly a nation of innocent bystanders. It didn't matter.

In the end it wasn't the attacks from outside which mattered most, but our own. Those of us who were left, scattered; the loose morality that we held as a nation dissolved further with each fresh attack.

I eventually left Oscar. There was nothing left for me at my home. I tried to take him with me but I couldn't. He scarpered during a heavy bombardment and I never saw him again. That was the day I started to count; nine hundred and twenty-three days of freedom, I think, and yet this was only day eleven of my capture.

Eleven, had it been so few?

I stopped then, the stinging and heat from my now bleeding wrist was consuming me. Each time the metal made contact with the wound I jumped as though electrocuted. Pointless and futile. I cried angry tears.

When I woke on the morning of the twelfth day, I was alone. My back now merely itched and throbbed. I still hadn't seen the brand nor touched it. It was there and that was enough. It was my wrist that hurt mostly, a constant band of pain. I stood and looked down at the floor as the door clicked.

"I've brought you food."

It wasn't my usual mealtime. Why had the routine changed? I kept my gaze down as he approached, but he lifted up my chin and I found myself looking into his eyes. *I know your name, I win.* He frowned and touched my lip and eye, making me wince.

"I'm sorry."

He wanted to be forgiven but I wasn't going to be the one to absolve him of his sins and, instead, I remained silent. He sighed and kissed my cheek softly, lingering with his lips against my skin until I started to shake. Another tick for him. He won: again.

He locked the door and removed my chain. I allowed him to guide me to a chair where I sat with head bowed. As I ran my hand over the sore skin of my wrist a thousand thoughts skittered across my mind. I could try again, try to overpower him and steal the key. I knew this town and thought I knew where to run and where to hide. I almost did. Almost. I was Anna, I was weak; Anna didn't have the strength to try.

He dragged his chair opposite me and opened a can. Peaches today. I hated peaches. He scooped each slice out and placed it in my mouth. I chewed mechanically and swallowed, all the time staring at the can in his hand. The sharp edges glinted at me. He paused with his sticky fingers on my lips and I glanced at him. He locked his gaze with mine he continued to feed me until the can was empty.

"Why do you fight me?"

I licked my sore lip and continued to rub my wrists. He grabbed my hands in his and, jumping to my feet, I tried to pull them back but he squeezed tighter until I cried out. *Gracious, be Anna, be gracious.* I stopped and he started to rub my skin as I had done.

"I don't want to be here," I answered.

"But you are here, Anna." He ran his fingers around

mine and entwined our hands, just like my picture. The sickness rose and the taste of the peaches burnt in the back of my throat. "I'll protect you."

"I've felt your protection, I'll pass, thanks." Why the sarcasm? Where had that come from? Remember who you are. *Anna.*

"You won't always be so angry with me, Anna." He sounded so sure that I began to doubt my own conviction. Chip, chip, chip away. I will always hate you, *Daniel.*

He reached down to his belt and pulled out the cuffs. I tried to snatch my wrist away but he squeezed again, and stared at the mixture of flaking dry blood and fresh drops. Swapping wrists, he clicked the metal in place and stood up, holding the other cuff in his hand. I decided then that I preferred the chain.

"It's not safe right now."

He tightened the cuff to his own wrist and touched my face again, running a finger around my bruised eye. I didn't flinch or resist and hoped the lack of emotion would make him waver, make him stop or even, at least, get angry; instead he pulled me closer and ran his hands under my top, touching my brand. It burnt – not the brand, but his touch, it itched and burnt like acid on my skin. He ran his hand along my ribcage and I cringed as his fingers stopped at the underside of my bra, fingering the hole in the material.

"Did you think I wouldn't know?" He sounded amused again and I screwed my hands into fists. I couldn't hit him when cuffed, I would have to work out my rage another way and the stinging in my palms helped. He undid my bra and gently removed it, bending my arm and hooking it over my elbow and through my tee-shirt, his touch skimmed my breasts; it was deliberate, and I refused to react. Stuffing it into his bag he shot me a smile and grabbed me, kissing me hard on the lips. It was vile, but I stood there and took it. *Gracious and subservient.* I could taste him, even though his kiss was strangely chaste: but I could feel his excitement and that's when I resisted and pulled back.

"Many of the others wouldn't have waited, Anna. I'm a patient man."

Letting me go, he walked me to the door. As he shifted the backpack his jacket rode up and there was my chance to escape. His gun.

Walking down the stairs I stumbled and tried to reach to his side and grab the gun, but he pushed me against the wall and stepped back, we were the same height now. With my cuffed arm across my chest he started twisting my free hand, the ligaments protested with a click.

"No games." Low and calm. I stilled, but the moment he relaxed I tried again and this time he placed his arm across my throat and pushed. "No." A touch of anger flashed in his eyes and with one sharp push he cut my air supply. My legs slid again and with a sweep of his arm he carried me out of the library to the streets.

We were alone. He stood me up and cupped the side of my face. "Don't fuck around, Anna. Now's not the time for games."

There was something about his warning that I heeded. I took his outstretched hand without resistance. I needed strength and if holding his hand gave it to me, I'd take it. He pulled me towards the outskirts of a small housing complex.

"Where are we going?"

He looked at me in surprise, then smiled and traced my lip again. "You're talking to me now."

I didn't answer.

"We're waiting for them."

Looking to where he indicated, three figures approached: one turned to my captor and smiled. It was a genuine look of familiarity – even friendship – of a kind I hadn't seen in a long time. He removed his sunglasses and glanced at me, rapaciously: why did all these men have such cold and cruel eyes?

"It's been a long time, Will."

Will? I looked at my captor in confusion, but he grinned at his companion and nodded. No, that wasn't right. He was *Daniel.* I let go of his hand and he glanced at me, his grin becoming a gentle smile. No, he was *Daniel,* he had to be *Daniel.* I had to have something over him.

"She's not bad." He spoke again and I stared at the speaker, the man with the sunglasses. He looked me up and down.

"Where did you get her?" He spoke as though I wasn't there, or I as though I was incapable of speaking, or hearing. I locked my gaze with his.

"Unlands."

"Easy?"

"Relatively. Satisfied?" Daniel-Will, whoever he was, pointed to the box and the other man nodded, handing it to one of the others.

"Not trained her yet?" He glanced at my eye and lip. "Problems? I could tame her for you, she won't give you any trouble when I'm done."

He wouldn't, would he? He looked the type to take pleasure in cruelty. My captor narrowed his eyes and shook his head. The atmosphere changed, I could feel him tense, his anger was rising and my throat contracted in anticipation.

"Not necessary."

"She been branded yet?"

The man to his right moved slightly, his arms crossed but one hand touching the knife at his side. My captor turned me around and lifted my top, I shivered as the cold air stung my skin. He waited a few seconds and then turned me back around.

"Is that everything?" There was a dangerous undertone to his voice now and he kept his stare on the middle man. They were matched in height and build but my captor had a gun. I was glad.

"For now." He handed over a small scrap of paper. "Anything you can get from that list, send me word on the network."

The trio turned and walked away, Will didn't move until they were out of sight.

"They'll be back for you," he finally said, glancing down at me.

"I know." I had seen the looks on their faces, I wasn't stupid. I'd spent over two years running from men with that look and avoiding the towns and communities. The first time I had been accosted by a man in the Unlands he had offered me food for my body and thought it a good trade. That was day twenty-two, when I had still thought there could be a semblance of normality in this place called home. When I refused, he had tried to take me anyway. I was stronger then, I fought him off and ran, but I remembered the touch of him on my skin and shivered.

"Are you cold?"

I shook my head and stood patiently as he rifled through his rucksack. A flash of black – he had brought the designer bag with him. I wondered what else he carried, would there be something in there to aid my escape? Pulling out a lightweight jacket he helped my right arm into it and then swapped the cuffs over – careful not to aggravate my grazes – and then put my left arm in, zipping it up slowly. It matched his. Of course it did.

"Your name is Will." I made it a statement.

"It is."

Will, I knew the meaning of his name and it wasn't right, not for him, but I kept quiet. I was Anna.

Neither of us spoke for several minutes, until finally:

"I've got some business to do on the other side of town. I want you to accompany me." It was a statement, yet something in his voice made me wonder if there was something more to come.

"How did you survive on your own, Anna?"

Our game was over, that much was clear. No longer could I answer a question and expect to be rewarded like a pet. If I gave in, gave everything, then I would lose forever, but I had to speak to him, I was tied to him out here and I relied on him to keep me safe. Finally admitting it to myself I screamed inside.

"I learnt not to talk, to move quietly." I remembered day one hundred and thirteen, the day I had decided to leave, try to move somewhere new. I avoided all the towns – anyone with sense did – and I ran as far as I could.

By day two hundred and seven, I was back.

The memories of that time were hazy. I remembered the Wanderers, the long nights I spent awake and hiding in pits in the ground and the feeling of complete and utter paralysing fear; fear like I had never experienced before. I saw my first dead woman back then; I can remember her face clearly. No one forgets an image like that. Her lifeless, naked body barely hidden by the scrublands, angry purple bruising to her throat and arms. I cried for three days: but not for her, I cried for me. I was selfish.

I told myself that my home was safe, but I knew it wasn't, knew it was in the town and therefore dangerous, but it was somewhere and something I could cling to. I could walk around the countryside of home and know where to hide and where to run.

So I'd gone back. I never attempted to return to my home, but I knew the area and as a creature of habit, it helped calm me.

"Do you have a family?" I wasn't going to allow him to be the only one to ask questions, for every question he asked me; I would now ask him one. I had to push back. He led me through the streets, avoiding the scatterings of people and Enforcers.

"No."

Just one word, abrupt and final.

"What did you do before–"

He grunted and pushed me to the ground, landing on top of me. It was my capture all over again, him straddling me, our wrists joined by the cuff and the smell of, *damn, what was it?* I was breathing heavily and sharp bolts of pain ran up and down my spine. He kissed me again, forcing his lips on mine and crushing them, making my bruised lip ache. *Gracious, be Anna.* My conscience warned me not to react, and I almost didn't. But I thought about the gun and I pushed through my repulsion and closed my eyes, I knew what I needed to do. I kissed him back. I could barely breathe with the weight of him on top of me and I was glad: because if I could breathe properly I would have vomited. Instead, the short, quick gasps of air I stole helped me maintain my composure. It was disgusting; at that moment I hated myself more than I did him, but yet, I didn't stop. *The gun.* He pinned both of my arms down to the hard ground. Nettles rubbed into my right wrist, taunting me with pain. I kept my eyes closed, and like a child I thought: *if I can't see him, it's not real.*

His kiss deepened, and that's when I started to cry. I could imagine it wasn't real all I wanted, but the smell, taste, touch and sense of him pointed otherwise. If I opened my eyes, then the illusion of a nightmare would be shattered. I couldn't do that. I had given in again; I shed more tears for the monster.

He finally broke away and I burst into fresh sobs, I didn't care that he was there, I was weak. His face was directly above mine and I turned my head to the side, eyes still closed, snot started to form and roll down my face. I just wanted this to be over. He kissed my neck, breathing in my scent. I continued to cry and slowly tried to move my right hand from his hold, but it was pointless. All pointless. He pushed down with all his weight as he moved his viperous touch across the top of my chest. I couldn't breathe and started to cough and desperately tried to gasp for air: I needed that gun, I *needed* it, otherwise this was all for nothing.

I choked on my tears and sobs and he hauled me to my feet. I'd missed my opportunity; I had given in and kissed him for nothing. I was useless, I was his Anna. He drew me into an embrace; I was too preoccupied to stop him. Huge, he was so huge, how did I ever think I might have gotten free from him? I couldn't move, my right arm trapped at my side and my left still joined to him. I could almost touch the gun, my fingers stroked the metal once but I didn't have the strength to reach forward and grab it. I was drained and empty. He murmured into my ear, trying to hush me like I was a child. I did quieten down, not through his attempts at consolation, but through sheer exhaustion – although I was sure he believed it was his words that worked. He kept me against him for a long time. My face was tacky, my skin covered in sweat and all I could smell was him. Where was my courage and my fight? When I had known I couldn't get the gun, why did I not fight?

"Anna, my Anna." He drew back and kissed my cheek; he must have tasted my tears. How could he not? "I'll protect you."

CHAPTER FOUR

HE TOOK ME to a small store buried deep in the centre of the worst bombed sites. As he rifled through the cupboards for supplies he would often stop to stroke me, like a fucking pet. No, he was a parasite sucking life and hope from me each time we touched.

The owner sat at the desk reading, not paying us any attention. Curiosity burned at the strangeness of this all. Since civilisation fell apart, manners and goodwill and honesty were scarce. This shop-keeper must know or trust Will. Or was scared of him.

"I need something." I put off asking him for as long as I could, but my lower stomach stabbed and churned with the familiar dull pain. I didn't want to have to tell him, ever. I had hoped I would be free before this happened. The shame at having to tell my captor made me blush furiously. "I need... toiletries." He had thrown my supply away with my rucksack.

"You don't need to be embarrassed, Anna." He replied, kissing me on the cheek. The hot and angry tears rose.

Not again! Weak, so weak. He searched the cupboards pulled out a small cardboard tampon box, shaking it with confidence as he led us to the desk and bartered payment terms.

"I need privacy." I clenched my hand around the box and looked out of the back of the store into the long and overgrown space. It was a mix of browns and yellows, and looked sick, like diseased skin, spreading as far as I could see. A fresh surge of pain cut through my stomach and I grimaced. "Please," I added finally. I would beg and pander to his ego if he wanted.

He guided me through the rubble to the coal store next to what once was a kitchen, finally releasing my hand and checking the store first – of course he did, ensuring there was nothing there with which I could hurt him or myself. Once satisfied, he removed the cuff from my wrist, gestured me to go inside, and closed the door, shutting out the sky and leaving me in the silence of the unlit room. I dealt with my problem quickly, and then sat on an upturned wine box with my head in my hands.

It was blissfully dark and quiet, and I was alone; alone to be myself without the shackles of Anna weighing me down. I feared that if I dwelled on my situation for too long I would float away and never be able to recapture *me*. I would be forever lost to pathetic Anna. I couldn't let him do that to me. Running my hands through my short hair the rage built again. Uncontrollable and unsustainable. I dug my nails into my palms; it took the edge off and I was able to think clearly. I could, no, *would*, get free.

Staring around the small room I searched for something

Will had missed; a shard of metal, a piece of glass, anything. I moved quietly and deftly: two boxes, a pile of newspapers, a broken vacuum cleaner and a hat stand. There was nothing. *Fuck.*

I exhaled and opened the door. He was there.

Gracious. There was a small sliver of space to his side and I considered running. Just running, but in the nanosecond it crossed my mind, it disappeared. No, I would wait, there would be other chances, better chances. I had to make it count. If I was to escape, I *had* to make it count. He locked the cuff and kissed my cheek. I looked past him into the distance. *I probably could have made it.*

"Are you in pain?" He sounded concerned, and that made me uneasy. Another weakness perhaps? Or worse still, a sign that he had emotions, that he was human? No, I didn't want to think that, a human who cared could never treat another person this way. I nodded. Yes, I was in pain, not just from my stomach, but my eye, my lip, my wrist and then my heart and soul ached. He handed to me two small white tablets. "For your pain."

I looked more closely at the tablets: *para500* was printed on the side. I didn't know if they were still in date, and I didn't much care. I swallowed them dry and worked the saliva around my mouth, swallowing again and grimacing.

ON THE MORNING of day fifteen Will took me out from my cell again. He hadn't demanded affection from me again and I stopped often when we walked through the town as he ran errands, feigning agony and rubbing my stomach.

I wouldn't tell him it was nearly over, I wanted him to think I suffered. He passed me tablets and I swallowed them: of course. My eye was no longer swollen and I could see clearly, and the soreness of my lip was nothing more than a memory. Strangely, though, my back started to ache and itch for the first time in days. I found myself touching the brand and tracing the thick, hard scab that had formed. I couldn't see what he had done to me and was glad. He was a butcher and I was a piece of meat, nothing more.

I stopped again and grimaced.

"It still hurts?" That soft, deceptive voice cut through me and I nodded. He handed me pills and I swallowed them dutifully, just like Anna. "How long does it last?"

My chance to lie and I took it: *liars never prosper*. I beg to differ, the longer I was unobtainable, the longer I had to gather up my scraps of strength and wits, and then the better chance I had to work out a way to escape and regain my freedom. I was good at lying as well, which made Anna a master.

"Another few days at most." I didn't want to exaggerate too much, and to my relief he nodded.

"It's so much better when you don't fight me, Anna."

I nodded. *If only you knew.* Without reason his expression changed, I don't know how, but it was as though he read my thoughts, saw my defiance and strength through the shields and disguise I had built up. I noted the now familiar tensing in his jaw and the deepening of the lines of his face. He didn't blink, and his dark gaze unnerved me. "You have stopped fighting me, haven't you Anna?"

I nodded again and held his gaze. I would placate him, and so gently I stroked his arm through his jacket. *Gracious and subservient.* He leant in and kissed me, he opened his mouth and I stepped back. My mask slipped. I couldn't keep the horror or disgust from showing. *Idiot!* He didn't do anything for a moment, and then he slapped me across the face, four times in quick succession and, as my head snapped to the side with each blow, the burning grew stronger and hotter until it was as though it touched my skull. I bit my lip hard enough to draw blood. It swilled around my mouth. I refused to shed tears, refused to cry when he beat me, and today I was strong, I absorbed the pain and allowed it to work into the constant rage I held inside. They were only slaps though, they didn't have the aggression and force of the beating in my cell.

"You make me so angry, Anna." He was apologetic again, and tenderly grabbed my face with both his hands. "I just want to protect you, to take care of you." I had no reply and instead ran my tongue across my lip to taste the blood. I was Anna, wasn't I?

There was silence again and as the heat dissipated from my cheek I allowed myself to recall another time, another slap to the face; a slap more painful than any of the blows from my captor. Even now, years later, the hate and anger of his face was as clear as the day it happened. It shocked me then, it still shocked me now, but I understood why he had reacted that way; I had deserved it, hadn't I? Absently I rubbed my bare ring finger.

*　　*　　*

HE MET WITH an Enforcer that day, and to my surprise uncuffed me, locking me in a small windowless room for hours. I had nothing to do but plan my escape and lament my failures. I needed to be strong – not only physically but mentally. I recalled my time alone, the speed and silence as I moved. I could be that person again. I had to be. A plan formed in my mind whilst I sat in the dark and as I pondered on the last few details the door opened.

"Come on, Anna."

Disorientated I stood, the light piercing my eyes and making it hard to focus. He cuffed us back together before I could gather my senses and leading me out the building in silence, we walked. I hadn't recognised this area of the town when we first arrived, but the route started to prick at my memory. There was a small tree-lined playing field further up and we walked that way slowly. The sea of green in a landscape so bereft of nature was a welcome sight.

Stopping by a tree he lifted several rocks and placed two small bottles and cigarettes under leaves and dirt before moving further on and doing the same again in different locations.

Suddenly, he stopped and held up a finger to his mouth. I didn't know what he had heard and when I started to speak, he clamped a hand over my mouth. His eyes went dark.

"I saw them come here, I swear it." A young voice, male. My eyes widened and Will backed us slowly into the hedgerow, moving me behind him, my wrist twisted.

"There's no one here." Another voice, male again, older, a city accent.

"There is! That man, and a woman!" The young one again, he sounded… excited. I recognised that tone.

"Wishful thinking you dickhead, desperate to pop that cherry aren't you?" Louder now, they had to be close. Will's grip loosened and he withdrew his knife. I remembered the sharpness of the blade and the coolness of the steel and started to shake. I grabbed his wrist and shook my head. Surprise flittered across his face but his dark eyes narrowed and he jerked my touch away. My back itched and I found myself holding onto his jacket to balance me. The gun was close, but I wasn't ready. I felt sick, dizzy, a memory of a wanderer leaning over me, his hands on me. I dry retched.

"Where the fuck are they then?" The older one spoke again and mumbled something to his companion. Will gripped the knife tighter in his left hand and, as the man behind the voice stepped into view, he dragged me around and grabbed the stranger with his right hand, holding the knife to his throat and leaving me hanging like a broken doll. My cuffed arm raised high, I stood on my toes to stretch but my shoulder clicked and a white hot pain shot down my body. I screamed.

It was the scream that made Will react and at once he pressed the knife closer to the man's throat. Agony blurred my vision, but I made him out: small, five foot six at the most, and slim. Like all the others he smelt of sweat, dirt and that smell that no one can ever identify, that grimy, all-encompassing smell of degradation and decay.

"Are you following us?" demanded Will. Still quiet, still soft, but his voice held an authority that demanded answers.

"No, no, the boy, he heard voices, saw you, we just wanted to see."

"You wanted her, didn't you?"

My arm ached, it hurt so much that I had difficulty remaining upright. There was another tug on the cuff as my captor grabbed the chin of the man tighter and pressed the knife into the soft flesh of his neck. I stared at the boy: he looked no more than fifteen and he was terrified and reminded me of a scared rabbit, wide-eyed and shaking and even his dirty brown hair looked like the colourings of a bunny. Why was I thinking of rabbits? I tried to pull myself together, but it was as though I was stuck in ice, a coldness was spreading from my shoulder down and from my feet up, encasing me.

"No, no, we didn't." He begged and struggled, Will pulled tighter, the pain grew stronger and I muffled another scream. I kept my gaze on the boy. *Don't do anything stupid, please.* But I knew that look on his face, I'd had the same expression. It was that moment when sense left you and all you had was fear and adrenalin. No rhyme, no reason, just the primal response, and the boy had chosen wrong. He had chosen to fight.

He charged towards my captor, drawing his own knife. I felt it first, a warm spray hit my face. The older man dropped to the floor and blood seeped into the ground. My legs started to give way, but before I had a chance to fall Will dragged me forward and he lunged at the boy. It could have been no more than a handful of seconds, but it seemed an age. I don't know why I watched but my eyes wouldn't respond and the lids wouldn't close. My captor dwarfed the boy and he struck out before the kid knew what was going on. The blade disappeared into his side. He cried out in disbelief and wailed. I saw Will's cruelty then: he twisted the knife and withdrew it sharply. No blood came to start with; for a moment I thought I had imagined the blow, but then it rushed to the surface and gushed from him, trickling between his fingers like water. Red water.

The boy staggered back, his face ashen and his lips so pale like the lips of a corpse. I was crying. The look he gave me made me crumple, the desperation, disbelief, fear and terror all mixed into one grotesque image which overrode and dominated my mind. I hit the ground heavily, throwing up as I did.

CHAPTER FIVE

"Anna, Anna, it's okay." Will's voice roused me and opening my eyes I found him rubbing my face with his red stained hands. I could smell the sweetness of the blood. I don't know why I hadn't considered the fact that my captor was capable of murder before: he had, after all, beaten me, cut me and chained me like an animal. The boy's face flashed in my mind again and I sobbed loudly, wiping my face. Never had I had such an urge to be clean before, not even when he kissed me did I feel so wretched. In panic I rubbed harder, unwittingly smearing the blood across my cheeks and nose. My shoulder burning as though I had been stabbed. Will knelt by my side, watching me with his expressionless face: *of course.*

"Get it off me, *get it off me!*" I was hysterical now. The blood wouldn't come off, my hands were tacky and I could feel it clogging up my pores. As my tears fell they carried blood and I could taste it each time I sobbed. "I can't get it off." I continued to wipe using the sleeve of my jacket. "Get it off me."

"Shhh, Anna, shhh." He grabbed my hands and squeezed them tightly. I didn't want him touching me. *Murderer.* Why hadn't he killed me? Why did I have to suffer this? He tortured me, every moment was torture and I would never be free from it. It was foolish to think I could ever escape him.

He held both my hands in one of his and wiped my face slowly and methodically with a small handkerchief. That immobilising feeling that trapped me like ill-fitting armour. Two lives gone. It was my fault. They had seen and wanted me. If I hadn't been here then they would be alive. It should be me. I should be the one lying on the ground with my throat cut.

I crawled to my knees, ignoring the pain from the cuff as it dug into my wrist, ignoring the sharp ache in my left shoulder. I'd seen dead bodies during the two years, who hadn't? There were thousands, millions of corpses in the cities and towns, and in the Unlands some of those who found it impossible to cope had taken their own lives. I had never seen someone murdered before though, never looked into the eyes of someone as they were dying and never seen their desperation or plea for help. *He was a child.*

"Anna, oh my Anna." His voice made me ill. I tried to scramble away. It was pointless, futile, we were joined and *I'd never be free.* He grabbed my jacket and pulled me closer. Twice my size, his grip was relentless. "I'll protect you, it's okay, Anna, it's okay."

Protect me? I needed protecting *from* him, not *by* him. I fought his embrace, pouring everything I had into it. I behaved just like the boy had, I couldn't flee so I had to fight. I clenched my fists and hit him. It was pathetic. My punches barely connected and I had no strength in my left arm. He was so very quiet throughout while I grunted and snarled through sobs. I don't know how many times I struck him, I didn't count, but eventually they became nothing more than cursory slaps. I needed to do it, needed to show him that there would always be a fight in me, even when broken. When I finally stopped he grabbed both my wrists and pushed me back down to the ground and onto my back, leaning over me and sitting on my pelvis, those lifeless eyes boring into mine. I tried to move my wrists, to dig my nails into his hands and arms, anything to cause him even the tiniest amount of pain.

"Enough." One word, that's all he said and it worked. I stopped. Why? I wanted to be free, I wanted him to end this once and for all. I wanted the peace and silence – didn't I? I had been so sure that I wanted to die, but I never actually had the strength to pull the blade across my throat, or across my wrists, something had always stopped me. Why? I was breathing heavily and the weight of him made it impossible for me to move.

"They would have hurt you."

"You killed them." I replied in disbelief, not thinking before I spoke, not behaving as he expected me to, how Anna would.

"They would have hurt you."

"But you *murdered* them you fucking monster, he, he was a boy, just a kid."

Something changed, his face held a flicker of an emotion

and he gripped me tighter, grinding into my pelvis as he leant closer. "They were animals, you heard them."

His face was inches from my face and his chest crushed mine. How I loathed him, how he terrified me. The fluttering in my stomach, the irregular beating of my heart, the palpitations: this was terror, pure terror. I couldn't let Anna be frightened; she had to be docile, gracious and subservient. I forced my body to relax, sag into the soft earth and I nodded meekly, swallowing my aversion to him.

"Are you hurt?" The gentle, concerned Will was back as he moved off me. How his moods changed. *Like the wind*, does the wind change that quickly? I nodded, I wouldn't tell him about my shoulder. He helped me to my feet, pulling on my shoulder. It took all my willpower – and there wasn't a lot left – not to cry out. Something crunched like a footstep on salt as the socket rotated.

I couldn't look behind me. I could feel the accusatory, dead eyes staring at me and I didn't want to see what I'd caused. He pulled his backpack on and tried to lead me past the bodies. I froze.

"Anna…" he started, but I shook my head desperately.

He took me the long way around the field and we bypassed the fallen men. I couldn't stop thinking about the boy's face, the touch of blood, my sudden comprehension that I did in fact want to live.

The pain from my injuries – the injuries that *he* had caused – flared up again. My shoulder, my back, my eye, I had suffered more in the days of his captivity than I ever had during my two years of freedom in the Unlands.

The boy's face haunted me. I'd never understood how someone could say something haunted them; it seemed such an odd expression. I understood now. Every time I closed my eyes the memory of what happened repeated on a continuous loop, it gave no peace, and it was my fault.

I allowed Will to touch me, to hold me close and embrace me when it pleased him as we walked. Why would I not? He stopped, pausing and staring at a patch of Sweet William flowers. Picking one, he tucked it behind my ear, his smile not reaching his eyes. *Sweet William*, the irony was not lost on me. He had finally shown me the extent of his brutality and I was too scared to stop him, too *weak*, but it no longer bothered me, nothing mattered anymore. He held me against his chest, stroked my hair, and whispered his promise to take care of me over and over again. I cried more tears. This time I didn't cry for me, but for the dead boy with no name.

THERE WAS A time when I never stopped talking; I'd use a thousand and one words when most people would use a hundred. My granddad would often smile at me and tell me to slow down and I'd laugh and grin at him with an inexplicable feeling of happiness bubbling inside. I was always happy, always laughing and joking; it was tiring, very tiring always being so happy. There were those days I felt like crawling into a hole and never coming out, but I forced myself to smile, to bounce into work and flirt outrageously with my friends – why? Because it was expected of me. All that time I spent pleasing others, precious time I should have been with Stephen. If I had poured as much into our relationship as I did my friendships perhaps things would have been different… But what did that matter anymore?

"Anna."

I looked up and he cradled me again, his hand on my head as he crushed me. Why did he play these games of false affection? As his hand brushed my ear the flower fell to the ground. I watched the purple petals curl as they hit the hardening mud. Staring down I moved my foot slightly and crushed his gift, grinding it into the dirt. I wanted nothing from him. The inevitable was coming. I wasn't stupid. It was a matter of waiting, a matter of time.

"How are you?"

Why ask? He didn't care: it was a failing of society, our never-ending politeness. *'Are you well?' 'How are things?' 'Hope you're okay.'* Perhaps we should have been more honest, more transparent, no hiding behind banal conversations that, if we were truthful, we cared little for, things would have been different.

"I have a headache." I didn't, but I had to reply, part of me had got used to the routine of tablets. And I wanted something to take my attention away from the memory of the boy.

"I only have a few left; I'll get some more." He passed me the two little white tablets and I swallowed them and then let him kiss me the way he wanted, all the while staring at his face. He closed his eyes as he kissed. I hadn't expected that.

"What we have is very special, Anna."

Special, something different from what was usual or ordinary, yes, what we had was special. I nodded in reply.

"Thank you for agreeing," he replied, whispering into my ear as he held his cheek against mine. The coarseness of his stubble sent itching through my skin and the itch ate away at my anaesthetised and dead skin. Rubbing life back into me – did I want that though? To feel again after what I had seen? I didn't deserve to feel.

"I need to trust you, Anna, don't fail me." I didn't understand, but that tone was back; the danger in his voice. I nodded again. "Good girl."

Those of us that survived tried to rebuild a society of sorts, but the gangs had taken control of anything and everything they could use as leverage – including the now-scarce medicine. Infection was rife and the vulnerable suffered. The first waves of cholera killed almost as many as the bombs themselves, and then the fear killings started. The weak and unfit were culled like livestock over the course of almost a year. Those with sense hid in the Unlands, and so the segregation started. Them versus us. Wanderers and townsfolk. The civilised and the brutal.

Absent with retrospect I slipped, but gripping my hand he helped me over the low fence and onto the pavement at the outskirts of the settlement. It took what little energy I had not to shout out as he hoisted me by my arm. When we approached the group standing outside waiting for Will, I watched with interest.

"This is Anna." Will squeezed my fingers. "Say hello,

Anna." Gentle and kind again, the fury gone. He smiled encouragingly but I could see the warning in his face.

"Hello." It came out like a whisper, my voice bruised with the injury of crying and tired from little use.

"Hello, Anna." A deep voice said my name slowly, dragging out the vowels. I glanced at him: he was at least twenty stone in weight, but clean, like Will, and well dressed. He licked his lips salaciously. I stumbled back and grabbed Will's arm, *no, no, no*. I had to be gracious, subservient, I was Anna, but Anna wasn't strong enough for this, I wasn't strong enough for this. He laughed. "Looks like this one likes you."

This one? I continued to grip his arm and he held my fingers tightly. *This one?*

The large man walked with us towards the small scattering of houses. I tried to be subtle as I looked around for a familiar location or site. "You're late, I was almost worried."

"It took longer than I thought," Will replied.

"But it's done, isn't it?"

"Yes."

"Good. Did you pass on my message?"

"Yes." Will stroked my fingers tenderly again.

"And?"

"He cried like a fucking baby and promised there would be more next time."

"Excellent. You'll find food and entertainment here for as long as you need them." He paused and looked at me thoughtfully. "I'll make sure my boys don't touch your piece."

"Appreciated as always."

"Would Anna like some company while we discuss business?"

Will looked at me, his hand strangely still, his face devoid of emotion. I didn't know how to answer. How he wanted me to answer.

"You're being spoken to, Anna." Will smiled, but it was an empty smile. Was this a test? Would he beat me if I failed? I hesitated, but something started to grow inside me; flickering and then expanding until I couldn't help but nod.

"Yes please," I whispered, casting my eyes down again. I didn't know if I had answered right or if I had angered him, but I wanted nothing more than to see and speak to someone other than the man who made it impossible for me to be me.

CHAPTER SIX

WE STOPPED OUTSIDE a nondescript brick house and the large man knocked on the door. A small, lithe teenager opened it cautiously. I bit back a gasp. His face was a mess of bruises and scars, accentuated by his mousey brown hair.

"Ben, I've brought Anna to you." He smiled widely, stretching out my name again; perhaps thinking it seductive. I thought it revolting. "I want you to look after her while we're busy. Where's Matthew?"

"Upstairs with Katrina." His voice was young, younger than he looked, his hazel eyes darted across to Will and I.

"And the others? Why are you opening the door?" The lightness in his voice was gone now and I watched Ben cower, shrinking back and trying to protect himself with the door. I slipped my hand back into Will's.

"Playing cards."

He barged past Ben, sending him flying. Shouts and banging soon followed, and I gripped my captor's hand tighter. Feeling again was excruciating, I didn't want it. After a few moments a skinny middle-aged man stumbled through the door, hauling up his ill-fitting trousers and scowling at Ben as he went.

"Imbecile, I've told you before! They – are – not – to – answer – the – door. What if he'd left again?"

"Sorry boss." He mumbled something further I couldn't make out and Ben disappeared into the house. The middle-aged man glanced at me: the same look they all had out here. Will tensed and stepped forward.

"If you touch her, I'll know." That silky, soft voice again. The man nodded fervently.

We followed them into the house. Musty, with an underlying odour of cheap perfume lingering in the air. The mismatched Parker Knoll furniture scattered with crocheted throws and cushions clashed horribly with the carpet and wallpaper. I loved it. It was normal, untainted and undamaged. I could lose myself here, pretend things were all right. As I looked around Will unlocked my cuff and rubbed my wrist.

"There are seven of Olly's crew here in this house, Anna, and they all have weapons and appetites. If you try to leave, I won't protect you from them. That would be your punishment, do you understand?"

"Yes." Oh I understood. How could I not? I had seen Ben's face. He pulled me close, wrapping his arms round, lingering in the embrace. He hadn't done this before. He held me so close it hurt; my hands limply at my sides.

The door opened and Ben stood in the doorway. He smiled at me nervously and I noticed how he crossed his ankles and tapped his foot. Will let me go and walked past him without acknowledgement.

"We have tea, would you like some?" A polite monotone. His face scared me: I was ashamed to admit that to myself, but it did. The bruises were so extensive that they covered half his face; his swollen cheek and eye reminded me of a badly crafted mask, and yet still the lines of his brand dominated his face.

"Yes, please." Tea, so civilised: was this now civilisation? I followed him into the kitchen and stopped abruptly. There were five men sitting around the kitchen table playing cards, laughing and chatting. They paid me no attention.

"Anna?" Ben spoke and I tore my gaze from the men.

The way he looked at me, the pity in his eyes, made my anger rise. I didn't want to be pitied, not by *him*, not by Ben who had been beaten, it wasn't right. I dug my nails into my palms. My legs responded then and I walked towards the stove where the old-fashioned kettle whistled away. I turned my body as I passed the men, I couldn't have my back to them, and the thought made my skin crawl and my capture flash into my mind.

They casually threw pennies into the middle of the table, taunting and jeering at each other with jokes and corrosive banter. They were carefree and calm; I was fascinated yet sickened. I had spent over two years alone, two years with nothing and no one because I feared being caught, and was this the life I could have had? Possibly even formed friendships? Been part of all this?

As quickly as the thoughts came I shook them away. There were no friendships to be made here for me.

"We've no milk." He handed me a mug and I took it with thanks. "It still tastes nice though."

Ignoring the men, he ushered me up the stairs. It was different now: the kitsch and homely touches of downstairs disappeared with each step. There were three bedrooms, and Ben opened the door to the one on the furthest right. Just two single beds and a wardrobe, nothing more. There were no pictures, ornaments or cushions. Just sterility. Voices from the room down the landing grew louder: two distinct male voices and one female voice. Ben turned to me.

"That's Katrina, she's Olly's."

She's Olly's. I repeated it to myself. She's Olly's like I was Will's. Olly owned Katrina, Will owned Anna. My brand itched and throbbed.

"Why does she shout?" My voice was quiet. I still felt uneasy talking. I'd said more in the last few weeks than I had in over two years.

Another shout from Katrina and a heavy thud.

"Don't worry. They'll stop soon, she doesn't fight for long." He sat on the edge of a bed, nodding to the one opposite for me to sit on.

"Where do they sleep?"

"Two sleep next door and two stay downstairs, one by the front door, one by the back." He smiled and then winced as the skin on his lip pulled. Neither of us spoke for a few moments and I sipped at the tea, not tasting it, not appreciating it.

"How long have you been here?"

"All my life, I lived here before... this was my grandma's house."

I regretted asking the question, his face dulled. He stared

at his tea, and tears rolled down his face. I looked away, willing my own tears dry.

"How long have you been with him?" he asked. I glanced at the lace and satin curtained windows: screwed shut, *of course.*

"Fifteen days."

He made a small noise and I looked at him with interest. I realised I had been wrong to be scared of his face. He was strong, perhaps stronger than I was. He had at least attempted to escape.

"Who did you belong to before?"

"No one."

"No one? How? You were on your own?"

"Yes."

"How did he catch you?"

I didn't want to answer any more questions, I didn't want to recall my shameful moments of weakness; the time I spent staring ahead instead of looking behind; the way he pounced on me and smiled; but I told Ben anyway, I told him the way he smelt, the touch of him, the slap to my face. I held nothing back and he remained quiet for a long while afterwards.

"Olly looked after me at the start. He was my grandma's carer and I've known him for like, forever. When things started to go crazy, he had to get firmer and firmer. I mean he was always so strong with her, you know? Took none of her nonsense. He had to show people he meant business, he told me to stay here so I did." Ben paused and sipped at his tea. "A few of the boys I went to school with saw how Olly was looking after me, how he'd cleared my school of the bodies and gathered up food. He took them under his wing and they respected him. They still respect him."

He was jiggling his foot up and down again.

"Then Olly told me I had to start earning my keep; that I wasn't doing enough to help out. I offered to help clear the town, but he got angry, said that I wasn't strong enough for that, said there was other things I could do."

As he looked at me, I nodded.

"It wasn't too bad, I mean, I liked Olly, he'd always been sweet to granny and he looked after me, I didn't mind. He's firm but fair."

I didn't want the rest of my tea, and warm, acrid liquid rose in my throat.

"I didn't like it when he asked me to do it with the others. We had a fight and he got really angry. I ran away afterwards but he found me and then he cut my face. He said all the men in the other towns were doing it to show who looked after who." His eyes were dead now. "He took me to the doctor who went mad at him. Like, she was really furious. She made him promise never to hurt me like that again."

A doctor. Images of the bloody and dying leapt into my mind. Those that hadn't heard or seen the bombs had fled to the hospitals for aid, only to find crumbling buildings and injury. I needed medicines to trade, and yet, as I approached the melee of the desperate, I stole painkillers from an insecure ambulance. Even now I felt sick remembering the blood-soaked sheet on the trolley and the despairing shouts of help from the paramedic as I ran away.

"Where's your mark?"

Happy for the distraction I switched away from my memories, stood up and lifted the bottom of my top. I still didn't know what he had done to me, what it looked like. I still didn't want to know but I would show Ben, share this the way he shared his scars with me.

"That's big."

Of course it would be, *silly little me.*

"But it's not your face." His voice was a sad whisper. "You're pretty though, he wouldn't want to cut your face."

I didn't know how to answer and instead pulled my top down and sat back on the bed, ignoring the fresh sting of pain. The shouts had quietened and instead muffled grunts and moans carried through the walls. It went on and on until finally there was silence.

"I told you she doesn't fight for long." I watched a sly smile creep over his face. "I fight all the time; some of them give up when I fight – not all, but enough. If they don't give up, I know just how to make them come quickly so it doesn't take long."

Enough. On that word the bedroom door opened and a tall, slim, forty-something woman walked in carrying a bag and a bottle of wine.

"Anna, this is Kat." Ben stood and moved next to me while Kat took his place on the bed. I watched as she opened a small toiletry bag and started to apply her foundation and lipstick expertly. I wouldn't have known where to start, but she used a lip pencil, a brow pencil, a primer, and a host of cosmetics I hadn't known existed, and within minutes her entire face was smooth and perfect, a beautiful mask.

"Who are you with?" Kat asked as she smacked her lips together and repacked the bag.

"Will."

"Oh, *him*." She looked. She may have covered her face, but her gaze was unmistakeable; she was curious. There was something else: fear? "Well he's always been a weird one. So how long you been with him?"

"Couple of weeks." I didn't want to have to repeat it again.

"What's he like? Is he moody and quiet when he fucks you?"

"Kat! Stop!" Ben's face twisted into more of a mess and he looked at me nervously. "You're so cruel at times."

"He's not done that." I didn't need to add the yet, the implication hung thick in the air.

"Lucky you." Kat swigged from the bottle again and looked me up and down. I blushed, I don't know why. "I have to wash, Matthew stinks." Kat stroked Ben's cheek, cupping the knotted and scarred skin as she brushed her thumb over the angriest looking tissue. Leaning down, she kissed his forehead and tucked the teenager's hair behind his ear before leaving the room.

"Kat doesn't mean to be so mean."

"It's okay." I had seen the hardness in the older woman's face, the jealousy when she looked at me, but I'd also seen the sadness. "Where's her brand?"

"On her thigh, Olly didn't want her to stop working."

I just nodded again. I could hear Kat shouting and the

grumbled responses of the men. I looked at Ben for an explanation.

"They don't want to go and get the water for her wash. Olly got the well working, it's a pain but it means we have fresh water and we can bathe. Kat will make them heat the water too."

I remembered the feel of warm water down my face and back, and the coconut smell. Why did it hurt to feel? Should I not be able to remember without pain? It wasn't fair. "What do you know about Will?"

"He comes and goes, never stays long. Olly likes him, he brings news and good trades. He protects us sometimes, and he sent Enforcers here when we needed help from some looters."

"Where does he come from?"

"I don't know. He doesn't talk to us, he doesn't like Kat much. Olly offered us both to him and he refused. I think that upset Kat in a way. I like Will, he turned me down too."

He liked my captor, really? He couldn't be more than seventeen, so young: *experience comes with age.*

"So you've always lived here?" I asked and he nodded.

"Since before I went to school. My dad used to work away and my mum looked after me and my sister at home."

I didn't ask where they were. No point.

Walking to the wardrobe he pulled out a battered board game: Monopoly.

"Want to play? Kat doesn't and the men aren't allowed. It passes the time."

No, I didn't want to play, but for Ben I would; as I nodded he grinned again, contorting the scars and bruises.

"Awesome. I'll be the dog." He pulled out his keyring and unclipped the small metal Scottie dog from the chain and placed him proudly on the board.

"That's sweet." I smiled at the blank faced dog with a chipped ear and set up my piece: the boot.

"I love Monopoly. I used to play every day with Eric from down the road. We went to school together until he left and apprenticed at the munitions factory 'cos he failed the mid-year aptitude tests and couldn't stay in school. So he went to work, but we saw each other every night. He would have dinner with Granny and me and we'd all play Monopoly. Anyway, he made me this keyring. It's cool, right?"

"It's lovely."

He stroked the dog gently and placed it back on the board, grinning at me as he did. "For luck."

"Of course."

"He joined up when he was sixteen and left, just as things got really bad. He wanted me to go with him, but I couldn't, you know? Granny needed me. I needed to stay with her for as long as I could." He stopped and stroked the dog again. "Anyway, let's play."

It took hours with just the two of us. He told me about his life before. His grandma had raised him from young, and yet he still didn't say what happened to his parents. He had been at school the day it had been bombed, trying to grab some sort of education. Olly had broken the news of her death to Ben, and buried her. He loved music and played the violin, until Olly took it away to use it in a reward system. He spoke of his love of board games and reading, his hatred of the dark. I learnt more of Ben in those hours than I had of Will during our fifteen days.

As the light disappeared we crouched closer and closer to the board until it was impossible to see the moves.

"I guess we have to finish, who won?" Ben screwed up his face as he started to count the money.

"You did, I mortgaged all my properties."

"Oh wow, I never win!" He sounded genuinely pleased and I couldn't help but smile. "I have to go and cook tea now. Will you come downstairs and talk to me?"

"Ok." I didn't want to, not with the men in the kitchen, but for Ben, I would. He re-clipped the little dog on to his keyring and packed away the pieces.

"Here, you keep the boot. It's your piece now."

I took the small metal piece from his hand and slipped it into my jeans pocket without thinking. It was only as we walked down the stairs in the dark and into the kitchen that I panicked and thought of how he would search my clothes tonight.

Three camping gas lights lit the room and the men were still sat at the table, but a woman had joined them. I made the mistake of catching her gaze and I almost stumbled. Pity. Was I imagining it? I looked at her again and her eyes followed me, no, it was as clear as day.

"What are you cooking tonight, Ben?"

"Pasta and fried corned beef." He held out two huge pans to those at the table. "I need water."

One of them stood and took the pans wordlessly, leaving

the house. The others had stopped their jokes and instead looked me up and down.

"What's your name?" It was her, the pitying one.

"Anna."

"Nice to meet you Anna, I'm Ella." She nodded to the two who sat in the corner. "That's Stu on the left and Jay on the right."

"Where's Matthew and Kris?" Ben interrupted.

"Olly wanted them for something."

Five, no, six including the one who had taken the pans. Will had told me there were seven.

"Thirsty, Anna?" She held up a shot glass and nodded to the bottle of whisky on the table. I shook my head. "You sure? It'll help relax you."

"Anna's off-limits Ella, Olly *and* Will say so."

Her face relaxed; this wasn't a dream. Perhaps she could help me escape, leave this place tonight. We could run. I added the numbers together in my head, we could make good time before anyone realised we were gone. I held the plan in my mind, covering it with hope and holding it tightly. I realised the betrayal of my thoughts. I'd looked towards a stranger to save me, someone unknown and untested. Why did I turn to her for comfort? A woman I knew nothing about. I stepped back, hoping to create a small distinction of space between us.

"Hear that? No one touches Anna." Ella raised her voice and the others nodded.

The man returned with the water. Ben lit the stove and leaned against the cupboard, waiting for the water to boil. It was a standoff, all eyes trained on us both, no one speaking. I crumbled first and stared at the floor. A few moments later they resumed their conversation and I looked at Ben. "Where's Kat?"

"Probably asleep, she doesn't do much other than sex, and sleep."

"Do you need a hand?"

"Actually, can you set the table? Ella will set up the camping table."

"You all eat here?" The panic set in again, a room full of men, a room with Will in; my false freedom would slip away again.

"Yeah, it's Olly's idea. We eat together every night, we're a family."

Right. A family.

THE TWO TABLES were pushed together and with Ella's help I laid out the tablecloths and cutlery.

As the food was served, Stu went and brought the other men to the house. The temperature rose, and the heat from so many bodies made me uncomfortable. Will was at Olly's right hand. His dark eyes locked onto mine and he smiled. I had to hold his gaze, there was no other option. If I looked away he would be angry, he would wonder why.

He took me in his arms and held me again; as though we were long lost lovers instead of predator and prey.

"Have you been good, Anna?" I nodded into his chest and he held me tightly for a while, finally releasing me and taking my hand in his to lead me to the table. In the few hours I was free of him so much of my independence had returned. I didn't want to be led like a pet.

Kat emerged, and sat next to Olly, her make-up immaculate. As I sat down, Ella took the seat to my right. It was a tight squeeze at the tables and her thigh pressed against mine, a silly and dangerous gesture, but it warmed me inside. A person whose humanity had yet to be eroded by circumstance. Foolishly I pressed back. Just a little. There was a feminine solidarity that comforted me.

Olly spoke of rebuilding the world, showing humiliation and understanding; being firm and decisive and showing no weakness. The men murmured their agreements, while Kat, Ben and I stared at them. The conversation flowed between the men with Kat and Ben joining in, but I remained silent. The heat and touch from Ella scorched my skin. Too hot now, I tried to shift but she continued to press against me. I couldn't move any more for fear of Will seeing us touch. I was trapped.

CHAPTER SEVEN

WHILE BEN MADE coffee, they sat and spoke of trades and the other villages. I listened for news of any women that had escaped, to hear if any had been recaptured but there was nothing. Instead I learnt of a new community twenty miles north of there. I listened attentively as Ella spoke in hushed tones to Will. It was a fanciful tale, one of a new town run by women, for women. I didn't look up, and the way Will spoke with amusement and derision made me feel it was a game of sorts. Perhaps a cruel way to see how I would react: and so instead I tuned them out, only paying attention when the men stood and left one by one.

It would have to end, and Will pulled me up and clicked the cuff around my wrist, tying me to him again.

"If you need anything, let me know."

I stole a glance at Olly, he had the same dead look in his eyes as my captor: an absence of compassion.

"I will."

He led me out of the house and I allowed myself one look back over my shoulder, catching Ella's gaze. It was there all right: pity. The warmth she'd given me with the truth of her leg disappeared as we walked back towards my prison cell.

"Did you enjoy speaking with Olly's pieces?"

Pieces. I pushed my nails into my already sore palms and allowed the haze of sharp pain to calm the anger.

"Yes. We played games."

"Did you speak to the men?"

"Only to tell them my name."

Ella. I thought about her again; her tall lanky frame, her mouse-like face and those pitying eyes. I squeezed again and cleared her from my mind.

The journey back disorientated me. We turned right when I thought we should go left and we passed two buildings that looked so similar I thought them the same one. Was he leading me in circles? Trying to confuse me further? We reached his base and walked up the stairs in silence.

Without saying a word he un-cuffed us, placing the metal shackles next to the bed and taking off his jacket and backpack. I stood by the chain and shackles on the wall expectantly, but instead he pulled off his jumper and I stepped back in horror as he moved towards me. *No, no, no,* not now, no! I had a few days, surely, he didn't, he wouldn't. *No.*

"Anna, I just want to hold you." There was no anger, just a gentle, pleasant voice. He didn't fool me. The dead boy's face echoed in me again and I screwed my eyes shut. *Please no, please go away, I'm sorry, so very sorry.*

"Anna." My name again, Anna, submissive and gracious.

I kept my eyes closed as he pulled my top over my head. Empty, it was as though I wasn't there. I covered my chest with my hands, wrapping my arms around me. I couldn't think, but tried to concentrate on my life, *my* life. Stephen's touch, Stephen's kiss, but each memory of us together melted away and Will reformed in his place. I shivered. The room was cold and my exposed back and chest were covered in goose bumps, and yet my brand burnt and prickled.

He pulled his tee shirt off. I didn't need to open my eyes to know that. He gripped my wrists tightly but I didn't move my arms, and instead let the pain remind me that I wasn't numb, that I wasn't empty or the un-living puppet. I shook my head and screwed my eyelids tighter.

"Anna, please don't make me angry. You want to see Kat and Ben again, don't you?" Ben, yes, I wanted to see Ben again. I hated him, *I hated him.* I screamed inside, pushing the face of the boy away, pushing Stephen and Will away, until there was nothing.

I could feel how close he was to me. *Crackling heat*, that's what they said; they were right. He continued to squeeze my wrists; yes, *yes.* I was torn. I didn't want to feel, but I did. I needed to know I wasn't a shell, a husk. I held out for as long as I could until I felt my wrists burn and the pressure build. He waited. He knew he would win. I expected the crack of a slap, the bite of a pinch, but nothing.

"You are so delicate, Anna. Just let me take care of you." How I wished he wouldn't speak, that voice made it all so real. *Delicate*, yes, Anna was delicate and docile. Not me.

Yet my strength ebbed away, my arms starting to shake and he tightened his grip again. I forced my eyes open and stared at his face. He was smiling.

"I won't hurt you, Anna. I want to take care of you."

Oh, how I had a reply for that; fuck you! But Anna, Anna didn't. This was Anna's predicament, I gave in then, relaxed my arms and his grip loosened, but he didn't let go.

"That's it, good girl," he breathed, pushing my arms to my side. I closed my eyes again as he pushed me against him, skin on skin. I stared at the door as he stroked down my back, touching my brand. "It's nearly healed." I didn't reply; my face against his chest disgusted me. It was like a thousand ants crawling and nipping at my flesh. "Hold me, Anna."

I wrapped my arms around him and fixed my gaze on the door: the dark imperfections of the knots that twisted and curled inside themselves, then the wavy grain of the wood, like rows of sand after the tide held my attention. I concentrated hard on the wood, trying desperately to ignore the feel of his touch, the smell of his skin, and the way he kissed my hair. I couldn't though and, as his lips moved down the side of my face, I jumped and squirmed. *Cheat.* He said he just wanted to hold me, not kiss me.

"What's wrong? Am I not gentle?" He held me tightly again. No, he was cruel, uncaring and unfeeling. "Do I not take care of you? Stop them from touching you?" I continued to struggle and he held me tighter. I couldn't breathe. Where were my tears? Those betraying tears that usually fell when I didn't want them – I wanted them now, but my eyes were dry. "Anna?"

"You said you wanted to hold me." I leaned away as far from his face as I could, but he pulled me in tighter. I was still holding him, I didn't stop, *what was the point?*

"I just want to show you that I care."

"Let me go." I squirmed again, it was too hot being held this way. I needed air. "Please, let me go, I need the bathroom." His embrace loosened but he continued to stroke my back.

"Still hurts?"

Why did he have to sound like he cared? And why did he make me feel like a liar? A fraud and a cheat, like I was the one who should feel bad? "Yes, it still hurts. I need a moment's privacy." I swallowed. "Please, Will."

He paused for a moment, and then released me. I lowered my arms, grateful for the space between us as the cool air dried my skin. And then I covered my chest again, but this time I looked up at him and mirrored his expressionless face.

"Please Will, I just need a few moments." Carefully I reached into my jeans pocket and withdrew the now battered cardboard box. "Please?"

He nodded and I grabbed my top from the floor, turning my back to him, and pulling it down in relief.

Nodding to the bucket, he turned his back and stared at the wall. I swallowed quickly, excuses failing to come. Instead I winced at the dryness as I pushed a tampon in with a tiny gasp.

"Anna?"

I cleared my throat and pulled my trousers up.

"Are you all right?"

"I'm fine, sorry."

He turned around. His backpack was in the corner of the room. I still itched to go through it, see what he carried.

He interrupted my thoughts and sat me on the bed, removing my boots and socks.

"I can do it." I grabbed his arms. "Please, I can do it." Helpless, Anna was so very helpless, but surely I could give her some strength? Some small amount of independence? That wasn't cheating. He nodded, watching me as he removed his hands from me and crossed his arms. I worked quickly, the quicker I went the shorter the amount of time he would spend staring at me. I stuffed my socks into my boots and kicked them under the bed. He leant forward, hooking his thumbs under the waistband of my jeans. I grabbed his wrists and shook my head.

He ignored me this time and pulled down my jeans, running his hands over my skin. The hairs on my legs prickled as my skin pimpled. I was powerless, there was no strength to give. Time, that was all there was. What was the point in fighting? I wouldn't, couldn't win. These two weeks I'd spent wishing I was free, wishing that there was a way for me to remain me, was a farce, and it was *pathetic*.

Staring at the artex ceiling I traced shapes; animals and clouds in my mind. A cat, an elephant and a rabbit. As he removed my top again and touched my skin I lay there and let go. It was futile fighting, pointless. Another cloud, and a sheep. He kissed my neck, my shoulder, my breast. My legs continued to dangle over the bed as he knelt between them. I was with the clouds, I *was* a cloud, floating, carefree and light, weightless, wandering. He removed his own jeans. *Wordsworth:* I remembered the poem and repeated it over and over in my mind as he continued to possess me.

He interrupted my dream, my wandering, and as he stood he blocked my view of the ceiling and my blessed world. The dance ended. All I could see now was his face and I blinked repeatedly, hoping that he would disappear. Pushing me further on the bed he wrapped his body around mine, pulling me into his chest. I stared at the wall this time, creating roads and paths on the flowery wallpaper. I was a cloud, wandering above the roads and paths, I was weightless.

I woke often that night to find him staring at me in the dark, and following the curves of my body with his fingers, his touch light and hesitant – but I felt it, of course I did. When he caught me watching he pulled me closer and pushed his lips against mine, hauling me onto him and forcing his tongue in my mouth. I could feel his body under mine and the way it responded to our kiss. I was grateful for my underwear, so grateful that I didn't resist. I was pliable and submissive, like a *good girl,* how he wanted me. He was sickeningly tender, I wanted him to hurt me, cause me pain, *beat me*, but he didn't. He kissed my face, my eyes, my neck, and my hands. I let him. I could have fought, scratched his eyes, beaten him. But what would have been the point? I wasn't leaving. I was his, like Kat was Olly's.

He curled his body on his side around me: *spooning.* How had that phrase come about? Who had looked at spoons and thought of lovers?

Lovers. Why had I used that word? He wasn't my lover, he was my captor, my puppet-master and abuser. How had he worn me down and brainwashed me into accepting this hell? I stared at the wallpaper again, following the stems and petals of the flowers. The hatred that burnt inside me was enough to comfort me. No, definitely not brainwashed. The morning came and I woke to find him dressed and wrapping me up in the sheet.

"I'll be back shortly. Do you need anything?"

Perplexed, I shook my head and he continued to tuck me in. Was I now a child? I was glad though, as the light streamed through the window I didn't want him to see me half naked.

"I won't be long." He stood, and pointed to the chain and shackles. "I'm going to lock the door, but I won't put these on. Can I trust you, Anna?" He glanced at me and I nodded again. "Good." Picking up his backpack he pulled out fresh clothes and underwear for me and left them on the drawers. "I've taken your dirty clothes. Ben will wash them."

"I can do it." The thought of Ben washing my clothes upset me. I sat up, dragging the sheet around my body and he smiled at me, that warm smile which didn't reach his eyes. Sitting on the bed he tucked my hair behind my ear.

"It's Ben's job, Olly will be angry with him if he doesn't do his chores." His hand lingered and slowly he touched my arm, trailing it down and across my body, tugging at the sheet. I closed my eyes as it dropped and he put his hands on me again. I tried to picture the clouds but it wouldn't work, the brightness of the day and lack of shadows turned this into a harsh reality. "I do care for you, Anna. I watched you for three days. I had to be sure, but you were the one, you needed me."

That worked. I opened my eyes in confusion: *watched me?* He was the hunter, I was the prey. How long would it be before he killed me? Skinned and gutted me?

"We get on so much better when we don't fight." He walked from the room, locking the door behind him and leaving me shaking. I dressed in the new clothes he'd left and laced up my boots.

I made the bed, pulling the sheets tightly, the evidence of the night smoothed away with each tug and pat of the cotton. I lay down and stared at the ceiling, searching for my clouds and animals. I found them, all bar the rabbit. He had gone, escaped perhaps. I couldn't help but smile. The rabbit had escaped.

I don't know how long it was – it could have been minutes or it might have been hours – but eventually the door clicked. I could smell the food, soup, hot soup and... coffee? I watched as he carried the tray, balancing it on one hand while he locked the door behind him; *of course.*

"I've brought you something." He smiled and placed the tray on my lap. I was right about the food, but there was also a perfect yellow rose. My favourite, but he didn't know that. How could he?

"Thank you." I touched the soft petals and picked it up. "It's beautiful."

"Just like you."

I wasn't beautiful. I was too scarred, too wretched, too dirty and with badly cut hair. No, I wasn't beautiful.

"After you've eaten, I'll take you over to see them." He sat down and watched me. I was so conscious of him this morning that my hands shook and I had no appetite. He had fed me many times, but this was different. Each time I raised my arm he followed my movements with his eyes. I think I spilt more than I ate.

"I can't eat any more." I put the tray on the drawers and sat back down on the bed with the coffee, sipping slowly and concentrating on the carpet. It was plain, with no swirls to distract me. "I'd like to have a bath today."

"I think Olly can arrange that."

"Can I have the shampoo?" I wanted the smell of coconut. I needed that memory, something, anything to help wash away the scent of him. Immediately he reached into the backpack and pulled out the black designer bag he had given me and handed it over. "Thank you, Will."

"Is there anything else?" I hesitated. "Anna? You can ask."

"Please can I have the photo of Oscar?" I blushed, it sounded so stupid. I couldn't ask for Stephen's photo, and I didn't want to see my parents or my brother. I just wanted the comfort that my cat gave me. I missed him. He eventually handed over the photo. "Thank you." I was gracious.

I finished the coffee and clutched the bag close to me as Will shackled my wrist to his and took me back to Olly's patch of the town.

Ben was in the kitchen kneeling by a huge metal tub and washing a pile of clothes. He looked up and smiled at me in delight, waving with soapy hands. I couldn't wave back, instead I grinned.

Will removed my cuff and kissed me gently on the lips before leaving me alone in the living room. The front door closed behind him and I sighed. My heart suddenly hammered and I shook, I don't know why. Adrenaline surged through me and I had to sit to stop my legs from trembling. What was going on? Without warning I burst into treacherous deceitful tears. I couldn't muffle my sobs and Ben walked in, a look of horror on his face.

"Anna? Anna? What's wrong?"

His gentle voice upset me even more and I shook my head furiously, *no*. No sympathy from Ben, I hadn't suffered half as much as he had. I still couldn't stop though: Will's touch and smell covered every inch of me, clawing and pushing its way inside. I hated it, hated him, why did it have to be like this? Why? I never understood women like this. And now I was one.

Ben came and sat next to me, jiggling his foot. Looking up at him nearly undid me, concern was etched on his features and he threw his arms around me, hugging me. I almost pushed him away, I didn't want to be touched, not again. But his was so very different to the monster that owned me. He was gentle and caring. Hesitantly I held him back. It helped.

"Oh Anna, what happened?"

I shook my head. "Nothing." He pulled away and looked at me again in disbelief. "Really Ben, nothing."

"Ok." He didn't believe me, I could tell, but he forced a smile. "Some are off getting you some water for a bath. Will told them to."

"Thank you." The thought of washing away his touch and

replacing it with a memory made me ache with impatience. "Will they be long?"

"About twenty minutes I think. Want to come and talk to me while I wash?"

I followed him into the kitchen, picked up my clothes and knelt by the tub with him, taking my jeans and scrubbing them. I emptied my mind and concentrated on the sudsy water and my filthy clothes. Eventually Ben shook me.

"Anna, your bath is ready." I stopped and stared at him, disorientated. "Are you sure you're all right?"

"I'm fine." I dropped my clothes and stood up. "Ben, I'm fine." *Liar*. What happened to telling the truth? I couldn't though. Not to Ben, Ben with the ruined face and life worse than mine. No, this time a lie was easier.

I stripped in the bathroom and sank into the hot water, closing my eyes and allowing the heat to comfort me. I leaned over the side and washed my hair. I was back on my honeymoon with Stephen. I used the shampoo as soap, scrubbing my body and paying attention to the areas he had touched. I couldn't stay in the water for long: it was filthy in minutes. I hadn't asked for a towel and in frustration I sat on the toilet seat shivering until I was dry enough to dress.

He followed me for three days before capturing me. Why had he waited so long? I'd seen him hunt: he was controlled, dedicated and concentrated. He wouldn't have missed an opportunity. Why hadn't he caught me when I slept?

Two days, that's all I had left before he would want, and undoubtedly take, even more from me: but what was the point in trying to escape? I was weak and submissive. I was Anna.

CHAPTER EIGHT

IN SILENCE HE led me away from both Kat and Ben and out of the town settlement across the fields and up a hill. Peering through my badly cut hair we passed a long disused farm; a huge rust coated combine harvester stood in the centre of a field, with crops starting to rise from the split ground and throw the wheels.

Outside the old farmhouse he reached inside his jacket pocket, dragging my arm through the air as he did. I ignored the grinding and gritty pain, it didn't matter now. I didn't see what he withdrew, but he held it so tightly that his knuckles went white.

Knocking twice on the door, we waited. Finally it opened and a large, portly woman holding a shotgun greeted us, and a waft of antiseptic and cotton hit me. It was a welcome smell. "What do you want?"

"Just here to see the doctor, Sue."

That gentle and placating voice of his. It grated like metal on metal. He smiled at the scowling woman and held out his hand. A ziplock bag full of white pills nestled in his palm. "For the doctor. One hundred morphine tablets in payment for her services."

She relaxed then. The barrel of the shotgun wobbled slightly as she looked into the street.

"We're alone," he added. Satisfied, she ushered us into the hallway and snatched the pills from my captor and walked away.

"Wait here. And don't touch anything. I'll know if you have."

I looked around. There was nothing to touch anyway. That smell of antiseptic was stronger now, but then so was the smell of urine and blood, both sharp, both acrid, and yet so different. There was a stain on the once-cream carpet by the door. Sanguine. I pictured a woman then, opening the door to guests and in her haste to greet them dropping her glass of wine.

But I knew the mark was too large for wine, and the tell-tale drips that trailed into the closest room allowed the words to form in my mind, brightly coloured and bold: *stain the white snow with the blood of their wounded feet.*

The woman called Sue returned, her shotgun at the ready still. "Doctor wants to know what else you've got."

There was a long silence, I counted to forty-three before he reached in again and withdrew an old tobacco tin and threw it at our hostess.

"Two hundred morphine tablets, and five needles. Nothing more."

"That'll do nicely," and with that she beckoned us through. I followed, how could I not? My feet were not bloodied, though my hope was blasted.

Perhaps once a sitting room of sorts, it was now a large light and sterile space that stretched from the front to the rear of the building. With tall ceilings and ornate coving it reminded me of my mother's house. Not a welcome memory.

Sue left the room, and with the click of the door I found myself staring at the slim middle-aged woman seated at a desk. Her nose was slightly too large for her face, and her pockmarked skin was caked in foundation, yet she had the prettiest eyes I had seen in a long time. We didn't move until she indicated the two plastic chairs in front of her. The trail of red had disappeared, and badly fitted grey linoleum covered the floor. I wondered then what else it hid and as I started to form the images, she spoke, shattering them.

"What can I do for you both?" she asked in a concerned and pleasant voice. A perfectly manicured hand covered in expensive rings lay poised with a pen above a pad as she looked as us both.

"I need Anna fit and healthy. She is in pain, it makes her slow."

"Where is the pain?"

He slid his eyes to mine and indicated the doctor. I turned and she nodded to me encouragingly.

"My back," I whispered, the colour rising to my cheeks.

"I want her checking as well," he added, unlocking the cuff that bound us and standing. "For sexual infections and anything that looks untoward. I'll be outside." He ignored my blushing.

Outside? He left and in stunned silence I stared at the UPVC door at the far end of the room.

"Now now, there'll be none of that. Let's get you sorted shall we?" With professional authority she led me to the examination table and handed me a gown. "Strip off and pop this on." There was no curtain, and the gown smelt faintly of cheap washing powder.

She didn't leave and I knew why. The door was twenty feet away and I had spotted the silver key in the lock. It called to me, the sunlight lit it up like a beacon.

"This won't take too long. Are you on any medication? Do you have any illnesses or conditions?" I shook my head as she put the thermometer in my mouth and checked my glands.

The questions continued, my family history, my childhood illnesses and vaccinations. I was tempted to fabricate something that would mean I was unwanted and surplus to requirements but that fear and want to survive refused to let me lie. And so I answered truthfully and stared at the ceiling. As she probed and prodded I bit back my tears. I had tried so hard and yet failed. My legs started to close and she rapped on my knees with her palms. "Open them up, just a little more. That's it... hold it there."

She was so close, her fingers probing and pulling.

"Everything seem fine? No pain on urinating?"

"No. It's fine."

"Itchiness? Burning?"

"No."

It was building: the pool of humiliation welled and bubbled. The heat flooding my face. She checked for disease or a sign that I was unsuitable. I wished that she would find something, but there was nothing to be found.

"And when was the last time you were sexually active?"

Squeezing my eyes shut I replied. I didn't want to see her. "Nearly three years ago."

"He can't hear us, dear. What went on before doesn't matter now." Her voice was patient and yet there was an underlying tone of disbelief.

"Nearly three years ago." I didn't want to repeat myself again. "My husband, no one else since."

She didn't reply, but continued to probe and then inserted the speculum. One hot tear slid down my face and I fought the urge to wipe it away. She didn't believe me.

"I can see you menstruate, yes?"

"Yes."

"No problems there? Excessive or irregular bleeding?"

"No."

Withdrawing, she sat me up and checked my arms. "Were you on any form of contraception?"

"No."

"Good good."

She checked my mouth then. "Any ulcers, unusual redness or soreness?" I shook my head. "Excellent, you have lovely teeth, dear," she added, before asking me to remove my gown. I stilled.

"Come on now, you don't want me to call Sue in. I need to make sure there's nothing untoward going on."

Shaking my head in refusal, she sighed and slapped my face. The sting scorched my skin and flinching I allowed her to check my breasts, stomach and thighs as I stood shivering. She checked every freckle and mole, and every scar and bruise received meticulous care and attention. I had seen the physical effects of those infected not just with disease from the land and water, but also the sexual diseases. The purges and culls had almost eradicated the incurable, yet precautions were still in place. If I had shown any signs then I would have been put down like a sick animal.

"Excellent. Now there's a relief, nice and clear. There we go, all done. Now, pop back up and flip over."

She then examined my brand. There was just one sharp intake of breath, followed by a tut, and then she worked in silence. I didn't squirm. The stinging and ache as she injected my fragile skin sent a warmth along my spine. I could see the thin silver straight lines of self harm on her calves through the tan tights.

"Have you been with your man long?"

Your man. Surely she knew what he was? What I was?

"Not long."

"I see the way he looks at you. You will be fine. Not like some that come here. Oh no, thrashing and kicking, screaming and fighting. Right little madams. Ungrateful too. I clean them up, and they still fight. Some of them though… well, riddled they were. Horrible way to die, much kinder to put them out of their misery."

Swallowing my anger and bitter reply I stared blankly at the floor. Anna, I am Anna, only Anna.

"Now, are you sure there hasn't been any fumbling I should know about out there? If I know, I can help you see. Unless it's one of the incurable, of course."

"No one since my husband," I repeated.

"And was he clean? No HIV? Syphilis?"

"No. He was conscripted." The conscripted were all of

perfect health, carefully screened and chosen for strength and stamina.

"Good, good. Right well. I think we're almost done. This is good, the right way for things."

"The right way?" I mumbled, a cross between sarcasm and incredulity in my voice.

"If we all sacrifice just a little bit, give just a little bit then it helps the greater good. A fairer deal for us all. This is our new start."

That was what the posters had said. Almost a decade ago we had been told to sacrifice just a little each month to help those suffering. I recalled how the price of rice based goods had risen sharply, and how my parents had voluntarily given ten percent of their wages to the government war fund that was meant to help orphans and those in need abroad, but unsurprisingly we never received confirmation from the government as to exactly where these donations went.

"… once a day."

"Sorry?"

"This antibiotic cream needs to be applied once a day to the inflamed area. I've given you a tetanus injection and a mild painkiller, but the wound must be kept clean and allowed to heal naturally. Don't pick or scratch. You have a small infection." She spoke quickly, changing tone and subject too quickly for me to gauge her.

"Will it scar?" *Stupid question.*

"Well yes of course, but it's neat and cut well. He's no butcher that man of yours."

Those words again. "He's not my man."

She ignored me and, as I dressed, she dropped the used speculum and tissues in a small plastic bag and neatly tied the waste. Waiting until her back was turned I ran to the back door and fumbled with the key, pulling at the handle. I was too slow, I knew that the moment I had failed to turn the key. She dragged me away and I fell to the floor. *Pointless.*

"Stupid girl. It's worse out there than it is in here. Try again and I'll call for your man. I've got a reputation. No one leaves unless I allow it," she hissed, kicking me once with force.

There was no point arguing. Instead I pulled myself up and sat back on the plastic chair by her desk. The pain in my shoulder rippled through me.

There was a tiny framed photo of a boy soldier, about sixteen years old, dressed in brown and black fatigues with the military police emblem proudly displayed on his chest. He had the same large nose and thin lips as the doctor. As he held his gun across his body with one hand and gave the thumbs up with the other, I recognised the silver ring he wore. The doctor now wore it on her right thumb.

"Now. He's paid well for me to make sure you're fit. Is there anything else? This is all in confidence, of course." The last part she added with an earnest smile.

"Is that your son?" It wasn't what I wanted to ask, but it's what came out of my mouth.

"Yes. This is Thomas, he's one of the Enforcers now in a community near here."

I swallowed and covered my surprise. I had presumed him dead.

"Are you married?"

"No. His father died when he was young and I've not found another man." A genuine smile this time, her eyes crinkled and she sank back in her chair. "These aren't really the sort of questions I had in mind."

"And yet you are bound by no chains." I ignored her last comment and let this one slip, looking up at her face. Her gaze pierced mine.

"I worked hard for my son, long hours, little reward, precious time with him lost, and then the wars started. I was needed. People needed me, my country, my friends, my son. So I did what I could to ensure I would always be there for him when he needed me. Whatever the cost. I worked hard for this, all of this."

The words were spoken pleasantly enough, but a hard feeling resonated within them.

"Do you see your son often?"

"Not as much as I would like. He travels a lot; mostly through the towns like ours and the new communities and settlements. When he returns we spend time together. Family. It's important you see, that's something we all forgot. When things go wrong, it's family that matters."

Another poster, another lie. I nodded meekly and remained quiet. The doctor then called to Sue who stood by me as she spoke to my captor in hushed tones. He kept his gaze on me the whole time, his face blank and hard. I allowed myself to be chained to him again. I would fight him, of course I would, but I needed strength and hope and I was drained of both.

*　　*　　*

HE RETURNED ME to the town. The day wore on and the hours passed too quickly. I didn't want them to; I wanted to drag each hour out for as long as I could. Each precious minute away from him a gift. We played more games, Scrabble, Cluedo and Pictionary. I let Ben win, I wanted to make him happy.

Not once did he pry into my past and instead would deflect questions away when he realised I didn't want to talk. I couldn't help but ask him then if he was happy.

"It's not so bad here, Olly tells me of stories in the towns of how things are worse, how the trades work. I sometimes watch the traders from the bedroom window, some are nice and bring presents and games. Others just walk by. There were two that looked like police used to and a soldier a few weeks ago. One looked up at me, I waved but she ignored me, I know she saw me. Some can be rude."

"Are you two still playing games?" Kat stood in the doorway walking to sit on the bed, bottle of wine in her hand and face immaculate.

"Anna likes to play them too, not like you."

"I'll be back in a moment," I mumbled, staggering out of the room and into the hallway. I knocked into someone, apologising and looking up. Ella.

"You all right?" Her hands were on my arms.

"I'm fine." I looked past her to the bathroom. I just wanted to be alone. Somewhere quiet, somewhere calm. Somewhere I could gather my senses.

"I saw you look back last night." She didn't move. I looked behind me and Ben glanced my way then cast his eyes down quickly.

"I need to be alone." I tried to go past but she held out her arms and stopped me.

"Wait." She looked around as she pulled out two bobby pins from her pocket and grabbed my hand, forcing them into it. "It's the best I can do. I'm on the outside patrol tonight. If there is any way you can get out – go behind the block of garages and through the trees. Do you understand?"

No, no I didn't understand. She was helping me? Why? If caught she risked everything, risked becoming like me. The pins were heavy in my hand. How would I hide these? When would I get a chance to try and pick a lock? I was never alone at night. Did she not know that?

"I can't." I tried to hand them back but she stepped away. "I can't. I'm never alone, he'll find these." I kept my voice low. "Please, take them back. I can't."

"But…"

"I can't. He'll hurt me if he finds them, take them. *Take them.*" I grabbed her hand, warm and soft, and forced the pins back into it.

He had found the Monopoly boot and frowned while gripping my wrist. That deceptive and soft voice demanding to know who had given me the gift, and my meek and rushed response as I spilled the story of the game to him. He had been satisfied with my earnest pleas and the promises that I hadn't spoken to the men, yet he still kept the boot.

"I just want to help you."

"Help Ben, get him out of here."

"I tried."

Looking up at her mousey face, there was pain there: a different pain to mine, and so very different to Ben's and Kat's, but it was there. She couldn't save me. I was damned. But I wanted to save her, to save the compassion within her. That was the rarity of the Unlands. I had been wrong. Good health, immaculate clothing, those things meant nothing. Ella needed Ben. He deserved her.

"You can't touch me or speak to me. You don't know what he's like."

"You shouldn't be here, Ben shouldn't, Kat shouldn't." She looked into the room again and then to me. "It's not right."

Oh she didn't need to tell me what was right and wrong. I didn't answer and stared at the carpet. She finally sidestepped and I rushed into the bathroom, closing the door behind me.

My legs trembled, my hands shook. Too close, what if someone had seen? What if Ben said something? I put my head between my knees and breathed deeply. Why couldn't she be on the patrol duty this morning? Why couldn't she have told me about the pins last night? I would have had a chance: *hindsight is a wonderful thing.* That's what they say, how true that was, but they only say it afterwards.

I removed my tampon and realised, with cold horror, that my tampon box was missing. Shit. Where had I left it? I cleaned up, hoping it had fallen out and was in the bedroom.

Eventually I opened the door. She was gone. Did I really expect her to stay? *Idiot.* As I walked back into the room I forced a smile. Kat knew. Her face said it all and she was unhappy. I panicked again, would she tell Olly? Would Olly hurt Ella? Or worse, would she tell Will? The dead boy and his companion haunted me again and my fear rose. *Please no, please no.*

"The girl's an idiot." Kat scowled at me and then at Ben, who quietly packed the game away. I didn't say anything, I didn't know how much she had heard. "It's her fault Ben's face looks like shit. She tried to *help him*." She emphasised the last two words sarcastically. "Now look at him, he's a mess."

Kat was cruel; and wrong, for Ella was no idiot. I looked at Ben again. His face went scarlet and he struggled to keep his face impassive.

"At least he tried."

"What?"

"I said, at least he tried. Ben is stronger than both you and me." I sat on the bed and held Kat's glare. The hostility in her was clear, but I needed to hold my own, show her that she was wrong.

"You think I'm not strong? I put up with more shit than either of you two. You think that because I don't try and run that I'm weak?" Leaning forward, she sneered. "Tell me, Anna, just how many men have you had fuck you? How many times have you been used as a reward, a prize and a way to give thanks?" She spat the last few words out and I recoiled. I was wrong to start this conversation, I was wrong about Kat. I started to speak but she laughed bitterly. "Because Ben is so *strong*," she said mockingly, "I have twice the amount of shit to deal with. And you think I'm *weak*?"

"I didn't say that." I was backtracking, I had built up an image of an uncaring, unemotional drunk: but I was wrong. And now I was ashamed. "Kat, I'm sorry. I was wrong, I didn't know."

"No, you don't know, you don't know what it's like, so don't you dare tell me that Ben is stronger, how dare you!" She stood up and returned to her room, slamming the door behind her. I winced as it reverberated through the house. I looked at Ben who shook his head at me.

"Don't worry, Anna, she's always like that."

"But she's right, what do I know?" I wanted to apologise, find some way to repair the damage. I looked at Kat's door, if I went to speak to her, would she shout? Would the men come running? Demand to know what had happened? But then... if I did nothing, would she tell Olly about my conversation with Ella? My desperation to say sorry wasn't completely altruistic. I had to make sure she wouldn't say anything.

I knocked on her door and opened it without waiting. She sat at a dressing table, delicately applying her make-up. It looked odd without a mirror.

"What do you want?" She was cool and detached, so different from a few minutes earlier.

"You're right, I don't know what it's like." I stood in the doorway as she deliberately slowed down and took her time with her make-up. I understood and waited. Eventually she turned to me.

"You don't have to worry, I won't tell him. I know that's the only reason you're here."

"I didn't come just for that, I was wrong, it was out of order–"

"It's not easy Anna." She interrupted me and I closed

my mouth. "I was married, with a toddler. I had money, status." Her voice was softer now. I closed the door and leaned against it. "After they died, I drank and drank. I was nothing more than a lush. I used to live a few miles from here and Olly's boys found me. I was so drunk I couldn't walk. They carried me here and I've never left." She slowly packed her cosmetics away. "If I'd had more strength at the start, resisted the drink, I would never have been caught. I could have been like Ella." I glanced at the wine bottle and she stroked it fondly. "Now all I have is the one thing that trapped me. Well, there is Ben I suppose, and now you."

She walked towards me. The smells of wine and old sex mingled with her perfume, creating a nauseating mix. I shrank back, unable to stand up straight. She grabbed a tendril of hair in her fingers and let the strands fall around my face. Her breasts pushed against mine and her breath laced with cheap, sweet wine. "Now piss off, go back to playing games. I won't say anything, don't worry, but don't think that this means we're friends."

CHAPTER NINE

As I WALKED down the stairs he waited with his arms outstretched, that disingenuous smile covering his face. *Welcome home, darling. Good day at work?*

I didn't eat that evening. Every time I lifted the fork to my lips my stomach cramped. I hadn't suffered from this sort of anxiety for a long, long while. It was such a waste of good food.

"Not hungry?" Will leaned in close and murmured into my ear, his lips close to my skin. I fought the urge to pull away and instead shook my head.

I neither spoke nor looked at any of them for the rest of the night, even when he shackled me and took me away.

Not until we were back in the cell and Will had locked the door did I even think properly. That dread covered me again and I started to shiver.

"You're fine now, aren't you?" He removed the cuffs and placed them on the side. I rubbed my wrist. *Damn, shit, fuck.* How could I lie? He would know. *Stupid, stupid, idiot*: the look of horror must have been clear. He frowned, and the false kindness disappeared instantly. "Did you think you could hide it from me? Hide the fact you'd finished your period?"

I shook my head and backed further into the room until I was pressed against the cold brick wall. He trapped me and I had no choice but to maintain his gaze. I feared what he might do if I looked away.

"I thought you were playing games. I hoped you weren't. I hoped that you were starting to understand that I want to look after you, make you happy. Instead you took me for the fool."

I had underestimated him again. Crossing my arms in an attempt to stop shaking, I wanted to show him I wasn't scared.

"No."

"No?" His voice hardened.

"No, I didn't need them today, it was the last day. It's not so bad on the last day. I didn't think I needed to tell you every little detail." I almost regretted the last comment until his gaze softened.

"Oh, Anna." Will grabbed my arms and held me. It was awkward and uncomfortable. I didn't uncross my arms. I liked the barrier between us. He didn't say a word, didn't force me to embrace him, didn't hurt me or shout. For some reason, it made me feel worse as he then let me go and said: "Get undressed, Anna."

The blood roared, my legs buckled and I grabbed the radiator. This wasn't fair, I had another day, another day with Ben, with Kat, with Ella. Another day before he did this. I shook my head, this couldn't be right. This was the final punishment wasn't it? The sentence for my crime.

"Anna." He walked to the door, leaning against it, crossing his arms and frowning. "Do it."

"No." My voice cracked, disappearing into nothing and all I could do was shake my head again: *legs like jelly*, such a stupid saying, so true. My bones had dissolved to mush.

A stalemate. Why now? *Why now?* But it didn't matter; I had no more time to wallow in self-pity. He walked over and grabbed my arms, twisting them behind my back and forcing me to the bed.

"I won't ask again, Anna." He turned his grip, releasing me and I cried out as my already sore shoulder cracked in pain. I curled up on the bed, facing the wall, tracing the roads and paths on the petals. I needed to escape, which path could I take? I blocked out his voice, he was talking to me and I didn't know what he said. I followed the paths and twisted along the flowers. I reached out and traced the petals, his voice grew louder and angrier, I ignored him and instead travelled away from this, from him. I tried to think of Stephen, but he had no place in this cruel world.

Then he tore me from my sanctuary, grabbing my wrists and forcing me onto my back. The truth-telling tears didn't disappoint. They streamed silently down my face. I wouldn't make a noise. I would be silent, gracious and docile; I would be unliving, like a puppet. He had straddled me again, just like my capture. My arms were pinned above my head, aggravating my shoulder. A tug at my jeans. I stared at the ceiling. I can't. *No.* I kicked, over and over again, it did nothing. The cold air covered my legs and instinctively I curled them together, twisting and rotating my hips. The skin of my thighs rubbed and caught against his jeans.

He grunted in anger and shifted his weight. It gave me a small amount of freedom and I folded my body up as tightly as I could, arms still outstretched and pulled taut.

"Fucking stop."

I almost did. I hadn't heard him swear with such venom before. But this was really it, this was the one time that fighting really mattered, *chip, chip, chip*, my resistance was nearly all gone. I only had the tiniest amount of strength left to fight. It was futile; it was pointless, but I had to.

I wouldn't win.

I struggled and thrashed against his grasp – *screw Anna!* I refused to look at his face, staring instead at the ceiling. He undid his trousers and my struggling increased. Then came the first blow, the cracking sting of a slap to my right thigh. I almost bit through my lip muffling my scream.

"Don't make me do this, Anna." He was panting now, struggling to contain me and I knotted my body even tighter. His breath was acrid. The stench of dinner, of him, of everything I ever hated from now and before assaulted me. I couldn't block it out. I thought of coconut, but the sweet smell curdled to sourness and then to him. My thigh blazed as though it was on fire, he slapped it again and I jumped. He forced his knee between my legs, pinching and bruising the delicate skin. He pushed his weight on to me, crushing my ribcage and I was choking on the smell of him, the closeness. I was suffocating. *Just die*, at that moment that was all I wanted, I wanted to die. He kissed my face, covering me in wet kisses, spreading my tears, I heard the wail escape, and I shook my head from side to side furiously: *don't kiss me, don't try and make this right.* He stopped, and instead fumbled between us, removing the last barrier. He liked this. A grunt of pleasure escaped and my sobs intensified. No matter how hard I tried; I couldn't block it out.

It was over, my fight was over and my defences destroyed. Every movement from then on heightened. Wet. I could feel it, smell it. Coppery. Blood. He wasn't gentle. There was no kindness. He drove me into the mattress with strength and force. It was agonising, fiery and seemed eternal. The pain wasn't confined to my shoulder now, my stomach, my thighs, my chest, it consumed every part of me. My tears didn't stop, but with each one a small part of *me* left. The ceiling was an empty expanse of white. I closed my eyes, I looked for Stephen but he was gone, why would he stay? Stephen had seen my punishment, his revenge was complete. I couldn't escape. There was no place to hide. Every smell, every drop of sweat that fell from him to me, every creak of the springs, every small noise he made burned into my mind.

Begging for it, she was! She likes it that way!

It finally ended. I still burnt, still ached, but he collapsed on me and lay there. I didn't bother moving, it was over, and I was still alive, regretfully.

Eventually he moved, releasing my hands slowly as though he expected me to fight. I didn't. He propped himself on his elbows and I closed my eyes: how could I look at his disgusting face? As he moved off my stomach the pain intensified and even though I tried not to, I grimaced. The waves of affliction crashed on me until the barbed stabbing pain started to numb. I was disgustingly grateful. I had to force myself not to touch; not to wipe away the trace of him and feel the blood and semen between my legs. Humiliation, anger, loathing and horror, a raft of feelings choked me into silence. But inside I sobbed and wailed. I was curled around my consciousness and unable to move.

"Anna, I told you not to fight." Loving again, quiet and gentle. He kissed my lips softly and slowly. "It doesn't have to hurt."

I nodded and he hoisted me over, pulling me onto him. Everywhere ached and I could feel the bruises start to form. A handprint covered the top of my thigh. He cuddled me, stroked me, kissed me and whispered his affections in my ear. I didn't hear any of it, I just stared at the wall. This was my life now, I was Will's, I was *Anna* and he had won.

CHAPTER TEN

I DIDN'T BOTHER to count the days that followed. There was no point. Time has no meaning when you're in hell; I'd passed through purgatory and now I was finally where I was meant to be. He owned me completely: *body and soul*, that was the saying. He had my body, but I had no soul to give.

The morning after my breaking he showed his dominance again and I submitted. He enacted tenderness and kindness, but my tears angered him. I didn't fight, unless my tears were a show of defiance? He hit me anyway until even my tears dried up. There was no point in resisting, each time I tensed, shook my head or whispered *no*, he still won.

I didn't leave my cell. I watched in dull fascination as the colours of my bruises changed over time until there was no sign of my fight left.

Cleaning became a daily occurrence; he would wash me daily, like a ritual to wash away the evidence of his crimes, forcing me to lean back against him as he dried every inch of my skin. He never used the coconut shampoo, instead I smelt of strawberries, a false sickly sweet smell. I was glad it wasn't the coconut.

I didn't bother to count the number of times that he *showed me just how much he cared*. It didn't matter, there was nothing I could do, but when my bruises had faded he started to demand more – how could he want more? I never looked him in the eyes. Instead I held him the way he demanded and stared at the ceiling; the animals were all gone and I was alone. It didn't last as long if I didn't fight. Stephen was gone, I couldn't see him anymore when I closed my eyes. Had he truly left me? I'd begged for his forgiveness, we'd talked through our problems, we had been moving on, why had he left? I truly must have deserved this.

One day when I knew it would be some time before he was back to clean me, I curled on the bed and stared at the familiar wall. I could smell him everywhere, on everything, all over me and the bed. Stripping the sheets and linen I lay on the bare mattress and covered myself with the duvet. He was still there; but less. I struggled to count how many days it had been and realised there was no way to tell. It could have been a handful, or even weeks. My brand was healed now, and I still hadn't looked at it. I stared at the wall until my eyes glazed and I heard the door lock click. Turning away, I faced the opposite wall. I didn't want to see him. He entered, and locked the door behind him; *of course*. I smelt the food and my stomach churned and heaved. I didn't want to eat today, but he had other plans.

Sitting on the edge of bed he pulled the duvet down and started to stroke my back. He made the simplest of touches feel like torture. I concentrated on ignoring the route he traced. I didn't want to know what he had carved into me.

"Anna." He shook me gently. "You need to eat."

I didn't need to eat, I didn't need to do anything, but I sat up anyway and fixed my gaze on the pile of crumpled sheets. He fed me the food, some kind of rice and sauce, I didn't taste it. It was a chore, the repetitive chewing and swallowing.

"Shall I bring Ben to see you?"

Ben, *Ben*. I'd forgotten him and a small yearning crept into me. I wanted to see him but I continued to eat in silence.

"Are you going to talk to me, Anna?" I almost looked up at him then, but managed to resist and continued to concentrate on the bedding. Conscious of the cold, I pulled the duvet around my bare skin, covering everything but my head.

"Anna?"

I couldn't ignore him forever. I wasn't stupid. I forced my eyes up to his face.

He was smiling as though this was normal. He put down the tray and sat next to me, worming his hands under the duvet and pulling me onto his lap. He wrapped his arms around me and my food threatened to come back up.

"Please talk to me."

A finger under my chin guiding me to look at him.

"I'm cold." He pulled the duvet around us both and leaned against the wall with me cradled on his lap, it was ridiculous. I realised how little I knew of him so I asked, "What do you do out there?"

He didn't reply immediately and instead took my hand in his, stroking the back of it over and over again until it became painful.

"I fix things for people, help settle disputes, find things and people that they need, patrol and carry messages."

"Why?" I couldn't fathom why I was getting into a conversation with him, why I didn't just ignore him. Another long pause.

"Because I'm good at it." He didn't want to talk anymore and pulled my face closer to his. I stared up at the ceiling as he kissed me. There was no point in counting. He broke away and instinctively I wiped my mouth on my hand. He noticed but said nothing. "This is the first time you've spoken to me in over two weeks."

Two weeks? How had so much time passed? I'd now been with him almost a month.

"You hurt me."

"I've only ever wanted to take care of you, you caused it to be painful. There was no need to fight." He wasn't accusatory, merely soft and explanatory. "It doesn't hurt when you don't fight, does it?"

There was only one answer I could give him. He wouldn't accept the truth, so I shook my head and he squeezed me tighter.

"Ben has asked after you, he was worried. I told him you've been unwell but that you're better now and that you'll come to dinner tonight." I nodded. I wanted to see Ben and yes, I had been unwell. "I've brought you new clothes." He moved off the bed and went through his backpack: a dress. I looked outside, it was nearly October, and yet he had brought me a dress. "I thought you'd look pretty."

"It's cold." I didn't know what else to say and I immediately regretted speaking. His face fell and a dark cloud of anger covered him. "It's pretty... but it's cold, I'll need a jumper." He stared at me and I swallowed anxiously. "I do like it."

He left the room and I stood on the bed by the window and watched the sky turn from grey, to blue, to orange and finally back to dark grey and then a velvety black. It was so clear that the constellations shone like beacons. Craning my neck and standing on tiptoes I made out Pegasus clearly; winter really was approaching.

He eventually returned with bedding and the wash bowl. I knew the rules. I helped him undress me and he sat washing me. I wasn't allowed to interfere. My hair first, then my neck, back and chest. He worked his way down methodically, ritualistically.

As he dried me and I dressed, he stood behind me, wrapping his arms around my waist and drawing me closer to him. "I have a gift for you."

I didn't want another false declaration of affection, but I remained quiet as he forced an ill-fitting ring on my finger. Though it was a simple diamond band, I hated it.

"I want people to know that you're mine."

"You've already branded me," I replied softly.

"This is prettier than the brand."

When he released me I tried to twist the ring but it was stuck.

"It won't come off," I blurted out.

"It's not meant to." He had his back to me and I almost, *almost* felt my own anger, but as soon as it rose it disappeared in a haze of pain and memory. I stopped trying to pull at the ring. My finger already red and puffy.

"Are you ready for dinner?" He held up the cuffs.

"Please… not the cuffs."

He lowered them and beckoned me over, I didn't argue and walked over to him.

"But you'll run."

"No, I won't." I shook my head eagerly, trying to convince him. "I won't."

"Oh, Anna." He clicked the cuff around my wrist and then his. "It's written all over your face, you'll try and then we'll fight."

We left the house, the shackle chafing my wrist and my finger throbbing at the tightness of his *gift*.

This was day one. I'd have to start again.

ON THE SECOND day I counted a rotation of thirty-three different Wanderers and Enforcers, including four women. Why were they different? Why weren't they branded and locked in a cell? Greeted with open arms by Olly and shown the same hospitality as Will, they looked no different to me, perhaps larger, stronger, but they were still female.

A husband and wife team pulled a third woman with them, her hands tied together, and her face awash with fright. A beautiful mane of red curly hair fell halfway down her back. Her limbs were so thin that surely, she would break. There was a large cut to her right forearm, and I couldn't tell if it was the start of a brand or whether she had injured herself. I found myself grabbing Ben's arm as Olly negotiated terms for the woman, pawing at her body with the eagerness of a child at a sweet shop. Ben held me back, whispering a warning, as I involuntarily forgot who I was meant to be and tried to step forward as Olly grabbed at her breasts and remarked that she would be a worthy addition to his toys.

She begged, her words an echo and memory to the way I had begged my captor not to hurt me, to let me go. Olly ignored her, even laughing at her tears and running a finger roughly across her cheek.

The deal was sealed. Her freedom traded for a repaired house within the town for the couple.

One of Olly's men, I can't remember his name, dragged her away to Olly's house, her screams growing quieter and quieter until I couldn't tell if it was her crying in the distance or another unfortunate soul in this hellish town.

THAT NIGHT AT dinner, the couple and female wanderers sat laughing and joking with Olly and his crew, ignoring Kat, Ben and me. That night, after he had shown his *affection*, I asked Will why those women were free. He chuckled and kissed my hair with his reply:

"Not all women suit being branded, the same as not all women are strong enough to be alone."

I didn't even have the will to be angry.

*   *   *

ON THE THIRD day I asked Ben where Ella was. He told me Olly had sent her to another town on an errand and she would be away for several weeks. A small pang of longing for a sympathetic face stabbed into my dead heart, jolting it slightly but not enough of an ignition to start it.

"Don't worry, Anna. Ella will come back. I hope she brings some honey like she did last time." He moved the Scottie dog along the board and I glanced at Kat on the other bed. She was silently watching us both over the top of her dog-eared magazine. When the door opened and Matthew nodded first at her and indicated the bedroom next door, she shot me a withering look and threw her magazine to the floor. It slithered open on a glossy shot of a mother and baby on one page, and an army recruitment poster on the other. As the door closed and Ben continued to steal from the bank while thinking I wasn't looking, and while he slid another handful of notes onto his already bulging pile, I picked up the magazine and flicked through; lies, all of it lies.

Reluctantly, I walked down the stairs with Ben and back into the kitchen, preparing yet another meal. Will stood and pulled out my chair. This was new, where had the chivalry come from? Sitting I looked around – Ben stared at his plate and Kat smirked as she sipped her wine. But it was when Olly began his nightly reflection on life and thankfulness of family that I really started to feel the hatred burn in me again.

*　　*　　*

THE CHIVALRY DISAPPEARED soon enough, for the following days I remained locked away and alone in my cell. He would come and check on me, remove the bucket, and leave food, but always silent. I wept like a child, huge sobs dragged through my body. Each minute I was alone, and without distraction, I could only focus on him and his vile touch.

It was late into the night of the fourth day I started to panic. My captor wasn't back. I banged on the door, shouting and calling for anyone to come and release me. More tears, more anger, more sadness and loneliness raged through my body. I had to get out. If he was dead, I was trapped. As much as I hated the thought of him returning, I willed and wished him to walk in. If it was him, I knew how to please him, what would happen. It was a cold comfort but comfort nonetheless.

The door was eventually unlocked. I didn't move from the bed.

"You left me all day," I blurted, without thinking.

"I had business to attend to."

"Why couldn't I be with Ben?"

He didn't reply and climbed in behind me and pulled me close.

He finally spoke.

"Ben's run away."

Those words were like I'd been punched in the stomach, like he had delivered another winding blow.

"Ella took him."

I screwed my eyes shut and screamed inside. They'd left me behind, *they'd left me behind!* My selfishness shamed me, but that shame was soon wiped out by fear.

"Do you know where they went?" He turned me around to face him and started to stroke my face and hair. It wasn't tender. It was threatening. I shook my head. "Are you sure?" His hand moved to my throat and I shook my head harder.

"I don't know where they went, I thought Ella was away, working for Olly."

"Olly wanted his men to question you. I said it wouldn't be necessary. You wouldn't lie to me would you, Anna?"

I shook my head again. His hand lingered around my throat. I found myself playing with the ring and thinking of the dead boy. He was a murderer, I could never forget that.

"I'm not lying, I don't know where they went."

Part of me was glad they had gone, escaped and run away, the rest of me was overwhelmed with loneliness.

"How can I trust you, Anna? You've played games with me before." His hand moved to my brand and he pushed me onto my back, leaning over me.

"I'm not lying, I promise, Will, I'm not lying." I pressed as far back into the mattress as I could, creating a small amount of space between the two of us. I'd tensed up and he could sense that, the heavy lines were back on his face.

"You promise? What do you promise, Anna?"

"I promise I'm not lying to you, I wouldn't lie to you."

"No?" He kept one hand on my throat and the other on the inside of my leg. I was too scared to close my eyes. "So tell me Anna, have you ever had a conversation with Ella with no one else around?"

Kat, that bitch. Instantly, guilt rose, I didn't know what they had done to her, and after a warning squeeze to my neck I nodded.

"What did you talk about?" He continued to move his hand on the soft skin of my inner thighs and I desperately wanted to clamp them shut: but I didn't.

"She offered to help me escape, I said no."

"And why did you say no?"

"You'd find me, you'd hurt me."

He relaxed the grip. My heart was beating so fast I was lightheaded and nauseous. He continued to irritate my skin and I grabbed his wrist and shook my head.

"I'll do more than hurt you, Anna."

He lied to me, it did hurt if I didn't fight, and there was no attempt at gentleness. I held him, I tried to push him away, begged him to stop, I even begged him to kiss me, anything to appeal to the man, but nothing worked. He dug his fingers into my arms, clawing at my skin. The sickness and pain spread from my stomach up my back. It went on forever, longer than ever before; eventually he gave up and released me. I pulled my knees up and curled on my side, crying softly into my pillow. I pictured Ben and Ella, far away, somewhere together: alone. They had left me.

I didn't sleep that night. When I was sure my captor slept I gradually inched out of the bed and knelt by his bag. Every part of me ached. Too scared to open the zip in case he woke I undid the toggle and opened the small compartment at the front: maps, compass, fishing line, hooks, a sewing kit, and a pot of paracetamol. I paused, slowly opening the pot, conscious that the tablets would rattle. There were only six – why, when I finally had the strength and momentum to end it all, were there only six?

I didn't get a chance to put them back. There was a sudden tearing and pulling feeling as I was lifted by my hair. Screaming, I dropped the bottle and clawed at his hands. My toes scraped the ground and he threw me across the room. I hit my head on the edge of the bed and blood poured down my face. In an instant he grabbed me by the arm and punched me in the ribs. I coughed and choked as my body crunched. A white hot pain burst through my side and I started to cry; blood was on my lips and shock set in. I was shaking violently. He hit me again and again in the same place. I didn't think it could hurt any more. I was wrong.

I collapsed. I couldn't see properly, it hurt so much that everything blurred. He threw me on the bed as though I weighed nothing and backhanded my face over and over. I tasted blood. Everything went black.

When I finally woke, I couldn't open my left eye and my face was swollen and inflamed. I tried to sit up but cried out as a searing rush of extreme coldness engulfed my right side.

Alone. It was day and the low winter sun streamed through the tiny window. Will was gone. I looked down, the angry purple and red bruising to my side glared up at me. Gingerly touching my face I could feel the heat trapped under the surface – my jaw throbbed and I ran my tongue over my teeth, feeling one wobble at the back. I stared at the ceiling. Why had I gone through the bag and made him angry? I was *stupid*.

At the sound of the door being unlocked I tried to scramble for cover, but the pain prevented me. He entered, face blank, with a tray of food.

"I'm sorry," I blurted out before he approached. "I didn't mean to make you angry." My voice was slurred, muffled.

He didn't speak, sitting next to me and forcing two painkillers into my mouth, followed by a sip of water.

"I'm sorry, Will." I really was sorry.

Not a word. He spooned soup into my mouth and even though I wasn't hungry I swallowed, wincing as my side pulled. When it was finished he helped me to my feet and I cried out and panicked. I was desperate to placate him, to keep him calm. After dressing me he checked the back of my head as he brushed my sticky, matted hair.

"Will you ever learn, Anna? I never thought you'd give me so much trouble. You seemed so lost, so quiet when I watched you. I just wanted to take care of you. Instead you make me angry, push and test me all the time."

"I'm sorry."

CHAPTER ELEVEN

"WHAT HAPPENED?"

I didn't speak, or rather, couldn't speak. My face was too swollen and I feared what he would do if I did.

"Business went wrong. Olly's lost Ben – his rent boy with the fucked-up face – and one of his crew, Ella. If you see them, get Sue to send him word on the network. There's a reward out for their return." He didn't unchain me this time, and instead accompanied me to the table. I drew back as her gloved hands touched my ribs and side. Blood filled my mouth as I bit my lip in pain.

"Most likely a fracture or two. I suggest rest and painkillers. I would give you some morphine tablets…" She trailed off and locked stares with Will while I concentrated on her paisley shirt, not wanting to look up. There was a long silence. "But no, I think just ibruprofen and paracetamol will do." She then proceeded to check my neck and scalp, her careful fingers slowly probing. It took all of my strength to remain still and not cry out. She took an agonising amount of time and made carefree chit-chat with Will: about the weather of all things. The doctor was worried about the anticipated frosts and her seedlings, and when he offered her supplies via the network she called him her hero.

I still didn't cry, not when the doctor caught the side of my face with her ring, nor even when I slid to my feet and jarred my ribs.

"I recommend that she takes it slow and steady. No heavy lifting and, as I said, lots of rest," she addressed Will, ignoring me. "If you must travel then be patient. She'll not be able to travel at the pace you're used to."

"Fine. How long until she'll be healed?"

"Difficult to say. The pain should subside after a few weeks. If she needs further breaking in then I strongly suggest you avoid that area – you could do real harm."

There was no emotion in her voice. Just that professional authority again, and Will clasped her hand in both of his with a declaration of thanks. The doctor hadn't charged him this time and she seemed warmer to him than she had before.

I could barely walk. Each step left me gasping for air and I shuffled like an old woman. He was still angry with me and would often pull on the cuff and quicken his pace, forcing me to stumble and cry out at the blinding bolts of pain in my chest and stomach. I didn't want him to be angry.

"I'm sorry, Will." I apologised often, but he ignored me.

*　　*　　*

I COUNTED THE days that followed: four came and went before I was able to walk without constant pain. I could see clearly out of my bruised eye and had managed to keep Will happy: a magnificent feat.

Locked back in my cell in the old library, it was the same routine. I would be alone and chained to the wall during the day, but at night he would come to me. Some nights he would do nothing more than hold me, others he demanded my affection in the form of kisses and a massage: but more often than not he would possess my body and control me the way he loved to own me.

On the twelfth day in my cell, which was day twenty-six since I had started counting again, everything changed.

I sat on the bed slowly brushing my hair when the door opened and Will entered. He carried the black designer bag.

"I've brought you a few more things."

"Thank you," I replied graciously as he handed me the bag: more toothpaste, more cosmetics, shampoos and creams. I pulled out the small box at the bottom and my blood ran cold. A strange saying that, but so very true. My mouth was suddenly dry and I tasted bile. *No, no, no,* it had been twenty-six days. It still had time to come. The relief warmed my veins and my pulse steadied again, soothing the sickness. I almost relaxed, until I remembered the two weeks I hadn't left the cell.

My hand gripped the box and I stared at the floor. The shuddering started, and then the coldness again. Everything was muted for a moment, everything other than the irregular beat of my heart pounding and roaring like a chorus of bells.

"Anna?"

I heard his voice, but it didn't register in my head. All I could think of was the numbers and days, where had I gone wrong? I must be wrong. I started again, slower this time, but no matter how hard I tried, they didn't add up. It had been just over forty days since my last period.

"Anna?" He repeated my name. I heard the echo but couldn't respond. I was weightless again, floating above the room, away from hell. My ears hurt, the fierceness of the pounding caused them to sting. I dropped the box and pushed past Will to the bucket in the corner where I threw up repeatedly until there was nothing left.

"Anna, what's wrong?"

That hollow concern. I shook my head. There was no way I could tell him. He'd never let me go, and, besides, it might be nothing, it could just be stress. Yes, stress; I'd read about this before: *traumatic emotional incidents can affect the cycle.* That must be the cause.

"I feel sick," I lied. I couldn't tell him. I stared at my hands on the rim of the bucket. The diamond band mocked me. He pulled me to my feet, feeling my temperature with the back of his hand.

"What's wrong?"

"I just felt unwell, I'll be fine."

Pulling me against him he murmured concern and I squeezed my eyes shut, willing and begging whatever force there was for my period to come. I hadn't thought of Stephen in days, but his face appeared now. Was this his final act of revenge?

By the morning of what I counted to be day fifty-two I was still waiting. Each night when he touched me I forced myself to smile at him and bend to his will. I told him my period was here, and so he had me please him in other, equally disgusting ways. I wanted to break down and cry, but I was still so tense that I couldn't force the tears to come, even though I had tried. It was slowly tearing me in two. I begged and wished and willed my body to prove me wrong: but it didn't. I was terrified he would realise. He wasn't stupid, he'd called my bluff before and he could read me. Every time the door lock clicked I jumped and swallowed the sickness plaguing me, thinking he would come in and demand to know why I hadn't refused his advances in over a month and a half when I had made him wait at the start of my capture.

As the days passed I sat back and tried to work out the mathematical probability of *it* happening, but without a pen and paper I started to confuse myself and my stress heightened. I was obsessed with my body. I spent hours scrutinising every inch of my stomach, looking for a change, a sign. I knew there wouldn't be any, but it didn't stop me looking: *just in case*. The thought of a baby filling me left me empty, completely empty.

He owned me, he would own a baby as well, *my* baby; he would never let me go. My entire future mapped out and carved in stone, chained to a wall in a cell like this, used by him, forced to play happy families for the rest of my life. It was all suddenly too real, and I threw up again. I hoped he wouldn't notice and, again, I willed it all to be a horrible mistake.

That night, when the door was unlocked, the nausea rose again. I stared at the floor until he sat on the bed and stroked my back. It had become his way of telling me he wanted me compliant and willing. I was exhausted: the anxiety made me constantly tired and the demands on my body were too much. I wanted to turn him down, but I was frightened of how he would react, frightened of what might happen if he beat me. I lay there as he squeezed and fondled my body, trying to stop the crawling disgust that swamped me as he kissed and lightly touched my still tender ribs.

He was too attentive that evening. I had to concentrate on not tensing up my body as his lips moved to my stomach. Against all sense I panicked: *did he know?* My heart started to skip and I gasped for air. Thankfully he misunderstood and perhaps thought I enjoyed his attentions as he continued with a perverse enthusiasm. I just wanted it to be over so I could wash my body in the bucket of warm water he would undoubtedly bring to me afterwards.

I knew how to please him, to speed up the torture, but tonight he unnerved me and instead he crawled like an animal to my side and cradled me, his hand between my legs. It irritated me, but I could do nothing. I longed to squirm and bat him away – my skin itched and was clogged with the very essence of him. I didn't like this attempt at a conscientious lover, but he continued to ply me with kisses and measured strokes. Each touch increased the pressure and tempo. The palm of his hand was moving in time with his fingers, one probing, the other rubbing. My breathing grew faster and I struggled to slow down my heartbeat as shame flooded my cheeks, shame mixed with the unwanted primal, physical desire for more. I moved but he held me tighter and I went limp in his arms. If I didn't move, if I refused consciously to submit then it would be fine, fine, it had to be fine. I closed my eyes but the feelings intensified. The flutter of physiological pleasure rising and building, and my body unwillingly responded to him: the final punishment, the betrayal of my own body. Unwittingly the muscles contracted and the burst of heady satisfaction left me unable to breathe properly, my gasps were ragged and uneven. I matched that traitorous feeling, clitoral and vaginal, with one of humiliation.

I finger fucked her and she came, fucking loved it!

He had won, and I felt him smile as he kissed me. It was then I burst into tears of disgust and mortification, encompassing the agony of my secret and my fear for the future. He muffled my cries with his abhorrent mouth until I couldn't breathe. When the heat left me and the overspill of my grief with it, he then took his own pleasure. I was grateful it was quick, until he whispered the words:

"Tell me you love me, Anna."

I forced the words out, dragging each sound from somewhere deep inside and he replied with a sigh and a kiss.

I SCRUBBED MYSELF that night harder than I had done before, not caring that he noticed. What did he know of love? I cringed as I recalled my words to him. *Disgusting*, I was *disgusting!*

The water made the skin under the metal shackle of my wrist rub and become sore.

"Can you take this thing off?" I snapped, rattling the chain as anxiety bubbled again.

But he knelt by my side and unlocked the chain, rubbing my wrist tenderly afterwards: *get away from me!* I shrugged his touch away and he started to stroke me, *again*, I growled and shifted irritably.

"Anna, what's wrong?"

"Nothing." I was furious, but I considered his temper and counted. "I just feel sick, I have a headache, I'm sorry."

"You've been ill a lot recently." It was a casual observation but I fumbled and dropped the flannel regardless.

"I think it's just my body's way of healing." I matched his light tone and continued to wash, but slower now as I thought of what to say next. He stood by my side with water and paracetamol. I thanked him and took them silently.

"If it gets worse, you must tell me. I couldn't bear anything happening to you."

I dipped my head and scowled, a thousand inappropriate replies in my mind, but instead I told him that I would, and smiled. *Anna, I was Anna.*

CHAPTER TWELVE

I WOKE WITH a start as a huge bang echoed through the room, followed by gunshots. Will was already dressing. I grabbed the closest thing to hand, my dress, and threw it on.

"What's going on?"

He didn't reply, pulling two large hunting knives out from the bottom of his bag and fastening them onto his belt.

More shots, followed by shouts.

"Will?"

"Most likely just a disagreement."

I laced my boots quickly and grabbed my jacket. It was freezing in the stupid dress.

"What are you doing?" He stared at me and I looked back in confusion. "You're not going anywhere."

"You can't leave me locked up in here." There was another gunshot, closer this time.

"You'll be safe here." He walked to the door, pausing and staring at the chain on the floor. "Anna."

"No, Will, no. What if you get hurt? Or die? I'll be chained to a wall, unable to move and I'll be found and taken."

"I'll be fine, you'll be fine. Come here."

"No." I screamed at him and he stared at me in fascination. "Take me with you."

"What?" He fastened his bag on his back. "Have you lost your mind?"

"Take me with you, don't fight, and just take me away from here. We can go somewhere new, somewhere quieter, just the two of us." I gabbled, I don't know what I was saying, I hadn't considered any of it.

"You want to leave? With me?"

The shots were in quicker succession now and I wrung my hands together.

"Yes, yes I want to leave with you."

"You want to start a life with me?"

Wait, what? I almost backtracked, but this was my chance, I truly would be stupid not to grab it.

"Yes." *I'm sorry Stephen, I don't mean it.* "I love you."

"What?"

"I love you. Take me with you."

He paused for a moment, his hand on the door and then, tutting in frustration, he strode over and grabbed me by the hand.

"Do exactly what I say."

I nodded and as we walked he took his gun from an alcove in the main library. I hadn't exerted myself this much since he brought me back here. The pull on my ribs and my still sore shoulder tested me. Instinctively I ducked when the next flurry of shots cracked through the air. I couldn't see where the shots came from, nor who fired them. Will's hand was as tight as a vice, but I preferred it to the cuff. It was so dark every shape blurred into a huge expanse of grey and black like a lump of charcoal. I could almost taste it, bitter, coarse.

Will knew exactly where he was going. We passed several houses like Olly's. Those men and women not involved in the fighting stood at the doors and the faces of broken souls stared down at me from the bedroom windows.

I tripped over a fallen lamppost and skinned both my knees on the ruined pavement. *Stupid fucking dress.* I swore through gritted teeth as Will helped me up. The shots were closer now and I pulled on his hand to get his attention.

"Why are we walking towards the gunfire?"

"This way is safer than the other exit."

Safer? Really? I couldn't argue, he knew this town, I didn't. He paused for a second and released my hand. I saw the gun clearly: *a Glock 17, 9mm.* He grabbed my hand again. We were deep in the centre of what had been the residential area of the town and now the houses were nothing more than piles of charred rubble.

For some reason images of the police, armed and patrolling the streets prior to the bombings and the riots came to me. Dressed in black from head to toe, an intimidating force. I knew a policeman, he lived opposite us; tubby and cheery he would wave to me every morning as we both left for work. After the implementation of article six of the new police reform act, he never smiled,

ANNA

never waved and soon I became too frightened to smile or nod to him in public. People were arrested or shot for the simplest of things. The first few shootings were subject to national outcry and huge media interest. But then article six was amended, and all reporting banned under a counter terrorist guise. Things got worse and for the first time in twenty-two years there were empty cells in the prisons. I learnt to shoot. My neighbour invited me over one night and showed to me the Glock 17, 9mm, standard issue. By the end of the evening I was able to strip the gun, clean it and reload it. He couldn't teach me to shoot it, his ammunition was rationed, but he did help me perfect my aim and shot with an airsoft handgun. I didn't see my neighbour much after that. A few weeks later we were attacked and the police, and what was left of the military, combined forces. Declaring martial law, they patrolled the streets and dealt out instant justice. It was easy now to look back with clarity and unclouded judgement: the police were meant to protect *us*, the military meant to fight the enemy. Combined, their role was hazy: the people became the enemy, the enemy became the people. Yet we did nothing to stop it.

SOMETHING GRAZED PAST my arm and there was a loud ping as it hit a wall by my side. I jumped and grabbed Will's jacket in fear, pulling him closer to me. I tried not to think about how I had instantly looked to him for protection; and how ludicrous that was. I glanced at my jacket: the passing bullet had torn the thin material.

He grabbed both my arms and pushed me through a hole in the wall, fervently checking my arms for injury. The pings ricocheted off the brick and the brick dust fell like rain around my head. I slowed down and looked around in bewilderment.

"Anna, what are you doing?" He dragged me by my arm and as I stumbled and tripped, my head finally started to clear.

"This is safer?" I asked as he marched me over and through another pile of debris.

"Yes."

I could hear voices now, shouts accompanying the gun fire. It still didn't feel completely real and only the smell of the dirt, the cold wind and the touch of my captor's firm hand grounded me, bringing me back into the warzone. I almost slipped again, but he grabbed my arm and held me up as I skidded down the demolished bricks, taking a sharp right at the bottom where I saw a glimpse of the main fight, before he pushed me back against the side of a garage, his hand on my chest as he stared at the scene.

So much fighting, so many *people*. There were fires raging throughout the housing estate, thick acrid smoke poured into the sky. It was noxious and it drowned my lungs. Sickened, I watched as two men beat a third with golf clubs as he desperately tried to crawl away; they were relentless and rained a barrage of blows until he stilled. I turned my head away and into Will's jacket. He stroked my hair – I didn't want him to touch me but my stomach was churning and I was struggling not to throw up.

He didn't move, and continued to survey the area,

rhythmically stroking me. My curiosity won and I looked again. I shivered in the cold but he misunderstood and pulled me closer.

"Don't look if it scares you, Anna." He spoke gently and stroked my hand with his fingers. *He was always stroking me*. His pet.

"I'm fine."

At least a dozen thugs in the melee were firing at each other, and into the crowds, from vantage points in the ruined homes. The popping and crackling of the fires, the cat calling and shouts worked in grating counterpoint to the gunfire. Not everyone wanted to fight. Three different groups tried to pass through, crouching and covering their heads with their hands; but they were attacked. A small lad, maybe eighteen years old, was thrown to the floor and dragged by the hood of his jacket into the midst of a baying mob and attacked by three men twice his size and a thin woman with a heavy wrench. I couldn't stop watching. His friends tried to help. *Heroism, here?* The smallest of them grabbed the arm of the nearest attacker and tried to pull him off. The light from the fire caught something in the attacker's hand, for a moment I struggled to identify what it was he held, but, just as I did, it cut across the face of the smaller of the two. I winced and looked away.

"When will they stop?"

"When the Enforcers turn up."

Enforcers worked for the gangs and new communities as security and self-proclaimed police. Whoever paid the most received the most protection. They attacked for pleasure *and* payment.

He squeezed my hand and then dragged me to the right as we threaded through the outskirts. I glanced at the faces of those fighting; I wished I hadn't. So much anger and... delight?

I tripped again and lost my footing, landing on already sore knees, and the stinging intensified. Will pulled me up. The soot and dirt clung to my skin. I'd become accustomed to being clean so quickly again that I was suffocating. While Will readjusted his backpack I leant against the side of a long ago burnt out car. Two men were throwing punches: one grabbed the head of his opponent and bit savagely into his ear, tearing away the lobe. Blood poured from the wound and the man grunted, grabbing his now ruined ear and running away. The attacker turned, locking his gaze onto mine.

"Will." He looked at me and I nodded ever so slightly upwards. "There's someone behind." My voice was almost a murmur. I needed him if I wanted to get out of here. He didn't say anything but he drew one of the hunting knives and I closed my eyes. I counted and got to twenty-eight before there was a pull on my wrist and I opened my eyes. It was Will, he dragged me across the next street where the people slowly thinned out. I didn't look behind me, I didn't want to see what he had done. What I helped him do.

At the end of the next street I realised why no one ever seemed to escape the towns. This was where most of the vehicles had been moved to, a wall of cars, buses, vans on their sides stretched as far as I could see around the perimeter. There was a small huddle of teenagers sitting in the bucket of a digger. One of the girls lit a cigarette and shot us a glance. Her bright pink hair visible in the dark. She looked so unperturbed with the terror in the town. Instead she laughed and joked with her friends while keeping an eye on Will. We didn't run now, he raised a hand to the four guards by the only space in the wall, they looked up and signalled above us, I followed their nods to another row of armed men in the top storey of a nearby house, their guns trained on Will and me.

"Daniel, not seen you around for a while." They shook hands. I watched my captor swap his gun hand over and then back again.

"Been away on business, I'm looking to leave now."

"Before the Enforcers get here? You could earn a bit helping them out. There's been a call on the network." The guard glanced at me with interest. I looked at the ground and counted the lumps of dirt by my feet.

"I don't enforce any more. Want to settle down. What will it cost me to leave with her?" I still didn't look up. Will reached out and took my arm, pulling me closer and against his hard body.

"No one leaves or enters until the Enforcers arrive. I'm sorry, Daniel. I doubt you'd give what I want."

He crushed my hand then and I fidgeted to show him my pain. He realised and loosened his grasp; the anger was back, the jealousy too.

"No, but I'll tell you where I've left thirteen bottles of whisky, six magnums of champagne and over four thousand cigarettes."

That got the attention of the guard. His eyes brightened and he hesitated before nodding slowly.

"Follow me." So we did. He took us into the nearby house and I sat patiently on a plastic chair by a large old dining table. They spoke quickly and quietly. Will pointed to three different spots on his map and the guard called to one of his colleagues and relayed the locations to him. After the second guard left Will looked at me and smiled, nodding confidently.

I forced a smile and leant against the wall, closing my eyes. I'd soon be out of this place, away from the noise, the barbarism and cruelty. I'd be back in the Unlands, back in the quiet and dead world where I belonged. The feeling of relief didn't last, now we had stopped my anxiety and sickness caught up and crashed into me.

There was nothing to do but wait. Placing my hands on my lap I cradled my stomach surreptitiously, yet again willing for it all to be a mistake. Closing my eyes I tried to picture Stephen but all I could see was a murky, unfocused blur. Out of everyone I had known and loved, only Oscar was clear in my mind. I reached into my jacket pocket and pulled out his picture. I'd lost so many memories being alone, each day that passed I lost a little of myself to the Unlands. If this was real, if my nightmare was to continue, then I could regain some of what the dead land now gripped tight – couldn't I? Regain some sense of me through my... punishment?

My thoughts were interrupted by the return of the guard and Will held out his hand, helping me to my feet. The handshaking and grins told me it was a success, and we were escorted out of the gates. The moment I stepped out of the town and back into the Unlands my anxiety slowly ebbed away.

"Can I trust you not to run away?"

"Yes."

"Good girl." He released my hand. I didn't know if this was a test, I hoped that if it was then I passed, if not, well: *never interrupt your enemy when he's making a mistake.* That was another one of those sayings.

I looked back. The glow of orange and the black smoke rising from different areas were wispy arms reaching to the sky, touching and polluting it with the evil the town struggled to contain: *stroking it.*

He allowed me my freedom as we walked, asking me repeatedly if I meant what I had said in my cell. I forced a nod each time. My ribs ached, reminding me of the *love* he had shown me just a few weeks ago. I touched his arm as we reached a small copse and he stopped.

"Just a few minutes." Stretching my arms up I winced as a sharp spike of pain lashed my side. Sitting on the ground I hunched over. He stood by me and he swore softly. Looking up through my arms there were three figures approaching, their silhouettes vaguely familiar. As they got closer I recognised the sunglasses man and his companions. I also remembered the way he had looked at me and I scrambled to my feet and stood behind Will.

"Will, thought you'd be in there, having fun at the party." Sunglasses man smiled at my captor.

"I'm leaving."

"You've tamed her then?" He stared at me. I glanced either side of him. There was something wrong, the lines in all their faces, the planes of their bodies, were rigid and strained.

"What do you want?" The friendly tone of the first meeting was gone and my captor pushed me further behind him. The man's stare flitted from Will to me and back, an amused expression spreading on his face.

"Her."

"I knew you'd be back." Will shifted and I continued to hide behind him. "Why her?"

"Because she's yours, and you know why."

I scouted a route through the scattering of trees. I could probably get past the first few rows of trees and into the scrublands before I was caught; but maybe not. I could possibly get further. I was fast, maybe I could outrun them. I used to be fast.

"I wouldn't, sweetheart." The amused voice of the main one, Sunglasses, cut into my thoughts and I scowled at him, making him chuckle. "If you run, I'll catch you, I'll break your legs and then you'll never run again."

He meant it. It had started to get light, and I could see his face properly now. There was no life in him; he was like my captor. Everything was quiet for a moment. I could hear the sounds of the town on the wind, the faint popping and cracking of gunfire.

"What's the issue Will? You can find another one, you caught her easy enough."

"Anna, run." Will's voice was low and firm and he stepped back, causing me to stumble.

"What?"

"Run, now."

So I did. Sunglasses shouted to his companions, but I had already sensed them running after me. Fixing my attention on the clearing I forced my feet forward. I hadn't run in over a month, my lungs were already hurting and my tender side screamed in agony. I couldn't stop, the thought of being captured and broken all over again pushed me harder than I thought possible. I skidded down the side of a small ridge and into the long-dead field. The tiny sprigs of rotten crops crunched under my boots. Each step was already getting heavier and heavier. I was running towards the sunrise – it was the most beautiful thing I'd seen in all the days I had been alone. A stretch of yellow and red, gold and ruby. It was freezing and my breath flowed back past me like a mist; but the image in front warmed me.

Then hands on my jacket pulled me, and I fell forward into the ground, smacking my face off the cracked mud and scratching my cheek on the crops. Fighting, screaming and kicking I broke my way free. Why had this never worked with him? Scrambling to my knees I cried out as my wounds reopened, and got to my feet before landing heavily on my front as the second one jumped on me. I snapped my elbow back and connected with his face causing both of us to cry in pain – I'd jarred my shoulder yet again. He let go of me and grabbed his nose, blood pouring from between his fingers, cursing me through his hands. A sense of satisfaction and pride at my strength burst through me. It was short lived for the first one grabbed my legs and I fell again. The second one took my arms and twisted them behind my back. I screamed as something tore in my shoulder, instantly losing strength and going limp.

"She's got spirit." The second one spat, a mouthful of

blood landed on my face and I cried out and thrashed again. I felt another tug on my shoulder and screamed.

"She'll be fun." The other one laughed quietly and he twisted something around my legs tightly and stood me up. I didn't look at either of them and stared at my legs, he'd used cable ties around my ankles. The second one started laughing and I glared at him, spitting full force in his face. You're not fucking this up for me now. Not when I'm so close to escaping. So much for the saying: *the enemy of my enemy is my friend*. He swore and pulled my arms again, digging his fingers into my bicep. I screamed, again.

It was slow and torturous, I could barely shuffle and the grip on my arms was burning, the fiery pain in my shoulder and ribs all consuming. I'd only managed to run five hundred metres or so. How pathetic. Pointless and futile. As we reached the clearing I couldn't see Will or Sunglasses. My new captors stopped in confusion.

"Where are they?"

"I don't know, do I?"

Pulling me around roughly they searched the area: nothing. We had been minutes, barely any time. Two gun shots bounced through my skull, a dull yet constant and quick thud of pain in my ears started and the hold on my arms melted away.

Both my captors were dead. I shuffled slightly and then fell to the ground, landing on my ribs and crying out as a rock dug into my side. I was grateful and yet hated him even more. He cut away the ties to my legs and checked my knees, my face, my side and my arms. His touch was disturbingly gentle. He leaned over me and kissed my cut cheek, the smell of him rolled through my stomach and I grasped at the ground by my side: *never underestimate your enemy.*

I struck out with the rock as hard as I could to the side of his head. He fell to the side of me and I rolled over, groaning and gripping my ribs. I looked down at his unconscious body and the gun at his side.

Snatching it, I pointed it at his head. The rage was all-consuming and my fingers tightened and twitched on the trigger; but I couldn't pull it. An indescribable barrier refused to move, refused to allow me to pull back and seek my revenge. Why? Why could I not now have my pound of flesh? My hand shook with the pain my shoulder sent shooting down my arm. I lowered the gun and swore over and over again, screaming out the words into the stillness.

I took his bag. It was too heavy for me to carry, so I emptied out his clothes and belongings, not having time to check them, and the black bag he had given me. I kept the knives, tins of food, the maps and compass from before and the smaller, useful things. Strapping it onto my own back I gave him one last derisory glance and kicked him hard in the back.

Then with a sudden fear, I ran.

PART TWO
PART TWO
PART TWO

CHAPTER THIRTEEN

LETTING GO DOESN'T *mean giving up, but rather accepting that there are things that we cannot control.*

It was a cold, wet and dark day, and yet it was perfect. I wiggled my toes as the wet sand tickled and leeched onto my feet, seductively pulling me further down into the freezing water. The cold numbed my ankles and I watched the water rise higher and higher before lifting my feet one by one and then repeating the process. The warmth of the rising sun behind me crept across my back. Eventually, the iciness became too painful and I walked back onto the beach, carrying my shoes and battling the wind which tried to wrap me up in its embrace and whisk me away. The smell of salt carried on the air and I breathed deeply, revelling in the scent.

I waved over to Old Tom sitting on the edge of a nearby rock pool with his net and bucket, hunched over, smoking a cigarette, but he sat staring at the almost black water and paid me no attention, too intent on catching one of the little dark greens that scurried around in the early morning waters.

"Kate!"

Hayley ran over to me from our house, her red hair blowing wildly around her face like a halo of fire. She was my guardian angel.

"What are you doing out here in the cold? Kate, are you mad?" Her voice was full of concern but also held a hint of disapproval.

"I just wanted to walk for a bit." I tucked my hair behind my ears and smiled at her reassuringly. "I'm fine, it's a lovely morning."

"It's freezing!" she replied in disbelief. "When I woke up and saw you were gone, I panicked. Are you sure you're ok?"

I broke my gaze from the curling waves. "I'm sorry, I was just thinking. I'm fine. I promise."

"You must be hungry." She reached up to me and hesitated. When I had first arrived she had stroked my arm and I had burst into tears, and even after two months I couldn't bring myself to allow her to hug me.

"I'm fine." I had eaten more here than I ever had, even before the devastation.

I walked in silence by Hayley's side as she chatted about the chores for the morning. The council convened at ten and we would be discussing the plans for the allotments and regeneration. Excitement and nervousness fluttered into me; today I was going to pitch the request for clearing the library and asking for Wanderers to collect books from nearby villages and towns. By replacing a small part of what had once been the heart of this place, I could help heal my own.

"Are you nervous, Kate?"

"Yes." I rubbed my stomach self-consciously as I walked. The baby had started to move again.

"Don't be, everyone loves you being here."

Everyone. That had to be a lie, but it wasn't why I was nervous. I hadn't spoken to such a large group of people in so long. At the thought of all their eyes on me, watching me, heat suffused my cheeks.

We walked along the old towpath, past the partially rebuilt terraced cottages. It was too early for the builders to be working but their wheelbarrows and sandbags scattered the ground, creating an obstacle course. Hayley slowed as I zig-zagged my way through; twice I stumbled, twice I refused her offer of help. As we reached our home I turned back and stared at the sea, the sun glittered and bounced off the water, sparkling and mesmerising.

"Breakfast is ready."

I followed Hayley into the kitchen and smiled at Glen who nodded politely. Glen was a wanderer and part-time Enforcer. I tried not to hold it against him. The Enforcers would disappear for days and return with all sorts of forgotten 'necessities' from the world before. I could never understand what went through their minds. But Glen didn't send my heart racing nor terrify me the way the others did. He was simply... Glen.

"You have to eat more, Kate, for the baby." Hayley continued to mither as we ate, and I sighed. Yes, for the baby. I pushed the scrambled eggs around the plate and eventually forced them down, each mouthful a tiresome task.

"Hayley, leave the poor girl alone." Glen glanced at me

and rolled his eyes. I smiled. "Honestly, you do witter on, woman."

"I do not." She gathered up the plates. "I'm just excited, is all. I can't wait for the baby to arrive... it's about time we had a baby in the house." Her words weren't lost on me and she winked at Glen with a smile.

"I'll be away for about a week," Glen said. He didn't react to Hayley's not-so-subtle infant hint. "Do you need anything, darling?

"No, thank you." She kissed his cheek.

"I'll have the radio. Contact is five miles so if either of you need me or remember you need something you'll have about an hour at most."

"Ok." There was a small silence, and I too nodded in understanding.

LATER I FILLED two buckets with water from the well in their garden and struggled back into the house to wash the crockery, losing myself in my thoughts as the strong smell of bleach and citrus filled the room. The floorboards above me creaked and there was loud humming and singing from upstairs. It was nearly time: Hayley always hummed when she was excited. I was right: she bounded down the stairs and tutted loudly, causing me to hide a smile.

"Kate, you're not even dressed properly! C'mon, you have five minutes."

I sighed loudly and theatrically, pushing the hair behind my ears as I threw the tea towel at her.

"Hurry up!"

"What are you? My mother?" I teased lightly, pushing that small amount of memory and pain deep inside.

"Cheeky mare! I'm far too young to be your mother."

Upstairs, I stared at my face in the mirror. The first time I had seen my reflection I cried. It wasn't me in the mirror, it couldn't possibly be me. Every morning since then I had sat and forced myself to look. Opening a jar of face cream I slowly moisturised my skin, paying attention to the discoloured skin by my left eye. The baby kicked, and I frowned, massaging my stomach and staring at my reflection again. What would I wear? I needed to look professional, but approachable: friendly yet firm. I wanted this so badly.

"Kate."

She was impatient now, and my nervousness sliced through me as I pulled on a pair of plain leggings and a white tunic. I brushed my hair and thought of everything I had lost, and everything I had gained: sometimes we can't control what goes on around us, or even to us. I had to remember that. Just before we left the house I stood over the chessboard on the sideboard and calculated my next move. We'd been playing the same game since I arrived. Hayley had told me how Glen loved to play, but that she had never learnt the rules – so on my third morning with them I had moved my white pawn and waited. It hadn't taken long for him to realise we were equally matched.

"Kate! Come on."

I moved the pawn protecting my queen and closed the door behind me.

It was almost nine a.m., and as we walked towards the

old council building I smiled and nodded to the workmen and listened to Hayley talk. She shared everything with me: her life before the war, her love of French poetry and cheese, her hatred of The Beatles and spiders. Today was the story of how she met Glen. I had heard it before, of course, but I listened as she recalled the moment they met, in the queue for the toilets in a nightclub. It was hardly the most passionate of stories, but the way she spoke, and the adoration in her voice, made it so romantic that she could tell me the tale of their meeting a thousand times and I'd never grow bored.

"What about you, Kate? Anyone special in your life?"

Subtle Hayley, the same question after the same story, time and time again. I shook my head.

"No, just me." I didn't want to drag up the past and I forced my memories back into Pandora's box, away from this place. If I released them they would infect everything, ruin the sanctuary.

"Do you know what you're going to say? How you're going to ask?"

"I'll just ask. Mr Henley is chairing today and I've heard he likes to read. I'll play to his love of books."

"You'll have to win over Simon though. He'll not be happy that you want them to search for books when they could be getting supplies or enforcing."

Simon, which one was he? So many faces and names shot through my mind. There were more people here than in any of the other towns I had passed through.

"Which one's Simon?"

"Head of the Enforcers." I must have continued to

look blank, because she added, "Average height, bald, big bloke with the huge tribal tattoo on his right arm. He never smiles, always scowls. He's not around a lot of the time, goes to Blackwood a lot." She paused, and then made me chuckle by adding: "I think he used to be ginger, he's got ginger eyebrows." As if that fact would suddenly jog my memory.

We were nearly there, and I looked up at the Victorian Gothic building, the tall and narrow arched windows and ornate stone pillars a stark and cold contrast to the brightly coloured cottages and houses surrounding it. It reminded me more of a church than a council building. I was used to cheap and lacklustre architecture in my hometown: flat roofs, symmetrical and boring windows, pre-fabricated with the same bolt-together fascia panels. This was beautiful, carved stone with hand chiselled designs around the frames – and yet I found it strangely grotesque.

As we reached the steps I considered a prayer, something to invoke good luck, but I brushed the thought aside as quickly as it came. There was no one listening, no divine entity to intervene or jump out and say 'Surprise! Only kidding, this is all a horrible nightmare, time to wake up!' And besides, there was no time.

The lobby was surprisingly bright and modern, black and white framed photographs of the bay, the boats and local surfers covering two walls while on the third was a brightly painted mural of an underwater scene: many mermaids, disproportionate fish, smiling shells, strange plants, a whale and a seven-legged octopus filled the wall from ceiling to floor. I read the plaque underneath: *Octopus Group, Jennington School.*

Hayley held open the door and we took two seats near the front, tucked away in a corner by a large cupboard. More people entered, filling up the empty spaces, laughing and joking and greeting each other with air kisses and hugs. Rows and rows of bodies, turning and smiling at each other, some chatting, others laughing, and a few, like me, that just sat staring.

Calm, I needed to be calm.

"Oh, I'll be back in a bit." Hayley jumped up and waved towards the opposite side of the room. "Mrs Brooks is here and she promised me two chickens if Glen managed to find a bottle of Dom Perignon. No prizes for guessing what my wonderful husband brought back last week." I smiled and watched as she accosted a middle-aged woman dressed head to toe in Versace. I'd seen the same outfit on a picture of a supermodel once in a magazine; it looked better on Mrs Brooks.

"Kate, lovely to see you here."

I shrank back in my chair and grabbed my stomach protectively. It was Mr Henley. I exhaled slowly and forced a smile.

"I'm sorry, ducky, did I scare you?"

"No, no. I was just daydreaming." I swallowed and counted, forcing my heart to slow down. "Sorry, Mr Henley," I added for good measure.

"Ducky, I've told you – call me Roger, and don't apologise." He coughed and loosened his gaudy cartoon-adorned tie. "Here to discuss the library?"

"Yes. Do you think there will be any objections?"

"Not from me. I think it's a terrific idea, simply wonderful." He grinned. "Are you liking it here, Kate?"

"Yes, thank you." *Hurry up, Hayley, please, hurry up.*

"And how do you find it with Mr and Mrs Stenton?" He brushed his hand over his thinning hair and smoothed his wayward eyebrows down.

"They're lovely." I looked over to Hayley again and she threw back her head and laughed with a group of her friends. She was so animated – her hands flying around and her face open and grinning. I could hear the jingling of her bangles from where I sat. "I couldn't ask for better hosts."

"We'd best look at getting you a place of your own soon, eh? Somewhere for you and the little one to make home, leave Hayley and Glen to host another newcomer maybe?" I forced myself to nod in agreement. "Good, good. I'll mention it to the workmen, get them to hurry up with those cottages. I know you like being near the water."

He continued to talk and I smiled politely at his ideas for my full integration into the community. The baby shifted and there was a wave of nausea; I just wished he would leave me alone. Perhaps he thought that if I addressed him in the meeting it would then mean I wanted to be friends. I didn't want that. I just wanted to be alone.

After ten minutes of inane conversation Mr Henley left, promising to discuss books with me soon, and Hayley returned. The room was full now and the four other seats around Mr Henley at the council table were soon occupied. I spotted Simon sat at the end, with his ginger eyebrows and scowl: I recognised him now. Dr Bennett sat closest to me, smelling strongly of whisky and peppermints, looking distracted and strained. There was a man I didn't know between Simon and Mr Henley: he was young, Indian, perhaps thirty, attractive and impeccably dressed in chinos, shirt and cravat.

"Who's he?" I whispered to Hayley.

"That's Mr Henley's husband, Deven." My face must have betrayed my surprise as she giggled and then smothered it with a cough. "They married a few months ago. He was a newcomer, like you, and he hosted with Mr Henley and his daughter. It was a gorgeous ceremony."

"The man in black, the one just sitting down – who's he?"

"He's a floater. When we have council meetings the other safe community at Blackwood sends a representative. We do the same with them. Keeps things nice and calm between the towns. I don't know this one though, he must be new."

As the council took their place I sat upright and smoothed my top. No one seemed to pay attention.

"Quiet, the meeting is in progress," Simon shouted, making me flinch.

The room settled down. Mr Henley stood up, clearing his throat and holding two pieces of paper in front of him.

"Thank you all for coming. This is the sixty-ninth official town meeting to date and I'm pleased to see so many regular faces, and I'm overjoyed to see new ones too. Welcome!"

His jovial persona was replaced by one of firm authority and direction. He introduced the other members and listed the agenda. Volunteers were wanted for clearing the northern sector of the town, which had been closed off since they began settling here eighteen months ago. Several hands rose. Mine didn't. They'd be clearing bodies and rubble, so the volunteers were to be well rewarded: they would automatically be moved up the housing list and put into the lottery for one of the six eco-houses recently renovated. Those who were unsuccessful would be first in line for the next batch. Running water, electricity and heating. Hayley and Glen had a self-sustaining eco home but without the running water and, regardless of my conversation with Mr Henley, the cottages wouldn't be finished any time soon.

They then discussed the possibility of removing security from the boundaries of the town. My sickness was back: without the security, anyone could enter. I wasn't the only one who felt that way: various members of the audience stood to argue their points, and Mr Henley occasionally had to break in when things got too heated. After two hours it was agreed that the security would remain for another month – but that Simon would review the shift patrols daily and look to decrease the number of Enforcers. I held Simon's gaze several times during the argument. There was something in his expression I couldn't pinpoint but the way he looked, the way he never smiled and was so devoid of emotion, brought back my nightmares, dragging them from the night and into the day.

It was lunchtime before the council reached the issue

of the library. I was desperate for the bathroom and the mixture of perfumes and smells in the room had given me a headache. Mr Henley called my name. Standing, I twisted the ring on my finger and started to speak. It was too hot and sweat clung to my neck and back.

"I'd very much like to restore the small library on Two-Gate Road. The building itself is structurally sound, but the place was ransacked by looters and those that needed paper to burn for warmth." I was careful not to insult those that had burnt the books; I didn't doubt some of the arsonists were present. "With this new start, this new community we've built, it seems a shame to ignore such an important aspect of education and community spirit." I paused and watched several people nod enthusiastically. "I'd like to request for the Wanderers to consider bringing back books, and if everyone in the town sorts through their books and considers donating to the library, we can start up a new lending scheme. I've made a list of the classic reads, if we start from there we can build a new collection." My small speech had exhausted me. I glanced at the council nervously and sat down.

"Thank you, Kate." Mr Henley smiled at me. "I think it's a wonderful idea."

His husband nodded in agreement and smiled at me. It was a patronising smile, I recognised that much, but that was two votes. I just needed one more on the council to agree.

"Library, a bloody library." It was Simon who spoke and I looked up at him, still twisting the ring on my finger. "We have houses that need repairing, people who need supplies, food and running water and we're sitting here talking about books." He sipped at a glass of water. "Books are heavy, each book could be valuable space for food or medicine or another necessity. My Wanderers are already overstretched and now you want them looking for books?" He shook his head. "I can't agree to this. If, perhaps, we were to readdress the security issue again, I would reconsider, but as it stands – I simply don't have the men available."

Two – one.

"I am in agreement with Simon. I'm sorry, love." It was the doctor. "Once the town is back on its feet then you'll have my support. I'm a lover of books, but the Wanderers are better placed searching out supplies and medicines."

Two – two. It depended on the stranger, the man from Blackwood. I looked at him and crossed my fingers. *I need this, please.*

"It's a tricky decision, and I understand I'm now the one to make the casting vote?" He looked at Mr Henley for confirmation, who nodded. "In that case I have to agree to this. The library is an excellent idea. Simon, you know we started a similar renovation a few weeks ago. A group of teachers share your young enthusiast's love for books and reading and won the support of our council. Though we have no library, we do have a lending system. I believe you were there, Mr Henley?" He nodded and so the Blackwood delegate shrugged. "I vote yes. I'm sure you can come to some sort of agreement with the Wanderers. Our towns are of similar size and numbers and we've managed." He nodded at me coolly and I trembled with excitement.

"Excellent, excellent," Mr Henley said cheerfully. "Three to two, the library is agreed. We'll break for lunch and discuss the wind farm and crop harvest rotation for the next twelve months after. Reconvene at two."

As people left and the room emptied, I sat staring at my hands and nails. I finally had something, a reason for being here. Something that I could make mine.

CHAPTER FOURTEEN

OVER THE NEXT nine days I walked more miles around the town than I cared to count. My feet were swollen and blistered, but I was happy. Over six hundred books had been donated to the library just from the residents alone. I had nearly all of Shakespeare's plays, including *The Two Noble Kinsmen*. I allowed myself a surge of delight as I stroked the cover. Wistful that it was for the library and regretful that I had to share it, for the memories of Stephen reading it to me during our first summer together in the fields near my college flooded me with love and a yearning for the long-lost freedom from pain and sadness.

Everyone knew who I was. But, while most smiled and called me Kate, several still called me Katherine. I was the cold, unfriendly outsider; pregnant and alone; the one who refused to attend church on Sundays and refused to go swimming or socialise when invited. It was to these people I tried to smile the most, to relax and to let go. I wanted to show them I could be happy, that my caution wasn't for lack of want, but for self-preservation – but the more I tried, the more I realised it wasn't for their benefit but for mine.

During those nine days I discovered more about the little fishing town now called home. While it wasn't as big or tourist-focused as some of the more well-known seaside towns, it was just as pretty and twice as rich in the sense that some who lived here had *real* money. I'd known it from the clothes of the long-term residents, but now I passed garaged Rolls Royce and Aston Martin cars, eyed the huge eight and nine bedroomed properties with marbled floors and chandeliers as I knocked on doors in search of books. I don't know what happened to the people who lived in these houses before; I'd never seen them and now 'millionaire's row', as it was known, housed groups of resettlers and refugees. The largest house was used as the Enforcers' social club and it sat at the top of a cliff overlooking the water. There was no doubt that the views were breathtaking, but the climb was agonising and in the winter the country path-cum-road down to the main town would be treacherous. As I trudged upwards in search of more donations, I decided that I was happy to stick with Glen and Hayley, and eventually I would be happy in my small house by the beach.

I stared back down the path to the town, surveying the houses and buildings below, becoming aware of how far the town extended now. I could see the church and the council building, and then the older, smaller houses surrounding them in a semi-circle. The beach to the east with the small scattering of houses framing the large cove was mirrored by the western sector. From where I stood I could see the extent of the devastation to the new housing estate where most of the work was now focused to remove the last reminder of destruction from this tranquil place.

Tranquil. A peculiar word to use when the underlying unrest from the other residents bubbled, especially those who lived here before the resettlers, like me, arrived. None of the houses on Millionaire's Row had their original driveway gates: those gates were now welded to the walls and perimeter of the town. *A temporary measure*, apparently. The desperate attempts of those permanently resident in the town to stop outsider looting. And that many residents believed that the town would be a better place if the gates were closed for good to newcomers. *Community spirit* they called it, and they pushed for the traditional family values, for religion and a *woman's place*: for a small community built on trust and friendship.

With a sudden longing I stepped off the path and carefully slid down the embankment into the overgrown woodland that led back to the town.

ON THE TENTH day I sat in the library, covered with a huge blanket and surrounded by piles of books, with a flask of Hayley's homemade soup and a lunchbox of bread, when Glen's voice echoed in the huge expanse and dragged me from my ledger.

"How's it going?"

I stood up, rubbing my lower back through the thick jumper.

"Good, there's so many. I think I'm about half way through, though."

He walked over, his gun resting in his hip holster. He hadn't checked it back yet with the Enforcers.

"How did it go?"

"Well, I managed to get these." Turning his rucksack around, he pulled out three hardback books: all works by Tolkien. "The house I got these from has a stack load more; I thought I'd bring these first and then go back with some others and bring the rest. Looks like the person who lived there was a lover of sets. Dickens, Shakespeare, Brontë sisters, they're all there."

I ran my hands over the jacket covers and pulled the books close, holding them against my chest as though they were a shield.

"Thank you." I didn't know what else to say and he nodded once and turned to leave. "Glen, thank you. Seriously."

Puzzled, he turned back and nodded again. "It's okay. I have a meeting with Simon in a bit. Whatever you've done to piss him off, it must have been monumental. He's still seething about having us look for books as well as supplies."

I sat back down and drew the blanket over me again. "I haven't done anything other than petition the council."

"Well, I'm sure he'll calm down soon. He's a moody arse on the best of days." He ran a hand through his short blonde hair. "It's Hayley's birthday on Tuesday, I thought it might be nice if we had some friends round, made her a cake? I'm a bit shit with baking, but could you…" He looked both hopeful and sheepish.

Tuesday: three days away. Plenty of time. I nodded with a smile.

We agreed on the plan; Glen would make sure the ingredients were hidden in the outside storage cupboard by tomorrow night and he'd take her for a walk on her birthday, giving me time to bake.

After he left I stared at the ceiling for a long while, trapped in my own memories, remembering celebrations, remembering gifts. I hadn't realised that I was twisting the ring until the dull throb of pain grew stronger, and glanced down. My already-swollen finger was now a dark red. I let go and picked up the first book Glen had brought: *The Hobbit*. I didn't want to log acquisitions any more, I wanted to read. I *needed* to read and lose myself in a different world, to pretend I wasn't me.

Chapter One: An Unexpected Party.

I don't know how long I read for, but as the light crept away and the shadows grew, I had to close the book and leave.

It was pitch black and several times I kicked large stones and rubble into the water. I heard the faint whistles and laughs from the workmen growing louder. Then the loud drone of a generator drowned their chatter, although Old Tom was singing to himself as he dug the foundations for a garden wall.

"Evening, Katie," he called.

"Evening, Tom." I stopped and leaned against the side

of his cement mixer, rubbing my lower back. His wiry old frame relentlessly shovelled up the sandy mud. He was dressed in shorts and a tee shirt. "It's getting cold out, Tom. You warm enough?"

"I see yer every morning Katie, standing in the water with yer shoes in yer hand, staring at yer feet. Makes me chuckle it does, I should be asking you if yer okay, yer soft city kitten."

Keeping my face impassive I stared at him until he glanced my way. His face dropped and the wrinkles deepened and the concern spread. He started to speak, but I interrupted.

"Meow."

"Oh yer tease." He leant against his shovel and finished his cigarette. I invited him to Hayley's birthday party and watched as he ground the butt into the earth and coughed.

"Sounds fun, I can bring yer some squash, it goes out of date next month and it'd be best to use it up."

"Make sure you invite the boys for me, Tom. They're more than welcome, but tell them I don't want to hear their god-awful singing at the party. My ears will bleed."

OVER THE NEXT two days I prepared for Hayley's party. In the library I had drawn up a list of her friends. I didn't doubt I'd forgotten some and hoped that there was no one important missing. Each time someone brought me a book, I cross-checked them against my list and invited them. Thirty-three so far: that was a lot of cake.

"Kate, isn't it?" I looked up and nodded at the young

woman standing in the door. With a lovely, wonky smile she strode over to my desk, swinging two canvas bags as she approached.

"I've brought you a present," she declared theatrically, dropping the bags on my ledger and pulling out book after book. "Some of these are truly terrible, cheap trashy reads, but there are some good thrillers in here." Her southern accent warmed my insides.

"Oh, thank you."

"That's okay. I've got some more kiddy books at my home, but I'm taking those to the school."

"School?" I looked up from the books with interest. She grinned again, her slightly crooked teeth displayed.

"When I heard you'd started up the library, I went to the Henleys and told them we should look at re-opening the school, or at least a classroom somewhere. There's thirty kids here, none of them learning."

She continued to talk about her ideas. She needed a space to teach: somewhere open, bright, and welcoming. Her hair flew around her face as she spoke and her mannerisms reminded me of Hayley. *Knowledge. The one thing that could never be taken away from them.* I mused, recalling my own education and the joy of learning and reading. We had all lost so much, but not our education. She was right. The children were our future and they deserved our best, whatever our circumstance. I rubbed my bump absently.

"What about here? In the library?" As the words left my mouth, I regretted them. My refuge, my own little place, would soon be overrun.

"Are you sure?" She looked at me in excitement. "Really? Oh God! I bet you thought I was hinting, didn't you? I wasn't, but that would be great." There was a long and awkward silence. I heard the workmen down the road; they were singing again. "I'm Nikky, by the way, sorry, God, I didn't even introduce myself."

She held out her hand and I stared at it for a moment before reaching out and grasping it. The skin was cool and soft, nothing like how I expected: I still didn't touch her for long and after I let go, I fought the urge to wipe away the sensation from my own skin.

"There's a party at the Stentons tomorrow afternoon, would you like to come?" I don't know why I asked.

Nodding and grinning, Nikky took down the address and then left, promising to bring fairy cakes. Had I made a friend? I sat back down and stared at the new additions, and struggled to wipe the smile from my face.

I WAS HOT, sweaty and tired – but I had baked three sponge cakes, put together a collection of sandwiches, and scrubbed the kitchen.

I balanced on the sideboard and the back support of a dining chair and pinned the 40th banner into the coving. I giggled as I imagined the horror on Hayley's face if she saw me. *Kate! What are you doing? Think of the baby!* I heard her panicked voice in my head and, typically, nearly toppled over. I climbed down and looked around the living room. Multi-coloured ribbons and decorations covered all the walls, the banner hung low – albeit wonky

– and screamed 'happy birthday' in bright, bold lettering.

Yet there was something missing. I ran my fingers over the glass framed pictures of Hayley and Glen covering one of the walls. Presents. But what could I give her? I had nothing. Hayley wouldn't be interested in presents… would she? Doubt filled me, and I found myself wandering around the house aimlessly as I desperately tried to think of something to give her. There was nothing. I hoped she wouldn't be upset that I had nothing for her. I couldn't relax, and brushed my hair and massaged my bump; staring at the unfamiliar curve of my stomach in my bedroom mirror with a fastidious interest.

"Kate, are you in?" Nikky. I ran down the stairs. The back door was open and the cool breeze swept through the house, bringing with it the nauseating smell of fresh fish. It was two p.m. The fishing boats would be coming back to shore soon.

"Sorry, was I interrupting?" She pulled Tupperware boxes full of cakes out of her canvas bag. "I brought these as well." Shooting me a sly, excited look she pulled back a tea towel and a huge red jelly wobbled at me.

"It's great." I couldn't remember the last time I'd eaten jelly. It must have been at least a decade. "Thanks, Nikky."

"Do you need a hand with anything?"

I shook my head and led her into the huge living room where the rest of the cakes and food were on display.

"Holy moly! You did all this?" She stared at the rows of sandwiches, full of tinned paté and fresh tomatoes, and others with homemade fruit jam.

"Yes."

"You're good." She beamed at me: I mirrored her expression, and, as she walked around the room gasping at the decorations, my earlier doubts washed away. Hayley would be pleased.

"Right then." She clapped her hands together in glee. "Where's the wine?"

Over the next hour the guests arrived and I played the part of hostess.

"Katie, yer look blooming." Tom's gravelly voice cut across the chatter and he stood by the kitchen door smoking a cigarette, his eyes flitting from the ocean to me. "Looks grand in there, dun' a good job girl."

He'd caught three crabs that morning, more than he had caught in a long time. It was a sign, he proclaimed theatrically, because it was Hayley's birthday – he would present her with a crab.

Mr and Mr Henley walked up the small gravelled path at the back of the house towards us. Deven was carrying a brightly coloured box, Mr Henley – Roger – hooked his arm in his husband's and nodded warmly to me.

"Thank you for the invite, Kate." Deven Henley looked me up and down and then smiled: it didn't reach his eyes. "I'm not sure we've been introduced properly. I'm Deven or Dev, but please, not *Dev-on*." They stood in the doorway, blocked by Tom who refused to move. An awkward silence followed.

"Tom, can you please take these into the other room?" I picked up a small bowl of boiled sweets and, grudgingly, he flicked his cigarette butt onto the stones and took the dish from my hands, shooting unhappy glares at the Henleys.

"When does the birthday girl arrive?" Deven walked into the kitchen, followed by his husband, and placed the box on the table.

"Shortly, they're due back in about twenty minutes. Would you like a drink?" Flicking the kettle on, I tried to busy myself, not knowing what to say.

"Actually, I'll get some prosecco." Deven touched his husband's arm before walking away; he didn't look back.

"I'd love some tea." Roger watched his husband leave and then turned to me. "It's been a while since I've been here, Glen's done a lot to the place. Have you got running water yet?"

"Not yet. The electricity is sorted and the insulation, but Glen said something about a pump and a UV filter for the water, I'm not sure exactly."

After making him a drink, he thanked me and wandered into the living room. Hayley's laughter down the path grew louder.

"Kate, what's going on? Why's the door open? You must be freezing!" She continued to laugh as she stumbled in the doorway, grabbing Glen and pulling him close. He wrapped his arms around her and kissed her neck. "Can I hear voices?"

Glen gently pushed her into the living room: there was a squeal in delight, and a roar of laughter and cheers from the guests erupted. Everyone crowded around her, like moths to my flame-haired guardian angel.

I played hostess for a while, making sure tea and wine kept flowing. I was just refilling the kettle for the fifth time when a dark figure at the edge of my vision caught my attention. Deven and Simon stood by the stairs and spoke in low voices: I couldn't hear what they said, but Simon wasn't happy. Deven kept trying to move but Simon's huge frame blocked his and he gently touched his arm. Deven's gaze flicked from his husband to the head Enforcer. Just as Simon's murmur grew louder, the stereo blared and their whispers were drowned in a sea of pop music. The young Mr Henley leaned closer to him, and he turned and scowled at me before storming away and out of the house. I flinched as he went past.

The music pounded through the room: I vaguely recognised the band and the beat from a long time ago.

"Kate, come and dance with me." Nikky pulled at my arms. Instinctively I pulled back and hugged myself. "Oh, sorry." She let go and continued to bounce by my side. "C'mon Kate, this is a great song."

"I can't dance," I mumbled, and shook my head. "I'll look like an excited hippo."

"Oh don't be silly, you're pregnant, not fat, and there's nothing to you anyway. Dance with me, please?" She paused for a second. "I'll stop bugging you if you dance for one song. I'll even get Tom to dance."

We both looked over to where he stood eating sandwich after sandwich, nodding his head to the music, but woefully out of time.

"Dance with Tom first, then I'll dance with you."

"Promise?"

I hesitated, and then replied: "Promise."

With a bounce, Nikky danced to Tom and I watched as she cajoled him into leaving the sandwiches and stepping to the small space in the centre of the room. He flailed his arms around and started to rotate his hips like a professional. Hayley joined them, and then Glen: soon the room was dancing.

I headed over to Deven Henley who stood by the stairs, alone and apprehensive, rubbing his left forearm.

"Are you all right?"

Looking up, he frowned. "Of course I am, I just have a small headache, Simon had some pills to help." He grabbed the nearest bottle of wine and filled his glass up again. "You look rather beautiful, Kate. How far along are you?"

"Seven months, thereabouts, maybe a little more according to the doctor."

"I run a small social group every Tuesday and Thursday evenings. We discuss books, sewing, gardening, anything wholesome." He took a deep glug, the corner of his lip curling upwards and his eyes creasing. "We like to think of it as a new women's institute." His smile reached his eyes at his own joke. "I'd love for you come and join us, you and Nikky."

I sat down on the stairs. I didn't want to go to a social club, I didn't want to discuss sewing, or gardening, nor did I want to sit in a circle discussing the trivialities of our town: but instead of declining, I found myself nodding and agreeing to provide a cake for Tuesday. He chatted, describing how he had come to the town just over a year ago and married Mr Henley six months later. He was from the mid-country, was a year older than me and used to be a part-time legal representative and maths tutor. He wanted to know about my life and as I hesitated, a crash from the table caught our attention: one of the Enforcers' wives had fallen to the floor, one hand clutching a beer bottle and the other grasping at the tablecloth, slowly pulling the food down with her. Downing his beer and balancing the bottle on the shelving unit, her husband pulled her up in one fluid movement. I watched as he gripped her arm tightly, digging his fingers into the soft flesh, all the time laughing and joking with his friends and ignoring his swaying and sobbing wife.

I stood to go to her, but Simon strode into the room from the kitchen. I hadn't noticed him return. He grabbed his Enforcer's black jacket by the collar, murmured into his ear and left again, without looking at anyone else. The couple followed, the wife stumbling as she was dragged. The chatter closed around them again as if nothing had happened.

Nikky was chatting to a young builder, flicking her hair and laughing coquettishly, but he scoured the room and his gaze stopped at the sofa where three of Hayley's friends were laughing and giggling, two bottles of wine on the floor by their feet, and a third on the windowsill – all empty. The young builder strode over and pulled one of the women up to her feet and started to dance with her.

I held my breath, glancing at Nikky, and then exhaled. She'd moved onto the next builder and this one grinned and engaged with her banter. I cast my eyes around the rest of the room. Glen was busy chatting to several of his friends while Hayley stood desperately trying to wipe red wine out of her white top, cloth in one hand, a slice of cake in the other.

"Excuse me." I walked away without waiting for Deven to reply, and went to the kitchen. The back door was open and as I stood outside and leaned against the kitchen window, I stared up at the dark grey sky and enjoyed the silence.

CHAPTER FIFTEEN

CLOSING THE BOOK in front of me I shook my head and sat back. It was morning, and I had read all night: it was nearly six a.m. Walking softly downstairs, the morning light was just filtering through the curtains. I flicked through the chore and trade ledger on the kitchen worktop as the kettle boiled. Hayley had agreed to work for the Mallorys for twenty hours this week in exchange for a share of a pig. Already my mouth watered at the thought of bacon. Looking further in the diary, week by week the trades petered off as summer approached, and instead certain days were circled and kept clear. I'd ask her about it later.

On the doorstep I watched the sunrise across the water, the coffee mug cooling in my hand. We were on the very last container. I never thought freeze dried coffee from the army base would taste as good as it did, and I'd miss it when it was gone. As the light got stronger, I couldn't see Tom at the pools, but it was a Tuesday and he liked to write on a Tuesday. The boats were out already, getting earlier and earlier and bringing back more and more. My stomach rolled at the thought: fish was the only smell that stirred up pregnancy nausea, and yet I now lived by the ocean. The brightly coloured sails clashed and waved in the wind. I liked the blues and reds: they matched the beach huts. A lot of the town was coloured: pink, cream and blue render on the old buildings that wound around and up the incline. The brightly coloured buildings lifted the fishing town out of the grey haze and into a rainbow.

"Morning, Kate." Glen poured a mug of coffee and indicated to me.

"No thanks, morning though. You good?" I walked back into the kitchen and started cooking as he murmured his reply. Each day that went by I found it easier to talk to him.

Hayley followed, the smell of ginger and coconut followed her into the room and I inhaled deeply, savouring the smell for as long as I could. We worked in unison, Hayley toasting muffins and washing the sides while I plated up. Glen sat reading and occasionally offering to help as usual, but Hayley poured him a fresh mug and fussed around him. He rolled his eyes and muttered protestations, but she ignored him. It made me giggle.

"We're having some friends over tonight, bit of a social thing, we used to try and do it monthly but things have been hectic recently, what with the nicer weather and regeneration of the town. Glen and I thought we'd start it back up, after my party I realised just how much I missed it."

"Do you want me to go out?" I thought about sitting in the library and working my way through my mental list of books, and relished the thought.

"No, not at all! I was inviting you along, silly."

"Oh." I paused. "Sure, that would be great."

After they left I cleaned the house for the rest of the morning. Each wipe of the cloth gave me purpose and pushed away the tiredness. I could sleep later that afternoon before guests arrived. Once I'd finished, I walked slowly along the path into the town to the northern sector, the place where the bombs had been relentless – even in this small town – and the place where the schools and the hospital once stood. A fire was already burning in the centre: I knew what the flames eagerly consumed, and grimaced. Hayley stood by a chest of drawers, sorting out clothes and bedding. Deven was standing and laughing at her side, dressed as beautifully as ever in a long-sleeved loose kaftan and skinny jeans; as he caught my gaze, he beckoned to me.

"We were just talking about you, Kate." Smiling, he made eye contact with Hayley and my chest hurt. *Laughing?* I swallowed and started to help fold the clothes: they smelt of decay, of dirt, and of death.

"We think it's lovely that you're letting Nikky set up a school in the library."

"I'm not really letting her," I mumbled quickly and they looked at one another, confused. "I mean, it's not my library, it's everyone's. It makes sense is all."

"It's good." Deven nodded, I got the feeling he was patronising me again, but there was nothing I could say. They talked on, gossiping and whispering about the other wives and townspeople: the doctor's daughter had been found wandering the streets last night wearing nothing but her robe and carrying a bin liner full of old newspapers and costume jewellery. The Enforcers and her father had taken her away, but not before the news had spread. I think her name was Amy, she was young, only twenty and very sweet. She ran the animal shelter with two of her friends and re-homed those she could. I'd seen her around and meant to ask her if there were any cats suitable for me. I tried not to think of my Oscar.

I managed to work for a few hours, sorting out clothes and then moving onto the piles of tins and packets of dry food from the ruined homes, checking the dates and organising them accordingly. There was a man to my right who wouldn't stop sobbing. I tried to block it out but it was constant and irritating; sighing, I looked over. He was hugging a doll and sitting in a pile of sheets. Opening my mouth, I wanted to speak, but there were no words. Gripping a tin, I turned it in my hands and listened. I didn't want to, but I couldn't stop, nor could I move. It took me several minutes before I was able to speak.

"Are you ok?" *What a stupid thing to say.*

He didn't reply and instead the noise subsided. Eventually, with a nod he stood and walked away, carrying the doll back into the northern sector. I watched him go and looked beyond him to where the handful of Excavators cleared the houses, carrying heavy rolled blankets and rugs to the huge pit in the centre of what was once the neighbourhood's park. There was something indescribable in the air: it carried me on the breeze and a small part of me tore away into the pit. I choked then, gasping for air and drawing it deep inside until it hurt: for a moment I couldn't get enough. One of the blankets slipped and I glimpsed a mottled and wizened limb, something that I'd hoped not to see again, not here. I couldn't help but look, it was out of place, awkward and... not right.

Turning around I headed back home. I needed to sleep.

I WOKE TO sounds of chatter and laughter and the smell of smoke from the pit. Undressing, I emptied the small amount of water from my bottle onto a cloth and washed in my room, away from the visitors. My meagre wardrobe was woeful, but I picked out a green tee shirt and a pair of stretchy jogging bottoms.

"Kate, you're awake." Hayley grinned as I reached the bottom of the stairs and peered into the room, counting the heads: fifteen, not too bad. "Just in time, everyone has just arrived. Games night begins."

She sounded so excited. The Henleys and Simon were there, and a group of younger, attractive townspeople I hadn't seen before and whose names all merged into one during introductions. They were apprenticed to the doctor but they looked far too young to be medical students to me. There were labourers and then a mixture of nobodies like me, those without a reason or purpose in the town.

There were three groups in total, one six and two fives. I ended up with Hayley, Deven, a man called Louis who was a mechanic, and Karl and Mia who were both of no consequence... like me. I vetoed the games of Monopoly and Cluedo and so we started with Jenga. Once the wine flowed, the atmosphere eased, and soon the three tables were rowdy and alive. Between the moves Karl shared his life before; he was an I.T. manager for a local pharmaceutical company and had lived in the northern sector for nearly ten years. I hadn't truly realised the extent of the attacks on the country: when the bombs dropped, the lifelines to the world outside of our little bubble went with it. The internet terrorists hit, viruses, open doorways into government databases and security systems, the stock exchange crashed and never recovered. What started as an apparent joke by a group of teenagers at the height of internal unrest and externals battles escalated the meltdown.

"There's nothing left, no telephone lines, no satellites, nothing," he declared simply as he pulled a brick from the tower and held his breath. It wobbled precariously but remained standing. Just.

"But what about the back-up systems? Surely we had something... I dunno, something secret?" Mia asked as she slid her chair back and walked around the table, hesitating and pausing at the bricks.

"How do I know?" Karl stood behind Mia, placed his hands on her waist and tickled. The distraction caused the tower to crash and the group to whoop in joy.

"Cheat," she grumbled as the others laughed. She swatted his hands away while he grinned and winked.

Deven lent forward and brought his lips close to my ear. "Look at the way they stare at each other, it's so sweet."

Mia chose the next game; some dice-based nonsense with plastic pigs and chance. I found myself looking at the other tables. Simon, Glen and some of the others played Risk. I knew that game, Stephen would play it every

Wednesday night with friends. The others were arguing over Trivial Pursuit.

I overheard Simon and Glen discussing raiding parties within fifty miles of the town, Wanderers who had banded together to loot and pick at the carcasses of towns and villages. He intended to send out a strike force of ex-military and police and *deal* with the problem should they approach. Glen frowned and several times opened his mouth to reply but ended up merely shaking his head and remaining silent.

"Kate, when's your birthday?"

"My what?" I blurted out in horror, turning to face Hayley.

"Your birthday. The day you were born." Hayley held a pen in her hand and a small pink fluffy diary. "I'm trying to get everyone's birthdays recorded so we can do something as a community. My party was amazing, and I just want everyone to have something to look forward to."

She continued to look at me; the whole table did. I had just a few seconds to reply or look rude, or worse, as though I was hiding something.

"November the 23rd," I finally replied.

"How old will you be?"

Paranoia kicked in. Mia stared at me and then raised her eyebrow, sharing a look with Karl. I had to answer. "Twenty-nine."

"Great." Hayley beamed and went around the table noting down birthdays, anniversaries and special occasions. Why hadn't I lied? Now, written in that book was something I couldn't erase or hide behind. I could feel eyes on me and as I looked up Mia smirked back. I decided I didn't like her. The feeling was compounded when she spoke.

"Are you excited about the baby, Kate? It must be lovely having a reminder of your husband." *Bitch.*

Everything went quiet. My face was hot and the roof of my mouth and nose tingled as I forced myself not to burst into tears. Our eyes met and I saw the challenge there. She wanted to know more. She poked and prodded for answers to the questions I knew they gossiped about behind my back.

"My husband would have loved a baby." It was a truth which told a lie. "Do you have children, Mia?"

"Not yet, I'd love a baby though." Flicking a look at Karl, she winked and he looked uncomfortable. "We'll see."

His face was ashen and he kept dropping the dice as he tried to slip them into their tube.

"Good luck with that."

Trivial Pursuit next. I set up the board and listened to the conversation behind me with interest.

"We heard from a military camp in Rennes. Couldn't understand much of what they said, but Teresa is going to try and re-establish communications."

"Rennes? Where's that?"

"France. Yeah I fucking know, right?"

I missed the next exchange as a roar of laughter drowned out their conversation.

"... they've got some kind of message on loop, something

about needing medical supplies and vomiting. It cuts off every now and then and you can hear people talking."

"How are we getting their transmissions? Bit far, isn't it?"

"I don't fucking know, I'm no scientist. Terry says it's something to do with the atmosphere. We're going to try and extend contact. Might even get the ol' Morse code going. Proper retro."

They started to talk about Terry and her tight fitting jeans then. I tuned out of their conversation and went back to the one on my own table.

IT WAS NEARLY midnight when people started to leave. There was more talk of supplies and of the northern sector. They were going to flatten the area, all four hundred houses, and with the help of the builders, renew and rebuild half that amount with solar panels and self sustainable resources. The town architect and the council wanted the land to be cleared and a large proportion of it turned over and worked for food and resources. The three trainee doctors would have a surgery there.

I THOUGHT ABOUT the doctor's daughter over the next few days. I was too nervous to ask after her, though, afraid that people would wonder why or – worse – that they would engage in conversation.

CHAPTER SIXTEEN

AFTER BEING BADGERED several times a day every day, I finally gave in and agreed to go to the social club with Hayley and Nikky.

They discussed the up-coming celebrations for Easter in two weeks time. The group decided to bake cakes and decorate the town hall for the children. The more I listened, the more I realised how boring the day would be. I only knew half of those present by name and, as the list of attendees went around the room, I struggled to remember names and faces. I recognised Mrs Carroll, sitting by the window in her finest clothes with a trolley at her side and a serious expression on her face as she organised refreshments. She was to be 'pourer' for the meeting and she sombrely nodded in my direction. Swallowing a laugh I continued to listen to the plans without interest.

"Perhaps we should have an Easter egg hunt?" I blurted out, inwardly cringing; boredom had suddenly made me crack. Several of the group swapped looks and rolled their eyes.

"What do you have in mind?" asked Deven, looking up from his pad and smiling at me.

"Maybe we could decorate some hen's eggs, leave a trail of them for the children, plant a few clues, make it a treasure hunt." I glanced at Nikky. "Nikky told me a couple of the older boys miss their games consoles, so perhaps instead of sweets and toys we could sort something out with the Wanderers and have them find one?"

"What about the younger ones?" It was one of the Enforcers' wives this time, Shelly I think her name was. "I mean, we can't ignore the little ones."

Accepting the tea from Mrs Carroll with thanks, I noticed how Shelly held her teacup: her thumb and fingers grouped together but her little finger was curled. A voice from a long time ago floated through me: *It is an affectation to raise the little finger, even slightly, never forget that. Again.* That was history though, the rules could be rewritten now.

"There are plenty of salvaged toys and games held in the block of garages by Simon's home." Deven smiled brightly. "We can sort something out for each child. I think it's a great idea. Thank you, Kate."

The chilly exterior of the group thawed a little as my idea was developed and expanded. The day after Easter Sunday, Deven reminded us that it was the Sikh New Year and he agreed to approach the small Sikh community and suggest a wider celebration involving the whole town. As Mrs Carroll handed me my tea, I thanked her and sipped quietly, listening to the allocation of jobs and crafts. Sharon and Tina, who sat opposite me, volunteered to paint the eggs for the hunt, and Nikky would create the clues for the trail. As the jobs were handed out one by one, I realised that I was the only member not involved.

"Is there anything I can do?" I twisted the ring on my finger.

"I think we've delegated everything, I'm sorry, Kate. I thought you'd want to relax and put your feet up." Deven stared at my bump, and a flicker of envy crossed his face. "I don't want you overexerting yourself. We need to look after you."

I didn't speak for a moment, and then, swallowing the anger, forced a smile.

"I understand. I'll help Hayley with the food."

"That's a great idea; I don't think anyone will argue that you're the best cake maker here." He looked around the room and everyone nodded.

When the official meeting ended and the socialising started, I struggled to talk and smile.

"Are you okay, Kate?" Nikky touched my arm, her fingers burning against my skin. "You're awfully quiet."

"I'm tired," I lied. "I think I need to go and lie down."

THE BEACH WAS quiet. I couldn't even see the fishing boats on the horizon or Tom by his rock pools: just a huge expanse of sand and ocean. It was nearly lunchtime and I was hungry, but I ignored the pangs and wandered along the coastline, walking further than I had since I arrived. I didn't know how long I walked for but the curve of the beach changed and thinned, and the sand along with it, replaced with slippery rocks and pebbles. I couldn't walk any further. Turning around to return my heart hammered in surprise: I couldn't see the town. Only my footprints in the sand. Sitting on a nearby rock, I leaned back and stared at the sky. It was nothing more than a dark grey haze. No shapes, no colours, just the sheet of cloud stretching out across the water.

The rain started to fall. Huge fat droplets splashed around and on me and within a couple of minutes I was soaked. There was no point trying to hurry back, there was no shelter and there was nowhere I could hide. So I embraced the sensations, water rolling down my back and arms, each drop chasing the one in front. A bright flash caught my eye, followed by a deep rumble through the skies: *God moving his furniture around*. I started to walk back for, as much as I loved the rain, I didn't want to be alone in a storm. I moved as far from the ocean as I could. The angry water foamed and lashed at my ankles.

More flashes, more rumbles: I laughed. My skin was stung by the cold and my clothes stuck to my flesh, but I didn't care. This was good. This was loud and unpredictable. This was peaceful and pure. Like Katherine: pure. I started to run, shaking off the wet and beating the cold, my hair rhythmically whipping my neck.

I couldn't run for long, those days were gone. The baby squirmed in annoyance and I slowed to a walk, rubbing and placating the grumpy sod. The rain was relentless.

I thought back to the months I had spent alone finding this place. When I left the comfort zone of my home county, I clung to the thought of a place where everyone was equal, and the whisper of safety and acceptance of a small community pulled me through the dark days and nights. I had started to fear it was nothing more than a fanciful creation of my imagination and then, as the desperation and loneliness had began to eat away at me, I'd found Glen. Recalling that first meeting, the way he had placed his guns on the ground and spoken firmly with his hands open and welcoming, and then caught me as my legs bucked in relief and tiredness, a ghost of a smile crossed my lips.

I realised I could now see the town, a hazy outline in the distance. Lights twinkled at me through the rain like little beacons guiding me home. It was nearly dark.

Home: this small part of the world that was now home, miles from my life before, from my family and friends.

"Where the fuck have you been?"

I flinched and opened my mouth to apologise, but closed it again. That voice wasn't meant for me. Reaching the corner of the main road that converged with the beach, I stood half-hidden behind a crumbled wall and watched as Mr Henley grabbed Deven's arm and pushed him along the path.

"I asked you a question." Roger, the sweet man who called me 'ducky' now slapped his husband's face.

"I told you, I was going to see Bethan. I needed to speak to her about prepping for Easter." He was crying. I could hear it in his voice. "I stayed a bit longer than expected, I'm sorry." He cowered as Roger struck him again and I flinched with him, twisting the ring on my finger and feeling the pain as if it was me he beat. "Roger, I'm sorry!"

"I told you to be back by four, it's nearly nine."

He didn't get a chance to reply as he was dragged along the towpath towards their home. I heard his cries and apologies merge into constant sobs. I didn't want to be outside anymore.

WHEN I GOT back home, I faced Hayley's tears, suffered the hugs and was swamped in guilt. She had been hysterical, telling me how she worried all afternoon. I hadn't thought, and hadn't realised just how long I'd been out. Nearly eight hours. I apologised repeatedly and she just cried and cried before sobbing in the living room.

"We care for you, love, that's all. You can talk to us." Glen followed her out of the room.

Freezing and soaked to the bone, I sat in the kitchen dripping onto the floor and staring at the table. I felt like a scolded child. I didn't want to go upstairs as I'd have to walk through the living room and see them. The gentle ticking of the wall clock grew louder with each minute that passed. Slowly I stood, careful not to make a noise; I didn't want Hayley to come and shout at me again. It took an age before I made it to the living room doorway and peered in. Glen sat with a book, alone.

"She's gone upstairs."

He didn't look up and I walked past him up the stairs, feeling the hairs on the back of my neck stand up. I hated having my back to anyone. In my room I stripped and dried myself and dressed in a huge pair of pyjamas. Sitting at my dresser I brushed my hair and plaited it away from my face. I missed make-up now; I could see a flurry of spots starting to break out on my chin. I hadn't had spots since I was a teenager. I curled under the blankets of my bed and tried to sleep, starving and miserable. The baby kicked. Eventually I closed my eyes and allowed exhaustion to take me.

THE FOLLOWING MORNING we ate breakfast in silence. Glen left halfway through, pushing his food away and walking out of the house without saying a word.

"I'm sorry, Hayley. I didn't think, I just went for a walk and lost track of time." She stared back at me, her face softening slightly. "I didn't feel great and wanted fresh air, needed to clear my mind."

To stop the waffling I sipped at the lukewarm tea, hoping she would speak.

"Do you know what Glen did before the war?"

I shook my head.

"He was an undertaker. We ran a funeral home together and I co-owned one of the florists in town. He had the contract for the local authority and coastguard rescue. When the weather turned bad, we thought the worst. Do you understand?"

Nodding I started to speak but she shook her head.

"Glen did a solid nine months' body identification and clearance, three times his allocated amount. It got us this house, electricity, heating and soon the water as well. He's volunteered for the northern sector clearance in exchange for a UV filter. It got us so much, yet cost too much. He's not the same." I continued to sip the tea. "He went out looking for you yesterday afternoon, just picked up his bag and left without saying a word to me. When he came back without you he sat in his chair reading with his music on. Not a word, Kate. He didn't say one word. I was worried sick about you and the baby; and then I had him to worry about as well. Please don't walk that far without a radio again, Kate, promise me."

"I won't, I'm sorry Hayley. It was stupid, and irresponsible. I really didn't mean to upset you. I'm fine though, the baby's fine too."

"Yes, but what if you'd got lost, hurt yourself, fallen over? So much could have happened." She was almost crying again and yet irritation wormed through me. I had survived long enough on my own, endured far worse than a thunderstorm. I wasn't made of glass.

"Hayley." She looked up at me, and I almost faltered, but if I didn't stand up for myself now, I never would. "I spent years alone, Hayley, when everyone I loved was taken from me. I'm not a child, please don't treat me like one. I've apologised, I know I should have thought, I didn't, I was wrong. But if I want to go for a walk in the rain, then I will."

It was as though I had delivered a blow to her face. I pinched my thigh under the table, digging in my nails and clearing the emotions that filled me. Expecting her to shout or cry again, I steeled myself, shutting down and smoothing my face to a mask. I hated to think what I looked like, what I had become yet again.

"Oh Kate, I'm sorry. I don't want you feeling like a

child, I'm sorry. I know you've been through so much."
The pain in my thigh spread now, up my side, across my
ribs and back and settling in my skull where the start of a
headache bloomed. "Just, please, the radio. I don't want
to fight about this, and I don't want to patronise you. You
mean so much to me, and to Glen."

As she hugged me, I forced myself to relax and pat her
back clumsily. We both continued to utter futile and now
empty apologies until Glen walked in, tutted, called us
daft and pulled Hayley into an embrace, muttering for
forgiveness for his moodiness. They disappeared upstairs
and I cleared up the kitchen. As the giggles and bangs
grew louder I struggled to block them out and sifted
through the CDs until an old album of favourite rock
anthems caught my eye: that would do. At the chessboard
I tutted, shook my head, slid my knight across the board
and dropped his bishop in the wooden box. Humming
to the songs I scrubbed the kitchen, dusted the living
room and dining area, and washed the windows inside
and out.

It was a good three hours before they re-appeared
downstairs, carefree and glowing. Together we walked to
the town hall. Simon had called an Enforcer meeting and
invited several of the residents along, including me.

Settling into the corner next to Hayley, I was relieved
to see that he didn't sit at the top table and instead he
moved all the chairs into a large circle and took a seat
directly opposite me. Nikky entered with a few of the
wives, tradesmen, and then, finally, the Henleys. Deven
looked tired, but he smiled and laughed and charmed his

way around the room, his husband close behind; smiling and waving as he always did.

The seats were filled, and the Enforcers stood around the room behind us. Shifting my weight on the chair, I was able to see the outline of who stood behind me: it was Paulina's husband, Mick? Or Mike? I counted over thirty Enforcers in their khaki shirts and black combats, outnumbering us two to one. Most of them were ex-military and police; that's the way Simon liked it. Those who weren't, like Glen, were men with excellent local knowledge and a healthy set of usable skills. Their guns were visible in the holsters at their hips, why were they armed? I glanced at Glen, who stood behind Simon with his hands clasped behind his back and a frown on his face. He shook his head at me, the tiniest of movements.

"I'll keep it brief. I got back yesterday from Blackwood and it's been decided that the security team on the perimeter will be reduced from a twenty man, twelve hour rotating pattern to a ten man team. Those released ten Enforcers will move to wandering and gathering supplies for the school and library." He glanced at me and held my gaze, his face impassive. "This isn't up for discussion or votes. It's been decided."

"Wait a minute Si, you can't just—"

"I can, and I have." He cut off Roger Henley. "It's decided."

"Simon, really…"

As Roger started to speak again, the Enforcers around the room moved: some grabbed their handgun hilts, others crossed their arms or gripped the back of the seats.

My stomach lurched and my legs shook and head swam. A coup? Now?

"My men want a life away from patrolling the border to the town. In the last two and a half years we've never been attacked. Why? Those in the Unlands know we're strong and unafraid. They know that they are welcome here upon surrendering their weapons. We have no significant crime. Why? The Enforcers. Who ensures that the communication network between towns and gangs is open and transparent? Us. My men have built links, groups and Enforcers for hire across the entire country, ensuring that *you* are safe and cared for. They deserve more than they're getting." He stopped and sat back, crossing his arms and frowning at us all.

"Just what's going on here, Simon? Why the guns?" It was Deven who spoke, and they shared a look. I glanced at Roger, who appeared oblivious.

"Mr Henley," replied Simon. "Many of my men have come to me over the last few weeks, angered and upset that their request for reduced security was denied. And now they are to look for books on top of their usual job role." He shot me a derisory sneer. Now I knew why I had been invited. "While I agree with the principle, and admire Katherine and Nicola's enthusiasm, I told you I didn't have the numbers to sustain everything, and Blackwood is now in agreement and they suggested a compromise. Nicola." He turned. Her face was deathly pale and her eyes darted around the room like a trapped and frightened rabbit. "Over the next couple of months I have to do several supply runs and trades with the other town. Their teachers have agreed to help you set up a proper timetable and syllabus and share teaching aids. I suggest you come with me and spend some time in their school."

"Simon, this is highly inappropriate." Mr Henley spoke, but there was no fight in his voice.

"Nicola? What do you think?"

She stared at the Enforcers with their guns, at Henley's face and Simon's wide and empty smile.

"Okay."

And so it was decided, she'd be leaving me for ten days a month for the next three months, but Simon had promised that the ten relieved Enforcers would be transferred to wandering for books and school supplies. *Every cloud has a silver lining*. That was the saying, wasn't it?

CHAPTER SEVENTEEN

THAT NIGHT I wished I lived alone. I lay in bed listening to the shouting through the walls. Hayley screamed at Glen to stop enforcing and start labouring, but Glen didn't want to, his low voice made it hard for me to hear, but several times he repeated the word *restraint... out there... kids*. They continued until the early hours. His involvement in the Enforcers' show of strength had upset Hayley. I heard my name several times and each time clasped my hands over my ears and counted – childish, but I didn't want to know what they said about me.

Eventually, with a slamming of doors and a volley of curses, it quietened. I crept from my bed and stared out of the window. Glen marched away down the shingled path towards the beach, and then sat on the sand with his head between his knees. He looked defeated.

"Kate, are you all right?"

I jumped. Hayley stood in my doorway, puffy faced with red-rimmed eyes, clutching a handkerchief.

"I'm fine. I heard you both arguing." I glanced back outside. "Glen's sat on the beach."

"Oh don't you worry about us. That wasn't an argument. You should hear some of the arguments we've had. Good God. We'd rattle the windows sometimes with the shouting!" She blew her nose loudly, her voice wobbling as she tried to smile, but failed.

Instinctively, I walked over and held her, she cried again and I ignored the anxiety trying to swallow me as she held me back.

"Will Glen be ok?"

"He's under a lot of stress, I've not seen him like this for a long while. I just wish he'd open up and tell me what's on his mind. This is killing me." She cried again and I continued to hold her, looking out my window at Glen's hunched form.

I SLEPT IN the following morning, a rarity for me. When I finally woke the house was quiet and empty. There was a note.

Gone into town. Glen's with Simon. Breakfast in the oven.

A smiley face at the end and a huge kiss made me grin, and, peering into the oven I sighed with happiness: bacon and scrambled eggs. I opened the kitchen door and allowed the light and cool air to sweep through the house. It was quiet outside but for the water and the seagulls. Soon though the crunch of gravel drowned the birds and a dark shadow filled the room.

"Morning, Kate."

It was Nikky. I pushed my empty plate away and invited her in, flicking on the kettle as I did.

"I leave this afternoon. I'm going to miss the Easter egg hunt. I was looking forward to that. Will you plant the eggs and do the clues for me?"

"Of course."

"Paulina's coming with me, her husband is in the convoy so it makes sense. Glen's coming too. I didn't think Hayley would want him going again so soon."

Nikki didn't want to go, and over the following hour she told me repeatedly how she was scared. She hadn't left the town since the Enforcers had arrived, about the same time the council had been set up and the renovations started. In a way I envied her fear at the unknown world and the Unlands.

"I wanted you to meet the class before I go. I haven't started anything concrete yet, and only had a few mornings with the kids, normally before you start work in the library. In case they turn up when I'm gone I thought it would be nice for them to say hello."

"Sounds great." I scribbled a note to Hayley telling her where I was and left with Nikky.

Scanning the rock pools, my heart sank a little: Tom must have come and gone already. I loved how close we were to the beach – only the cottages were closer, and everything in this part of the town was compact and clean; but the further we walked towards the library and the centre, the dirtier the buildings became, salt stained with rusted and ill-maintained metal framed windows. The plan was to replace the windows in this older part of town with the units from the northern sector. It made sense, I guess. As she told me about the background of some of the children I nodded and tried to concentrate, but the dark outlines of the Enforcers patrolling the streets distracted me. They were out early today. They were armed as well.

It was a little after nine a.m. when we got the library, and already there were three teenage boys waiting outside.

"Morning lads. Josh, Mo, Lee – this is Kate. She's sorting the library out so we have lots of books to read."

I forced a smile at the three boys, who grunted their replies. I think they said hello.

"Josh lives next door to the Henleys with his mum, and Mo and Lee live with Artie, the builder, they sort of apprentice with him, don't you?" Nikky opened the library door and ushered us in. Mo and Lee nodded in response as they stared around the library.

"Cool window, Miss Daniels." Lee nodded at the curved and shaped window frame. "That's old, right?"

"Very early 1900s, so yes, quite old. Art Nouveau I think."

"Yeah, it's cool," he repeated, looking pleased with himself.

Nikky chatted to them while I stood next to her smiling and nodding. It wasn't long before others arrived, mums and guardians escorting in the younger children. There were more than we initially thought: forty-six in total, ranging from three to nearly sixteen. Mr Henley's daughter was the oldest and the moment she saw the three boys, her scowl was replaced by a grin and wave.

Over the next few hours I was introduced to so many

children that I forget all their names. All except a little boy who solemnly shook my hand and introduced himself as 'Alan Philip Olney', before adding that he was six years old and he loved apples but hated peas. I shook his hand and promised to bring him an apple the next time he came to see me.

Nikky was amazing with the children. Some of the parents stayed and watched. Nothing fazed her. She told them that she was going to get books and crayons, toys and teaching aids and would be back soon, but she made her audience part of her speech, inviting them to talk and discuss where she was going. She had already introduced maths into the morning by calculating the distance and time aloud. None of the children had an education to speak of, though they seemed keen, and their enthusiasm cheered me.

Late in the morning my attention was drawn to the door; Simon was staring at us. I placed my hands on my bump.

"How's the baby, Katherine?" Simon asked.

"Fine."

"I'm glad. A new baby will be wonderful and just what the town needs."

I went to stand: I didn't like him looming over me. My ledger slipped from my lap and instinctively I bent down to pick it up, my top riding up at the back as I did. I pulled it down quickly, placing the ledger on my desk as I glanced at his face. It was blank, as always.

"Is there anything you need, Katherine? From the other town? They have a lot more supplies."

"No, thank you."

"What about for the baby? Do you need clothes? Nursery equipment?"

Disliking this sudden interest, I shook my head and stepped back, creating space between us. He smiled, his eyes creasing in the corners. It was a genuine smile, of that I was sure. It confused me.

"If you think of anything, let me know." He paused and added: "Or Glen or Nikky. Anything at all."

"I will, thanks."

We watched Nikky interacting with the parents while the children ran around the library chasing each other. Giggles echoed through the high-ceilinged room.

"Sorry if I come across as a moody bastard at times."

I looked at him and frowned. "No, it's fine." *I don't want to talk to you, go away.*

"No, I know I'm a shit sometimes. Deven tells me I need to relax." He met my gaze and smiled again. "This is a lovely town, Katherine. Everyone gets on well, we don't have any problems, everyone's happy. I just don't want us to end up like them out there, animals."

I nodded, unsure why we were having this conversation.

"I know there are terrible things that go on in other towns. Things like that just don't happen here. We honour the sanctity of marriage, obey the law and live by an honourable code. It's taken time of course, always takes time to set these things up, always some resistance. We ironed out the creases though, got things nice and smooth."

I thought back to the Henleys. Did Simon know? Of course he did, stupid me. Both of them at the party, the slap to his face by Roger Henley, the look they shared at the meeting.

"You're not stupid, are you Katherine? You know that things like that don't happen here, wouldn't be tolerated. Those involved would be excluded and asked to leave. Wrongdoers are punished. I've seen it before." His voice was steady and low, his gaze now on the children. "It's worse for the accuser you know, they're never forgiven, and eventually they leave." He grinned widely and waved in acknowledgement to one of the women in the corner with Nikky, before looking back to me and gazing at my bump. "It's a nice place here. We're not like the other places, or even like Blackwood, you won't be judged because you're pregnant and unmarried. We love you and care for you."

I tried to shut him out and concentrate on the children playing. When the country closed her borders, the disquietude and defensive belief of different groups bubbled and grew until the unease morphed into hate and segregation. Those with common beliefs banded together, and new towns were formed. If I had found myself in one of those communities instead of here, I didn't doubt that I would be an outcast and my baby taken. I knew the stories. Unwed and unclean. I was a sinner in their eyes and unworthy of saving.

"I'd hate that to happen to you."

I nodded again. I had no reply.

He wandered over to the women, his hands in his pocket as he laughed and joked, so different to the man who stared and scowled at me. What had I done to offend him?

"Kate."

Nikky beckoned me over.

"Kate, this is Rose, Alan's guardian. It seems Alan's quite taken with you."

A plump, pretty middle-aged woman smiled at me; her perfect peaches and cream complexion made me acutely aware of the spots on my face. She reminded me of everyone's favourite friend who always remembered birthdays and special occasions, the one who brought cakes into work for no reason and bought little kitschy presents back from holidays.

"Alan thinks you're the prettiest lady in the town, Kate. He's intrigued by the bump, I don't think he believes me when I told him there's a baby in there."

I couldn't help laughing, it escaped before I could conceal it and Simon glanced over curiously.

"Bless him." The grave little boy sitting on my chair, flicking through a huge book and pretending to read; it was my ledger.

"Yes, he's an unhappy boy. Found by the Enforcers wandering the Unlands nearly a year ago. How he survived alone, I'll never know."

I kept my attention on Alan as Rose spoke. He sat and studied the other children, and when they approached his body language changed, he tensed and scowled.

"He hates men, and doesn't like other children. In fact, apart from me and you, Kate, he hasn't spoken to anyone else here."

"Really? No one?"

Nikky shook her head. "No one. When I saw him

introduce himself to you, I told Rose, and well, we hate to ask, but…" She trailed off and looked guilty.

"C'mon woman, spit it out." I smiled lightly.

"Well, Rose is exhausted, really exhausted, she could do with a few mornings to herself, and when it comes to teaching, if Alan won't talk to me, I won't be able to teach him, so…"

"You want me to teach him?" I couldn't hide the incredulous tone from my voice. I was useless with kids, I couldn't teach him.

"It'll only be a few mornings a week, just so Rose can get on and do some chores. Please, Kate." The wheedling in her tone dissolved some of my anxiety, and the giggles started to bubble up again. I looked back at Alan: obviously the book had proven far too boring, he'd moved onto a boxed-set collection of Beatrix Potter's books.

"Ok." I nodded. "Ok, two mornings a week, whichever days suit you, Rose."

She grabbed my hands and I jumped, unsure what to do. As she gabbled and thanked me I brushed aside my reservations of Alan and my fear of Simon. This was a good thing: I just needed to convince myself of that.

EARLY THAT AFTERNOON Nikky dragged me back to her small house behind the football pitch and I couldn't help but gawk at the walls as she organised her clothes and toiletries into a holdall. Every conceivable surface was covered by artworks. The countryside in watercolours and oils, charcoal sketches of buildings and pencil portraits of people from the town. I touched the flat faces of two of the builders smoking on the site near where I lived; she'd captured every nuance of their features.

"Nikky, these are fantastic."

She looked over and snorted. "Oh those, yeah, they're okay. I did art and design at University. I try and do something every day." She stopped suddenly. "That reminds me…"

As she bounded up the stairs I walked into her dining room, continuing to admire her art. I wandered to her easel to see what she was working on. It was the library. Instead of depicting the grey, cold stone she used bright and vibrant Indian ink with a host of colours, the stone shaded to look like opal. It wasn't hard to see why she was kept at university. Only the higher echelon, both in talent and social class, had remained in education as more and more of the working classes and adults were conscripted and forced to fight. My local art college had closed early on in the conflict, with those who were enrolled moved to apprenticeships on the military bases or in the government offices that sprung up all over.

"Oh no," she groaned, standing in the doorway and making me jump. "That's terrible, don't look at that!"

"Are you mad? It's gorgeous." I traced the library windows and the rainbow of ink that ran down the page.

"Really? Have it." She broke into a grin. "Consider it a gift for you looking after the kids for me."

"Are you sure?" I stroked the sheet again.

"Yeah, course. I don't like it anyway." She dumped her bag on the circular dining table and struggled with the zip. "I think I have too much."

"Wait… is that the kitchen sink I see?"

"Ha-ha." She grunted as the zip finally gave up the fight and closed. "Done, I've got my pencils and pad, I'm working on something extra special at the moment. I can't wait to show you."

"What is it?" I asked, immediately intrigued.

"It's a surprise."

I don't like surprises, but seeing her face light up and the anxiety of this trip melt away, I stayed quiet and nodded, screwing up my face a little in mock irritation.

"I meant to say, Kate. Thanks for agreeing to look after Alan. Rose is drained, I mean, really drained."

"It's all right, I don't mind."

"You're a star, you know that?" She grabbed her holdall and kissed my cheek. Without thinking I jumped back and failed to hide the horror from my face. "Oh God, I'm sorry, Kate." She looked confused and crushed. "I didn't mean anything by it."

"No, no, I'm sorry Nik, I just don't like all that sort of stuff. I've got my own shit to try and sort out, sorry." I waved my hands around and shrugged. "I just, I don't… sorry."

The colour rose to her cheeks as she nodded and mumbled her understanding. I don't think she did understand though, and I didn't blame her. Following her through the small house I took her backpack while she heaved her holdall and locked her front door before handing me the key.

"Do you miss your home town?"

The question hit me as hard as a truck and I stopped dead in the middle of the deserted road.

"Yes." The familiarities, the sights, the shortcuts, separately they were nothing but together they were home. I remembered the crumbling wall I always walked beside on my way to work, remembered digging and scratching the mortar between the bricks as I went.

"Is it far from here?"

"Mid-country."

"Cool. I had a boyfriend from around there. Well, he was sort of my boyfriend for a bit. He joined the military police about a year before the bombs started and we split up. Turned into a right arse."

"Yeah, I can believe it. I knew a few people like that."

"I wanted a baby," she blurted out. "But he didn't. Said we weren't married and it wasn't proper. Said that people thinking like me was the reason things had gone so wrong. We needed to go back to our roots, family values."

Family values, again.

"I'm not stupid, he was just spouting that poster crap plastered everywhere. He didn't believe in it any more than I did. Especially when we were in the field by his house, and his parents' room when they were away." A faraway smile crossed her face. "But he split up with me anyway. I wasn't the sort of girl he should be seen with. That's what he said."

"I'm sorry." And I was. His behaviour wasn't uncommon though, and many thought as he had. That somehow staying at home and ignoring what was happening around us would make everything all right. I had thought that way. There were demonstrations in my town. Those who spoke out, those who disappeared.

"What happened to your husband?"

I licked my lips and mulled over my reply. "He was conscripted a week before the bombs dropped and was shipped to a base. I never heard from him after the first wave hit. I waited for days, weeks for him to appear on the doorstep. I prayed to anyone who would listen, I begged for another chance, for him to be okay and I dreamed he would make his way home. I pictured him on the doorstep, I imagined myself in his arms. He never came, though, and when things started to go to shit I had to leave."

"So who..." she trailed off and glanced at my bump. "Sorry, that's none of my business."

Swallowing I replied: "No, it's okay. The father is dead. What we had wasn't love." I couldn't tell her the whole truth, not yet. Not when I was still so judged with silent stares and whispers.

Thankfully, she didn't ask anything more.

HER BACKPACK WAS heavy. After a few minutes I found myself swapping it from hand to hand and wrapping the straps around my palm. I didn't want her to leave. A small darkness crept across us as the sun disappeared behind a dark grey cold. Moving quicker we made it to the steps of the council building before the skies opened.

"Just in time! There's been an incident." The owner of the voice appeared from behind the door and I tensed: it was Simon. "An emergency meeting has been called." He flicked a gaze to Nikky. "One of the fishermen is dead, things are getting messy."

As he walked back inside I said, "Dead?" and looked at Nikky as she stacked her bags by the underwater school painting. She ushered me into the room and I inhaled sharply. It was packed already and my usual quiet corner occupied: everyone I knew was there.

"Dead?" I repeated, but she shook her head and sat down, indicating for me to follow. It was eerily quiet, and only a soft murmur of voices grumbled through the space. "Nikky, what's going on?"

"It's been months since a trial. We're the jury, and the council the judges." She bit her nails and tapped her right foot, the silver buckle on her flat pumps catching the sunlight through the window and reflecting onto the ceiling. I stared at it until three loud taps of a gavel on the top table commanded our attention. The four from our town council were present, but the Blackwood representative was missing. The Enforcers lined the room like sentries and no one spoke. Only the shuffle of bodies and the sounds of coughs and breathing could be heard: growing louder and louder, crawling under my skin.

"What should be a happy day, is in fact a sad day. An hour or so ago the fishing boats came back with one less crewman, there's been some confusion over what happened, but it appears that Alex Marshall is dead."

There were several sharp intakes of breath around the room and my stomach churned as he cleared his throat and called: "Bring in the accused."

The doors creaked and I forced myself not to turn around as two Enforcers escorted one of the fishermen in. It was Neil Proctor, Hayley and Glen's neighbour who gave me apples twice a week. This couldn't be right, he was no murderer, surely?

"Mr Proctor." Mr Henley pointed to the single chair at the side of the room and Neil sat down, twisting his flat cap in his hands. From the back of the room I could see his legs shaking, and found mine were shaking also. With all the people in the room, the air was heavy and oppressive. He looked terrified, and so very alone. Roger spoke again, his voice cold and clipped. "Are you Neil Proctor, of Betterly House, North Lane?"

"Yes," he replied, scanning the room. From my seat I could see the thin sheen of sweat across his face, and the furtive glances at the armed Enforcers at his side.

"You have been accused of the unlawful killing of Alex Marshall. We, the council, have decided upon this charge and your peers shall decide upon the true verdict according to the evidence."

Why not murder? Simon had spoken of such a crime, what was an unlawful killing if not murder? Nikky was still, her head bowed and her eyes closed as though she was in prayer.

"How do you plead?"

Craning my neck around, I watched. Neil still scanned the room as the doctor, Simon and Deven sat at the table and Mr Henley paced the small space in front of them. Nothing was said, and the smell of fish and sweat grew and I licked my lips to stop myself from gagging.

"Mr Proctor. How do you plead?"

"Not guilty."

"You plead not guilty." Roger nodded at Deven who was scribbling furiously on a pad and making notes.

"Mr Proctor. You have been accused of the most heinous of crimes. My position is one of impartiality. I shall ask you questions and you will have the chance to reply. Do you understand?"

"Yes."

"You left this morning with Alex?"

"Yes."

"Following an argument with your wife?"

He remained silent and stared at the ground.

"Mr Proctor, three people have come forward and sworn to the council that they heard you arguing with your wife as you left this morning. Is that true?"

He looked up then and scanned the room once more, no doubt looking for his wife who wasn't present. Eventually he nodded, but he still refused to look at Mr Henley.

"And you left the harbour angry with Alex, only to return four hours later with his body."

It wasn't a question. *Tell them Neil, please, tell them what happened.* I could see where this was going, from the tone of Mr Henley's voice, the feeling in the air. It was deathly quiet, every shuffle and cough echoed in the room and I couldn't tear my eyes from Neil.

"What happened, Mr Proctor?"

And then he spoke. Initially calm and controlled, his voice finally cracked and he sobbed. He had argued with his wife that morning. A small disagreement over the dinner plans for the week. He wasn't angry when Alex had arrived; he was flustered but not angry. They'd set sail just before six and spent several hours casting the nets out. He'd seen two other boats and spoken on the radio to the other skippers. Alex had complained of feeling sick, and so they packed up and started to prepare to return; then he had slipped on the deck and hit his head. Neil hadn't been able to rouse him and so he had sailed back and alerted the town. The doctor declared him dead on arrival. Several of the townspeople started to cry.

"We have a statement from a resident who claims you were in fact angry at your wife, and it was more than a disagreement over dinner."

Simon beckoned to a woman on the front row. She stood and turned to face the room. She started to read and I closed my eyes. A statement. She documented how she had heard him shout at his wife. He'd called his wife a *whore, liar, ungrateful.* I found myself shaking my head. Neil? I'd never heard him speak in anything but quiet tones. The entire room was focused on her and she loved it, that was clear in the way she stood, the way she paused every so often, glancing at Neil and then at her audience.

I looked at Nikky and found her shaking her head and muttering under her breath. I searched for Hayley and, finding her gaze on me, I raised an eyebrow. She frowned, shaking her head slightly. The woman finished and sat down; the person to her right rubbed her back in a comforting manner.

"Are you a violent man, Mr Proctor?"

I sat up straight and crossed my arms.

"No," he shook his head, "no, never. Ask Nazia, I've

never laid a finger on her. Never."

"I'm asking you, Mr Proctor. Not your wife. Is it not true you were involved in the Capital Riots four years ago?"

Silence. *Just reply. It doesn't matter what you say, just speak.*

"And is it not true you spent three weeks in prison for affray?"

"It weren't like that. It was a pub fight, I was only a—"

"I asked you if you were a violent man, and you replied no. Have you just lied to the court, Mr Proctor?"

"No, I—"

"You were convicted of violent disorder in the Capital Riots and you have spent time in prison for affray. You are a violent man."

"It weren't like that, it—" He stopped twisting his cap and stared at us. "Honest to God, I didn't hurt no one. I just needed food, we all needed food. It were a bad time and no one listened. I just—"

"One hundred and thirty-eight people died in those riots, a further eight hundred were injured. Over half of the city suffered extensive and expensive repairs, shops were ransacked, women raped, and yet you sit here and tell us that it was all for food?" Mr Henley chuckled and glanced at us, his eyebrows raised. "Mr Proctor, come now."

No further questions were asked. Neil couldn't even defend himself against the accusations. He had stopped twisting his cap and inexplicably he looked up and directly at me. There were dark circles under his eyes. A small bruise framed his right eye socket and he looked tired and defeated. I looked down first.

Mr Henley read out two other statements, though the witnesses were not present. They confirmed the account given by the first woman. Then the doctor spoke. *Head trauma, aneurysm, internal bleeding.* I concentrated on only a few of his words. I couldn't tear my eyes from Neil whose bloodless lips trembled as he muttered silently at the ground.

"Extensive bruising, unexplained post mortem bruising, no evidence of an accident." Mr Henley rifled through the papers in his hands. "Post mortem bruising? Did you kick him when he was down, Mr Proctor? Did your anger get the better of you?"

He didn't bother to reply.

"Indeed." Clearing his throat, Mr Henley summed up the case; emphasising the Capital Riots and Neil's aggression. "I ask the townspeople, those that agree with the guilt of Neil Proctor, stand."

I had been on jury service before. I knew that more questions were to be asked of the defendant, and they were to have the opportunity to speak if they so wished. I wanted to know who else had seen Alex with Neil, why unlawful killing, was Alex sick before leaving shore, where was Neil's wife? These were questions I should be free to ask; these were the principles of our law. Where was Neil's defence? Yet so many of the room stood, only Glen, Mrs Carroll and I remained sitting. Glen shook his head, his lips moving wordlessly. Hayley stood to his right, chatting animatedly to the woman to her left. Mrs Carroll looked across at me, dark circles under her eyes and tears rolling down her cheeks. What was this? Through the standing bodies Simon watched me, frowning.

"What the hell is going on…" My voice trailed off. He looked down at me, then back across the room and down again before staring straight at Mr Henley.

"Mr Proctor. You have been judged by your peers. The guilt is decided, you will be exiled from the town this afternoon. We will not see or hear you." Three strikes of the gavel and he was taken away by two Enforcers who guided him through the side door and out of sight.

That was it? Within a quarter of an hour his guilt was decided and he was banished to the Unlands. Someone whispered the words 'scrupulously just,' with venom in their voice.

I wandered with Nikky to the main gate. We didn't speak for a long time until the guilt ate away at me. "I should have said something. How can that be it?"

"It's the way of things here, Kate. When we started to rebuild this place, it was no different to the other towns. We, I mean women, were treated like those in the other towns, like we were some kind of reward for the men to claim. So the rules were set. No leniency, no second chances, all crimes treated the same and equality for all. The test of a society is how it deals with its enemies. The right choice is the one that keeps us alive. That's what Simon said the day he set up the Enforcers."

The right choice is the one that keeps us alive.

I waited with Nikky at the side of the road as the convoy of trucks were loaded with supplies and trade. Eight wheelbarrows of rice, six of flour and three of fresh fruit and vegetables were packed into the last vehicle.

I said my goodbyes and waved to her leaving the town, then walked to the beach. Sitting on the sand, I hugged my stomach and stared out at the water.

CHAPTER EIGHTEEN

THE FOLLOWING TWO days rolled into one, and Sunday, usually my one day a week to spend away from everything and everyone, was instead crowded with rowdy celebrations, screaming and cheering children and raucous laughter. The main street in the town was alive with people – over three hundred – and I sat at the children's table, with Alan to my left colouring in and drawing. Groups formed and split away; the early twenty-somethings sat by the cider barrels playing cards; the builders kicked a football around further down the road, while the off-duty Enforcers stood by the food tables and systematically made their way through the piles of pies, sandwiches, cakes and salads. Old Tom sat on a deck chair at the end of the road, sleeping in the sun with his filthy hat covering his eyes and the top of his nose.

Since the trial I avoided the Henleys as much as I could. I didn't want to speak to Roger. He wasn't the man I thought he was.

A long extension cord stretched from my table to a

generator behind a block of garages and a stereo blared out a compilation CD of old songs, reminding me of my teenage years spent in the middle of a field, staring up at the sky and laughing with friends. Sipping my water I eyed the cider, and patted my bump: not long.

"Kate?" I looked down at Alan, who had stopped drawing and was holding his hands together on his pad. He stared gravely back at me, his big brown eyes wide and his mouth smeared with jam.

"Yes?"

"Is that really a baby in your tummy?"

I tried not to smile. He was so serious all the time.

"It is."

He nodded, picking up his felt tips and drawing again. He fastidiously coloured within the lines of the pad and replaced the lids to his pens with care when he changed colours.

"That's very good."

"It's okay."

I struggled to think of something more to say and instead we both remained quiet. I went back to watching the townspeople. It was just gone two p.m. and the handful of elderly churchgoers walked out of the vicarage and made their way to the party. The young vicar trailed behind, stopping to talk to everyone who smiled and waved to him. He scanned the crowd and made eye contact with me. I dropped my gaze and watched Alan again who had discarded the colouring and moved back to drawing.

"What are you drawing now?"

"Me and you," he replied, cocking his head to one side,

sticking his tongue out and concentrating on the pad. I watched as he coloured my brown hair on the page. I was alarmingly round, but I was smiling and holding what I presumed was his hand. He was smiling too.

"You look happy in that picture, Alan." I pointed to his grin and smiled at him, ruffling his hair.

"It's because you and me are going home and we are going to bake a cake and then read and I'll make you some hot chocolate."

"Are we?"

"Yes." Stopping he looked up again. "Why did mummy leave me?"

I had no reply and shook my head slowly.

He then decided that he was going to live with me. I panicked and reminded him that he lived with Rose. I stood and waved Rose over from the new W.I. table and repeated the conversation, begging her to speak to him. Before she had a chance to reply I strode away to a small section of patchy grass near the church and sat down. I watched as Rose spoke to Alan, he kept looking over at me, and then up at Rose again, until confusion and hurt crossed his face. He slowly replaced the lid to his felt tip and then pushed back his chair, it toppled to the ground and he ran down the road with Rose following. A shadow cut across me.

"Katherine, isn't it?" said a deep voice. It was the vicar. I nodded in response. I wanted to shift to one side but I couldn't, and instead a waft of cinnamon and apple hit me.

"I'm Richard." He held out his hand and I shook it. "Rich, though, please."

He stretched out his legs and I found myself staring at his dark blue-black jeans. I had thought he was wearing trousers earlier, but now he wore designer jeans. *Go away, please.*

"I prefer Kate," I finally replied.

"I haven't seen you at church, not a believer?"

He didn't mince his words. I found it refreshing and shook my head.

"It's not for everyone, but it helps some."

I hoped he wasn't going to preach. I'd suffered the ramblings of a believer during my time in the Unlands; his name was Eli and he had followed me around for a week. He was harmless, but the amount of time he spent telling me to believe in the Lord and I would find salvation wore me down to the point where I waited until he slept one night and left. I'd felt bad for days after, worrying about him and how he would eat and survive, and I'd tried to find him again just to reassure myself that he was all right. But after four days of looking I gave up. Eli was gone. Sitting in the town watching everyone laugh and play, I didn't want to be reminded of the world outside of this haven, of people like Eli. Rich spoke again, asking questions about my time in the town and offering information on his life as a form of enticement.

"Where are you from?" I asked eventually, his accent betrayed that he wasn't from around here.

"A small town in the south. Well, my family are from there. I left some time before the wars and moved here. One moment," he added, jumping up and walking to the food. I watched as he piled up a plate and poured two plastic glasses of water. Returning, he handed one glass to me and placed the plate between us.

"I won't eat all this, please."

I thanked him, but didn't touch the food. "Are you married?" He nodded to my ring and I touched the painful reminder of my time with *him*.

"I was."

"I'm sorry." And he truly sounded sorry. I shrugged and looked out at the road. It didn't hurt anymore: the pain of losing everyone had finally eased away. I couldn't see his face now; it was nothing more than a haze of black and white. Everything that reminded me of home and my life before had been traded, lost or taken from me. I had one photo, and that was it.

"It's a good place to restart, rebuild and rejoice." Rich rolled the sleeves of his shirt up: his right arm was a mess of thick and twisted burn scars, and his left was covered in a full tattoo sleeve.

"I tried to help at the school when it was bombed." Lifting the edge of his shirt, the scars continued across his side and stomach. "A small price to pay for Lara and Daisy."

He pointed to two girls painting at the crafts table, both were around ten years old. I remembered Daisy: she was one of the giggliest and loudest girls in the library.

"Your hand seems fine." What a stupid thing to say. I should have commented on his bravery or something. He burst out laughing and I jumped.

"You know, no one ever notices, everyone always goes on about the girls and my *brave act*." He rolled his eyes and grinned. "I've got so used to people asking that I automatically feel the need to tell them it was for Lara and Daisy, sorry if I sounded a twat."

I shook my head. "No, it's fine. I didn't think you were being a twat."

"My hand was protected. I'd wrapped my jacket around it as I opened one of the doors in the school. I didn't think about things falling."

"Sorry."

He smiled widely again, and I maintained eye contact for longer than I had in a long while with anyone.

"So when is the baby due?"

His words broke the spell. "About six or eight weeks."

"Excited?"

I looked down at the stretched white top I wore, the bottom of my stomach peeking out over the top of my skirt. "I suppose so."

We chatted for an hour or so. I didn't deny him this time, and I told him snippets of my life before the war, carefully editing out anything personal or interesting. I made my story beige and boring, but he listened as though I told him I was a superstar. I caught myself staring at his tattoos on more than one occasion, making out a koi carp, a lotus flower and a huge cross, a mix of beautiful blues, oranges and greens.

"A throwback from my wild youth."

"What?"

"My tattoo, you keep looking at it."

My cheeks reddened.

"I got it during my discernment period, and then I realised that it might not be a great idea."

"It's striking."

"That's very diplomatic of you."

"No, I meant it's lovely. Really bright, I like it." I was going redder, I could feel it.

"I'm just teasing. It was a mistake is what it was. I was caught up in all the excitement of finding my calling that I thought I'd get inked. There were three of us that found each other during those dark times, and we celebrated our path with light – lots of light and bright colours. It took bloody ages and four sittings." He gave me a rueful smile. "Now, I've kept you far too long." He stood and held out his hands. "Easter egg time."

I reached up and allowed him to pull me to my feet, startled at my body's lack of protest at his touch; my top rode up my back. He said nothing and instead escorted me to Deven with gentlemanly grace. Soon the children were lined up and the clues handed out. They were banded according to age and when the older teenagers saw the maths questions there was a collective groan. Then the sharp-eyed Mo spotted the games console tucked away behind my table. I watched as he nudged and whispered to his friends and, suddenly, the maths looked good.

Alan and Rose were still missing. I would have to make it up to him. He couldn't live with me, I couldn't take care of him. I almost heard my voice say *"I can't take care of a kid,"* but I stopped myself.

Rich stayed nearby, chatting to the older women and laughing with the Enforcers. He was the male equivalent of Hayley: *lambs around the shepherd.* I snorted aloud at the image and looked for Hayley, eventually finding her with her friends and the remainder of what looked like a case of wine. Her cheeks were flushed and she was giggling uncontrollably. As the parents moved around the safe areas of the town with the kids I found myself replaying my chat with Rich; talking to him was different. I'd only felt that same way around Old Tom.

As the groups started to file back with the clues and prizes from the trail, I handed out the rewards to them. Nikky and I had decided to give all the children a gift. It didn't seem fair to reward just the winners.

It did, however, make me laugh to see Lee and Mr Henley's daughter race each other back to the table, out of breath and shouting. Apparently, Nina was a 'dirty cheat' and the argument escalated until I cut in and softly told them there was a console for each of them, and one would be permanently installed in the library once the solar panels were fitted. Suddenly, all was right with their world and Nina was 'cool' once more. Christ, I was old. With the children occupied, and some begging to go home, the streets thinned and soon there were just twenty of us left. On my insistence, Hayley staggered home and I started clearing up the mess. The paper plates and torn paper decorations were thrown away in black bags, for the first time I wondered where the rubbish was taken; I'd have to ask Hayley when she was sober. With so few it took hours. My feet were swollen and every part of me ached, but I ignored Laura's pleas for me to relax. It was only when a stern-looking Rich dragged over Old Tom's deck chair and forced me to sit that I paid attention. Tom stood behind him tutting and shaking his head at me. I felt guilty sitting and watching the others work.

I WAS COLD: I'd waited for the arrival of the convoy for several hours, sitting out in the dark with a blanket and thermos of tea. It was nearly midnight before the crackle of static on the radio and Glen's voice roused me:

"Sweetheart? Are you up?"

"No, it's me, Kate, I'm by the main gate."

He told me they were five to ten minutes away. I switched the radio off and waited. When they arrived I was stunned to see so many new faces, at least twenty, and eventually Nikky appeared.

"Did I miss much? How did the Easter egg hunt go? Were the kids good? I've got so much to tell you." Nikky embraced me with a tight hug and the words tumbled out of her mouth. "Kate! You've got so big in ten days, this baby is going to be huge!"

"I hope not," I replied, laughing and screwing my face up in mock pain. "And you didn't miss much. Easter was good, the week after okay, and you'll be gobsmacked to know I went to church yesterday."

She teased me with gross stories of childbirth as we walked back to her house. I nodded to Glen and he continued to unpack the vans and relay orders to the Enforcers; he raised a hand in response.

I then pressed Nikky about the other town; it was more heavily populated but lacking in natural resources and sustainable energy. There was a school with over ninety children and seven teachers. Nikky excitedly told me that on the next trip back two teachers would be coming for resettlement; and once the northern sector was clear we were to expect the arrival of another fifty to sixty re-settlers. The relief at no longer being the newcomer was overwhelming, and I found myself grinning.

"You'll never guess what?" She didn't wait for me to ask. "Honestly, this is good... Simon's got a step-son and fiancée in Blackwood."

"A fiancée?" I thought of Deven, screwing up my face in confusion and wondering whether he knew.

"I know! She's lovely too. Really sweet and loves helping out at the school. Simon runs the Enforcers from Blackwood. They all live in one area there but Cali, Simon's fiancée, makes sure only those on duty carry weapons. Cali is basically treated like royalty because she's just so lovely, and Simon's the King of Blackwood. Everyone listens to him, even the Council there."

The grimace on my face was clear and she nodded. "Yeah, exactly."

"Why doesn't he stay in Blackwood then? He's here more than he is there."

"Apparently he's been busy recruiting more Enforcers and because we're closer to the other towns here it's easier to work out of here. He goes back loads though. His second-in-command is quite dishy. A big tall blonde guy. Looks like a movie star. He was lovely to us when we were there."

I rolled my eyes. "An Enforcer, though. They're all the same."

"Yeah, but some of them aren't bad." She winked and I groaned in disgust. "What? I'm only human! A girl has needs."

"Nikky!"

"What? I'll seal up soon."

I snorted in disgust as she grinned and winked at me. I'd missed her.

She then asked about the children. Alan hadn't forgiven me; he refused to talk to me, or even look at me. It was only this morning at church that I made any progress when I gave him an apple, receiving a small 'thank you'; but nothing more. Even Rose couldn't persuade him to open up. I'd ruined everything.

"What's this about church?" she asked as I unlocked her front door and she dumped her bags in the hallway. I collapsed onto her huge sofa, kicking off my sandals.

"Rich convinced me to give it a try. I'll admit it's not as bad as I thought. I expected him to cry and shout about the end of the world and fill the service with doom and gloom, but it was all right. Bit too much God-speak, but it was doable."

"Rich? He's cool. Makes church a community thing." She dragged the footstool over and sat next to me, both of us groaning as we lifted our feet. "I'm not tired yet, I feel pumped. I slept a bit in the truck but I've got so many ideas for the school, wanna see?"

I was exhausted. My limbs were like lead but I nodded. I could sleep soon. She knelt by her bag and pulled out her drawing pad and a small notebook. She had a timetable organised, with dedicated lessons in English, maths, science and general studies, split into three age groups and colour coded with topics to discuss and possible lessons on history and art. I was impressed.

"There's this really nice bloke who used to teach in a school with loads of troubled kids and he had a small timetable. He was really helpful."

"Was he 'dishy' too?" I teased.

"Very. In a broody, intense and manly way. Don't think he was interested, though. I tried." She pouted and pursed her lips. "Ah well, always next time." She lifted her pad onto her lap. "Now, you ready to see my surprise? I finished it the day I got there."

She handed me the pad and I flicked it open. It was me. She'd drawn me sitting in the library with a book in front of me and a hand on my bump. It was excellent, as though she had copied a photograph; she'd even captured the way the right side of my mouth curled up as I smiled when in thought.

"It's amazing, really amazing. When did you do this? I mean, I know you finished it there, but when did you start it?"

"A few days before I left, I saw you sitting there with the light behind you and you actually looked happy." I screwed up my face. "No, you did! You looked so peaceful."

She then told me how she had been finishing the picture in the communal canteen when the teachers had arrived; they'd seen her drawing and begged her to do more. She received three commissions and the promise of more work when she returned.

"Peter – the dishy teacher from the school with the

troubled kids – tried to trade for my pad! He loved it and suggested that I give art lessons as well, so I'm going to try and fit them in."

"It's a great idea." I held the pad. "Will you look after this for me? I only have my room and I don't want it getting damaged."

"Yeah, course."

I listened as she told me about the way the other community lived, further inland. They had no wind farms nearby and the use of generators was rationed; there were no eco-homes or running water. It reminded me of the towns from the Unlands, but the streets were full of Enforcers who ensured those who lived there abided by the laws: a zero tolerance policy. She witnessed three people excluded from the town, an adulterer, a thief and a fighter, gone with only the farce of a trial that poor Neil had suffered. We spoke then about how Amy was still missing and her face fell, but there was something else hidden there. I knew better than to pry, and she continued to talk until I finally fell asleep.

The following morning I woke with a stiff neck and sore back. At some point Nikky had covered me with a huge fleece. I crept from the house and walked to the beach. It was early, and Old Tom with his bucket and smokes walked across the sand. Calling out to him, I waved eagerly, and he slowed and waited for me to catch up.

"Mornin' Katie, yer up earlier than usual. Babby keepin' yer awake?"

I told him about my night at Nikky's and he chuckled as we walked to the rock pools. I climbed up next to him and dangled my feet in the water.

"Katie, now you'll scare the crabs away." He slapped my legs lightly and I stilled and apologised. "Ah, don't yer worry. They were probably sleepin', yer woken them up for me." He lit a cigarette and inhaled deeply. "Yer want to talk about it?"

Cocking my head, I looked at him.

"Whatever's on yer mind."

"No, I'm okay, really. I just wanted to come and say hello. It feels like it's been ages."

"Only a week or so." He coughed and flicked the rest of his cigarette away. "Still, I know what yer mean. Told Hayley 'bout the nightmares?" I shook my head and he tutted and sighed. "What 'bout Nikky?" I shook my head again. "Honestly Katie, yer can't keep all that stuff quiet."

Absently, I splashed my feet until he rapped my knees with his net. Tom never shied around me but knew when to stop asking or probing – he reminded me of my old next-door neighbour. I used to have tea with Arthur every Wednesday afternoon when I finished work early; he would sit and tell me about his week and we'd share stories. He always knew when I was down, and Tom was just the same. He'd cajoled me into joining him for tea one afternoon and made me laugh with stories of his wife, children and grandchildren. So it was our pattern now, tea and stories once a week.

I told him about the new people who had arrived, and the others who would follow in a month. He sat in silence and lit another cigarette, nodding slowly as I told him about the school and the new plans.

"It'll be good for yer Katie, mixing with more people. Yer won't get hurt."

"Because of the rules?" I couldn't hide the bitterness from my voice: he knew how I felt about Neil's trial.

"Not just them, but because we love yer."

His words mollified me and, as he nudged my arm, I smiled and rolled my eyes at him. The sun was up now and the water glistened with a crystal hue. He hadn't caught anything so he packed up his nets and helped me down to the sand, joking that it was my fault.

"It's yer feet Katie, they scare the crabs away, it's the green nails."

He pointed at my nail polish and I wiggled my toes. He was the only one to notice. It was stupid painting my nails and it had taken forever with my burgeoning stomach getting in the way, but I liked them and I stuck my tongue out and tucked my hair behind my ears. He walked me back home and I stood waving until he was out of sight.

CHAPTER NINETEEN

"IF YOU DON'T want to, I'll understand."

Rich leaned against the wooden veranda on the back doorstep, his hands in his jeans pockets and his baseball cap pulled low. His low-cut tee shirt showed off his scars and tattoos. He looked so different in casual clothes that I almost forgot he was a vicar.

"But c'mon, you know you'd like to. It's only a picnic."

That was the problem. I would like to, and I didn't want to *like* to go on a picnic, especially with Rich.

Eventually I spoke. "I'm sorry, Rich. I don't feel that well. I have some work to do at the library, and Nikky wants a hand with her classes this afternoon."

Rich continued to look down at me expectantly, his face still calm, still optimistic and pleasant. I almost buckled.

"The fresh air will do you good, Kate." Hayley appeared by my side, beaming at Rich and nodding eagerly at me, her eyes wide and pleading.

"No, it's okay, Hayley." He bent down and picked up the basket. "It's okay, I'll rearrange. Kate won't always be

so difficult." He winked but his words left me cold, and
the memory of another smiling and confident face replaced
his. I gripped the side of the kitchen worktop and clenched
my other fist. He wasn't that person, but his light-hearted
assumption left me rooted to the spot. My breakfast lodged
in my throat; I couldn't swallow or speak.

"I was kidding, Kate."

I knew that, and yet I was immobile and my skin itched
all over.

"I know." I replied at last as Hayley laid her hand on my
forearm. "I'm sorry, Rich. I really can't."

Shrugging off her fingers I turned and left them both at
the door. Sitting in the living room I listened to their low
voices until eventually Hayley walked in and the footsteps
on the gravel faded away.

"Don't say anything, please."

She walked past me and up the stairs, just stopping briefly
to squeeze my shoulder. Why do people do that? Why do
they feel the need to touch each other to show that they
care?

After lunch I left an apology note for Hayley and scribbled
a second one that I took with me. I walked down to the
library but, instead of taking the usual route by the towpath,
I wound through the streets to the main road and stopped
outside the church. I walked up the steps to the vicarage
and then posted the crumpled note through the letterbox.

I SAT ON the floor and sorted through the new book arrivals,
watching Nikky leaf through a textbook and explain a

quadratic equation formula to the older children. After a while, a shadow caught my eye. Simon sat on my desk flicking through my ledger and records; anger boiled up and I found myself marching over and snatching it up and holding it against my chest.

"You're doing well, how many books now?"

"Over thirteen hundred."

"The Enforcers bringing you decent stuff? Not any trashy romance shit?"

"I accept everything they bring. Some people like romance."

"You don't, though, do you? Not a fan of having people look after you. Quite an independent creature."

I thought back to Rich and nodded. Already the gossip had spread, and all doubts I had about saying no disappeared. How did he know so soon, though?

"Is there anything I can help you with?" I placed my ledger on my desk and sat on my chair, crossing my arms. His smile widened.

"I just thought I'd make sure you were all right. Not long till the baby's here." He nodded at my bump, and continued: "I hope you don't mind, but I asked around at Blackwood and on our next run I'll bring back a few things, maternity supplies mostly. I've got a friend relocating here who'll make sure they get to you."

"It's quite all right, I don't need anything." *Especially from you. Everything from you would come with a price.*

"It's not for you. It's for the baby and for Deven, he's begged me to make sure you're both cared for." The smile was gone now, and all I could concentrate on were the dark shadows around his eyes. "I'd very much like for us to be friends... for Deven's sake."

There was a small moment of silence. He was gauging my reaction, waiting for my response, and there was only one sensible answer I could give. He would win this round: will these games ever end? I was suddenly swamped in tiredness. I wanted silence and peace.

"Let's see where friendship takes us then." Forcing a sickly smile, I watched as he matched my grin, insincerity and all. He stood and opened his jacket, pulling out a leather-bound book and leaving it on my desk as he left. I picked it up. *The Velveteen Rabbit*. I turned it over and over in my hands before placing it back on the to-be-sorted pile.

WHEN I HAD locked up the doors and started to walk home, Rich stood waiting for me at the corner. Against my better judgement I walked over.

"Rich, I just want... shit, I'm sorry. Sometimes... I get... things get a bit... much." I struggled to verbalise what the emotions and feelings were that I struggled to contain. "I was rude, I'm sorry."

He held my note in his hand and shook his head. "Kate, no. You've done nothing wrong, please don't apologise. I shouldn't have pushed so much. You said no and I was a dick to not listen to you. I didn't mean to upset you, when I ask I don't want to force you I just want to... I dunno... get to know you and just relax. It's me that should apologise." His voice cracked a little, and glancing up the remorse washed his face. His cheeks were flushed and his mouth set in a line. "Please, forgive me."

I started crying. I'd promised myself that I wouldn't cry in public ever again, but I failed. I had broken so many of my promises, failed so many of the tests I set myself.

"Sorry, Rich. It's pathetic me crying. You haven't done anything wrong. I just... don't like feeling trapped and like I have to say yes when I'm not ready, you know?"

I liked him more when he didn't try to console me with a touch or a hug, and instead he leaned against the wall in silence, nodding in agreement. It forced me to quell the tears, to rebuild the barrier without the suffocation or closeness of another.

"Sorry." I wanted the ground to swallow me up before the anger of my weakness consumed me.

"Please stop apologising." He was gentle but firm, and as he smiled I found it burnt away the anger and the tears slowed to nothing more than blurry blinks.

He walked with me back home, all the way to the door, where I thanked him.

"Do you want to come in? For a coffee or something?" I paused, with my hand on the handle as I looked at him.

"I can't. I've got to see Deven and Roger about some Council business, but I'd love to come over soon?"

I nodded and we said our goodbyes. He walked away and I found myself watching him until he disappeared from view. Glen and Hayley were out for dinner with friends, and I was alone, the way I liked, the way I always loved. But tonight it didn't feel right.

So I walked to the beach and spoke quietly to the ghosts of

my past for the first time in longer than I cared to remember. When I now thought of my parents, the bitterness and hate I had carried no longer weighed me down; instead, regret and pity filled that space. I never told them just how sorry I was and that I didn't blame them for what happened. I pretended I did – it's easy to hurt those we love and those we're closest to – but the truth was, I never blamed them for the breakdown in my marriage. They were right to tell him about my infidelity. I had dragged them into my lies and games by using them as my scapegoats, my shields, my pawns. It wasn't mum's fault she got confused and muddled that day on the phone to Stephen and called him Stuart. I deserved it. Now, I could look back clearly without the raw emotion clouding my judgement and understand why he slapped me. I had broken his heart. We were supposed to be trying for a family and yet I had cheated and betrayed him. Everything we worked for was for nothing.

To the outside world we carried on as normal, that thin facade of happiness always precariously close to shattering, but never quite fracturing: behind closed doors we lived separate lives. The day he received his conscription papers was the day I realised just how much I loved him. It was too late. He had forgiven me, told me he missed me and wanted to try again and I readily agreed, but I never got to tell him just how much I loved him too, and that I was desperately sorry for my cruelty and selfishness.

So, alone on the sand and staring at the sky, I told him and said my goodbyes.

*   *   *

THE FOLLOWING MORNING I was forgiven by Alan Philip Olney. Rose appeared at the backdoor holding his hand and smiling, they were earlier than I expected.

"Do you want to come in?" I asked, trying not to smile too much with relief as he acknowledged me and shrugged, looking around the kitchen with interest. His eyes stopped at the fruit bowl. With gentle persuasion he came and sat by me and bit into an apple, his little legs swinging as he did. I walked with Rose down the drive and she told me that since the Easter egg hunt he had closed back down; it had been nearly three weeks and now he was finally talking again. He believed that he was going to live with me and nothing she said could change his mind. She wanted me to talk to him again. I didn't want to talk to him again about that, but I agreed.

"Alan, what do you want to do today then?" I smiled brightly. He shrugged and continued swinging his legs and munching at the apple. "How about we go down to the beach and gather some shells, then make Rose a present?"

"Ok." He jumped down and walked over, holding out his hand and looking up at me.

"Oh, you want to go now?" I glanced at the clock. "I just need to get changed." Walking upstairs I realised he was following me and as I pulled on my leggings and long baggy tee shirt, he sat at my dressing table and started to apply my face cream to his cheeks, dabbing it on expertly and rubbing it in.

"My mummy used to do this."

I didn't reply and dipped my fingers in the cream. He

watched and mirrored my expressions and actions as I massaged my eye socket.

"Ready?" My hair was long enough for a ponytail now, and I pulled it away from my face and tied it back, ruffling up his hair as I did. Nodding he slid down and held out his hand again. I took it and the stickiness of the apple clung to my palm and fingers as we left the house. I didn't mind, his warm hand in mine fired up something deep inside of me.

When we got to the beach I was pleased to see we were the only people in sight, I let go of his hand and he walked by my side, matching my steps and pace. I took him to the rock pools. The tide was low.

"Now, go and collect as many shells as you can, bring them to me and we'll go through them and I'll tell you what I can about them."

He glanced at me and then at the wet sand. "My trousers will get wet."

I knelt down and rolled them up and then took his trainers and socks off.

"Better?"

Nodding, he ran out by the pools and started to hunt in the sand. I sat down on a dry patch and tucked my legs to my side, watching him use a stick and dig into the sand. After a short while an inexplicable sadness washed over me and I went and joined him, kneeling and collecting the shells and making him giggle with stories of fish that used to nip toes in beauty spas and the crabs that were scared of my green nail polish. Hearing his laugh was the opiate that I craved, each giggle and chuckle making me smile more than the last.

"Now, let's sort through what we have."

Sitting back down, I sifted them into piles and explained the difference between the grey top and flat top shells. He had found an enormous, beautiful top shell, and I praised him enthusiastically – his face glowing more with each encouraging word: neither of us bothered to put our shoes back on, and walking back to the house he skipped and hummed along the grass verges all the way to the gravel path, pausing and waiting for me to catch up and, when I did, we slowly walked along the small stones and both moaned as they dug into our feet. I washed the shells outside and took them into the kitchen where Alan sat eating another apple.

"I had an idea. How about I ask one of the builders to make a nice frame for these, then you can give them to Rose and she can hang them in her house. How does that sound?"

"Can I give it to you? Not Rose."

"But Rose will love it."

"Won't you love it?"

"Well yes, but..."

"You have it."

Sitting down I took an apple and bit into it, keeping my eyes on him. He moved the shells around the table, making patterns and smiling faces. It was nearly time for Rose to pick him up and I still hadn't addressed the problem of where he wanted to live.

"Alan, can I talk to you about your home?" He nodded but didn't look up. "You know that you live with Rose, and can't live with me, don't you?" There was silence again and he stopped playing with the shells. "Just because you live with Rose and not me doesn't mean that I don't want to spend time with you. Rose cares for you and loves you very much."

"But I want to live with you."

"And why's that, sweetheart?"

"Because I do."

And so the conversation continued and we went around in circles. When Rose appeared at the back door I shook my head at her and she sighed. When they left he didn't grin and laugh like he had on the beach, though he did wave.

That afternoon I cleared the backlog in the library while Nikky taught the middle group of children. I listened to the chatter and buzz as they ran from box to box swapping poster paints and pencils. When all the books were documented and shelved, I helped the younger ones with their pictures. Some drew their homes, others themselves, all brightly coloured and smiling.

They left and I was pinning the pictures to the walls when there was a loud knock at the door.

"Hi Deven." I greeted him at my desk and piled the remaining pictures up. "What can I do for you?"

"We've missed you at the meetings. Tonight's Paulina's birthday and we're having a few drinks and snacks at my house. We're going to watch some films and relax." He ran his hand along the edge of my desk. "Will you come? And bring Nikky?"

"Um, okay." He had caught me off-guard and I couldn't say no. I hated being unprepared and as we sorted out the time I tried to think of an excuse, but my mind went blank. After he left I waited for Nikky to return and told her.

"Oh no! I was going to go over a few lesson plans. I told some of the other teachers that I'd have timetables worked up for them."

"Do it another night. You're coming," I grumbled, pinning the remainder of the pictures on the walls. "This is the last night I'll see you before you're off again."

"Nah, screw it. I'll go through the timetables with them when I'm there. There's only one of me and loads of them. Still, soon to be two teachers here and more time off for me."

We walked back to her house and shared the remains of a stew for dinner. As we discussed the school and library I suddenly realised that sometime in the next five weeks, I would become a mother. For a while I replied with one word answers until Nikky realised something was wrong. I thought back to my morning with Tom and the way he disapproved of me keeping everything inside. I pressed my mug of tea against my forehead and mumbled that I was fine, just a headache.

Sitting in a room full of drunk women leering over long-dead or missing actors in movies felt surreal. I found myself staring around at those present and wondering just what was going on. I was disconnected and yet, with everyone asking me questions about the baby and my plans, I was treated as though it was my evening, not Paulina's. Nikky remained sober. She was leaving early the following morning and her gaze followed mine around the stuffy room. I was sandwiched between Deven and Lydia on the only sofa while the carpet was crowded with women in various stages of drunkenness.

"Do you have a moment?" Deven asked, indicating the back door as he poured another glass of wine and I nodded.

As we stood outside, he drank deeply, his dark eyes thoughtful. The moonlight bounced off his cheekbones and accentuated his beauty.

"Thank you for not saying anything about Simon and me."

I nodded, not wanting to be drawn into the games, but he took my hand and kissed it, his eyes glazed.

"He's taken care of me and he loves me. He knows about Roger's rages, of course, but I've begged him not to say anything." He continued to drink and talk as I wrapped myself in a cardigan.

"I never thought I'd be accepted for who I am, but it's different here. Gentler than out there, you know?" he paused for a moment. "Yeah, you know." He was more astute than I realised.

"I really need to go, baby needs rest." I didn't want this conversation, not yet.

CHAPTER TWENTY

I SPENT TWO mornings with Alan, suffered two meetings of the social club, and taught the older children on three of the five weekday afternoons. Tom and I met for tea and lunch on Friday and whilst drinking tea and resting my weary feet, I worked out my pregnancy dates as best as I possibly could using an old calendar. If I was right, I was thirty-six weeks pregnant and my due date around the thirteenth of June. It was all rough of course, but suddenly, seeing it written down made me want to stretch out the last few weeks, regardless of my displeasure at the humid weather.

After lunch that day I made my way home; Tom had told me that the northern sector was nearly finished, and that huge amounts of edible food had been found within the rubble of a small supermarket. There was enough to ensure we got through the winter. Body recovery had ended and the pit was filled in; the next council meeting would involve suggestions for a memorial. I had some ideas but was unsure if I should propose them. I didn't know the victims, and so perhaps it would be better to let the old residents decide. There was a small group of people at Mr Proctor's house moving furniture in and out, and the woman from the trial stood laughing with a smaller group while watching the handful of men carrying in a hideous flowered sofa. Seeing me approach she waved cheerfully. I ignored her. I still hadn't seen Neil's wife since the trial. As I reached home, Rich sat on the doorstep looking at me, dressed more like a surfer than a clergyman today; jeans, tee shirt, blonde hair loose and in desperate need of a cut.

"Hi." I couldn't hide my surprise, and the small thrill that shimmied across my body. We hadn't spoken properly since I turned down his picnic and cried in front of him. I hadn't been back to church, and deliberately bypassed the main street as best I could.

"Hi." He stood and stepped down next to me. I was so frumpy, and so very fat next to his tall, lean figure. "I've not seen you around for a while. Everything all right?"

I nodded absently. "Would you like to come in?" I still hadn't broken the habit of politeness. When he followed me inside I made us both coffee. Creaks from upstairs followed by footsteps made me close my eyes. I almost feared opening them, but I did on hearing Hayley's gasp of joy. She stood in the doorway smiling widely at us both.

"Well, this is unexpected." *Smooth, Hayley.* I glared at her, but, typically, she was oblivious. "Fancy seeing you here, Rich. What brings you over?"

"I just wanted to make sure Kate was okay. I didn't see her at church and hoped that my sermons hadn't put her off."

"Hayley, don't you have something to do? Out in town?" I suggested.

"What? I don't... Yes, I need to see Mrs Brooks... for... something." She grinned and slipped her shoes on, leaving us in a now awkward silence. Eventually he cleared this throat and I looked up.

"So, are you all right?"

"I'm fine." I ran my fingers across the rim of my mug and then, throwing caution away, added: "Well, a little bit nervous, I guess. I worked out that baby is due in just over four weeks and I'm really unprepared."

"Four weeks? Plenty of time. Baby will be fine, you'll be fine." He sounded sure and firm, I raised an eyebrow. "Kate, seriously, we won't let you be alone."

"Won't let me?" I echoed, a fizzing of irritation starting. "I don't need your help, I can take care of myself. Everyone always thinks I need taking care of. I lived alone in the Unlands for over two years, for Christ's sake!" When I opened my mouth, the words flooded out and I couldn't stop them. Even when I tried to close my mouth, it didn't work. "I'm not weak, Rich! I'm just lost and trying to find my place here."

"You're not weak. I've never thought that."

"Why are you here, Rich?" I tried with desperation to keep my tone light, but a wisp of clipped wariness crept in.

He was nervous. His Adam's apple bobbed up and down as he swallowed, but without missing a beat he smiled.

"I want to make you laugh. Make you smile. Make you forget whatever it is that makes you so sad."

Impossible. His words made me uncomfortable, and sad, and irritable. Everything made me irritable today. "You don't want much then." Sarcasm infected everything. "Is this your good Samaritan act? Help a desperate newcomer and earn some brownie points?"

"It's my human act. We're not all monsters, let's just talk. Anything you want." He dragged the chair across the tiled floor closer to me.

"For fu…" I trailed off, and he grinned wider, raising an eyebrow.

"Ok, fine. Why are you so friendly with the Enforcers? You know what they do in other towns, surely?"

"The Enforcers protect. Simon chooses those with disciplined military and police background. Do you remember what it was like at the start of the war, our war at home I mean? The fear that everyone felt?"

I nodded. Flashes of mobs and crowds: desperate, angry, greedy.

"The Enforcers stop all that, before it escalates. They protect and–"

"And control." I interrupted. "They don't always arrive before it escalates. They're professional mercenaries, Rich. Thugs who work for whoever pays the most." He was still so calm that my voice raised an octave and I found myself clenching my teeth.

"That's not fair, they're good men and women. They're just doing what they can for us."

"They're animals and thugs." I snapped back with more viciousness than he deserved.

"What were you doing when these *thugs* stepped forward and risked everything? Were you one of the quiet and peaceful ones calling for help and berating the government for not doing enough before things escalated?

Men enlisted, some voluntarily, most forced, and tried to protect and calm those complaining for more action. And then those vigilantes who tried to protect their homes started fighting the army. But that wasn't the end of it. No, those who harped on for peace then complained they needed more protection, but when the army tried to protect, when the police tried to make the streets safe they complained *again* about the violence used. And the gangs knew then that they could do what they wanted, so the violence continued. And force was used to quash violence. No one stepped in and said *enough*. What were you doing when this went on?" He stopped and I looked up at him, his hands were clasped and his voice still level and calm.

"How could we stand up to them? There was nothing I could do."

"Did you try? We did nothing and the strategies used by the government undermined everything. But they tried. They did something to stop what was going on. Then those pacifists and pencil-pushers complained about their rights, they wanted the violence eradicated, the violence punished, but not by fighting back. No, by sitting around and talking about the problems and holding hands?"

"What did you do then, Rich? You seem to have a clear view of what went wrong. Where were you?" I snapped back.

"I was doing the sort of things that created the problems. I walked as far down the road as a man can before he loses the ability to turn back. By the time I did, it was too late."

I hid my surprise at his admission. He remained quiet and looked at me expectantly.

"So… what are you now?" I finally asked, turning my body around and closer to him.

"A man of peace, in a world of war. That's why I'm so close to the men of violence."

"You're not sodding Gandhi, Rich." He watched me, the corners of his eyes creasing as I grinned. I breathed easier, the thorns of the irritation falling away. "But they, the Enforcers I mean, are meant to look after us. Meant to be the perfect guardian and defender and yet…" I trailed off and shook my head. "It doesn't matter. Why are you friendly with men who kill other men? Surely that goes against what you believe in."

"The alternative is to fear them. It is not my place to judge. That's for Him." He glanced at the clock. "I guess I should go, just know I'm here to chat to whenever you want. I'd still like that picnic, Kate. If you'd be more comfortable with others coming, that's fine. I just think an afternoon away from this place will do you, and me, good."

I clenched my fists under the table and fought the sigh that inevitably escaped me.

"No, seriously. It's okay, forget it. Just know that the offer is always there – as a friend. I want you to know that, anytime you just want to get away and talk, or just get away and sit there, I'm here. I meant it when I apologised for pushing you, I don't ever want you to feel trapped."

I wanted to ask why but didn't, and so just murmured my thanks. After he left I went upstairs and looked around my room. I had nothing for the baby, not a blanket or a stitch of clothing, and my lack of preparation angered and bewildered me. My baby deserved better than this. It wasn't their fault, none of this was their fault. I needed to do better. I made a list that afternoon of things I needed and wanted, and walked to the Henleys' house.

Nina answered, and told me that her dad and Deven were out and probably over at the storerooms. Making my way to the storage warehouse, I spoke to the Enforcer on duty and asked to speak to Deven. Waiting patiently for him to return I looked around at the chicken and barbed wire fence surrounding the supplies. There were over thirty lock-ups full to the brim with collected goods and I watched as sacks were hauled from one to the other. It reminded me of a jumble sale of sorts. Deven and the Enforcer returned: he wore a huge sunhat and gardening gloves. How did he always manage to look so glamorous?

"Kate, lovely to see you, how can I help?" He kissed both my cheeks and I caught a waft of his aftershave: I recognised the scent and pictured the tall blue bottle it came in, so sure that Stephen once wore the same, but couldn't remember the name.

"I've made a list of things I think I'll need for the baby. I was hoping you could help see if there's anything in the storerooms." As he scanned the list, he nodded and then chuckled.

"You'll need a lot more than what's here. What about a basket for baby or a pushchair? Nappies and babygrows? What about you? You'll need maternity pads, loose clothes, towels..." He reeled off a list of things I hadn't even considered. "Oh Kate, I'm sorry. I didn't mean to sound so dismissive. I remember my mama having my baby brother, and another, and another. It's a scary thing." He sorted through and pulled out a pushchair full of baby items. "I put this together a while ago, thought you might need it."

I stumbled with my thanks, but he brushed it aside and instead grabbed and pulled me into a hug. I didn't quite know what to do, so I stood there.

"I'm so glad we're friends." He pulled away and stroked my arms. I froze: the slow controlled movements up and down my skin repulsed me.

"Me too." I replied, breaking away and grabbing the pushchair.

"I know I was a bit off when we first got talking, I still find it hard to talk to people. Out there it's... not like this." He offered with a shrug.

"I know. It's okay."

"I know you know. No one speaks about the monsters in here, but I know you know." He was quiet as he rolled up his left sleeve and showed me his mark on his left forearm. It was a small traditional hot poker brand. "Birds of a feather, Kate."

I didn't speak, couldn't speak. I didn't want to confirm our solidarity vocally and instead lifted my top and showed him my brand. He was silent as he covered his arm. I waited for the shortest moment, but then threw my arms around him. He sobbed. We didn't need words, and I just held him until he calmed.

"Let's see what else we can get you. Perhaps some new clothes, because those old things are just... no." He elaborately wagged a finger.

The subject changed, I forced a smile. The effervescent Deven was back, though his eyes were red-rimmed.

WORD SPREAD, AND all afternoon things were dropped off for the baby. My bedroom and the spare room were soon full to bursting. Hayley was in heaven, cooing and *ahh*-ing over the tiny clothes and wishing for a baby of her own. We sat organising them into piles according to age and left the "unknown" items to last, a mixture of pinks and blues – I hadn't really thought much about whether baby was a boy or a girl.

I slept well that night: no faces haunted me and the following morning I took the radio, left a note and walked for miles along the coastline. I left my shoes by the rock pools and splashed through the water. I could feel the warmth of the sun all over, the sounds of the seagulls and the pull of the coldness around my feet emptied my mind. This was home, the place where I wasn't chased or coveted, wasn't owned or ordered. I didn't need to hide anymore. On my walk back the radio crackled into life and Hayley's voice cut into the silence.

"Kate, are you there, Kate?"

I replied and she told me that she'd prepared lunch and wondered when I'd be back. I estimated an hour and the radio clicked off. I reached the rock pools and slipped my sandals back on. Bending down, a stabbing pain in my stomach made me groan and I rubbed the spot firmly, but another wave rippled through me. The usual short walk to the house took an age but by the time I got the to path the pain had subsided and I thought nothing more of it. I'd had twinges and aches before. I walked in and jumped to a chorus of:

"Surprise!"

The kitchen and living room were packed with the women from the club, banners and streamers in baby blue and soft pink covered every inch of the ceiling and balloons scattered and floated around the floor. I spotted the strawberries on the table and grinned. I loved strawberries. So many people kissed my cheeks and patted my bump – I couldn't control the contact, it was overwhelming and yet I didn't pull back, I fought my protective measures and won. Hayley thrust a glass in my hand and I sniffed: lemon?

"It's homemade lemonade." She guided me into the living room where a long lean figure leaned against the wall – could he never stand up straight? "This was all Rich's idea," she whispered. "He even made the cupcakes." I looked over to the table and guffawed at the badly iced monstrosities; the icing had slipped and pooled on the surface of the plate.

I met him in the middle of the room and indicated the table. "Are they edible?"

"I hope so." He went to kiss my cheek but hesitated and pulled back. Relief tinged with the most imperceptible amount of disappointment surged through me, leaving me short of breath. He was the only one who knew when to stop, when not to touch me. "Hayley and I thought it would be nice for you to have a little fun before baby turns up." He whispered: "I know you aren't keen on big groups, I suggested just a few people, but you know how things spread in this place."

I sipped and nodded. I could feel the eyes of the room on us and turned my back on him, smiling widely at Paulina and Laura, forcing a banal conversation on the summer weather. Presents had been brought: a pile of toiletries and baby toys sat on the table and I wondered whether they had asked for them out of the storerooms or if they had come from their own allocated supplies – not that it mattered.

By sunset, people started to leave and I sat back on the sofa watching Hayley and Rich clear up with Deven and Laura. Closing my eyes, I gave in to the tiredness that covered me like a heavy veil and when I awoke with a start, it was dark outside. The kitchen light was on and I could hear voices. I walked through and Hayley and Rich sat at the table drinking coffee and playing cards.

"Hey, sleepyhead. Want a coffee?" Hayley asked.

Hayley poured me a mug as I joined them. They both looked disgustingly fresh and wide awake. Another surge of pain cut through my stomach and I knocked my mug over as I grabbed my bump.

"Kate, are you all right?" They both jumped up and Hayley knelt by my side while Rich cleared up the coffee. My legs were soaked and burned. Another wave of tightness and red hot stabbing made it impossible for me to speak and I shook my head.

"Rich, get the doctor!" Hayley grabbed the towel off him and started to dab at my legs.

"I'll be fine, really." I pushed off the chair and walked

around the kitchen until the agony ebbed to a dull throb. "It's gone now."

"Do you think it's time? I mean, is the baby coming? Should I prepare the back room?"

I shook my head again. Hayley paced with me, wringing her hands and muttering.

"Rich, get the doctor!" she snapped.

"No, I'm fine. The baby isn't coming, it's Braxton Hicks, I'm sure. I read about it in the library." I wanted fresh air.

"Are you sure it isn't labour?"

"Pretty sure."

"You must see the doctor." Hayley wouldn't calm down.

"Hayley, no. If it makes you feel better, I'll see him tomorrow. Look? I'm fine now." She tried to speak but I held up a hand. "I'm going to get some air, I won't go far and if I have any more pains I'll let you know."

Leaving the house before she could reply, I nodded to Rich in thanks. It was cooler that night and lying on the sand I watched the stars; it was cloudy and the grey wisps covered Bootes; I couldn't see the ploughman. Searching the darkness I named and pinpointed as many constellations as I could remember, but my concentration was interrupted when I sensed someone approach. I scrambled and tried to sit up.

"It's only me." I relaxed and Rich lay down next to me. We both stared at the sky in silence.

"That's Corvus, we won't be able to see him for much longer." I finally said, pointing up to the crow.

"And that's Hercules," he replied.

I turned my head to one side and watched him smile in the silvery light.

"Yes, it is."

I was relaxed, and the sudden realisation warmed me.

CHAPTER TWENTY-ONE

"So, I HEARD you come in quite late last night." Hayley commented, swirling her fruit teabag around her mug. "Heard Rich too."

I choked a little and coughed, looking up from my plate at her. Patiently, she smiled and nodded like a cute toddler. *Oh how wrong you are.* When I stopped coughing I said: "You're beyond belief. He was walking me home, nothing more."

"Home from the beach? All two hundred metres away?"

I didn't bother to reply. She was smiling now and the more I protested the more she would read into it something that wasn't there. So I finished eating in silence, ignoring the little 'mmm-hmm' noises from her.

"So what are your plans for today?" I asked. It was already muggy outside and I was too tired to face a room full of children. I hoped she would sit with them.

"Not much. I'm out this evening with some of the girls. Rachael has just got engaged to Tim – you know Tim, the butcher – anyway, there's some drinks and stuff at the Enforcers' club. It was so sweet. He took her to the watchtower and spelt out 'marry me' in shell pieces before getting down on one knee. It was just gorgeous." She continued to chatter, describing the engagement ring to me in detail. I nodded.

"I thought the watchtower was off limits?"

"Off limits? Oh no, no that was lifted a few weeks ago. Simon decided he didn't have the men to keep watch up there. They thought it would be better for the Enforcers to patrol the streets at night, double up on the protection."

"Oh." Piling up the plates, I crossed my fingers and asked her to look after the children.

"Of course. Are you off with Rich again?"

"Oh for... no." I stopped and exhaled, ashamed that I almost snapped at her. "I just fancy a day alone. Bit tired."

She didn't tease again. I gave her the keys to the library and ran through the loose plan of the day with her. I rushed through my chores and by eleven the wind was sweeping through the house, cooling me and inviting me outside. I knew where I wanted to go.

LOOKING THROUGH THE telescope I watched the town like a voyeur. Every so often I paused and mumbled the names of the people I observed, reminding myself of who they were and what they did. So many faces, but they all stopped and smiled at each other, shaking hands and laughing.

I swung the telescope to the northern sector and fed another fifty pence piece in the mechanism. The demolition was well underway; huge piles of brick and rubble. Lee, Josh and Mo rode up and down the mounds of destruction on their BMX bikes.

"Kate? What are you doing?"

Deven stood at the cast iron bench and beckoned me over as he sat down.

"Just having some alone time."

"I can understand that. It's lovely up here. You can see for miles across the water on a clear day. It's so peaceful to just come up and think."

Deven repeated Rachael's engagement story. I pictured Tim on one knee, at this spot, opening up the small box and asking her to share the rest of her life with him. For some reason I couldn't concentrate on the voice to my right. Instead, Stephen's silhouette appeared. On his knee in the car park of our local cinema, a ring on his flat palm and the same question uttered. A huge lump formed and I blinked away the tears. Just one escaped down my face and hastily I wiped it away. Deven hadn't noticed – I hoped not anyway.

"Yes or no?" he asked. His voice was a little louder this time and dragged me away from my thoughts.

"Sorry?"

"Tonight. Are you coming to the Enforcers' club for the engagement party? I know you don't know Rachael or Tim that well, but Tim enforces every so often and I'm sure the others would like to get to know you. Rich will be there."

"No. I think I need an early night." I didn't explain. He nodded and was silent for a while.

"Thank you, for the other day. I'm sorry it's hard for you, Kate. I can't imagine what it was like for you out there. I know I was lucky to find a place here so quickly. Lucky to find safety with Roger. I made so many friends through him." He stopped and picked at a loose thread on his white trousers. "I've hurt Roger. I know that. He cares for me, probably loves me. I do love him, in a way. I know that I shouldn't make him upset or angry. I just feel so trapped at times that I don't know what to do or even who I am. It's not like it was out there, but it still feels like a prison at times."

I licked my lips but didn't make a sound. It seemed wrong to interrupt. I wanted to know more, even if it was just to understand what he had to say.

"Anyway. I should probably go. If you change your mind switch the radio to channel 31 and let me know. I'll come and get you. Roger's given me a little car to use 'when absolutely necessary,'" he quoted. "Can you drive?"

I replied with a nod.

"If you ever need to use it, it's parked in a garage behind our cottage, the one with the red door. Key's on the top of the front right tyre."

"Thanks."

He started to walk down to the beach.

"Deven?"

Turning, he looked back. I walked over. "Thank you for everything. When I came here I know I wasn't the easiest person to be around, not after out there. You know?" I hoped he'd understand, and with relief he nodded. "I never thought this would happen," and placing my hand on my bump, I sighed. "It's not easy talking about stuff, but thank you for trying to make me feel welcome and sharing with me. One day I'll be okay."

"You'll never be okay, Kate," he murmured, "but you'll learn to live with what happened and find some sort of peace." He went to touch me, but thought better of it and said his goodbyes. His words echoed inside.

Ignoring the band of tightness across my stomach I looked down at the town and Roger Henley emerged from the church and shook Rich's hand. My attention turned to the woman at Rich's side; she was young, pretty, thin. As I struggled to remember her name, Rich placed his arm around her waist and squeezed before letting go and walking back into the church. I inserted another coin into the telescope, following Roger and the woman as they walked towards the doctor's house. That was it. She was one of the trainee doctors and one of the doctor's daughter's friends. She disappeared into Dr Nicholl's house and Roger walked away towards Glen and Hayley's.

There he was. Deven stood on the edge of the beach near my home talking to two of Simon's Enforcers. Pointing up to their club house he laughed, and when they shook hands they passed something to him, small enough that he was able to pocket it discreetly. His face was the perfect emotionless mask, and for a brief moment I thought of Kat and hoped she was all right. Then of Ben and Ella: *please let them be safe.* I pushed them to the back of my mind again as Roger appeared and stood at the small pavilion watching his husband and the Enforcers. I couldn't see his face clearly, and so I panned back to Deven and watched him say goodbye to the Enforcers. Looking back, Roger had gone.

*　　*　　*

ALL DAY MY baby had turned and twisted, and now, when I wanted nothing but peace, a nerve in my back throbbed, causing a deep knot of pain in my backside and down my leg. I stood up from the sofa and hobbled into the kitchen, sifting through the drawers looking for painkillers. It was nearly eleven p.m. and it hurt too much to sleep. I was too hot. Opening the backdoor I listened to the waves and focused on the moonlight bouncing off the inky waters. Rubbing my bump I tried to force baby to move. It didn't work and I slammed the back door in anger, with the bang echoing through the house. I was lonely. The music carried on the wind from the party and I desperately wanted to talk to someone.

Channel 31. I spoke: "Hello?"

Damn. No, I'd just go to sleep. As I went to switch it off, there was a voice.

"Hey, Kate? Is that you? Everything ok?" Rich. Why did he have the radio? Where was Deven? How did he know it was me?

"I'm fine." I paused. "I'm just saying goodnight."

"Ok… goodnight."

I switched off the radio and sat in the darkness, my mind empty and only the quiet ticking of the clock reminding me that I was awake. I couldn't move, I wanted to, but I had no energy and instead it was so much simpler to sit back and stare at the ceiling.

One need not be a chamber – to be haunted.

CHAPTER TWENTY-TWO

ON MONDAY I was too tired to teach and sat in the library letting the children play. There were no new books to organise so I started reading *Middlemarch*. I recalled first starting and stopping with it in my early twenties and laughing at the ideals of Dorothea, but as the wars raged through the country I found myself wishing for a better world, wishing I could achieve something for the greater good.

I didn't get very far: the screams and shouts from an argument caught my attention and I spent the following two hours placating Daisy and Lara who had fallen out over the ownership of a plastic bracelet. Eventually, I confiscated it so neither owned it, tuning out the whining and grumblings that followed.

By Tuesday night I was exhausted; my ankles were swollen, my back ached and I disliked everything and everyone. I spent the night crying in my room with the door locked, ignoring Hayley's pleas to help. Little Alan hated me. He had refused to do anything I asked and on our walk to the beach had thrown himself to the sand and rolled around, screaming in temper at the smallest thing. I sobbed harder that night as I remembered dragging him to his feet and shouting until his little face was white with terror and he submitted; his body limp and his voice a whisper as he apologised over and over again. I tried to win his forgiveness with cuddles but he squirmed and fidgeted away and didn't speak to me. When Rose collected him, ashamedly I told her what happened and she brushed it away as though it was nothing and cheerfully proclaimed he would be fine on Thursday. I wasn't so sure, nor could I forgive myself. How could I have behaved that way?

As I sat waiting for the convoy on Wednesday night, Rich joined me. Instead of spending hours by the main gate we sat on the beach with a small fire, watching the waves and the sky. It had clouded over the last few nights and instead of stargazing we discussed music, films, and then Alan. He made me feel better. I hadn't forgiven myself but I would make it up to him. Soon the crackle of the radio cut through our chatter and Glen announced they were five to ten minutes away. With Hayley we walked down and watched as the trucks unloaded. There were more newcomers this time. I thought that Nikky had said they were coming on the next trip. Simon ushered them to one side and they were led away to the council building where they would be offered hosts or houses.

Nikky shouted and waved, dragging her holdall over and throwing her arms around me, almost knocking me over. Glen pulled Hayley close and I watched as she closed her eyes and rested her head on his chest, her arms encircling his waist. He rested his cheek on her head and accidently made eye contact with me. I looked away.

As Nikky pulled away and fiddled with the strap to her bag, I hoped Simon hadn't planned another trip in quick succession.

"Oh, hi Rich." She slid her gaze to him, grinning in surprise. "Who are you waiting for then?"

"No one. I came with Hayley and Kate. But I am going to go and have a word with Si and see if he needs a hand with the newcomers. I'll see you all soon." He jogged towards the council buildings. I counted.

"The vicar?"

It was less than ten seconds before she said something, and I shook my head.

"No, nothing like that at all. Rich has just been helping me out a bit while you've been away." I couldn't recall exactly what he had helped me with, but it sounded better than *Rich helped organise a party for me, kept inviting me on a picnic and when he realised I would keep saying no, we lay together on the beach stargazing.*

She made a disbelieving noise. Back at her house she told me about the teachers and the new timetables. Peter and Gloria had relocated on this run and a full 9–3 pattern had been worked out for all three age groups. She was excited to be in charge of art and sports, while Gloria would do the science and maths, with Peter teaching English and history. They had brought back almost a whole truck of school supplies and books; Simon was friends with Peter and, with persuasion, Nikky had got her way and even the sports mats and skipping ropes were added onto the transport load.

Under a fleece throw, we talked. She leant against my shoulder and went through each day in the other community, describing the way they taught there, the strictness with uniforms and badges. I couldn't see how that would work here, but Nikky assured me that the badges were already made and a simple dress code would be implemented: order into chaos, apparently. They had also decided that the children needed a firm hand and guidance. There would be punishments and detentions and a book of rules. Nikky explained that it was to set boundaries. My stomach turned at the thought.

She then showed me her sketches of Blackwood. It was hillier than I imagined and with less damage than our own and I recalled what she told me about Simon and how he had set up the Enforcers during the tail-end of the bombings when the looting bands had started swarming through the country, stretching his network as far as he could.

As it grew light outside, I said goodbye and agreed to meet her teacher friends in the afternoon after I had rested. Instead of sleeping she intended to drink copious amounts of coffee and struggle through the day. There was no chance I could do that. I needed breakfast and then my bed. On my way home, I saw Rich opening the doors to the church. He waved but didn't come over. He was talking to a group of resettlers who looked tired and drawn. I watched as he joked and laughed with the young women and they giggled and flirted in response. It made me smile, but that smile soon turned into a yawn. I was so tired, and my eyes cold and dry. By the time I got home I crawled quietly into bed and slept, too tired to eat.

* * *

WHEN I FINALLY woke, the house was silent. Light crept through the curtains, forcing me to sit up. Nearly six p.m. – I had slept all day? Washing and dressing I went downstairs and read two notes while I ate leftover cold pasta. Hayley and Glen were out together for 'couple time' and would be back very late. The other note was from Nikky, she would catch up with me tomorrow, but had left a present for me on my desk in the library.

On my way over I saw many new faces. They showed a mix of emotions: fear, excitement, longing, curiosity. I was stopped and asked directions, some asking when the baby was due, others ignoring the bump.

I unlocked the library door, walked in, and dropped my keys in shock. The huge room had been reorganised. My books were now displayed on custom built shelves and were closer to the door. There were more tables and three distinct areas of study, partitioned with bookcases and shelving units. I had a bigger desk, drawers and a bureau. I laughed at the surface of the desk. Nikky had organised the drawings I loved and had the top of my desk covered in a sheet of glass – how? Where? I sat down and examined the pictures: the library, the view across the rock pools, the church, all the places I loved. In the centre was the sketch of me reading.

"It's a beautiful picture, I wanted it the second I saw it."

My hands stopped moving, my fingers splayed flat on the glass. I couldn't lift my head to look up. The paralysis started from my head and worked down, a film of terror covering and possessing me. Controlling my body it wormed, gnawed, forced its way inside, making each breath laboured and painful; each second passed slower than the last. I was freezing and yet my palms sweated and beads of my fear rolled down my neck. I closed my eyes. If I couldn't see him, he wasn't real. Perhaps I imagined that voice. I was tired. A thousand thoughts, fragments of memories, rolled though me, images, conversations. I was tired. I couldn't look up. It wasn't a nightmare. I needed to move, move, *for fuck's sake, move*. My lips didn't move, but I screamed, silently, move, but they didn't. My hands didn't move, not a millimetre.

"I didn't think it was possible. I put out so many messages for you across the network, but no one had seen you. I know why now."

Shut up, shut up, shut up. His soft voice cut into my skull. Closer this time. He was getting closer to me and all I could do was stare at the glass. My chest rose and fell, faster and faster, the baby moved in irritation. I wanted to rub my bump, reassure my baby, *my* baby, that it was fine, that I was fine, but I still couldn't move. I couldn't protect myself; worse, I couldn't protect my baby. I was trapped. There was a shadow in the corner of my left eye and soon the outline of a body. But it was the smell that made me gag, the smell which released the tears – that spicy, fresh scent.

The trembling started. I couldn't stop my legs from shaking but I still couldn't move my hands or head.

"You look so healthy, so happy. I watched you walk here like you didn't have a care in the world."

He didn't move. It was pathetic, but for that I was grateful.

I needed every precious second I could gather. I watched as my tears hit the glass and spread across the clear surface, obscuring my face in the sketch. Why was this happening? I thought back to my goodbyes and screwed my eyes shut again. *I'm sorry, Stephen, I'm sorry.* Was this his way of telling me he wasn't gone?

He touched me then. His hand ran down my face, my hair and skin. Stroking me. Move, fucking, move!

"Don't you have anything to say, Anna?"

Anna, Anna is docile and gracious, Anna replies, she submits. I was Anna, *was* Anna. I'm not Anna now. I'm Katherine, I'm Kate. And yet, I was still his. I had no strength, it was as though each tear took a small piece of my defence away, *chip, chip, chip.*

"Anna?" He knelt down now and his smell hit me like a tidal wave, assaulting my senses, I tasted the pasta again and swallowed furiously. My eyes wouldn't close, they wouldn't respond and I could do nothing but watch and feel as he ran both hands down my face and forced me to look at him.

It was real. He was real. He was there. Those dead eyes stared into mine; his hair was shorter, he was thinner, but it was him, an empty smile on his lips. I blinked away the fresh tears and they rolled down my face. Memories I had tried to lose flooded back. Ribs ached, back itched. He let go of my face and touched the bump, the smile grew and he bent down, inches from skin. I saw the road outside, the open door, and my escape. I just had to move, to yell, to shout, to hit back, anything to show him I wasn't Anna, I wasn't submissive and I wasn't his.

But I still didn't. I'd failed to protect my baby. His hand on my top burnt through the material, tainting my flesh underneath.

"Anna?"

I found my voice. I swallowed down the pain and shock and spoke: "I'm not Anna."

It's all I could say. Why didn't I scream? His hand started to stroke my baby, it responded and moved: *traitor*.

"No, you're Kate." He tilted his head and knelt then, moving my chair to face him and taking my hands in his. I pulled back and a small jolt of excitement rushed through me: I could move, I could do this. But he squeezed my wrists and I stilled, ever the faithful dog. How did someone who I hadn't seen in so long affect me so? Was I that weak I couldn't move? My body just didn't respond.

"You're Katherine, and I'm your Peter."

Peter? He was Peter? No, no that couldn't be right. Peter was a teacher, Peter looked after children. He was Will, and Will murdered a boy.

"Kate." Gentle and calm. I tried to fight, tried not to give in, but I responded. I looked up as he moved forward. "Kiss me, Kate."

PART THREE
PART THREE
PART THREE

CHAPTER TWENTY-THREE

GET AWAY FROM me, I don't want you; I don't want this, not again. Turning my head to the side I refused to look at him and instead stared at my pictures, my home. I pushed back in my chair but the more I struggled, the harder he squeezed until I sobbed.

"Kate, you mustn't fight."

He held my face and I remembered the way he pinched and twisted my skin, the backhanders to my face, what he had done to my hair, my beautiful hair. Chopped. Gone.

"You are so beautiful."

"Please, let me go," I begged.

"Did I not look after you?"

"You hurt me." The tears continued, hot and wet as they slid away. "Leave me alone, please, just fucking go, please." My voice was a whisper as I begged, *good doggy*, I begged for my master, again.

"I can't leave you, you need protecting, our baby needs protecting."

My baby, MY baby, not ours!

"My baby. Not yours. I don't need protecting." The words came before I had a chance to think, a primal rush of hatred, anger, violence assailed me.

Sickness came and I pushed him back and threw up on the floor, the taste of food lining my throat and mouth. Hunched over, he touched and rubbed my back, the scars I tried so hard to ignore were raised and hard against his hands, I could feel the outline and trembled.

"It's all right, I'm here now."

"Don't touch me, leave me alone."

It was only then I took in what he wore, a pinstripe shirt, trousers and grey jumper. He looked professional, as though he belonged here in my library.

"You don't belong here, just leave me alone," I repeated.

"I thought Nikky told you." He continued to rub my back, his other hand on my leg, scalding me, I imagined peeling his fingers away but I couldn't. "I'm living here now, teaching again." He paused and I stared at the mess on the floor, ignoring his hand. "I like Nikky, she's a lovely girl."

"What do you want?"

I had my voice. Now I just needed my strength. He couldn't hurt me, not here, he couldn't. I was safe, this was home, my sanctuary.

"We're a family."

He pulled me to my feet and I stared through the open door. I could just see the grey water across the horizon from here, and several figures moved in the distance, a blur of colour, indistinguishable, they could be anyone, friend or enemy. That smell again. I preferred the bitter stench of sickness to him. He pressed against my bump, aggravating baby and touching me. I was grateful for baby, but ashamed at the relief the barrier gave me: he couldn't pull me close. I didn't try to fight though. I had nothing to fight with, I couldn't risk harming my precious baby.

"I've missed you."

I nodded automatically, under his control; the puppet, again. I hadn't stopped crying, the tears still flowed. I'd lost the fight. He'd won, I always knew he'd win, I shouldn't have left him, not alive. Why didn't I pull the trigger?

"I like Kate, it's pretty." He kissed my forehead. His lips wet and vile. Nausea rolled again and my breathing became erratic. Hot. It was hot, suffocating. My cheeks burnt and my head throbbed like it was going to explode. My hands, my hands were on fire. Too tight, his grip was like stone.

"I can't breathe. Let me go." He ignored me and stroked my hair again, that rhythmic stroking, *why me, why me, why me?* "Please, Will, please."

"I'm Peter now, you're my Katherine."

"Please, Peter." I didn't care, a name is just a word, it doesn't define a person. I needed air, space, distance. He released me and I stumbled back until I hit the cool wall behind me. The door was near, I could make it; but I couldn't force my legs to work.

"Kate?"

He sounded confused, and wary. I turned to the door and started crying again in relief. I'd never been so happy to see anyone.

"Deven."

He walked over to me, and stared at Peter. "What's going on? Who are you?"

There was strength in his voice. How I wished I had that strength. I listened as he explained who he was, and his lies about how he found me throwing up and how he'd scared me by approaching quietly. He never faltered, his mask was perfect. His smile open and warm but his eyes were dead: they were always dead to me.

"Are you all right, Kate? Do you need the doctor?"

Shaking my head I twisted my ring, abruptly stopping when he stared at my fingers. His face changed and the flicker of intense possession and realisation passed over his features and his breathing quickened as he smiled at me. *Please see him for what he is, please Deven.* I couldn't speak. I wanted to tell him, tell everyone what he had done to me – but the words were stuck, I'd been so quiet for too long that I didn't know how to tell him. Instead he reached out and shook his hand. I watched in disbelief as he introduced himself and he smoothly replied, glancing over at me and smiling yet again.

"I don't feel well, I'm going home."

I didn't wait for their replies; the terror subsided and I walked to the door. My keys were on my desk, but I couldn't walk past him again and so left them. He was watching me, my back was alive now and each time my top touched my skin it chafed and rubbed.

I made it home and locked my bedroom door. Lying under my blankets I curled my body and hugged my baby. I was empty. No tears this time, no cries, no pain or wailing, just my memories.

I ate in my room that night, and for the following three days. I could barely speak. I forced down bread and water for the baby. Hayley worried and cried, and Dr Nicholls diagnosed exhaustion. I just wanted to sleep. To be alone. On the third evening Nikky arrived and lay next to me, telling me about the children and the new timetable. Every time she mentioned his name the lump in my chest expanded and my head pounded.

"Honestly Kate, I think you'll really like him. He makes everyone laugh."

I stared at the ceiling blankly.

"Even Alan speaks to Peter, it's amazing, he spent the whole day yesterday with him. I told him that Alan loves you and was upset you were poorly, so Peter really made him feel special. Alan told him his mum's name. He's started opening up, isn't that great?"

My head swam and the room spun. I closed my eyes, but his face was there and so I opened them and concentrated on the space in front of me. As Nikky spoke, her voice became white noise and I could no longer distinguish words. Instead, I pictured Peter sitting at a table with Alan. His cold eyes watching and measuring, his smile luring Alan into the belief of safety and security. It was my fault, I'd brought him here, if I had remained alone then everyone would be safe.

"Peter asked if you were all right, he told me about finding you throwing up and how scared you were. He's so quiet though, I would have been scared too if he walked up to me when I was poorly."

I didn't want to hear about how amazing Peter was, nor

how everyone loved him. I wanted to tell Nikky who he really was, what he really was. Yet, all those weeks in his captivity and I knew so little about him. Perhaps now was the time, I could do this, surely.

"How did he introduce himself to you?" I finally asked, cutting her off mid-sentence.

"What? Oh, I was in the canteen at the other town, drawing your picture. He'd just arrived there, still had his backpack, and was talking to Simon. He saw me drawing and we got chatting, he asked why I was there and then who I was sketching. I told him, then he told me his name and said he was a teacher."

You're Katherine, and I'm your Peter. Of course. I closed my eyes before the tears betrayed me.

"Honestly, Kate. I think you'll really like him. He's just so amazing with the children, I've never seen anything like it."

"You've said that. I doubt it." My voice was flat and listless, I couldn't summon up any interest, and her enthusiasm for my captor started to eat away at my hope; now was not the time to tell her. "I'm sorry, Nikky. I'm really tired."

"I'll come and see you soon, I miss you in the library."

As the door opened I called out, "Nikky?"

"Yes?"

"I love my desk, thank you."

"Oh, that was Peter's idea."

Of course it was. I didn't reply and the door closed softly as she left.

*   *   *

THE NEXT DAY I slept and slept. I didn't want to be awake. It was real when I was awake. By three p.m. I could sleep no more and left my room to go to the bathroom. Glen had fitted the filter for the water and I ran a bath. Hearing the water roar from the taps was strange, curious and bizarre, and as I stepped into the bath I closed my eyes. I hoped the water would help me recapture some normality, but instead all I could feel and recall were his hands on me, the smell of strawberry shampoo and the touch of his body behind mine. As I bathed I wrote my name in the water and cried before struggling out of the bath and throwing up in the sink until there was nothing left.

Later, downstairs, I sat reading when I heard Rose's voice. Looking up, a smile spread across my face as Alan walked into the living room carrying a cake.

"I made this for you."

"Thank you."

So I sat in the kitchen with Rose and Alan, drinking coffee and eating cake. With each bite he beamed and I swallowed, ignoring the instinct to throw it back up.

"Kate, do you mind if I just pop down the road? I need to pick up some knitting, I'll only be a short while and there's no one else to look after Alan... I know you've been poorly but...?"

I nodded. Alan then started chatting nineteen to the dozen. He'd missed me it seemed and had drawn some pictures and left them on my desk. I ruffled up his hair and without warning, he threw his hands around my stomach and hugged me, his ear against my bump. The baby kicked and he giggled in delight.

"Hello baby, I'm Alan Philip Olney, and I'm looking forward to meeting you." He kissed my tummy and I burst into tears. He looked up at me in concern.

"I'm okay." I tried to reassure him.

"Why are you crying then?"

"I just feel like crying."

"I do sometimes as well."

We sat on the sofa and he cuddled up to me. He seemed to like just being held and I found myself enjoying holding him. I thought of Alan when he left with Rose later that afternoon. The serious little boy who had survived the Unlands, managed to walk through the wilderness alone. What the land had left was an innocent and pure child who knew only his name. Three words, six syllables and fifteen letters. Alan Philip Olney. All he had was his name, and yet it was all he needed. It was his umbilical cord and lifeline to the town: something to use as both a shield and a badge, his identity and his safety net. He wanted me to care for him; someone so uncorrupted as he had attached his life to mine.

Tom arrived, although he didn't stay long. I still couldn't drum up the energy to speak in more than one word answers. But he knew it was more than exhaustion. He didn't question me, other than to ask if it was the nightmares that troubled me so. It was easier to nod. Instead of simpering, he chastised me like a child. *I should tell Hayley or Nikky, they could help.* When he left I cried again, *chip, chip, chip.* Perhaps I could tell someone, but there was no one who wasn't enamoured with the kindly handsome teacher from the other town. No one.

*　*　*

CHIP, CHIP, CHIP.

"You need fresh air, Kate. Just a little, you must be going crazy in here."

I shook my head and tucked my feet further underneath me. I had been inside now for days. I couldn't go back out there: not when I knew he would be waiting, watching for me.

"Kate, please, just a short walk to stretch your legs, clear your mind." Rich continued to badger, his voice steady and firm. When I looked up there was simply all-encompassing concern in his face. His lips made a thin line and his eyes, so like mine, flitted between me and the back door.

"Stop, Rich. Please." My voice was quiet, but I scowled. "I don't feel like walking."

"Please?"

He was gently persistent and I didn't have the stamina nor true will to resist. Eventually I nodded and agreed to walk on the beach. It was two p.m.; Peter would be teaching. I would be safe.

After changing I stood at the back door and looked down the gravel path to the road and beach. It wasn't far. My heart hammered so hard that my chest was cracking under the pressure and as I walked down on the stones I held my breath and looked around. Though I couldn't see another soul, I still didn't relax. It was humid and stale outside, even by the water there was only the lightest of breezes. I moved as quickly as I could, out of sight and along my now-familiar path, following the natural curve of the sand past the rock pools. Rich stayed by my side, his presence an irritation but also a strange comfort. I walked further and for longer than I intended until the heat became unbearable. Searching out a patch of shade, I gratefully sat gazing at the bluey-grey water. We had barely said a word.

"Do you think people can change?" I asked eventually, shifting and kneeling on the sand, my head bowed as I now stared at my swollen belly. He was quiet for a while and I stole a glance at his face. It had clouded over and he narrowed his eyes, deep in thought.

"Yes, people can change, and they do change. Sometimes for the worst, but they can change for better. I did."

I looked at him openly then, and he mirrored my expression. Anxiety rose; *they* say that you can feel danger before it approaches, like a sixth sense. It wasn't danger I felt, but apprehension and dread. I didn't want the truth of his past to taint what I believed him to be.

"I wasn't always a vicar, there was a time when I was a lost and angry man. I did terrible things, Kate. Things I don't like to speak of, they shame me, but I have repented, I seek forgiveness. We're not perfect creatures, Kate. I don't want and will never allow myself to be that person again."

I wanted to ask him so many questions, but I didn't. I wanted to, but I couldn't.

I considered telling him then, pouring out my grief on to the sand and watching it sink away, but no matter how I tried to form the bubbling words they wouldn't come.

"Are you all right, Kate? Do you look for forgiveness?"

I started to shake my head, but then thought of my husband. He deserved better. I nodded.

"I cheated on my husband. His name was Stephen and he was a good man. I hurt him more than I ever thought possible." I had to give him something, some part of me. He stayed quiet, nodding, his eyes still on the water.

"No one is perfect. That's why understanding is so important," he said.

With precipitance, I pressed on.

"I was captured... out there. For over two years I'd lived alone, looked after myself and survived, and in one... stupid *fucking* moment it was all gone." I trailed sand through my hands, not daring to look up. "He took everything, *everything*, from me. My freedom, my belongings, my hair, my *name*. Everything. He beat me, over and over again. Pretending to love me all the while, telling me I needed him. I didn't need him. I was *fine* on my own. He..."

I trailed off, I couldn't bring myself to say it. Rich touched my hand and I didn't pull away. The warmth of his touch a balm I didn't know I needed. "He forced himself on me and I let him. I was disgusting and let him do it, but I couldn't stop him. At the start I tried but he always won. I was so tired, so... broken. Coming here was the only way I could be sure of safety, for both of us." I placed my hands on my bump. "But I'll never be safe. We'll never be safe. The past haunts me and I'll never be free of it."

The final words were on the tip of my tongue but

wouldn't come. I wanted to just tell him about Peter but I couldn't. The fear of disbelief, of rejection and ostracization muted that final admission. I needed this place, for my baby, everything was for them and though I craved to scream it, to be believed, I just couldn't. Still so shamefully weak. *This was what he had done to me.*

When he did finally reply, through tears of his own, he said just two words: "I'm sorry."

On our walk back we didn't speak, instead I reached for his hand. When he entwined his fingers in mine my chest fluttered – not with the girlish joy from a crush, but the triumph that conquering a fear brings. His touch didn't still me. Didn't burn my skin or make me want to run.

It couldn't last forever, and as we reached the rock pools, I looked at the porch. *He* was there. Waiting. I stumbled and hit the sand hard, the abrasive mineral grating and rubbing against me. My chest, my heart, again, it hurt so much, pain rippling through my body. Rich helped me up and it was only when he swore that I realised.

My skirt was stained and water rolled down my legs; a sweet smell carried on the light wind. For a moment I couldn't move, was this it? Eventually the pain returned my wits to me, and sudden understanding hit me. I grabbed Rich's arm and clung to him as he walked me back to the house. I squeezed tighter as I sensed him nearby, but all I could do was stare at my bump and the ground. Baby first, baby would always be first.

"Get the doctor, the baby's coming."

Without a word Peter left, running down the road and out of sight. I could do this.

*   *   *

PACING THE KITCHEN with Rich by my side I cried and moaned as the pain took me. It was worse than anything before, but, *baby first*. When the doctor returned, Hayley and Nikky followed, the anxiety on their faces doubling when they saw my face. However when *he* stood in the doorway with Glen, I demanded that the men leave, all of them. I couldn't help but stare at him then: the triumph in his eyes was nearly my undoing.

CHAPTER TWENTY-FOUR

ADAPTATION, LIKE CREATION and death, is one of nature's imperatives, part of the perpetual cycle. The world has suffered, we've annihilated each other and yet we've adapted and moved on, and the land renews, it forgives. Our fitness for the world is repeatedly tested.

Thirty hours later I finally understood sacrifice. Nothing but agony and misery. Each moment stretched and thinned in front of me. I remembered so much, much more than I cared to remember. Memories I had pushed away from my life re-appeared but with no creeping, no gentle meandering, instead they drowned me like hurricane floodwaters. I remembered friends, holidays, trips away, meetings at work, arguments, all the mundane details as clear as the pain coursing through me.

But, as I held my baby in my exhausted arms, I realised that none of it mattered. I trailed a finger down his sleeping face, marvelling at the softness of his skin. I finally had my baby, my hope. He was so small. The doctor weighed him in at just under six pounds and expressed concern at his small size for full gestation, but he was utterly perfect. He was strong and listening to his heartbeat on the stethoscope I beamed, unadulterated joy and relief with each beat. When the doctor left the endorphin crash kicked in, and the self-doubt started.

"Have you thought of a name, Kate?"

Hayley stood at the end of the bed, clearing away. A name. Something which could never be taken from him; but a name was just a word. I shook my head and she opened the window. The breeze brought a frown to his face and, stirring, he started to cry. I panicked. Every time he cried it sawed into me, his noises all sounded the same to me. I didn't understand and I looked up to Hayley. I held out my arms to her. Taking him, she shushed his cries and walked the length of my bedroom, up and down until he was asleep again. I was useless.

Terror stood behind me always. Would I love him enough? Could I love him enough? The nurturing bud of love had grown in my heart as he had grown inside me, but would it flower or wither away?

Deven visited next, and though I could barely keep my eyes open, he showed me how to feed him and take care of myself, citing his mother and six siblings as experience. I fought my embarrassment: baby comes first, and so I allowed him to show me how baby should latch. I needed strength. I would always have to consider my baby now, for everything I did would affect him.

When Deven held him, he seemed so at ease: he knew just what to do, and understood his cries. I was useless.

When he left, I begged Hayley to turn all visitors away.

I wanted silence, stillness, and my baby.

For three days I had just that. I grew to learn his cries and needs. When he looked up at me with eyes as dark as *him*, the wretchedness returned: unwanted, bitter and entirely unfair. I traced his face and arms with my fingers often, stopping at his little fingers when they wrapped around mine; indefectible nails, so tiny. I marvelled at the exquisite perfection that was this tiny human. My chest hurt, but I opened myself to it and revelled in it, and it was the sweetest pain. The nights, to me, were the hardest. I couldn't sleep and watched him often. When he woke I found myself holding him close and whispering my love to him, kissing his cheeks and forehead. I told him my name often, but I couldn't speak his. I still did not know it.

On the fourth day I washed and bathed us both and, with Hayley at my side. I took him downstairs to see Nikky and Rich. As they held him I counted the seconds he was away from me. It was too many but, nodding and smiling, I pretended I didn't mind. When Rich handed him back, I closed my eyes and kissed my child's forehead.

"Does he sleep well?" Rich asked. I shook my head. He barely slept during the night and only seemed to settle when close to me. I needed to get to grips with the sling that Deven had brought for me.

"He's gorgeous, Kate. Have you named him yet?" Nikky murmured, moving next to me on the sofa. I shook my head.

"Not yet."

They stayed for the afternoon and helped me open the mountain of gifts that had arrived. I had more baby clothes than he could ever possibly hope to wear. I picked up a small box and flicked it open to reveal a tiny silver bangle.

"That's from Peter, he wanted to have it engraved by the silversmith, but he can't until you name the little man. Are you going to have him christened?"

Staring at the box, I slowly closed it and placed it on the floor. I would have thrown it into the bin if I could, but they circled me, blocking my escape routes. Glancing at my baby as he slept soundly in his basket calmed me.

"I don't know."

"Kate, consider it at least, I'd be honoured to christen him." Rich's voice was low. I looked at baby and then at him, and shrugged. They left a short while after and as Hayley packed away the presents I slipped the bangle into the bin, where it belonged.

More visitors came and the following week was a blur of faces. He changed so much in those first ten days that I was glad we didn't sleep. If I had, I would have missed too much.

On the twelfth day I woke early, restless and irritable, my breasts aching and leaking with seemingly stubborn delight even though he had been fed just an hour ago. I changed my bra again, padding it out and cursing at the pathetic cotton pads. Standing by the window I looked out at the beach and frowned. Enforcers, at least ten of them by the rock pools. The doctor was there as well. *Tom?* Panicked I ran to the door and then paused; I couldn't leave him here.

"Hayley, Hayley!" I called, running down the stairs and

tripping as I missed a step. Grabbing the banister I steadied myself before running into the kitchen. Then back up the stairs as I realised the house was empty. I pulled on some jogging bottoms and a tee shirt from the dirty pile in my room and slipped him into the sling. He murmured quietly and, kissing his head for reassurance, I walked along the beach. It was early and the sun was low. As I reached the pools I saw Hayley's tired and drawn face.

"Kate, what are you doing? It's night." She tried to usher me back to the house. She'd been crying. "He'll get too cold out here."

"Tom?" I pushed back against her and she shook her head. "Is he okay, Hayley, is Tom ok?" Thick, the fear was thick in my throat and I cared not that Peter stood with the Enforcers staring at me. Tom.

"No. It's Amy, the doctor's daughter." Her voice low and tense. Pulling my gaze from the pools I stared at her. She shook her head sadly and squeezed my arms. "It's not pretty, Kate. Please, take the baby inside."

"What happened?"

"We don't know, she's been... gone a while. We think the tide brought her home."

I could only nod, and turned back towards the house. I didn't need to see, nor did I want to. *The tide brought her home.*

I made coffees and soup for those outside: ignoring him and his constant presence. It was nearly ten a.m. by the time everyone left and Amy was taken away. I hugged Hayley, and Glen placed a hand on my shoulder and patted. They left together. Dr Nicholls wanted to discuss arrangements sooner rather than later. I tried not to think about it and after they left I wandered around the house. I pictured Amy alone in the cold and dark, her skin translucent and the moon glinting on her jewellery. The diamond band shackled to my finger felt heavy then. Twisting it, I swore. My fingers still too swollen to remove it.

Later that day Nikky arrived, but she wasn't alone. Peter stood in the doorway of the living room, blocking my exit. I held my baby close and tight, my eyes darting from Nikky's beaming face to his smiling one. It reached his eyes this time, and as he looked at us both, it was predatory.

"Surprise! I thought I'd come and see you. Peter's been asking about you both all week so Gloria's covering the classes for a bit." She grabbed his hand – *how could she bear to touch him?* – and pulled him over to where I sat. I shifted away as he sat next to me on the sofa, his smell threatening to asphyxiate me.

"Scoot over." Nikky sat to my other side, forcing me closer. Baby slept in my arms, cradled against my chest, the warmth and weight of him soothing the fear. Peter moved his arm over the top of the sofa. I couldn't sit there and I tried to stand when Hayley, Glen and the Henleys walked in, laughing. His hand moved to my neck and skimmed the skin, freezing me to the spot.

This was my chance, my opportunity, I could tell them all what he was, everything he had done. I had to protect us both now, it wasn't just me.

As new guests pulled up the dining chairs, Hayley greeted Peter with a kiss to the cheek and questions about his resettlement. He had one of the new cottages Tom had helped rebuild. I remained quiet as they discussed the school. I had missed a council meeting where the remainder of the cottages had been allocated. I had been given the cottage nearest the water, next to his.

"Isn't that great, Kate? Your own place." Roger Henley spoke earnestly, reaching over and touching my baby's head and face with a gentle trail of his fingers. *What was it with him always being touched, being mauled by everyone. Stop it.* "Somewhere for you and little one."

"Are you kicking me out?" *Is that all I could say?*

"No, Kate. No, it's for when you feel ready." Hayley smiled. "Now, can I have a cuddle with the little man?" No. She held out her arms and I stood and handed him over, though. It was Hayley and she loved him. Sitting down I realised how close Peter was to me.

They spoke then of the funeral arrangements and the sadness of Amy. Convincing themselves that she was in a better place and she had been *a tortured soul*. Then they moved onto the town and the northern sector. A change of plans it seemed, only a third of the houses would be demolished and the rest renovated. The other community was close to overpopulation and needed to relocate over a hundred people here. They continued to talk, but I heard little after that. Their voices were close and yet so far away and all the while I could only truly concentrate on my own voice. Counting and watching him in her arms. It was too long and I was about to speak but his voice cut me off:

"Can I have a cuddle?" and he held out his hands.

I didn't want him touching my baby. Never. He'd own and possess him like he did me. How could I deny him without telling everyone what he was? No one would believe me, not now, I'd left it too long and he was now part of the town, and close to my friends, and so *Anna* watched as Hayley handed him over. *Docile and gracious.* The tension almost snapped me in two. He cradled him in the nook of his arm and stroked his beautiful tiny face, stroked the way he loved to stroke. A protective flare of anger licked at my insides, and I forced it back deep inside.

"He's so small." His voice, calm and assured, made me squirm and fret. I reached out and took him back, relieved the others were there for he handed him over without a word. Instead his gaze burnt into mine. "He's gorgeous," he added.

It was then he woke and cried. I knew that cry now. It was my escape.

"I need to feed him." Without looking around the room I walked upstairs. I lay on the bed, putting my child to my breast, and closed my eyes as his little grip tightened on my fingers, comforting us both. He was all I wanted. Opening my eyes and looking down at his long dark lashes as they fluttered with each gulp the bud inside my chest curled into bloom. I loved him so completely that I couldn't breathe without it riding on each rise and fall of my chest.

After a short while the floorboards creaked and he stood there watching me. I covered my bare chest with a blanket and shrank back. I had no defences, there was nothing to protect me, no one to stop him approaching. He sat on my dressing stool, leaning forward and clasping his hands together, still watching. The door was wide open, and I heard the laughter from downstairs.

"What's his name?"

I couldn't reply and instead kept my eyes on his; my fear was overwhelming. He knew it.

"Kate. What's his name?" The harder tone was back, the one I remembered, the one I had grown afraid of.

"He doesn't have a name."

"Why did you–"

He didn't finish. Nikky walked in and grinned at us both.

"Peter, we've got to go." She grabbed his hand again and pulled him up. All the while he was staring at us both. "'Bye, Kate," Nikky said to me. "I'll be around later – in fact, how about I cook dinner tonight? Hayley and Glen are going to be out with Deven and Roger. I'll come over."

I was going to be alone. "Please."

"See ya later!" she chirped.

No one but me saw him for what he was, and watching him with my baby sickened me. I had handed him over and allowed him to touch the purest thing in my world; would my little piece of hope now be corrupted? Was he already corrupted by blood? As he murmured and twitched, kicking out his legs as I swapped sides, I dismissed the thought as quickly as it came. He was pure and beautiful.

With the house now empty, I locked my bedroom door and slept fitfully. I don't remember my dreams, but each time I woke all I could picture was his watchful gaze as I fed my baby. He still stared at me as though I was his. I drew my blanket around me and checked on my child.

He slept soundly, his tiny fists clenched by the side of his head.

By mid-afternoon he didn't want to sleep anymore and I found myself smiling at his serious little face as he studied me with dark eyes, so unlike my own. Using the sling, I held him close and cleaned the house from top to bottom. My back ached at the weight of his body against mine, but to not hold him hurt more. I needed to breathe in his baby scent often. As I mopped the floor in the kitchen I looked up to find Tom standing on the porch grinning at me.

"Can I come in?"

He sat at the kitchen table while I made the cakes I had promised Alan. I stopped often to glance down at baby. He still needed a name.

Tom told me about the latest council meeting. With the newcomers so eager to ingratiate themselves they had offered to finish clearing the northern sector, twenty of them were from the building trade, including a female plumber. He made me giggle as he recalled the look on Simon's face when she stood up and asserted herself and her profession. "Looked like he'd chewed on a wasp," he cackled. There was a dentist and an optician in the group; both had agreed to enforce two days a week in exchange for residence. They negotiated terms of settlement while the Henleys nodded and acquiesced.

"Yer library looks empty without yer Katie, maybe you and the babby should take a walk down?"

"Maybe soon." I whisked furiously now, concentrating on the bowl. Something different attacked my insides now, and desperation swirled with a need to be accepted.

I tried to concentrate. I could do this, I could do this.

"Everything okay, pet?"

"No, no it's really not." I managed, biting my lip hard, and clamping my lips shut, to stop the tears. Baby had woken. Staring at me. "I know Peter from before, in the Unlands." I swallowed and continued, unable to look up and concentrating on the most pure thing ever to exist in this world. The words that came were different to what I had planned; I had no control: "He's a violent man, he had a girl called Anna, she escaped, but he did terrible things to her." My voice was a whisper now. "I saw him hurt her, over and over again. I didn't do anything to help. I should have. I should have fought him. People just let him do it. No one helped. I was the worst." For a fleeting moment I thought of Ben and Ella and the pain was overwhelming. I wiped away my tears. I needed to believe they were free, that they were safe.

Trailing off I looked up at him, hoping and praying he understood. The shame of my back prickled against my tee shirt. It would be so easy to show him, all I had to do was lift up my top and he would see the truth but I couldn't put down the whisk or bowl.

"Quiet chap he is, strange how some people behave out there Katie. It's a cruel place now, do what they can to survive. One of my boys was like that, got carried away with the fight, joined in the riots and one of them smaller gangs, disappeared off." He rolled a cigarette and the despair rose.

"Different rules in the Unlands now. Cut my boy out I did, didn't speak to him when he left. He came home one day with a load of cuts to his knuckles and Joe's boy had a black eye and a limp. Angry boy he was. I threw him out. Went to Simon, tried to tell him what happened but he laughed at me. Said mebbe the poor sod deserved a pounding. Men like Simon, and that man yer mentioned, and my boy, they just get away with it."

I couldn't speak, or differentiate the feelings inside me; they all merged together into one huge ball of poison that ate away my strength.

"Yer okay, Katie? Don't yer think about it. Nothing yer can do, that girl got away. Peter's here now, making a new start, like we all are."

"But he doesn't deserve to be."

"Don't yer go upsetting yerself about it. Now, I got yer a present." He reached into his inner pocket and pulled out a bubble-wrapped package. I took it with thanks and he cocked his head. "Yer sure yer ok?"

"I'm fine." *Fine.* Sitting down I carefully undid the string and unwrapped the parcel. Six small blue glazed tiles, each the size of my palm. I ran my hands over their surface, feeling the ridges and grooves, tracing the outlines of the shell designs.

"Thought mebbe yer could put them in yer new place? I know you like the sea. Been a while since I worked."

"They're lovely." I struggled to smile, and through the poison I forced a half-grin and touched his hand. He patted mine.

"I'd best be off. Come to the town Katie, yer missed."

Nodding absently, I continued to trace the shells as I replayed our conversation about Peter over in my mind.

I thought Tom would know, that he would understand. Nothing was fine. No one listened.

That evening Nikky cooked some sort of vegetable curry. I was starving but my appetite disappeared when she started to talk about Peter.

"I think he really likes you, Kate. You're so lucky, first Rich, now Peter."

"I'm not interested." I stopped eating and sipped my water. All I could taste now was a corrosive burn at the back of my throat as bile rose. "Please don't talk about him."

"You don't like Peter, do you Kate?"

I looked over at my sleeping child and shook my head.

"How come?"

I had so many answers. Because of my photos, my back, my hair, my ribs, my face, my baby. He'd taken everything that made me, me. I was silent and dug my nails into my palms for a while, until I finally settled on one truth. "I don't know who he is."

I wanted to tell her, to pour out my entire story and my tears with it but I found myself unable. She was clearly enamoured with him, and wouldn't believe me. I would be shunned, treated differently. He was everyone's friend, everyone with influence in this place warmed to him in a way they never had me.

"Give him a chance, Kate. Seriously, he's lovely."

"No. Leave it Nikky, please. I'm not interested in getting to know Peter."

"But why?"

"Because I'm not." I emptied my plate in the bin and stood by the back door, staring down the path to the beach. "I don't need him in my life. I'm thinking about seeing if Paulina wants to take care of the library for me as well. I don't think I can manage baby and the library."

"Is this because of him?"

"No." Hugging myself I looked at her and smiled. "Please though, I don't want to hear about how great he is."

"Are you jealous?"

"What?" I almost laughed, it was so far from the truth yet strangely true.

"Everyone likes him, he's settled straight in. He goes drinking with the Enforcers at night, he's funny, the women like him, the kids adore him, all the newcomers know him so he's not really had the problems you did."

"I'm not jealous. We know nothing about him, I don't trust him."

"We didn't know anything about any of the new settlers when they came, you were new too once, but look at us now! Best friends."

Best friends. I smiled.

"Will you just try, please Kate. I work with him every day, and I really want the two of you to get along."

"I'll try." I said the words to shush her.

"I knew you would." She jumped up and hugged me. "God, you're already thinner than me! I hate you! No I don't, I'm only kidding – but I am envious." She let go and helped me clear up. He wasn't mentioned again that night and instead she helped me with a list of names for baby. Some were ridiculous and I screwed up my face as she said them, but there were two I loved and I filed them away in my mind.

CHAPTER TWENTY-FIVE

"A SPORTS DAY for the kids?" I glanced at Hayley as I scraped the dinner plates into the compost bin and checked on him in his basket at the doorway. He was awake, staring at me. I found myself smiling down and blowing him kisses.

"We thought it would be a great idea, seeing how well the Easter egg hunt went down with the kids."

"We?"

"Oh, sorry, Glen, Peter, Nikky and me. We were at the Enforcers' house the other night and chatting about the school."

"Oh." I didn't know what else to say. I promised Nikky that I would try, and this was the perfect opportunity. Yet every molecule of my body and my conscience was on the qui vive. My jaw throbbed and I clasped the side of my mouth.

"Are you all right?" Hayley stopped knitting and started to get up. I raised my other hand and she stopped.

"Fine, just a bit of a toothache, it'll go in a bit." Running my tongue across the surface of the tooth I forced a smile, and she sat back down, seemingly mollified. "When are you thinking of holding the sports day?"

"Kate, you do make me laugh. It's not *you*, but *us*! We were thinking of having a meeting this evening and holding it soon before the holidays and before the weather turns. I'm sorry for not mentioning it sooner, it slipped my mind, but you are very much part of this. In fact, Peter was keen for you to be involved in all the preparations."

The pain in my mouth spread, and the muscles in my legs and neck tensed. Easing myself down into a chair, I forced that smile again. I must have appeared demented, or like some sort of animal.

"Slipped your mind? Or you realised I'd say no so you thought to spring it on me last minute?" Reaching over to my baby I traced his cheek with my finger. There was a silence. "Don't worry. I'll come to the meeting. I don't want to leave him though and it's too steep to walk comfortably. Do you think Deven would mind picking us up in the car?"

"No, no, not at all." She was gushing now and beaming. Always smiling, always so positive. "I'll just radio him now. The meeting is in an hour."

I raised an eyebrow and she had the decency to blush as she left the room. Sipping at my water slowly I pictured his face and that dark smile. No, not the smile, but those dark eyes. Was it a dark smile or did I just see it that way? Perhaps he had changed.

I tried not to think then and instead just stared at the moses basket by my side and focused on the white lace trim. I could hear Hayley getting washed and changed, but I didn't move. Instead I licked my lips and rolled the glass of water on the table creating damp rings.

"Kate, you not getting changed?" She entered with a waft of perfume. "I can watch the baby."

"No, it's okay." I stood and ran my fingers through my hair. "It's only a meeting. I'll be back in a sec though."

Grabbing the car seat from the back bedroom I glanced in the mirror and Kate stared back. She didn't smile.

"LOVELY TO SEE you all here, I know this was last minute, so apologies if it inconvenienced anyone," Peter looked around the table, smiling broadly, his skin stretching. "A couple of nights ago we thought it would be a great idea if we had a sports day. Lots of activities. Sack race, egg and spoon race, something for the kids and the adults. I've got the bean bag race in the... bag. " There was a smattering of laughter and he grinned even wider than I thought possible. "Kate, do you have any ideas?"

Addressing me pulled my gaze to his and his smile changed. The muscles moved in his face and I watched his lips. He saw that and his eyes widened. His smile became something for just us. Even at the other end of the table I could see the change in his expression. Deven watched us both, quiet and unassuming as he made notes.

"Not really. Just that there's enough planned to keep all the kids entertained."

"What about a three-legged race?" Nikky piped up. "They're always good fun. They'll have to work together to move forward." *Work together to move forward,* echoed in my head. But it was the voice of the war propaganda machine I heard, not Nikky's. *Working as one to solve the problems caused by just a few. Might is right. For home, hearth and happiness.*

"Great idea," Peter nodded and made a note on his pad. "We can have a host of team building exercises for the older kids. Problem solving and so on, what do you think?"

He was talking to me again and the eyes of those present were on me. "Great idea." I finally echoed, and from across the table Nikky relaxed; she mouthed 'thank you' and I found myself smiling at her.

The ideas continued to flow, and I joined in the conversation. I could do this; I was proving that I could. Conversation flowed and with people around there was a confidence in me I relished. Even when I was discussing a maths based race with Peter, Deven, and Nikky I ignored the unease building with every second I spent near him. My fear was rooted. It didn't grow, didn't encompass me. It was just... there. As Nikky laughed at another of his self-deprecating jokes and Deven wandered off I breathed deeply; there were people around, people who loved me. He wouldn't try anything here. I was safe. *Safe.* I studied him again. He was trying so hard to be a warm and kind person, open and welcoming. I too could pretend to be someone I wasn't, but I'd be someone with a fearless confidence. I could do this.

"Where were you before Blackwood, Peter?"

They both looked up and he cleared his throat. Hayley and Glen laughed with the Henleys behind me, but I resisted the urge to turn around and instead I shifted the baby sling and stared pointedly at him.

"I mostly enforced, ran errands on the network and delivered messages, that sort of thing."

"What made you come down here?"

"I wanted a fresh start and decided it was time to settle down." He smiled at Nikky, who blushed a deep crimson.

"And there was nowhere else?" The disbelief was thick in my tone, though my face still smiled.

"Nowhere like this."

"Do you have a family?"

"No." He glanced down at my baby's soft, dark head and smiled, his gaze moving back to mine. His pupils widened.

"*Did* you have a family?"

"No."

I paused for a moment, unnerved by Nikky who now stared at me intently. Her face unreadable. He then said,

"What about you, Kate?

I shifted again. My top clung to my skin and the cloying smell of baby vomit engulfed me but the heat of him, snuggled close, warmed me. "I was a mature student. I studied humanities."

"Interesting. Whereabouts?"

"Abroad."

"Were you married?"

"Yes."

"What made you come here?"

"Like you I wanted a new start. Somewhere I could forget the horrors of the past." I emphasised horrors, which elicited a slither of disapproval from him. It oozed into a thin line across his mouth but as soon as it appeared, he grinned, pushing it back deep inside.

"Kate's a pretty name."

It wasn't a question, yet I needed to answer. "It was my mother's name."

"What was your husband called?" He didn't bother to hide behind generic bland questions now.

"Michael." I smiled then, unabated.

He looked up from his pad then and his eyes locked with mine, eyes dark and thoughtful. I didn't break contact, not even when Nikky scraped back her chair on the floor and joined in a conversation with the Stentons.

"Anyone else in your life?"

"No one I've loved." The danger of this game pumped in my blood, I was heady with adrenaline.

"Where's the father of your baby?" He leaned forward, inches from me now. His voice was lower now and emotionless.

"Dead." I leaned back.

"Is that so." He too leaned back.

"Have you finished?" My words were clipped and my face flushed. It was anger.

"Come on now, don't be... waspish, no need to be angry." His tone was loud and cheerful again and I looked up as Nikky approached with three glasses of iced water. Ice. Such decadence.

"Thank you, Nikky." He took the glass, his fingers brushing hers lightly. She blushed again and shot him a lopsided grin.

"My pleasure. You okay, Kate?"

"I'm fine, feeling a little tired. I should be getting back; I need to put baby down for the night."

"I can drive you back if you want?" Peter sipped the water and then crunched on the ice. My tooth throbbed again. No fucking chance.

"No." I was aware that I snapped. "I can drive myself." Peter's face twitched and his eyes widened.

"I didn't know you could drive, Kate," Nikky exclaimed. She was sitting close to Peter, and his arm was draped casually over the back of her chair.

"My husband taught me."

"You must have been rich! My parents couldn't afford the cost of fuel, and when the wars started we sold our fuel rations so I could go to university. I wish I had learnt though."

"I can teach you." Peter nudged her and she clapped in excitement.

"Wow. Really?"

And so they started to discuss driving plans. Every now and then they'd stop and try to coax me in to conversation, but I didn't want to play any more and excused myself. Deven handed over the keys, asking if I was all right and raising an eyebrow at Peter as he rubbed baby's cheek. I shrugged a little and he promised to speak to me tomorrow about it.

My baby stirred a little as I lifted him out of the sling and into the car seat. His head sagged forward a little and so gently I lifted him back, wiggling him into the seat and resisting the urge to eat his chubby little thighs.

I manoeuvred the car down the track, flicking the radio

on. It was more habit than anything and when the static and crackle filled the car I wasn't surprised. Hitting the button on the steering wheel I switched to the internal memory and smiled at a playlist of songs still stored there. I skipped through until I found one I knew and tapped my fingers along with the beat as I drove.

THE FOLLOWING MORNING I was up, dressed and washed before either Hayley or Glen had woken. Opening the pantry I murmured in surprise. It was full. Pulling out the eggs I rifled through the boxes: pasta, bolognese sauce, tinned vegetables and soups, spices, stock sauces, gravy granules and dry pet food – luxuries I hadn't seen since I had hurriedly packed my rucksack while the shots and bombs fell around my home.

That was the day I first witnessed the cruelty of death. As I tried to catch Oscar in the midst of the chaos, three gunshots in quick succession rang out over and above the cries and screams from my neighbours. I watched Oscar dart and run through the remains of a block of garages – away from the noise – and I tried to chase him, I fell and cut both palms on chunks of metal debris. Sitting in the middle of the destruction a soft undercurrent of sobs caught my attention. The blood pooled and rolled from my upturned hands, and though I wanted to cry, the sorrow in the distance prevented me. I couldn't force my tears to flow.

I stood up and followed the cries, and wished I hadn't. In a tree lined alleyway a man sat with his back against the brick wall stroking the head of a woman who lay face down on the path. Next to the woman lay a young boy and a dog. The man looked up, the red and brown on his face streaked with tears. I held up my bloody hands and stepped forward, but before I could speak he raised his gun to his temple and fired.

Later I emptied a bottle of antiseptic on my hands, feeling nothing, and strapped my backpack on. Quickly emptying Oscar's cat food into bowls, I left.

Blinking I now stared at the rows of food and rubbed my palms against my jeans. Looking closely I traced the small white scars with my fingers before picking out the eggs and a packet of pancake mix. I could make them from scratch, but today I wanted ease, luxury and laziness, and besides, the packet wouldn't last forever.

It was still dark outside, and I turned the kitchen light off and watched the grey and midnight blue shadows ripple across the water. Perhaps it was more of a steel blue, or a Prussian blue, I wasn't sure. Opening the back door, I shivered and tucked the blanket in around him as he slept in his basket. It was just gone five a.m. Stepping out on to the doorstep, I glanced around and then went and sat on the sand. The smell of salt, wet wood and earth was strong and I closed my eyes and inhaled. The taste slid down my throat: metallic and bitter. As the fishing boats left the harbour, the shadow of someone I thought was Tom made his way across to the rock pools. I started to raise my hand to wave, but something stopped me and instead I watched the horizon alone. Eventually the warmth of the sun on my back and the colours of dawn seeping across the water stimulated me to walk back inside and cook.

Glen stood over the basket and instinctively I tensed before relaxing and reminding myself that it was Glen. He looked at me and the corners of his mouth tilted upwards. It wasn't quite a smile but it was more sincere than the broad grins I had grown accustomed to here.

"He looks like you."

No he doesn't. I nodded and washed my hands before starting to beat the pancake mix.

"You saw all the new supplies then? We found a supermarket about thirty miles from here on an industrial estate, practically untouched. Place stank, but there's so much food that we're going back later with the rest of the convoy and some of the Blackwood team. Clear it out and split what's left. There's a few houses nearby we're going to check out. See if there's anything we can use."

Like vultures stripping a carcass. I made a non-committal noise and nodded. This was perhaps the most he had spoken to me in a while, perhaps ever.

"Oh, before I forget, Deven is going to pop by and collect the car later. We'll probably need it for the trip."

"Ok."

"I didn't know you could drive."

"I learnt a long while ago."

"I learnt as a teenager when it was cheap, before your time and all the fighting."

"I don't know much about the history of how it started." I mumbled, blushing.

"How old were you when the Asia-Pacific wars started then?"

"When it first started bubbling? Ten. When the violence

322

started I was twelve." He looked at me, and there was clear disappointment in his gaze. "I wasn't really interested in the news or current affairs. Sorry."

"Not many of us were. I'm only fifteen years older than you, but even I wasn't bothered to start with. It was only when my mother died in the conflict I paid attention, and do you know what I did?"

I shook my head.

"I started an online petition to the government." He sounded so bitter that I slowed my cooking down and turned to him. "I wrote to the government and asked them to help mediate, sent it around the internet and gathered signatures. I didn't hear anything. Not surprising really, but I didn't stop there. I... I got involved in the Freedom and Independence Fighters."

I stopped completely and looked at him, really looked at him. The Free-Indies were the first of the groups to speak out, but they were cruel and brash. Speaking with violence and hiding their faces from the world behind masks and online videos. They started the wave of groups and rights movements that spiralled into vigilantes and crime gangs. Why was he telling me this now?

"I never told Hayley about the meetings. She thought I was having an affair with all those nights I spent away from home."

He poured me a coffee and pushed it across the table. "I eventually gave up, Kate. I came home, ignored the calls from the Indies and continued to bury the dead who just kept rolling on through. Now though, now we have all this and something worth fighting for again. We'll make the same mistakes again I'm sure, but we all have something worth believing in. Whatever happens, we fight. We don't give in."

He was earnest. I was confused. There was a hint of something in his voice, and he looked at me with knowing.

"What happens if we give in?" I asked.

"Then we are never free. We live our life in the thrall of others dictating what we do, what we say, where we go. This is the time for new beginnings." He nodded to my baby. "For him and his generation. Freedom is worth the price."

"Do you regret any of it though? I know what the Enforcers do."

"Yes I regret some things, but not most." He paused. "I've seen some shit decisions and actions out there. I've made some shit ones myself, but if I'm not out there helping, keeping them in line, there'd be carnage." He took another gulp of coffee, flitting his eyes to the kitchen door as the stairs creaked. "Freedom, it's worth fighting for, isn't it Kate?"

I glanced at the basket and then looked up at Glen: "Yes it's worth fighting for."

As promised, that afternoon Deven came by and sat with me on the beach as I fed my baby and tried on several different slings, finally finding one that didn't pull so much on my back. Roger had locked himself away with Simon and the doctor to discuss security protocols, and so he welcomed the company.

He told me about his life in the Unlands and what he had become after the wars. We weren't too different, he and I, both trapped by the actions of others.

"You learn to box it up, Kate. I promise," he said, smiling as he drew deep on a cigarette and I batted him and his smoke away from the baby with a grimace. "I was never quite so..." he indicated to his glamorous attire, "before the wars, and definitely not out there, but here it keeps me safe. Roger and Simon keep me safe."

Unsettled, I spoke. "But are you happy, Deven?"

"Are any of us really?" he replied.

He asked me about before, and so I shared with him my story as he had given his so freely. He knew that I had been captured, but now I also told him that my baby was a product not of love, but of possession and obsession. It seemed so easy to tell him whilst staring over the waters and holding the love of my life against my chest.

"Bastard. What happened to him?"

"I thought I escaped him."

Right now, sitting on the beach, there was nothing stopping me from speaking the whole truth, but Deven was close to Simon, and Simon close to Peter. If somehow Peter found out that I had told anyone who he really was, my baby would be in danger. So instead I didn't say a word.

There was nothing for a while, and glancing at him, his furrowed brow relaxed and his eyes widened in realisation.

"Shit."

CHAPTER TWENTY-SIX

IT TOOK JUST a week of planning. I saw Peter every day during that week for a total of thirty-two hours. Wherever I looked, he seemed to be there. Laughing, smiling, helping. Once I even found myself staring at him as he made sandwiches in the Enforcers hall for those planning the sports day. His sleeves were rolled up to his elbows and his top shirt button was undone. He looked disarmingly normal, but I was uneasy and it was as though I was skirting around a trap of sorts.

"Have you got a name sorted?"

"No."

"Gabriel's a nice name."

I didn't reply, but Hayley did. "Oh that's lovely! Isn't that a nice name, Kate? Is it a family name, Peter?"

"My father's." Chop, chop, chop, he sliced the cucumber quickly and with the precision I had come to expect of him. Each slice the same width and perfect. "He was a great man, real family values and always smiling. He was crippled in the Black Sunday terrorist attacks, lost both his legs, but that smile never left his face. Your little man's smile reminds me of his." He pointed the knife at the pushchair by my side and I licked my lips as my heartbeat quickened.

"Oh, Kate! Gabriel sounds lovely. You simply must consider it." Hayley beamed and I made a vague mumble about thinking about it, though I had no intention of doing so.

"Peter, do you have the notebook of ideas for tomorrow?" she asked.

"Sure, it's in the car outside." He reached into his pocket and pulled out a set of keys and threw them at Hayley. "On the passenger seat."

It was just the two of us again: well, three of us. The measured sounds of the chopping the only noise between us until he looked up and smiled.

"It's true you know. The story of my father." I said nothing, but there was no stopping him. "He was a great man until the attacks, until the Republic wannabes took his independence away. He got legs and a shit load of compensation, but it made no difference to his dented pride." Stopping and flexing his fingers, his eyes burned into mine. "He'd always been a very physical man, played rugby every weekend, climbed mountains for animal charities, cycled a thousand miles in aid of the Independence Movement, loads of that sort of thing. Afterwards he just wasn't the same, but he was always smiling and he loved us to the end; right up until he killed himself a month before I graduated university. I loved him through all that, you know. He was the one who said I should be a teacher, that

I had a natural talent for teaching. I loved it too. It's great to be back in a classroom. Thank you, Kate, for making that happen."

"Don't thank me."

"If it wasn't for you, I'd be out there still. We need to talk. I've missed you."

I didn't get a chance to reply, for Hayley walked back in and slid the keys on the worktop with thanks. I stared at the keyring and dry swallowed. The metal Scottie dog linked to his keys stared back at me with lifeless eyes and a familiar chipped ear. My palms moistened, but my arms and back were so cold that shivers racked me. I coughed in an attempt to swallow and force air back into my chest. With my head down and my hand in front of my mouth I hid the tears that had formed. Strong. I needed to be strong. Blinking furiously I forced the tears away as Hayley patted my back.

Hayley noticed my gaze. "That's a cute keyring."

"Oh this old thing? I've had it years. I was down in… God I can't remember where… it was some years back on a school trip and I bought it in one of those souvenir shops. In fact, if I remember rightly, all the teachers bought one." He lied with ease.

"I've not seen one as a keyring before." She turned it over in her hands and I sat on my hands to stop them shaking.

"I thought it had been lost. It took me quite some time to find it again, and I was relieved when I did. It has a lot of sentimental value." I forced myself to look at him and he grinned cheerfully, with a tiny, barely perceptible nod to me as he continued to slice.

The noise of the chopping intensified, blocking out the sounds of chatter and laughter from the others as they milled around and took their seats at the table. Their bodies blurred at the edges and faded to nothing as I held my memories of Ben in my mind. His childish laugh and innocence had been a balm to my wounds, but now I ached all over again. *Pain, pain continual; pain unending.* Merciless, determined and constant.

"I need some air."

Stumbling outside, I stretched my back and agony out and stared up at the sky, breathing deeply and burying the howl of anguish that sat on my tongue.

"Katherine?"

Turning, Simon approached. His hard face as expressionless as ever. He was dressed in the familiar black fatigues of his Enforcers, and I noticed the handgun strapped to his thigh. Tucked under his right arm there was a black file.

"Simon."

"How are you and the baby?" He stood far too close, and I involuntarily stepped back to create space between us.

"Well, thank you."

"Do you need anything? We do worry."

We? "No, I'm fine." Baby stirred a little and I stroked his soft head absently.

"Me, Deven... Peter." He answered the question I hadn't asked.

I shot him a narrowed glance then, he held my gaze with a cruel smile. "Beautiful baby. Deven speaks of him often.

Desperate for a family, that man. He'd be a wonderful parent and I'd love to make that happen." He paused, glancing to the building. "Peter, too. He lost someone he thought was special, oh about eight months or so ago. Been through a lot, he has. You both have. Perhaps something good will come from all this, hey?"

"I'm happy on my own, thank you."

"Not forever though, surely. Baby needs a father figure. All boys need a man in their life, someone to look up to and admire. Have a think about what's best for you and the little one, and what might make things... easier here in the town for you." He nodded, leaning close. "There's only so much the town can give before it asks for something in return, and if you're not a team player then we have to ask ourselves if we really need you on our side." He placed his free hand on my shoulder, squeezing, before entering the building.

I didn't realise I was shaking until he was gone.

REFLECTION, IMITATION AND experience. I think it was Confucius who said that there were three methods for which we may learn wisdom. Having suffered the bitterness of experience, today I reflected. Comparing Will with Peter, and Peter with Daniel.

The sharp trill of a whistle made me look up from my baby's feed to the children who ran and skipped towards Nikky and Peter. It was too hot. I sat under the gazebo and longed for a breeze to cut through the long disused cricket pitch where the town now congregated.

I watched Peter with the children, he would grab and swing them around, and they would squeal and yell in delight. The younger ones followed him around with their remote controlled cars, their colouring books and outdoor games. He played with each and every one as he moved from adult to adult. By the Enforcers' table he sat Lara on his lap as they all pored over maps of the area. She kept thrusting a picture in his face, but he patiently distracted her and pointed to areas on the map, deep in conversation with the other men.

So many townsfolk came to speak to me about the baby. I ignored the surprise and judgemental comments when they realised he had no name yet. I smiled when told it would be better wrap him in more layers given his small size, and then later nodded when advised to strip him down given the heat.

Deven would flit glances to me, Peter, back to me, to Rich, to Simon. When he had realised who I spoke of, I begged him not to say a word, said that I couldn't risk anyone else knowing. He promised that I would be safe, and that he and Roger would ensure that, but I found myself shaking my head and telling him I had seen Roger's darker side at the trial and with his violence, and I didn't trust his husband. It had taken an age before he unhappily agreed not to say a word. I wasn't entirely sure if he promised silence for my safety or his own.

Today I shook my head a little and he pursed his lips together, walking towards the group from the social club.

"Have you named your baby yet?" Alan walked up, balancing a hardboiled egg in his spoon, his little tongue stuck out at the side of his mouth.

"Not yet." I stroked my baby's head as he suckled. God his hair was so cute, the way it curled behind his ears and the nape of his neck flipped my stomach. I smiled at Alan. "You're good."

"I'm not as good as James. He can run really fast and zoom. His egg doesn't even move a tiny bit." His eyes were wide. "Not. Even. A. Tiny. Bit," he repeated solemnly with a sigh.

"Wow." I offered, lamely.

"Are you going to race with the mummies later?"

"I don't think so. It's too hot for me to run."

"But you can race instead of Rose. She'll be all fat and slow and you'll be fast." He ran his finger along the plastic rim of the chair and then walked his fingers along my arm to the baby's head where, hesitantly, he stroked it and looked up at me. "It would be really good if you raced with me. We could beat James and his mummy."

"Rose will be sad."

"Oh Rose won't mind. She told me to come and ask you." He looked guilty and then turned away. "But it's a secret. You can't tell her that I said that."

"Did Rose really ask?"

"Yes, really she did... but she might not remember asking so don't tell her. Rose is old."

I tried not to smile and instead I pursed my lips and nodded. "Ok, well, don't tell Rose she's old, she might get upset. If you promise not to tell her she's old – I'll race with you."

His face lit up then and a huge smile spread from ear

to ear. "Yessssssss!" Jumping up, he ran across the pitch to James and danced in front of him. Wiggling his bum and shooting his arms in the air with attitude. His egg rolled around my feet. I picked it up and balanced it on the plastic table by my side. My hand hovered over the barbecued vegetable skewers by my side. I was starving but Peter had cooked them and brought them over. He still sat at the table chatting with Simon's men. He spoke often with his hands, waving them around and spreading his fingers wide as he threw back his head and laughed, his Adam's apple bobbing up and down. The creases in the corners of his eyes softened his face and I caught several women looking in his direction with interest. Looking away, I focused on Rich. He was surrounded by several of the newcomers holding their plastic cups of drink in one hand with the other hand in their pockets as they watched the children and adults with uncertainty – as though they expected the children to grow two heads and burst into flames. Rich's hair was almost long enough to tie back and with the bright colours of his tattoo I could make out the shapes of the koi and the flowers from where I sat. He kept glancing at me as he spoke and when he caught me staring I then automatically waved, beckoning him over. He matched my grin and as he strode over I covered my exposed breast and baby's head with a small blanket.

"You look hot." Grabbing one of the skewers he dragged a tomato off with his teeth and nodded. "I mean, in a sweaty and red sort of way. Not an attractive way." His face dropped and his eyes widened. "Oh no, I didn't mean it like that."

"Why thank you, Mr Vicar." I said, blotting out the image of Peter in the distance and instead focusing on him in front of me. "You look very I'm-a-mature-student-wanting-to-recapture-my-youth-and-can't-accept-I'm-old... in a desperate way."

"Let me think of a reply for that."

Sitting next to me, he stretched out and crossed his legs at his ankles. A waft of Issey Miyake aftershave danced around me. It clashed with the salt air and the smoky smells of the food, but I didn't mind and instead I breathed deeply and slowly, savouring the tastes – acrid and yet sweet. Sitting in silence, listening to the laughter and chatter of the kids and the gossiping of the adults, I didn't know what to say. I glanced at to Peter every so often. He still sat with the Enforcers but three times he looked at me and then at Rich. Each time he did a lump caught in my throat and I found myself smiling at Rich and moving my chair slightly closer to his.

"You ok?" Rich finally asked, leaning forward.

"Yeah, you?"

"Yeah," he dragged his hands through his hair and coughed. "You know, we've still not had that picnic. There's a nice little spot on the beach." I noticed the tension in his smile and the nervous jigging of his right foot on top of his leg. I placed my sleeping baby down in his basket and ran a finger down his nose.

"Sounds good. Let me think on it?"

He smiled and stood up. "Sounds good, but at this moment in time it looks like I'm about to be replaced." There was amusement in his voice. Instinctively I looked for Peter, but he was with Nikky and a line of children on the makeshift track.

"Kate, Kate, Kate, Kate!" Alan shouted me, running over and making me jump. "Kate, Kate, Ka–"

"What's wrong?" I grabbed him before he careered into me. He was gasping and fidgeting.

"Now, c'mon. It's the race." He dragged me to my feet and hopped up and down. "We can't miss it."

STANDING ON THE opposite line with the other women I shot Alan the thumbs up and he copied me with a huge smile. I tried to concentrate on the race and not my baby. Alone. With Rich. I shook my head quickly, shaking my distrust away with it. Rich wasn't Peter.

There was a sharp blow on the whistle and Alan was still, his body solid and his fists clenched as he waited. He really wanted this and I had a sudden urge to win... for him, and, if I was honest, for me. The finish line was only a hundred metres there and then about one hundred and fifty back. I could do it easily, but my competition was likely to be Daisy's mother. She looked like a gazelle and her legs were longer than I was tall. Eyeing her up, I lingered on her flip flops. Mistake.

"Ready..." Peter called out.

"Set..." Nikky added, and Alan bent low. I tensed with him and as Nikky blew the whistle and Peter shouted 'Go!' I cheered with the others as Alan hurtled towards me. He was right, James was a little rocket and soon the distance between them grew but he clapped my hand and I ran faster than I had moved in months to the line at the end, turning and then running back to the start. Peter stood next to Alan, a hand on his shoulder as he jumped up and down screaming my name. I was neck and neck with Daisy's mum and, digging my nails in my palms, I pushed with all I had. My back protested and a dull pain ripped along my hips and stomach. I pulled from deep inside and threw the last of my energy out and collapsed over the line. Relief and surprise rolled together and I laughed. I still had it. I wasn't totally out of shape.

"Kate, Kate. We did it. We won!" Alan pulled at my arm until I stood up and then he threw his arms around me – head-butting my stomach in excitement and making me grimace.

"Well done, sweetie," I stroked his hair as we walked back to my baby.

"I was fast, wasn't I?"

"Yup."

Alan continued to chatter, then without warning he shot off towards Nikky and Peter and animatedly re-enacted the race to them both. Nikky grinned at me while Peter just glanced over and then took Alan's hand. Together they picked a prize from the table. Peter crouched face to face with Alan and whispered something in his ear. Alan looked over at me and giggled.

WHEN THE RACES ended and the children were taken home I sat on the grass with Nikky while she cuddled my little man, who stared up at her with his serious dark eyes.

The heat of the sun had burnt away, and a cool breeze ruffled the air. The sweat trickling down my back itched, and absently I rubbed the brand through my tee shirt. It was raised and hard. The Henleys and Hayley sat in the nearest gazebo drinking wine and laughing, while Glen and the Enforcers still huddled over the maps with Peter pointing out locations and scribbling notes. Rich had left at the request of one of his congregation – something about discussing another wedding. Other townsfolk paired off or sat in groups, chatting and drinking. I sipped at my squash and closed my eyes in bliss as another gust of wind passed.

"He's so cute. I think he just smiled at me," she exclaimed making strange 'bub' noises and tickling him. He just stared back, his fingers wrapped around hers.

"I think he's thinking 'who's this strange woman and what the hell is she doing?'"

She pulled a face at me and continued with the strange guttural sounds until a smell caught us both and she promptly handed him back to me for a change. "Not cute anymore. You know, today has been perfect. Peter's done really well."

"Wasn't just him, you did most of the organising."

"Yeah but it was all his idea. He likes you, you know. He asked me to put a good word in but you know me. I'm not that subtle."

"You're as subtle as a brick in the face. I thought you might like him." I remained as calm as I could.

"Well, yeah," she paused. "But plenty more fish in the sea. He's probably too nice for me. You need someone nice."

"I don't need anyone, Nikky." My baby looked up at me and wriggled restlessly as I did up the buttoned outfit. "And I don't want anyone either. I just like being alone."

"Yeah but, he's really nice, and there's Rich."

"You're like a bloody broken record. Rich and Peter, Peter and Rich."

"I just want you to be happy."

"I am."

"Are you really?"

I didn't reply. *When the truth is replaced by silence, the silence is a lie.*

LATER THAT NIGHT, I sat in the living room and read with just the side lamp on, the small glow illuminating me and the moses basket. My little one had started screaming and crying earlier that evening and nothing soothed him. With apologies and embarrassment I left the evening party and returned home. For two hours he had sobbed until his shuddering little body gave way to exhaustion. His pain was my pain and I cried with him, desperate to soothe him, let him know I was here and I loved him so completely. I stood by the basket long after he fell asleep, too scared to move in case it woke him. When finally satisfied I grabbed the nearest book and lost myself.

IT WAS NEARLY midnight when the door opened. I jumped up to greet them, desperate for some conversation, but instead ran straight into *him* and felt his hands grab the tops of my arms. I screamed and the baby woke, joining in with wails of his own. Peter stank of beer. Every cry from my little hope ripped me apart and pulled deep within. He grabbed my hair and silenced my scream with his hand. He'd been smoking; I could smell and taste the nicotine on his fingers: he pushed me roughly against the door frame. The wood slammed into my spine but the physical pain was nothing compared to the ear piercing screams from the basket. I started crying.

"Don't cry, Anna. I'm going to take my hand away, don't scream." He rubbed my face and leaned his cheek against mine. "Please, don't scream." He let go and strode over to my baby, grabbing him and holding him close again. He was impossibly gentle as he kissed the tiny face, the cries subsiding to snuffles and murmurs. So tiny, seeing him in his arms showed to me the glaring vulnerability of new life and the cold cruelties to which he could be subjected.

"He's my baby as well, Anna. You mustn't keep him from me." Laying him back down with a kiss, he turned to me. "We can stay here, settle down. I can give you what you want, but I need to be with him, with you."

Rushing to the basket I picked up my child and backed away again; he already smelt of spiciness, smoke and beer. I wanted my baby smell back, *my baby*. Not his, never his. I tried to leave then, but he blocked the doorway with his huge frame. "Talk to me, stop ignoring me." Marching us to the sofa he pushed me down and sat with his hand on my knee. I was forced to sit and hear his pain at missing me, of his loneliness: all he ever wanted was a family, my love. Was I meant to care? I stared at the clock. Eventually he grabbed my chin and forced me to look at him.

"Talk to me. Tell me about your family, your life. Why did you lie about the name of your job and your husband? What else have you lied to me about?" The hard, cold face was back, and his words carried the threat. I was mute. I wanted to scream *'everything'* in his face, but the warmth of baby between us acted as both a barrier and a connection, and no longer did the fear for myself engulf me – it had been replaced by the fear for my child. I glanced over to the clock again.

"They're not coming back tonight, Glen's taken Hayley away, camping on the beach, some shit about being romantic. Why do you think I'm here? This is the first opportunity I've had to truly be alone with you. I miss you, Anna, so so much. I think about what we had all the time."

I jerked my head free and his body stiffened. He grabbed my left hand, squeezing my wrist in his vice-like grip. His calluses were like grit on my skin.

Turning my hand over, he thumbed the ring he had forced on me. "You still wear it. When I saw you with it–"

"I can't get it off." I cut him off, unable to hide the way my lip curled.

He squeezed my hand, the pressure building and building until I gasped.

"I couldn't just take you back, God I wanted to. Not from here and the fucking pious rules they enforce. You've been clever, haven't you? Made friends with the councilman's husband, with Glen and Hayley, even the fucking vicar – have you fucked him? Tell me you haven't. I don't know what I'd do if you had." Alcohol made his tongue loose, and I wondered if it made his reactions slow, if there was time for me to run.

Shaking my head I didn't cry out, I was under that spell again, but this time I knew it for what it was, knew the games he played. He hadn't changed.

"Good. I knew you wouldn't. Not really. Don't you care how worried I was about you? I thought you'd been taken from me, or that you were dead. Do you know how hard it was for me to see your picture? When I realised that you left me and hadn't been taken? Did you know you were pregnant? Of course you did. You stole my son and left me." I wouldn't look at him and instead screwed my eyes shut. "Look at me, Anna."

I immediately opened my eyes and he narrowed his at me; glazed black eyes. "You ran. You told me you loved me, that you wanted a life with me. I trusted you and you broke my heart. If you wanted to come here, I would have brought you. A family, we could have been a family... but we still can. I can provide for you both."

"A family?" I echoed, my lip involuntarily curling again. "With you?" No. Stop. Think of the baby, don't. I quietened and smoothed my face to an expressionless mask worn by so many here.

"Just give me a chance. Enough with these games. We need to be together. Nikky loves me, the whole town loves me, I've proven that. They don't need to know about the past; this can be both our new starts." He was earnest, but I couldn't even entertain the idea.

The radio: they'd have theirs with them, if only I could

get to it. The purple set stared at me from the other side of the room. I didn't get the chance.

He led me upstairs, and the scab on the memory of my cell and my debasement rubbed away and I festered. Without so much as a complaint from me he had taken my baby and now held him with one arm and my hand with the other. In my bedroom he watched as I changed and fed him. I tried to cover myself, but he removed the blanket and instead focused his attentions on the two of us. He'd sobered up.

He shrugged off his lightweight jacket and pulled me close. I stared at the blank wall with his lips against my ear. Gripping my wrist he pulled my arm against my chest and his other hand rested on my brand, the ruined skin moulding to the shape of his palm, like it belonged.

"Go to sleep, Anna." It wasn't a request.

Closing my eyes before the tears escaped I stiffened as he breathed in my scent and planted a kiss on my shoulder.

"God, I've missed this. We're never going to be apart again, I promise."

WE HAD TO be free.

CHAPTER TWENTY-SEVEN

I DIDN'T SLEEP, and neither did Peter. Each time the baby woke to be fed I found him staring at me. Even in the darkness I could see and feel his eyes following me. He didn't try to talk to me, which unnerved me further.

It was five am when he left. Drawing me into an embrace, he tried to kiss me the way he kissed Anna. Not now. I forcefully jerked away. I didn't allow my surprise to show when he finally let go and left without a word or even a glance at the baby. It was light outside and I worried that someone would see him leave. Rubbing my now-bruised arms I watched him through the window. He held his head low and took a sharp left into the town and away from his house.

I knew what I needed to do.

Washing and dressing us both, I waited in the living room until Hayley and Glen returned home. All the while I could still smell him all over me. Touching me and possessing me. I'd scrubbed and scrubbed until my skin was a deep and angry red. The burning was an exquisite reminder that

I felt, that I was still alive. When Hayley and Glen returned I had bread baking and coffee percolating. She laughed, asking Glen to give her a few minutes and ran upstairs. Glen leaned against the worktop, staring at me.

"What's happened?"

I continued to wipe the same spot over and over and shook my head. "Nothing, just a rough night is all."

He didn't say anything more but removed his gun holster and left the weapon on the kitchen table and went up to Hayley.

Leaving it a few minutes I crept upstairs and into their bedroom, there were giggles and shrieks from the shower in their en-suite and I quickly searched through the top drawer of the bedside cabinet, grabbing the two clips, and crept back down again. I was light-headed, my blood was pounding in my ears, leaving me dizzy. My resolve started to trickle away but, looking across to the basket, my very reason for living reassured me with a light snore and a hiccup that I had to do this. We had to be free.

Lifting him into the pushchair, I left. I walked through the town, winding through the streets and stopping outside the vicarage. I almost stumbled as I hesitated. Rich was standing in the inner porch of the church wearing those designer jeans again, and he was deep in a heated conversation. I heard the voices rise and as he side-stepped a glimpse of Simon and Peter filled my vision. They were all armed – including Rich. Seeing the three of them so close spurred me on. I moved more quickly now, hiding my bag further under the blankets, tickling his covered feet as I did.

It was eight thirty a.m., and the library was open. Strolling in I glanced around and finally saw Nikky organising the worksheets for the day. Looking up, she grinned and rushed over for a hug, almost knocking me off my feet. When she leaned down to the pushchair I almost panicked but she just kissed his sleeping cheek and stood back up.

"So pleased you came back in. There's a load of new books for you." Glancing at my desk I estimated there was at least another hundred and nodded. "I'm taking the kids to the beach with Gloria this morning. We're meeting up with the fishermen and they're going to give a lecture on safety."

Alone, in here, with him.

"We should be back around ten. I'm meeting the kids down on the beach with their parents, so I'll see you shortly." Kissing my cheek and leaving her burning touch I went to speak, but she was already leaving. Sitting down, I pulled open my drawers and took out the book I had come for: *Middlemarch*. It needed to be finished.

"Anna."

My head snapped up. He was standing in the doorway, his dark silhouette accentuated by the sun streaming into the building from behind him. I'd recognise his profile anywhere, how could I not? As he strode over I straightened, but he stopped at the pushchair and glanced down. I forced myself not to panic.

"He looks so much like you now."

But he has your eyes, I thought.

"I'd like to talk again, like we did last night."

I nodded: anything to keep him away from the pushchair. He embraced me and I pushed back against him and tried to break free, but his touch was more a restraint than a caress. It brought the memories from before, when he was Will and I was Anna. Lifting up my top he touched the brand and laid his hand flat against the scar. I stilled.

"Let me go."

And, to my surprise, he did, he stepped back, a ghost of a smile on his face as he pulled up a chair and gestured for me to sit. I did, but the decision was mine and mine alone.

He told me then what happened. He was clearer today, the fog of alcohol burnt away.

"When I came to and you were gone. I thought someone had taken you. The pain was unbearable. I returned to the town and went to Olly, trading for searchers to look for you, for my mark. My every thought was for you, Anna. Only you."

He touched my knee and I scraped my chair back a little, shaking my head. He removed his hand, leaning forward and taking both of my hands in his instead.

"I drove myself crazy thinking about you and where you might be. Who might have you. Olly sent messages across the network to the Enforcers ensuring you weren't in any of the town whorehouses. Fuck, the thought of you in there…" he trailed off, shaking his head. "It kills me even now to think of anyone touching you."

I swallowed down my vitriolic reply. Not now. The silhouette of the pushchair in the corner of my eye was the visual reminder and grounding I needed.

"Simon, he helped me look for you, with the Enforcer

network down here and his contacts up north. Months of looking everywhere for a woman named Anna who matched your description. I should have realised, shouldn't I?" He searched my eyes, still shaking his head as he glanced over at my baby. "Your mark. He saw it and knew then. I came immediately."

"My mark..." I repeated.

"You have no idea how hard it was seeing you after thinking you were dead, or worse, with someone else."

All the while he held my hands in his, his placatory stroking gesture infuriating me. I didn't resist, though I wanted to. I wanted to hear two words, that was all, but if he said them I knew I would still take this path and be forever damned. Damned, was that right? Haunted perhaps, the way the boy from the field haunted me.

His voice was still soft and his gaze intense. My tooth throbbed and shoulder ached. "Say something, Anna."

I was doing this for me, for my baby, and for every person who had ever had their liberty stolen away by another human being who believed it their right.

"Morning Katie." Tom strolled up, his thin figure moving stiffly. He saw the swift movement as Peter withdrew his hands and sat back. "Am I interrupting?"

"No."

"Yes."

We spoke at the same time, my voice firm as I shook my head and Peter's level and cold. He looked over at the older man. Tom dithered at the side of my desk. As I readjusted my top, I caught him staring at the bruises on the tops of my arms.

"Katie, can I have a word?" He jerked his head to the door. I stood by the side of the pushchair and he moved in close. "Yer ok?"

"Fine."

"Yer sure?"

"I'm good. I'll come and see you later. It's probably best if you leave." I searched his eyes with mine but before he could reply, Peter clamped a hand on his shoulder and spun him around.

"Tom, isn't it? Good to meet you, but we're busy here. I'm an old friend of Kate's, we're just catching up."

"Old friends?" Tom coughed repeatedly, bending over and gasping for breath, eventually recovering and standing upright. "Katie's not mentioned you before."

Just go Tom, please, just go, you'll ruin everything.

"Tom, just go." I escorted him to the door and smiled brightly. "I'm fine."

He turned to speak to me once more, but I sensed Peter standing behind me.

"I'm Anna," I murmured, almost too quietly to hear. But I hoped Tom did hear; I wanted him to know, wanted someone to know, just in case.

WHEN THE CHILDREN returned I was exhausted, it took all my energy to assuage the rage and hatred I had towards him. When Nikky saw us talking she grinned and gave me the thumbs up in excitement. I stayed for a short while longer until he started to teach. I told Nikky I was going home to change the baby and that I would be back. He was watching, but I spoke loudly enough for him to hear. He caught my eye and I nodded once. I hoped it would work.

IT WAS DONE.

I CRIED UNCONTROLLABLY as I tucked him in his blankets and kissed his forehead, my tears dampening his head and hair. *I love you so much, so much my darling.* Writing out the note for Hayley I finally said what I needed to say. I didn't tell her everything involving Peter, but I told her the truth of the Unlands and what happens to those that are weak, and that I left in the hope to clear my head and heart of the demons of the past. I hinted heavily that I would be in the nearby woods looking for peace and that I would return. I hoped she'd understand. My backpack was heavy and cumbersome; I'd forgotten just how much it weighed. I'd grown soft and weak in the town, and there was no room for weakness now.

I made my way to the church and placed his note through the letterbox. I hoped he would understand, that he would believe me. I needed him to believe me and though I was only now ready to admit it, I needed him.

THE BEACH AND paths were clear and, grabbing the radio, I paused at the door and glanced back at his sleeping form. Already the pain threatened to be too much to bear but it was better this way, safer. I was leaving him alone. I never thought I would love someone so much as I did him, he filled my every thought, he was my reason for living now, the reason why I hadn't ended my pain so long ago. It was for him that I did this. He deserved better, he wouldn't understand, even I didn't completely. A part of me – the rational part? – was screaming for me to turn around, tear up the notes and stay, to accept Peter and accept his deal to assure my baby's safety.

Reaching the rock pools I continued to walk along the sand, if I was caught now then it would all be over, but he couldn't be left alone. He needed protecting. I counted and switched the radio on.

"Glen?" There was a short pause.

"Kate?"

"Can you ask Hayley to go home, it's urgent. I'm sorry."

"What? What are you sorry for? Kate –"

"He's worth it, Glen. He's worth the fight."

I switched off the radio, threw it into the water and carried on walking. He would be fine, Hayley would look after him. Hayley loved him. The steps fell heavier then and I struggled to lift each leg: it was done. I pictured her returning and calling for me, seeing my note. She would cry, I knew that. She would call Glen, and he would be forced to look for me, *he* would force him to look for me.

Reaching the rocky barrier, I cut my hands on the sharp and slippery black expanse as I crawled and lost my footing more times than I cared to count as I climbed across. The red water rolled away and disappeared against the black glossy surface. I gripped the stone tightly and dangled down the other side, my chest pressed against the slimy stone and my legs flailing desperately, the weight of my bag pulling me like an anchor. As my grip gave way I fell and landed heavily on my back, pulling and tearing my shoulder. The old injury flared up, and my vision blurred in agony. Weeping, I rolled to my hands and knees, sagging as my shoulder refused to support my weight. Gritting my teeth and swearing I dragged myself up and continued. I couldn't stay here.

The further I walked, the rougher the ground became. The sand thinned and the golden beach was replaced by an expanse of stones. Looking behind I could no longer see the rocky barrier. It had been five hours now, my back ached and my chest was sore. A searing burn scorched my skin and it was as though a dozen hands tore at my insides. I'd cried yet again, stumbling through my tears and further away from my hope.

It was too hot. My skin was slick with sweat and the backpack rubbed against my hips and dug into my shoulders, chafing and painful. I reached the edge of the beach and struggled up a sharp incline, tugging at the tufts of long grass which peeked over the edge, and hauling my body steadily higher. It was so very green that I found myself standing and gazing around at the expanse, not considering the enemy, not paying attention. A field of daisies. I would spend hours sitting in the fields by my home with my MP3 player, making daisy chains and crowns trying to recapture my lost youth. Now, as I stared at the carpet of grass and the sprinkle of white flowers covering it I realised how much time I had wasted back then just doing nothing.

I needed to move, out of sight and as far from here as possible. Walking through the grass I watched three rabbits jump and scurry away in fear at my impending threat. I hadn't seen rabbits since he took me hunting. Here there were two small ones, babies possibly, and one larger and darker furred bunny chasing them to safety. The flashes of their white tails made me smile involuntarily, but it was short-lived. I shivered. The rich smell of the small copse called to me, but he would find me there in the sparse collection of diseased elm trees. There was no place to hide or run should I be seen. I stepped through the shaded areas and savoured the quietness. No water, no wind and no chatter to distract my mind. I loosened the backpack and leaned against the nearest tree.

I still couldn't find peace. He filled my every thought with his tiny face, those serious eyes, the smell of his skin. The churning and fluttering in my stomach was more than nerves and anxiety. I shouldn't have left, how could I have left him? Alone and vulnerable? Emotions flooded me and I slid to the ground, crying into my hands. Loud, too loud, my sobs shuddered through me, echoing through the quietness and cutting the calm. The birds scattered and I flinched as two flew past my face, their wings flapping against my hands. I forced myself to stop, but moans still escaped as my body recklessly found a way to release the pain. I needed to be silent. It took an age. Each time I thought I was spent, a fresh melange of feelings rose and none of them soothing. My jaw was sore and my shoulder more so, while the pain was mirrored by that of my back and breasts.

He was overdue a feed, he would be missing me. I nearly started to cry again, but instead of a sob I took a sharp breath as a whistle carried through the air. Scrambling to my feet I tightened the clip of the backpack around my waist and moved through the trees, gripping and pulling at the bark and using it for leverage. I moved quickly, not stopping and not thinking until I reached a single track road now overgrown with brambles and hedges. Pausing briefly I took the compass from the small front compartment of the pack and headed north, turning left and crouching as far in the undergrowth as I could as I jogged. The high pitched sound of the far-too human whistle drove me on.

It was dusk when I reached the outskirts of a larger wood and what appeared to be an abandoned golf course. Long patches of overgrown grass stippled the flat area. Why had it not grown equally? I was standing in what once was a cared for fairway and instead the ground dipped and peaked like a badly fitted carpet. Useless now. The sun set low in front of me and I stumbled down the sharp incline into the partially covered sand bunker, where I sat and huddled against the dug-out curve of the ground. I couldn't be seen from above, but I could be seen by anyone approaching from the front. The sand was filthy; seed casings from the trees overhead scratched at my skin, and I kicked and sifted the animal dung from my space. Removing the backpack I pulled myself up to the edge of the wood and snapped several large branches from the nearby trees – ensuring that the branches I took were spread equally from tree to tree. Dragging them over to the bunker I covered myself from those approaching from the south and sat with my eyes closed. Every sound carried in the stillness. The rustle of leaves in the cool wind and the sound of the wildlife were so enticing, but I knew better than to be lured and seduced into the darkness. He would be waiting: perhaps not here, but he was out there, of that I was sure.

He'd watched me for three days before capturing me. That small voice in the back of my head, the one that made no sense and speaks when not invited, whispered to me then: *make it four before he finds you.* It was a challenge of sorts and part of me revelled in it. But I wouldn't, couldn't, play the game of before. There was no tally to see who would win, there was him and there was me. He would not be underestimated again, not by me.

I slept badly. My body was now unused to the harshness of Unlands. Over two years of survival and learnt behaviour had been pushed aside and replaced with that luxury and caress of a bed. Waking often to the sharp stabbing reminder in my chest I cursed my lack of preparation and stretched my body along the sand, loosening the stiff, sore muscles. When I woke again the blackness of night had passed. Moving the branches, I saw the thin strip of red and copper haze of the sky: red sky in the morning, shepherd's warning. That was the saying wasn't it? What would the shepherd be warning me of today? Dragging the branches back into the wood and hiding them in the undergrowth I smoothed over the sand in the bunker and made my way across the golf course, walking towards the sun and watching as it crept slowly across the sky.

The early morning chill melted away with each passing minute and I found myself thinking of everyone I ever knew in an attempt to stave away the ache. The morning I had met Stephen crept to the forefront of my mind like the sun creeping to its zenith. I recalled the way he had introduced himself in the coffee shop with an ill-timed and badly executed joke. I had forced a polite laugh and tried to walk away but something had stopped me. Fate? Divine Intervention? Curiosity? Boredom? I don't know. I agreed to dinner after college. It was so unlike me, he was a stranger, older than I, with no sense of humour – well, none I had witnessed. Yet I was attracted to his smile and eyes. I cringe as I think back to how naive I was. That afternoon he picked me up in his red sports car and I was sold, he had the full package and I was eighteen and shallow: a fast car, great looks and he liked me, really liked me. Even as I remembered the way he kept glancing at me as we drove through the back roads with the roof down I couldn't help but smile. He was funnier that afternoon, his nerves disappeared and he oozed a confidence that I found strangely intoxicating. What was the phrase? *He rocked my world.* I was enchanted from that moment onwards. Now I walked away from the only other person I had loved with such intensity, with more intensity.

I had moved full circle, in trying to push my thoughts from my little hope I had instead found my way back. But some of the pain had abated and instead I was simply tired and empty.

The golf course covered miles and it was mid-morning by the time I reached the far side. In the large clubhouse-cum-convention centre I sifted through the kitchen cupboards; they were all bare, stripped to the carcass by those who had passed through a long time before. I found two unlabelled tins which had rolled under the massive stainless steel fryer. Opening one, I smiled at the irony: peaches. Forcing the slimy slices down my throat, I emptied the tin and moved on, tucking the other tin in my backpack.

CHAPTER TWENTY-EIGHT

WHILE I HAD been inside, the smell of the morning air had faded, and the damp of the grass had been dried by the sun. It was bright. I should have brought sunglasses. I left the door open to the building and gazed around. There was a lot I should have brought with me, but were any of those things really necessary? I had managed alone with far less than I carried now: adaptation was the key.

I soon realised I was walking without purpose or thought. The woods had thinned and my dark red tee shirt seemed so conspicuous against the green and brown background. I could have been seen for miles. I needed to speed up and move back into the dense greenery ahead. Was this a forest? How would I tell? Why these thoughts sprang into my mind I didn't know. It was uncomfortable out in the sun, and I wanted a breeze and some moisture to cool down and cleanse my skin.

A whistle, again. Another human voice? Was this a game? Was the whistler looking to tease me? Was there more than one? Would I be rounded up like a frightened rabbit and skinned?

I fumbled with the straps to my bag, tightening them as I ran; the constant bouncing of the backpack against my body irritating my already sore skin. I was so out of shape, the months of regular meals, of sitting around and socialising had made me soft and vulnerable. By the time I was under the cover of the trees I was sweating profusely and my knees were shaking: *get a grip, for fuck's sake*. I was angry now, again, angry at myself and the weakness I displayed. I wasn't incapable nor was I stupid and yet every noise, however small, made me jump and cringe. Pathetic. I had spent months away from him, months I could have spent working on these errant and unwanted emotions, but I hadn't, and now I was weak; inside and out.

It was dark, crouched low by the misshapen trunk of an oak tree. The bark was soft under my hands and I found myself stroking it absent-mindedly as I craned my neck and struggled to hear the whistle again. A soft green powdery mould coated my fingers, and I wiped my hands on my jeans.

Silence again. What was the noise? Who was it? I tried to think logically, but I simply had no idea as to who would be whistling. Unrelated? Could it be another wanderer perhaps? Someone who wanted the peace and tranquillity of the coast? Yes. It could be.

That's all it was. How many people had I seen wandering during my two years alone? It must have been over a hundred: I'd seen those with cheery faced and happy grins, those who whistled and sang. I never approached them – they were the most dangerous.

Soon I could only hear the sounds of a woodpigeon and for a small moment I was lost. The ground beneath my feet seemed to tilt and my vision blurred. With a blink the feeling disappeared and my clarity and vision returned. Swallowing, I breathed deeply and exhaled, stretching down and rolling my shoulders: fine, I was fine.

Courage is resistance to fear; that's something 'they' said, or was it something I had read? I couldn't remember. It was ridiculous repeating the phrase aloud while simultaneously trying to control my breathing and check my surroundings.

The woodpigeon called again and, moving out of the darkness of the forest towards the rays of light that cut into the green, I followed his calls deeper into the woodland. The more I touched the trees, the softer they became, there was no sun to warm and dry out the bark and ground. It was gentler here and the atmosphere was different to the open expanses. The further I walked, the quieter it became. Even the bird was silent now and I was conscious that every movement needed to be measured and controlled. It was odd, I was calmer alone and without supplies, without comfort or the blanket of safety that the town provided. Slipping off my backpack, I crouched under a huge blackthorn bush and swapped my red tee shirt for a dark black one.

Sitting back and hiding from sight I rubbed the damp soil between my fingers. The texture was so different from the sand to which I had grown accustomed. This was smooth and moulded to my skin; whereas the sand was gritty and everything I formed fell apart when touched.

It had been over twenty-four hours. I pictured him sleeping, being changed, fed, and then crying. If he was crying then Hayley wouldn't know that he liked to have a finger run along his nose to lull him to sleep. He would miss that. Before I had a chance to stop them, tears slid down my face, I was crying silently but I was crying nonetheless. I wanted to kiss his cheek, to inhale his smell and hold him against me, the warmth of his tiny body merging with mine. The disquieting sounds of the world meant nothing as I worked at capturing that memory, making it my goal, my purpose. It was then that I knew his name, and that made me cry harder as the totality of my desperation for him hit me. I continued to cry, ignoring the milk from my breasts as it leaked through my clothes.

IT SEEMED HOURS before I was in any state to move, and my already sore body was now stiff and tired. As I went to leave the crack of a branch and a cough stilled me. I shrank back under, pulling my legs close and using the dark green canvas of my bag to hide my jeans.

A pair of boots: black and scuffed, well-worn and travelled. They were large, a man's and yet the wearer walked lightly, leaving barely a mark on the ground as they moved. I fought the urge to fidget. I wanted to look at the face of the wanderer and run from him, but it was safer to remain silent and still.

Twenty-two. That's as far as I got before the boots

moved, stepping to the right and facing the bush. I held my breath. If he bent down he would see me, the branches stopped almost a foot from the ground. One – he didn't move, but I could see the dark green of his combats through the leaves. Two – I swallowed and panicked; it was too loud. Three – a rustle of something to the side of my head. A crawling sensation tickled in my hair and my heart started to thud. Four – the crawling moved closer to my ear, irritating my scalp. I had to move, brushing my head: a large, strange looking bug flew away, causing the slightest of noises. A cry caught in my throat. Five – the boots moved away and towards the centre of the forest.

I didn't stop counting for a long time and it was only the dampness chilling me which forced me to move. I crawled on my stomach, dead fallen leaves sticking to my skin as my tee shirt rode up. I stopped and counted. I could hear the woodpigeon again, but no whistling, no coughing. I pulled myself up and brushed away the debris and mud. My left side was wet and uncomfortable. Twigs fell from my hair as I ran my fingers through and retied my ponytail. Kneeling, I secured my backpack. I ran my hands over the tracks of the boots. If I stayed to the left and worked my way around then I shouldn't cross the path of the wanderer; unless he changed direction. The ground started to dip to the right, perhaps I should take the low ground? Follow the contour and valley away from the direction of the town? There would be more places to hide, the ridges and rocks would provide shelter.

He dragged me through a wood similar to this, chained like an animal, my back a huge scabbed wound. My feet a bleeding mess. I rubbed my wrist absently. There wasn't a breath of wind and it was as though I was standing at a great precipice with no one to pull me back.

I took the high ground. I wanted to look down, not up. A crackling of leaves and twigs made me stop and crouch, darting my eyes at the plants by the sharp edge down. A flash of black and white disappeared into the undergrowth – badger? I didn't like badgers, their sharp teeth and claws terrified me, and they fought with a vicious desperation when trapped. I remembered several infected scratches and cuts from two years before when I was less experienced at hunting. I recalled how he had set the trap the first night we had hunted together. Not a word spoken. I watched as he wound the wire and tied the snare, hiding it in the grass. It was quicker than my method of sitting and waiting for them to approach, and even his way of skinning was skilled. I realised how much I had learnt from him. I doubted that was his intention.

I walked for several miles, stopping often and checking the ground for tracks. Only small paw prints greeted me. I was able to see clearly now. The dry lit ground contrasted with the darker, moist patches; it was strange seeing the light and dark areas, like a melting chessboard. There were puddles of water in the dips. It hadn't rained overnight.

I thought about my parents and my brother, how I had screamed and shouted on the phone to them the day the army took Stephen: ungrateful, that's what they'd said. Ungrateful traitor. A disappointment. I'd not spoken to them since. When the towns were hit and those who survived started to band together I thought of going to them, asking for their forgiveness; but I always held back. As the gangs grew larger and the danger grew thicker, I regretted not trying to find them. It was only when I stood and watched one of the gangs ransack and loot the local nursing home near to me for supplies that I truly started to realise the desperation of what was going on. Now, walking along an overgrown track I pushed the memory of the violence that day to one side and batted the hundreds of tiny flies away from my face.

The puddles were becoming larger, they were small ponds. My skin was greasy and my throat sore from fatigue. I stopped and knelt, washing my face as best as I could, and the grime and sweat peeled away. Glancing down at the rippling water I grimaced at the face that stared back at me. I hated mirrors, hated seeing what I had become, a timid and watered down version of me. The same dark brown wavy hair, blue eyes, and high cheekbones; the discoloured scar to the corner of my eye was obvious, a thick line of tawny brown. I followed my frown line with my fingers and then wrote my name in the water, watching my distorted mirror image dissolve. I allowed myself a small moment of satisfaction then. The water had an invigorating effect – both on my body and mind.

I carried on. The track continued upwards, and to my left I could see down the side of the hill. The many shades and textures of green created a deceptively flat looking path, but it was only when I looked closer that I saw the gaps in the carpet and the drop below.

Stephen: I didn't miss him anymore. The thought stung

me like a horsefly. I thought of him often, how could I not? But I didn't miss him. I could barely recall his face now. I was angry at him, for he had left me; not when he should have, but when I needed him. Through the pain of the realisation came the understanding that yes, I had cheated, lied and hurt him: but he should never have slapped me. I deserved the pain that came with the strike, but not the violence. He wasn't perfect. We both made mistakes but I had always forgiven him and washed the perfume scented shirts without the slightest protest or comment. I never searched for an explanation through discussion. That was where I went wrong, wasn't it? Communication. I wasn't logical, but I didn't care.

I tripped over a root, jarring my right ankle, forcing me to pull my thoughts back to the here and now. My steady pace meant I was at least ten miles from the golf course and close to the centre of the forest.

The slight twinge of pain when walking slowed me down, but I still managed a few miles before nightfall. I was on higher ground now. It was cooler. The air seemed moist and kissed my skin; it spurred me forward. I still thought of Stephen, but no longer did the melancholia of longing swamp me down, instead it was the icy awareness and understanding that I had grown apart from him accompanying me. It took until nightfall to walk off the anger and upset; but it was odd – with each step I left him behind and strength returned. This was achievable, more than a dream, more than a whim, I could escape this prison. I was flying higher and higher away from the confines of what my captor had created. I could be free.

The euphoria remained as I climbed a nearby tree and sat high in the branches and stared out as far as I could see. On my way up, my feet slipped from the gnarls and knots in the wood often, but I found my footholds and remembered how I first learnt to climb a tree in my gran's orchard as a child. The wide apple trees were perfect and I would hide in the trees all day, pretending to be a fairy hiding from the monsters. Steadily I pulled myself up, clambering onto the thick branches and ignoring the darker, almost black rotten wood. The sun was setting now and I could just about make out the sea through the mist and clouds. It was beautiful and calming.

I love you, Stephen. I just don't need you.

Long after the sun set I remained on the branch, my legs dangling down. I was at least twenty feet from the ground. I used to suffer with terrible vertigo, it jumped on me one day in my early twenties and stayed with me until I entered the Unlands alone: being forced to look after myself meant I had to tackle so many of my fears. Now I could hold spiders and climb twenty-foot trees: in some ways desperation had been liberating.

Still swinging my legs, I removed my backpack and took out the rope, tying the pack to the trunk and then to me. It was warmer in the trees with the shelter from the wind. There was no sign of movement anywhere but I could hear the forest nightlife. The rustling of leaves on the ground, and the high pitched clicking of insects, the calls of the birds, all surrounded me. I could hear more at night than I could during the day. I stretched my legs along the length of the branch and tightened the rope around my waist, using the excess around my thighs. I can't remember where I learnt this, a book, a television show, it didn't matter. It was habit now, a good one. Leaning against my bag, I closed my eyes and listened, allowing myself to think of nothing but the darkness.

"Will, this is ridiculous. Come back to the town. She won't leave the baby for long, she'll be back."

Simon. I opened my eyes. I had dozed off and not heard him approach. But now, now I could hear the material of his jacket rubbing, the scraping of his bag, and the heavy steps. I didn't move: if I could hear him, he could hear me. I stared up at the clear sky and the constellations. I couldn't name them, I couldn't concentrate. I wanted to hide. It was strange, but I was desperate to hear his voice.

"Will, are you listening? Jesus Christ. C'mon, forget it. Forget her. You've got your son."

He muttered, but I couldn't make out what he said, I wanted to look down, but I forced myself to remain still.

"Look, I'm going back to the town, it's been nearly two days. She'll come back. I'll shut Glen up and have Deven look after the baby, Glen can't protect him forever."

There was a silence, stretching across the distance between us and bouncing back again. I got my wish.

"I know her. She's in here."

I knew it, I knew he'd come. How could he not? His obsession ran too deep. There was small triumph in my mind, but it was smothered with paralysing terror. His soft tone still unnerved me, my fingers and legs cold and liquid. I could be free. I needed to remember that.

"She could be anywhere, this place is huge. Trust me,

she won't leave the baby for long." Simon sighed and then chuckled. "I don't think I've congratulated you, he's a good looking lad."

I didn't hear his reply, but they both laughed. I dug my nails into my palms. They would be armed, I couldn't do a thing. There was his voice again, deep and low as he murmured to Simon. Again I couldn't hear what he said.

"All right, that makes sense. I'll see you soon. I've got a crew looking for her back on the route she first took to the town. Dave, Morgan and Rees have fanned out on the other route. I'll keep them looking for as long as I can, but soon the council will ask where they are. I can't juggle this for long. I can't keep Rich locked up for long. Too many questions and problems. You owe me," replied Simon. "He did a good fucking job on your eye, that's for sure."

"He packs a decent punch. It causes a fucking problem I didn't anticipate. We need to find out who else she told and deal with it. If we don't, I'll have to leave with her and the baby, which isn't fucking ideal. No, this makes us even. You'd have nothing if it wasn't for me. Don't forget that, Sergeant." A hint of a friendly warning and then: "I'll be back with her. She knows I can give her what she wants, she fucking loves it." Followed by a laugh from them both.

"Good hunting."

Then there was silence again. There was no wind and yet that scent called up to me, and my nostrils flared in protest. One pair of boots walked away. The other person remained; I couldn't hear him, not a sound came; but he was there. I knew how quiet he could be when he waited for his prey.

What if he stays here? Till morning? He'll see me then.

I couldn't allow the panic to take over my senses, so I concentrated on my baby: I was doing this for him. The insects clicked and the ground still rustled, but he made no noise. I imagined him standing at the bottom of my tree, staring up at me. If I looked down would I see those dark eyes and darker smile? The black gave way to grey and I struggled to keep my dread in check. It would soon be light. I allowed myself to think. What were the chances of him finding me here? How had he known to go high and not low? To stop at this tree, here in this forest? Could it be fate again? That concept of predetermined events I didn't believe in? If fate was a possibility then this meant that everything I did was for nothing, I would be unable to change the course of what would happen. I should embrace it.

It was light now, so quickly did the sun rise in the summer. I slowly undid the rope from my legs and waist and twisted myself around, looking down to the ground. Nothing but dirt, leaves and plants. He was gone. I exhaled and massaged my stomach. Undoing the top button to my jeans I rubbed harder, and the pressure on my bladder eased. My spine, however, protested. Hours of sitting in the same position, tense and unable to relax, caused my muscles to spasm and a bolt of pain travelled from my back, down my backside and my right leg. I moaned and then pressed my lips shut. He could be nearby. I counted, one hundred and thirty-eight and then looked down: it was clear. With my bag secure I climbed down the tree and hit the ground softly, controlled and measured. He was around now. I was the rabbit, he was the hunter. I doubled back and, as I relieved myself, I decided to go wide, to find the edge of the forest to the west and follow the tree line around.

Walking on I remained alert, checking for tracks and signs that he had passed through, but there was nothing. The outskirts of the forest was a good choice, thick and overgrown with ferns, bushes and flowers. I was able to see both across the fields and back into the forest. There was no sign of him.

CHAPTER TWENTY-NINE

I STRUGGLED WITH the path and terrain several miles further along. I should have researched the forest, the layout and places to avoid. The ground was no longer soft and accommodating, and it crumbled as I gripped at the weeds I used for leverage. This was stupid. After sliding again and grazing my palms I sat with my head in my hands and swore repeatedly. I'd have to double back again and find another way around, the drop down to the fields was too high now and I didn't know if the land would reconnect with the trees. Too exposed, too obvious. Idiot. I couldn't stop. Reluctantly I stood and jogged down the path. Was this even a path? I wasn't so sure now, how could it be? I shuffled, moving to my backside as it dropped at both sides; what the fuck was I thinking?

I wasn't. That was the problem, I'd been too distracted with the painful longing for my baby. Several hours later and only half a mile or so along I found a way into the forest: there was a short drop into a tall collection of ferns, ten feet or so to the forest floor. I pulled off my backpack and threw it down. It landed with a thud; okay, more like fifteen or twenty feet. Twisting, I lowered my body down, grabbing the exposed roots of a bush and dangling. My breathing had quickened. The ledge cut into my chest. Pain. Gritting my teeth, I let go and fell. Hitting the ground hard, my head smacked off the mud and a heavy thud rattled me. I didn't move. *Hammer to the skull*: even that didn't describe what I felt.

Several minutes passed before the coldness wore off and I could move. Sitting up I rubbed the back of my head, no wetness – that was a positive. But as I ran my hands over my scalp I winced at the large spongy lump.

I wished I had painkillers. I remembered his fingers pushing the paracetamol in my mouth and my ribs flared up in sympathy and anger. I crawled to my knees and stood, my back spasming again. I ignored it though and hauled my pack on, my right leg buckling as the small of my back throbbed and the pain shot back down my leg. Shoulder, leg, back, head.

I MISSED THE first smattering of raindrops as I struggled with the weight of my pack and the aches of my muscles and scrapes as I slid down the makeshift paths. I couldn't concentrate, memories of my grandfather swirled to the forefront of my thoughts. He had trained as an air force pilot. He never saw the conflict, though he often said aloud to us that he wished he had. He longed to fight for freedom.

It was only when we were alone that he would pull me

onto his knee and whisper the truth. *'I'm glad I never had to fight. I was scared and I didn't want to leave your grandmother, but don't tell anyone, promise?'* I had promised. It was our secret.

The clouds embraced and a deep rumble rolled through the sky, followed in quick succession by the splitting crack of lightening and flash of white.

He spoke often of his time in service and the beauty of places he visited.

'Get out of here when you're old enough. Don't stay, go and get lost somewhere.' He made me promise to live my life, to never settle for second best.

I WAS SOAKED now. The rain was relentless. Rivulets of water chased down my arms and splashed on the floor, disappearing into the puddles and waterways that welled upwards. Rumble, one, two, three, four, five, crack. Swollen seeds, uncurled leaves floated and spun. Only the sound of the sky could be heard. It deafened yet thrilled me.

The wind lanced through the air. The grass bent. The trees twisted and curled, branches stooping low. The smell of smoke chased the wind, riding on the tails of its power. I stumbled over an exposed root, losing my footing.

Down, the side of the ravine raced to greet me, or I it. My hip and ribs were rattling as the falling stones ground against them. There was a blur of browns and greens. My hands clutched at the murky emptiness. I was falling. I was out of control. *I love you, you are my hope.* Leaves hit my face; the spray of water stung my skin as the smell of honeysuckle engulfed me. I ripped the bush from the ground, the roots giving in to the pull of my desperation and the soft earth. With a crash I stopped: a rotten tree trunk. Curling in the shade of the fallen tree I clutched my sides and breathed, greedily drinking in the air and soothing my raw throat. My hands were almost black, my nails broken to the quick and bleeding. Grit covered my face, I could taste the green, the browns and blacks of the forest.

The flaking bark fell like snowflakes on my jeans and top as I pressed my back tighter against the tree. My ankle too sore for me to walk, or move, I would have to wait. Back, shoulder, side, head, ankle, pain flared throughout. Minutes passed, the storm howled through the forest, hunting for something, someone. Rumble, one, two, three, crack. Wriggling free from my pack I glided it along the mud and under my head. The aroma of salt, fish and wood filled my nostrils. Closing my eyes I caught the scent of baby powder and pressed my face into the tightly woven material and breathed in again. It was gone.

It had changed. Sitting up, the wind had calmed, the rain thinned. Huge droplets splattered lazily on my skin. Rotating my ankle and satisfied it no longer throbbed and only ached I stood and shrugged the pack onto my back. My top was stuck to my skin and I longed for a hot shower. There was a silence that unnerved me. The symphony of the storm had quietened and now came the rests. I was sure there was more to come and I needed shelter before nightfall. It was time to move.

Looking up, I could see the crumbled path I had walked along high above. The winding root of the closest tree was exposed from the side. It was thick and gnarled. Turning, I pulled out the compass and headed west. I needed to get far away. Inland and away from the community. My boots sunk in the mud and with each step the resistance grew, begging me into the ground. I grimaced as my thighs protested at the exercise. I was so out of shape, stupid, so very stupid. I should have prepared better. For him though, I did this for him. The pain was back, deep and merciless. I had to leave him. Freedom: he deserved an unshackled life, and so did I. *I deserved it.* It sat uncomfortably within me, as though I was reciting the words and trying to convince myself I was worthy. But I was, wasn't I?

The rain was back. It answered me and the hunt was on once again. At first a light shower poured from the sky and released the damp smell from the nooks and crannies of the earth. Licking my lips I tilted my head back and drank: warm, dusty and smelling of strange chemicals. Unnatural. Rumble, one, crack. Rolling my shoulders and neck I pushed forward through shrubs and foliage I couldn't name, sliding in the deep tracks that pooled with water, snaking their way to the well-worn and forgotten road. I was sure I was lost. Shaking and numb I stopped.

Lovers curled around one another. Their heads bowed and touching, lips so close, eyes stared at one another, lost in dreams and forgotten promises. Arms splayed, legs like a marionette's. Eyes full of blame and hurt: yet all empty. My dreams burnt away in the rain, replaced with smiling families cold and drained. No laughter or life. Brown.

Yellow. Green. Grey. Slick. I turned and slipped in the wet ground, falling backwards into their embrace. Crawling now, the mud oozed through my fingers and my knees and shins rubbed against the hard and unrelenting bodies of the bloodless. Of fathers and mothers. Sisters and brothers. A welter of faces and more than I could count. A welt on the face. I paused and stared, a corrosive burn in my throat, moving inwards and deeper. She stared back and the stretched and split skin moved to accuse me as the earth moved around her. The smell, earth and mould, decay that lingers. Smoke and blood. I cannot forget this. Dreams are drained and yet I still moved. Surrounded, I was trapped and would never escape, never be free.

For a fleeting moment I thought this to be a massacre of the war, or perhaps a final resting place for those who had suffered a plague; but the barely sunken-eyes, the cool skin and recognisable red patched jacket of Neil Proctor told me this was the community's closet, and the place where they hide their skeletons. *Scrupulously just,* words on the wind, but it was an echo, just an echo. *How a community deals with its enemies.* Blind with ignorance I stumbled here as I had there. I allowed this to happen.

Another downpour, water rose, pulling us closer. The man at my side, he helped, and so I followed his outstretched white hand and grabbed the root that reached down to me. Pulling, I dug my cupped hand into the perfectly straight wall, but it fell away and a sob escaped as I landed face down on my guide who slept silently in the gloom, never to speak or be spoken to again. *Hope, my hope, I did this for you. I'm sorry.* Closing my eyes, I rolled to my side, and the smell of long forgotten sin lingered in the air between us. *I am everyone here and yet I cannot stay.* Opening my eyes, the rigid trees stand to attention.

The dark gloom of the sky continued to fall. I then saw the first bird of the afternoon. A black crow sitting on the branch of the oak tree. Dark eyes full of life stared back at me. Dark eyes. The mud, the grey, brown, white chalky earth had consumed me. My skin couldn't breathe and yet I continued to move in the rising water. My hands lost in the pool. *I'm sorry, I'm sorry.* To each of the fallen I apologised as I clambered and disrupted their rest. The touch of a hand, the feel of hair and unnaturally warmed and wet skin. *I'm sorry.* I didn't look for long, fearful that I would recognise one or worse, more, of those I clambered over. The crow watched, I could feel his stare. Judging from high, looking down, anticipating.

As I rose, standing on the shoulders of one who had fallen, I was carried high and could see through the rain and into the trees. Throwing my pack and reaching up I dug my hands into the ground and my toes into the wall of the grave. I whispered a final apology and, closing my eyes, I pulled my body from the despair. The mud slipped across my stomach and arms, and my wrists ached. I couldn't let go. Willing myself forward I stabbed my left foot higher up the barricade, twisting and turning. The mud gave way and my shoulder jarred. I stabbed again. Deeper. I ignored the tears that ran down my face and mixed with the rain. I ignored the taste of smoke, of ash, of mud, of lies and death that crawled around my mouth. The water continued to fall, *forgive me,* each drop washing a little more away. I was clean and yet the grey-brown soil enveloping my skin was still my shroud. I heaved again, stabbing the wall and thinking of those I had left behind, those I had left when they needed me. My family, Stephen, the man and his family, the women from the town, the boy in the field, of Kat and her scowl, of Ben and Ella. I dug deeper, my cheek now resting on the ledge of the grave. The lovers: they continued to stare at one another, grimly gay, their faces slowly disappearing into the swirl of grey. With one final pull I broke free and stared at the sky from the safety of the forest floor.

The crow hadn't moved, but as I turned my head and watched him, our eyes connecting, he called out and rose from the branch, flying free and away from the death. Away from me. I was alive. The old lie: *it is sweet and right.*

CHAPTER THIRTY

I STOOD AT the doorway of the small information hut, leaning against the wood and watching the sky. By the time I had summoned enough energy to move from the graveside it was dark, and yet, I had stumbled through the black and shades of grey to the open arms of the woodland and eventually, my shelter.

Pinks and reds swam across the canvas of the sky. The storm had broken and a ray of light pierced through the clouds, hitting the ground and creating a dazzle of blues and whites. The chirps and tweets of life called out – the scurrying along the floor, the cries from the skies. Each sound bright and crisp. Rubbing my arms the dried mud curled and scabbed away. I changed my clothes and dragged a brush through my knotted and caked hair. With each stroke, death and smoke were released. When I finished, the sun had broken through the red haze and burnt the morning warning away. I needed to keep moving.

I walked back to the grave and left my filthy clothes at the side, it was closer than I thought, perhaps four hundred metres from the hut and I stood far from the side, not needing to look in again. Scanning the area, a well-worn gravel path led to the main asphalt covered road.

The weather had slowed me down; yesterday I had covered just five miles. I didn't want to go too far from the settlement, and needed to make my presence known to him. He could be anywhere, close, perhaps even watching. It was a curious feeling. The all-consuming fear no longer stilled me and instead a flutter of eagerness and relief tickled me. I was tired, and filthy.

Months of cleanliness, of civilisation washed away in one night. Civilisation. I thought then of the horrors I had seen, that I had been a part of. The Proctors. Did the whole town know? Was this the price to be paid for peace? I had so many questions but hunger and thirst overruled my conscience and instead I dragged my feet along the road. I hadn't removed my boots during the night and my feet were still damp and sore. If I took them off now, I wouldn't be able to put them back on. I had blisters, I was sure. That biting sting mid-heel was too ripe to ignore, but I had to try.

With my compass in my hand and a head full of thoughts, I walked past the layby and continued along the road. Something forced me to stop, and turning, I walked back. A dark green and deliberately hidden car was partially covered with broken branches. Automatically I moved to the treeline and hid. I sat for a long time. Still and waiting, but it was just the forest. Opening the driver's door, the smell of well cared for leather and polish greeted me as I climbed into the seat. The backseats were empty, but in the foot well of the passenger's side there was a small grey bag. As I opened it, a mobile battery pack and radio lay cushioned in a case with a map of the area. Switching it on I recognised the frequency and channel: the town. The static hummed, and I crawled through the car checking for supplies, or better, keys. No voices, just silence. Checking under the car mats, in the visors, door cards, and chair pockets I searched for the keys, but there was nothing. Eventually I remembered: the front right wheel. My chest filled with relief as I found them there and, as I turned the key in the ignition, I thanked Deven for letting me know where they all kept their keys.

As the needle rose I grinned. Nearly a full tank, and with a car this size I could cover good distance if needed. Manoeuvring out of the layby I navigated with the small built-in dash compass and continued west. The radio still crackled and driving along the road I opened the window. The diesel engine knocked and chugged and that nagging fear was back. Too loud. Even the tyres spraying through surface water sounded like a roar.

Trees, trees, more trees, the countryside blurred as I drove through the forest. Pockets of water stippled the ground and twice I struggled with the steep inclines as the asphalt road changed to mud and gravel. As I shifted down a gear, a voice cut across the radio:

"Team two to control, negative on quadrant alpha three. Moving to four."

I couldn't stop. I needed the momentum. But I wanted to listen, to see what was negative, what they were looking for. Through the static I struggled to recognise the voice.

"*Control received. Believed that subject may be as far as quadrant charlie fourteen.*"

Was that Simon? I couldn't tell. It sounded like him, but also a little like Rich, or even Glen. Gripping the wheel tighter with my right hand I turned the radio up.

"*Team one to control, just checking in, negative up to quadrant charlie seven, moving westward and remaining in quadrants bravo and charlie.*"

That was him, of that I was sure. Sure and confident.

"*Roger that team one, further supplies have been dropped off at charlie twelve.*"

They continued to discuss quadrants. There were six teams out looking. I presumed they looked for me and I guessed there was no escape, no mercy for me. I had turned my back on Simon's caution, he wouldn't let me return unscathed. He had said as much. I could remember the smile when he warned me in the library. I didn't know how Simon and Will knew each other, but their bond ran deeper than camaraderie: they had shared something. Perhaps I would be able to walk back through the gates unmolested if I just stopped now and returned with him and forgot everything I had seen. Perhaps I *should* return with them and show them both that he didn't own me. That I was a free person; but it was an impossibility, there was no scenario I could think of where he didn't win and possess us both. My body reacted then, an involuntary sound escaped my lips as it protested at the thought and I allowed the grimace to remain on my face as I listened to the last of the radio chatter die away. *Quadrants, numbers, letters.*

Pulling over I unfolded the map and followed the hand-drawn grids. It looked as though a net had been cast across the paper and the curved lines were divided into sectors. I found my location and then his. He was close. He would be at the grave soon and he would see the car was gone. I needed to pause and give him time to realise. *Never underestimate your enemy.*

And so I switched off the engine and waited, he needed time to catch up with me, I wasn't thinking this through.

"Team one to control. I've found signs of the subject, and vehicle four is gone. Is it scheduled for service or in use?" My heart almost stopped as I waited for the reply. It was silent for nineteen seconds.

"Negative team one. Vehicle four should be in situ. Wait there. Wheels being brought to your location."

Time to move. I jumped out the vehicle. He would find it and follow me. I was sure. The aches from the day before tormented me and I smelt of stale sweat and sour milk.

I had to leave him. I would leave him if I had to get him food; I would leave him if I had to get some medicine which would save him; I would leave him to ensure his life. I must leave him to ensure he had the right life, to ensure he didn't become *him.*

In a fit of desperation I picked up the radio and spoke: "Are you there, Will?"

My only reply was static. I don't know if I expected him to reply, or even if he was listening and his radio was on, if he replied, I didn't know what I would say. Would I taunt him or simply give him my location? There was nothing. One hundred.

"I'm heading back to the grave."

Clipping the radio to my jeans I emptied the car of anything of use and circled the nearby woods on the map. Shaking, I left the map under the windscreen wiper and set off down the road with my pack.

I CAME ACROSS a small travelling community. The small collection of vans, caravans and large vehicles encased with portable metal fencing and solar lights protected their perimeter, and even across the field I could hear the laughter of children and the murmurs of conversation and music. During my time in the Unlands I'd seen several communities like this one and always kept my distance, declining their warm welcomes and encouragements to dine and travel with them. Right now, I surprised myself, for I yearned for company and strength in numbers, for rest and easy conversation and laughter, but it would be fucking stupid to stop and so with reluctance I kept moving.

The radio remained silent. What was I doing? He could have taken any number of roads, any number of turns. There were miles and miles of countryside between us.

It was already mid-afternoon, and I remembered something Will told me months before, when he kept me chained to the wall in his cell. *I'm a patient man.* That's what he had said. Every time he wore down my defences he had done so in a precise and calculated way. He had planned each move and I had reacted just the way he had anticipated. Except the night he first raped me.

Walking away from the traveller site and the possibility of refuge, I turned the radio down at my hip and stamped the mud from my boots on the tarmac. While it was warm, there was a cool chill in the air that left me feverish. The flaking picket fence that ran along the side of the country road looked sad. The brown of the paint and silver of the wood resembled a disease and stretched as far as I could see. A cracked and toppled telephone pylon seemed to balance precariously in the middle of the field while two horses grazed lazily between the slack thick cables. I hadn't seen a horse for months. I watched them flick their tails and twitch their ears with casual confidence. The large farmhouse was nothing more than a pile of ruined rubble and charred wood, but a tiny brick house stood alone just forty or so metres away. I sat behind the hawthorn bush and continued to watch them while picking and nibbling at the berries. The grass was damp and sweet-smelling; within minutes my backside was cold and wet. Closing my eyes, I listened and tried to block out the bitter aftertaste that assaulted my mouth. In the distance I could hear the familiar beat of music and the odd note. I was at least a mile from the travellers. There were so few people left and yet I was so surrounded.

A flash of blue to my right made me turn as the front door of the old farm worker's house opened. An elderly lady walked out with a young man – her grandson, perhaps? She watered the immaculate hanging baskets that framed her front door while he stood scanning the road with his shotgun in his hands. She struggled to raise the can, and with his other hand he reached up for her.

She patted his arm. With a final cursory glance he looked around and escorted her back inside with tender love, closing the door.

I needed to keep moving. If this was to end then I had to keep going. It was a little too late for apologies and mistakes. The walls that I had built came tumbling down, and I didn't have a choice. It was a risk, but one worth taking. Taking the long way around and avoiding the rectory I waded through the soggy field to the woods that curved along the roadside. It was dark and musty as I stepped under the canopy. Within moments my boots were caked in mud once more and it was cold. I tried the radio frequencies again and hearing nothing I switched the machine off and packed it away. I didn't need the distraction; it would slow me down to be regularly checking the airwaves for a voice and a sign that I wasn't alone.

I strode further back into the woodland. Bright berries and vines twisted around the trunks of the trees like a strangling snake. Yew berries. Poisonous. There were so many, they had overrun and smothered the other plants. I continued to walk and the further I went, the more hostile was the terrain. The land was guiding me to the grave and I couldn't deny it. As the trees became denser and thicker, I climbed up an oak and scanned the horizon. My attention was caught by the sudden bolting of a Muntjac. I almost slipped from the branch. It was him. He stood there at the edge of the clearing in his black lightweight jacket and his cargo trousers; he looked at home in the forest. Could he see me? I gauged that I was about a hundred feet away, but if he was to look up to his right, then he might just see my blue jeans.

He didn't though; he sat by the side of a fallen tree, removing his bag and hunting knife. The blade glinted in the sun and I watched as he deftly created a snare loop. His fingers moved quickly and all the while he gazed around, assessing his surroundings. I didn't move. I couldn't tear my eyes away. I had no way of approaching him without being seen, I would have to wait.

Staking the snare, he backed away from the trap and waited. My backside was numb and my legs tingled, but I didn't want to move.

It was close to an hour before anything happened. Then I watched as a rabbit became tangled and he strode over and killed it, attaching it to his bag and sitting down again. He massaged his right thigh and I noticed the way his body tensed and his shoulders rose as he did. After he stopped he spent over ten minutes with his head in his hands before setting off into the forest. As he disappeared I moved quickly and hit the floor with a thud. I couldn't lose him now. Running lightly, I followed his tracks and slowed as I reached the area where I lost sight of him and swivelled the bag around, taking out my own weapon and tucking it into the back of my trousers.

As I knelt and touched the indentations in the mud, I craned my neck and kept a look out, tuning out the whistling of the birds and the whisper of the leaves. I needed to concentrate on the abnormal sounds, human sounds. He'd headed this way, but then turned and walked back again. I slowly continued through the undergrowth, crouching and moving in the shadows of the trees. There was a flash of black ahead and I caught my breath. But I followed slowly, stretching and stepping in the shadows. The wind came from behind, cooling my back and neck. He stopped and I darted into the shade of the tall goosegrass. Fifteen feet ahead, that was nothing. Shit, if he turned around he would find me. Not here, this wasn't right. I shrank further back and waited, and through the gaps I saw him look around, frowning. I itched to step out and see the expression of surprise on his face: but not here. He moved and I increased the distance between us by another ten feet. I watched the rabbit swing limply from his bag.

The adrenalin was tiring; it flooded my being and controlled my body. I followed him instinctively, matching his pace and step, pausing when he paused, quickening when he quickened.

Later, from a tree high above I watched as he lit a fire and skinned the rabbit. He worked in silence. Of course.

I DIDN'T SLEEP. I concentrated on him and every movement he made. He ate the rabbit; the smell of the tender meat made me salivate, but I couldn't open a tin, not here, and I ignored my stomach. As he stamped out the flames and leant against my tree, pulling his hood down over his face, I smiled. The smile spread across my face and I found myself laughing hysterically inside. He had no idea, absolutely none. I could finish it here. Right now. He wouldn't know it was coming. But no, I wanted him to see me and see what I could do. *I win, your turn.*

My eyelids grew heavy. The long hours dragged and I struggled to remain awake, pinching my arm every so often. I rubbed away the stiffness of my head and neck, and kept my gaze on him at the bottom of my tree. Moving my hands to my chest, the heat and tightness had dissipated and I was healing; adapting.

When I had first heard of the gangs forming after the east fell, I was told not to worry, that this was part of the change, it had to change, and people would adapt to the new governments, the new regimes: that's what 'they' said. Those wanting to survive became susceptible to the new laws and ideals put forward by radicals and zealots, the violent and the politicians. I viewed it as desperation, but I was as bad as the others, I kept my head low and my thoughts private. We all did. That was how we adapted, and this was now the price we paid.

CHAPTER THIRTY-ONE

HE WOKE BEFORE the sun rose. I didn't realise he was conscious until he pushed back his hood and stood up. I froze, my hand still tying my ponytail and my legs dangling down. If he did look up then all he would have to do was wait. He didn't though; he leant against the tree with one hand and relieved himself. Looking down, the start of grey licked the sides of his dark hair. His hands were just as I remembered. I imagined those calloused fingers touching me, but now, seeing his fingers splayed against the bark, the faint scars were accentuated by the early morning light and his skin appeared paper thin.

His eye was swollen shut. Purple and black bruising ballooned across the socket and crept along his nose. My heart fluttered as I pictured Rich and his fury. I was grateful he had stopped, that I hadn't been robbed of my revenge.

He removed his jacket and tee shirt. His shoulders and chest made me shiver. His back and the planes of his muscles moved as he soaked a flannel and cleaned himself with small circular motions. As he removed his trousers, the new red and purple scar on his right thigh grinned at me, like a mutilated smile, angry and thick like rope against the pale white skin. He turned slightly and the dark line of hair to his groin made me heave. He adjusted himself and I looked away. I waited until he started to walk before looking again.

I hid in the bushes, undid my jeans and ate the cold beans, throwing over half the tin away and then snatched a handful of sea buckthorn berries, nibbling on them to freshen my mouth. Refastening my bag, I winced as it rubbed my hips, the stinging sharp and deep. I hesitated before running my hands to the small of my back and massaging the tightened muscles. His brand was cold, flattening my palms. I pressed and moved my hands along the scar and traced the outline before stumbling and vomiting up the beans and berries. The lumps, bitter and caustic, blocking my throat and making me gag. I wished I hadn't touched it, especially now when I needed to focus: instead I pictured the knife in his hand and the heat of the blade slicing into me.

Wiping my mouth, I concentrated on the ground, on the hazy and clouded images swimming in front of me. This needed to end. It had to. I followed him, skipping through the undergrowth to catch up. I kept my distance, watching the way he walked, his gait was uneven and the weight unequally distributed. He was still heading through the centre of the forest where the land sloped downwards towards the grave. He paused and surveyed the route ahead.

Glancing down, I watched as he sat again and thumbed through a collection of papers. Squinting, I realised they were photographs: my photographs. Rage filled me. *They're mine, you bastard. My memories, my life; not yours.*

I let him walk away and then took a wide arc to the right, speeding up and overtaking him. It was drier here, both the ground and the air. Sunlight cascaded down through the trees and sharpened the edges of every nook and crevice. The crisp crack of leaves dulled away; looking down, a track of woodchip and gravel twisted into the distance where the trees dispersed. I reached the next clearing and walked the perimeter. To the right, ragged patchwork fields: yellow, red, brown and green. I removed my bag and drank in the view. It looked so normal that for a moment I pretended that none of this had happened, but then the heat from my scar burning through the dark cloth of my top angered me. I needed a distraction and through the trees in the far distance inland, the tall spire of a barely visible church pointed upwards like a needle poised to pierce the sky. Throughout all the bombings it remained unscathed and perfect. Something constructed with such determination and pride in a time of death, suffering and sickness had survived the attacks and yet almost everything else around it was in tatters. I didn't need to believe in divinity to appreciate the architecture and simplicity of a time gone by, when people fought to better themselves and their surroundings. They had created beauty from brutality.

It wasn't far now. I was ready. Yesterday, I wasn't, nor the day before, but now the heavy weight of conviction grounded me and filled me so completely that there was no room for fear or failure.

Rolling the strap of my bag between my hands, I glanced down. Nothing yet. It was so very quiet. The wind had dropped and the trees were still.

Checking my compass I recounted my path from the town and closed my eyes. As I worked out my speed and distance a shadow crossed my back, cooling me. Opening my eyes I looked down and his reflection greeted me in the dull metal. I forced myself to remain loose and relaxed. The metal obscured his features, but I didn't doubt he was smiling again.

He was soundless as he approached. A true predator. His hand reached out towards me and, breathing in deeply, I clenched my fists and twisted to the left, kicking out and connecting with the tender flesh he'd massaged the night before. Stumbling back, he cried out a broken and vulnerable howl. I kicked again and he fell to his knees before falling on his side, gripping his leg. I scrambled to my feet and kicked again but he grabbed my ankle and pulled. I fell hard and pain shot through my hip. His other hand grasped at my jeans, bunching the denim and clawing at my skin. I continued to kick and using my arms I dragged my body away from him, kicking constantly and connecting with every grab he made.

On my knees I reached to the small of my back and pulled out my weapon – Glen's weapon – and seizing the grip, pointed the barrel at him. He froze and those dark eyes locked onto the gun. His hands lowered and I watched as his right slowly reached down to his waist.

"No."

He looked up at me and his hands rose, palms facing out. I couldn't help but smile at the small red scar by his left temple and swollen eye. I hadn't seen it before. It was my brand on him. Leaning forward I unclipped his gun and shoved it into the back of my jeans. I could smell him again, but I didn't let my reaction show and instead stepped back and signalled for him to get up. I'd waited so long for this moment, played this scenario through so many times in my mind.

This was it, I had what I wanted, my baby, my hope, and my reason for living was safe. A liberating split second of understanding and clarity; I was nothing like him, my hope needed protection, needed my love. What I offered my baby was pure. I was no longer just Kate, but before I could squeeze the trigger, before I could end everything, he spoke.

"Anna, don't. I love you."

Love? What did he know of love? I stepped back, my mind a cloud of confusion. So close, I just had to squeeze the trigger.

"Anna."

Anna, again. Anna, what was it with Anna? She submitted, she cowed, and she was weak. Blood rushed and covered my face, my vision was obscured.

"You know nothing of love. Nothing."

"I *never* gave up. I travelled from the north down. I was so sure you'd go north, I had to find you, you wanted to start a life with me, I wanted you. Do you know how much I missed you? The pain I went through? I—"

"Pain?" I cut him off, a year's worth of agony streaming through me. "You know nothing. I hate you. I hate everything about you."

"No, you don't." He was on his knees now, his hands still by his temples. I glanced at the empty holster at his side and the patch on his trousers by his pocket. "You don't hate me, Anna, not all of me. I can make you happy, I can please you, you know I can. We both made mistakes, but it doesn't have to be like that this time."

"You hurt me." I did hate him. It was a loathing I couldn't control, no matter how hard I tried. Hating him seemed so inadequate though. I couldn't put into words what I felt, what he made me feel. Mistakes?

"I kept you safe, you would have been caught. I waited. I waited until you were ready. You wanted love, needed love, and did I not give you that? Think of him, our baby." So soft, always so gentle and persuasive. Lies, all of it lies.

"My baby. He's nothing to do with you."

"He's my son too. He needs his father." His voice cracked with emotion and I swallowed hard. There was still time to stop. I didn't have to do this. I could negotiate with him. Maybe show him that I was strong and that I didn't want or need him.

"I don't want you. I don't want you near me or him all the time. I'm not weak."

He nodded. "Whatever you want, Anna. You can work in the library if you want and stay with the Stentons. It's all possible. I can tell the others to stop watching you. Just think about it."

He was talking too much. He never spoke to me like

this. He wouldn't really give me freedom... would he? I widened my stance and kept the gun trained on him.

"I enjoy teaching again, Anna. I don't want to go back to that life in the Unlands. I'm tired of it. I want a new life, to earn your trust and love. I want to start over. We all have blood on our hands, but it doesn't have to always be that way here. We can move on. We can change. *I* can change. For you. For him. Just give me a chance, please."

"A chance? You've had plenty of chances."

"Don't I deserve the chance of happiness?" he asked.

No, you don't. "What of Ben?" I asked, keeping the gun on him and pushing the searing pain in my shoulder to the back of my mind. "He deserved happiness. What did you do to him?"

"Anna..." he shook his head, pleadingly. "Don't."

"What did you do to him?" My voice almost a scream. "Tell me."

"I needed to find you, understand that, please Anna." He was slow, his voice pleading. "I traded with Olly. His men to search for word of you and I would deliver a message to Ben and Ella." He paused for the smallest moment. "Olly found them and wanted their treachery to be a deterrent to others." He stopped and swallowed. "Don't make me, Anna. Please."

"Finish, you fuck." I hissed.

He closed his eyes. "I found them not far from the town. I shot them both and Olly arranged for them to be strung up so they could be seen."

Tears ran down my face, I shook my head as though trying to wipe away the memory.

"He was a child." I finally said.

"Don't you think I regret things, Anna? I live with the deaths I've caused every day. Every day I see their faces. When I wake, when I teach, when I sleep. They're with me, always."

"Good. You fucking deserve it." I shifted my weight slightly.

"Anna, please. I want to change. I hoped to show you that. I didn't claim you when I arrived, I left you alone, didn't I? I wanted to show you I could be a good man, that I could provide for you and our son. I love you."

Love. He used that word so freely, but his words wormed into me, cloying at my resolution like the parasite he was.

"What if I don't ever want you?"

Pain crossed his face and he shook his head. "I'll make you happy. You know I can. I know you."

I didn't hide the contempt then. "You fucking know nothing about me, you're a piece of shit."

"I do, Anna, I do." He was pleading now and I didn't know who he was trying to convince. "You love roses, yellow roses. You hate peaches. You love walking on the beach before the sun rises. You—"

"You don't know *me*. Those are small details, they don't make a person." I took pleasure in the next statement. "You don't even know my real name."

Confusion replaced pain, followed by a cloud of realisation and anger. He started to lower his hands, then moving like lightning he lunged. Taken off guard the gun was knocked aside as I fell. I only just managed to keep hold of it when I hit the ground hard as he pounced, his steel grip on my wrists.

Fight. I could do it this time. I wasn't that woman from the Unlands anymore. I curled around and bit his arm, sinking my teeth into the flesh, tasting the sweat and the smell of him. He squeezed tighter and I clamped my teeth down, drawing blood and feeling it fill my mouth. *Fuck that's good!* I was elated, and the look of pain on his face thrilled me. He let go of my wrist and tried to grab my throat but, using the gun, I hit the side of his head again and with a hiss of frustration he released my other wrist and I kicked and squirmed my way free, his weight attempting to anchor me to the ground. Twisting onto my knees he grabbed my ankle as I stood and the gun flew out of my hand, bouncing along the earth like a pebble on a lake. I kicked again, tripping as I did, but I was lighter and his grasp was gone. I left my bag, there was no time, and ran back into the woods with him following close behind. The rabbit and the hunter again.

"Anna, stop, Anna!"

He called to me but I ran, my feet pounding, pushing into the mud. As I crashed into the trees the thin branches from the plants and bushes whipped my skin, stinging my neck and face and bringing unwanted tears to my eyes. I couldn't stop, wouldn't stop. I was nearly there.

Eventually I did: my lungs screamed for air and my back ached. I grabbed the closest branch of an oak tree and swung, hitting my side and scraping my hip on the bark, but I fumbled for a foothold and heaved my weight up. Sitting high above the ground I slowed my heart rate and watched. He had my gun in his hand and he moved quickly through the greenery, searching for me. He looked up then and everything slowed. I stared at him, and he stared back at me. The dark circles under his eyes and the sharp lines of his cheekbones showed me the stark truth of his vulnerability. I didn't wait, didn't give him time to pause or realise, I jumped and landed on him, pushing my knee into his chest and grabbing the gun. He wrapped his other arm around my waist as I turned and tried to get up. My back pressed against his chest, my arm was over the top of my head, contorted and jarred. His breath on my neck, he dragged me to my feet. I didn't let go of the gun, couldn't let go. It was my lifeline, my hope. His rough hand was on the soft and still tender skin of my stomach. I stamped repeatedly, trying to make contact with his feet.

Strong, he was impossibly strong, he was huge. I'd forgotten, no, I'd blocked out the sheer size of him. My arm burnt now, a knot of pain growing larger and larger as we struggled. Seconds dragged, neither of us spoke or did more than grunt. He forced us forward and slammed me into the trunk of a tree, crushing me further against him, melting and sculpting to his body. He spoke but I couldn't make out the words. The gun was trapped: I was trapped. Shaking, all I could see was the scaling bark of the tree in breathtaking detail, each layer and colour intensified. The weight of him, the shape of his body against my brand, the eternal reminder of him cooled my blood. And then I heard him.

"Stop." He pressed harder and I groaned in pain. "Why

do you always fight? Our baby needs us, come back. Just stop." He struggled to speak as I thrashed and squirmed.

I nearly did stop, a trickle of surrender escaped: he can live, I can go back with clean hands, and this empty space inside would fill in time, we can move forward. My baby, I could be with my baby, just the two of us, I could show everyone what this man really is, what he did.

"Come back, I'll protect you both. We can raise him together. Teach him, just us. A family."

I screwed my eyes shut and breathed in, folding into myself, creating a few centimetres of space. Enough, it must be enough. *Not us, me, he needs me, never you.* It came to me then: his hands on me, the unwanted and cruel response he invoked from my body and his smile at my tears of shame. Hot. The blood boiled again. I wrenched my arm down with all the force I could muster, fast, hard, his grip slipped and his nails caught on the skin of my hand, drawing blood to the surface.

Just me. Just the gun. There was a coldness of the metal against my stomach through the tee shirt. I jerked my head back and connected with his face. The already tender scalp was now a lake of red hot agony. He stumbled. I turned and fired. The explosion echoed through the forest and the birds scattered. One shot through the air, rippling and resonating. Then there was nothing. I stared as he fell back, holding his side and looking at me in pain and confusion. I had seen this in my dreams, of course I had. As I stood there with the gun it was inevitable.

Those black eyes bled to brown and his face relaxed, the hard lines disappearing. His right hand, the fingers that he splayed on my skin so often now covered his own, but they were red, a thick dark and almost velvet red. I thought of the murdered boy from the field, of Ella, and of Ben.

"Anna."

I squeezed again, firing into his chest this time and I watched as the blood trickled free of him. I watched him long after the blood stopped flowing and his body stopped moving. His skin, white and waxy, seemed stretched too tightly over his skull.

I'd failed. It was unequivocal and final. The greatest trial and though I had not walked the line of least resistance. I had lost and I was now no better than those I shied away from. But I had saved my baby. He would never be scared of my captor the way I was. Never have to experience what I had.

How long had I stood here? It was day, but the copper hues of the sky were spreading and darkening the light. I dropped the gun and burst into tears. Unexpected, treacherous tears. He didn't deserve them, nor my sorrow, or my pity. Not after what he had done. But I cried anyway. For what I had done, for what had become of us, for what we had made of the land, for what the Unlands had made of us, for everything that would never be.

Leaning down I closed his eyes, forcing myself to touch him. The skin was cool already. My fingers lingered on his eyelids as my hair escaped from its band and fell around my face. I thought of my capture, of the moment he chained me to him and marked me as his own and the way he humiliated and abused me. I thought of the way he had chained Anna and stolen a part of me *over and over*, and destroyed that pure essence we keep hidden and secret, the part we never show any other person. But I no longer hated him.

Every bone ached and my muscles wept with pain but I pulled him to the edge of the grave. Pausing to stretch out my back I couldn't look as I rolled him in, but winced at the thud of body on body. I allowed myself one glance and the lover's embraced him into their fold. He was home.

Searching his bag I found my photos and slipped them into my back pocket, but then something caught my attention and digging further I pulled out another bundle of photos: *his*. His father, mother... sister? I frowned, he had his arm around her, but they looked too similar to be lovers. Flicking through there were more photos of this woman with two children, and her husband. He was in so many of their pictures, laughing, hugging, smiling. His life before the wars laid out clearly before me. He was a brother and a son. He was loved and he loved in return.

Then the final one. My captor, alone at the top of a cliff. He was younger then, perhaps mid-twenties, and a smile danced across his face with pure unfettered joy. I turned it over, reading the inscription over and over, and finally cried. Tears of weariness, of relief, of pain and sadness, regret and resolution.

I WALKED AWAY, heading towards the setting sun which guided me like a beacon. I left him and not looking back I started my way back to my son. I had left him to save him, but that wasn't enough now. Even though I had saved him from my captor, there would be other dangers, other trials for him to face and he should never have to face those without me. To be alone in this world was to suffer. It is true that we are not perfect creatures, but to me he is perfect. He is pure in a world of hatred and lies. There would be questions and accusations, distrust and disbelief, of that I was sure. Simon would threaten me, intimidate me and never stop until my captor's death was avenged, but I wasn't alone, and me, the *real* me, would survive.

I AM NOT Kate.
    I am not Anna.

AND I KNOW his name.

ACKNOWLEDGEMENTS

THIS IS ALWAYS the hard part, and in true Sam fashion I'll probably forget someone. If I do, please be assured it is not intentional. I cherish and appreciate every single person who has helped me with this book.

My thanks to the very first beta readers for their positivity and cheerleading. Emma Brooks, Zoë Harris, Frances Kay and Robyn Fulton, you all offered insight and honesty, and helped so much with character motivations. Thank you to Robert Peett for his inspiration and help during the first draft.

My eternal gratitude to my friend and editor Kate Coe for her constant enthusiasm and support along the way which knows no bounds. I've lost count of the number of times I've emailed you with 'what about this?' and you've responded with such positivity and passion that you've spurred me on even when self-doubt set in. You'll never truly know how thankful I am! In fact, publishing a book is a group effort, and so huge thanks to Laurel Sills for her thoughts, honesty, and excellent skills when running through the manuscript with a fine toothed comb. For Hanna Waigh and her patience at my barrage of emails, and a big thank you to all at Rebellion (Solaris) who have taken a chance on this author and Anna's story.

And as always to John Smith, my partner in all things.